VIRAGO
MODERN CLASSICS
137

Molly Keane was born in Co. Kildare, Ireland in 1904, into 'a rather serious Hunting and Fishing Church-going family', and was sketchily educated by governesses. Interested in 'horses and having a good time', Molly Keane wrote her first novel, *The Knight of Cheerful Countenance*, when she was seventeen in order to supplement her dress allowance. She used the pseudonym M. J. Farrell 'to hide my literary side from my sporting friends'. Between 1928 and 1961 Molly Keane published ten novels under her pen name, novels in which she brought acuteness and good-tempered satire as well as affection to her portrayals of the ramshackle Anglo-Irish way of life. She also wrote several successful plays. But the untimely death of her husband brought a break in her career which ended only in 1981, when *Good Behaviour* appeared under her own name, triggering a revival of interest in and respect for her work. Molly Keane died in 1996.

Novels by Molly Keane

The Knight of Cheerful Countenance
Young Entry
Taking Chances
Mad Puppetstown
Conversation Piece
Devoted Ladies
Full House
The Rising Tide
Two Days in Aragon
Loving Without Tears
Treasure Hunt
Time After Time
Good Behaviour
Loving and Giving

THE RISING TIDE

Molly Keane
(M.J. Farrell)

Introduction by
Polly Devlin

Virago

VIRAGO

Published by Virago Press 1984
Reprinted 1984, 1985, 1988, 1990, 1994, 1997, 2002, 2006

A CIP catalogue record for this book
is available from the British Library.

ISBN-13: 978-1-84408-326-8
ISBN-10: 1-84408-326-8

Printed and bound in Great Britain by
Clays Ltd, St Ives plc

Virago Press
An imprint of
Time Warner Book Group UK
Brettenham House
Lancaster Place
London WC2E 7EN

www.virago.co.uk

INTRODUCTION

Molly Keane started to write in the 1920s, for "pin" money when she too was in her twenties, using the pseudonym M.J. Farrell which name she borrowed from an Irish public house as she clattered by on her Irish horse near her Irish home in County Wexford after a hard day's hunting. She needed a pseudonym since in her Anglo-Irish and somewhat philistine world, writing was no occupation for a young woman. "For a woman to read a book, let alone write one was viewed with alarm, I would have been banned from every respectable house in County Carlow." So, apparently casually, did her remarkable career begin, a career that has spanned half a century, though her creative powers quivered, almost broke and certainly lay mute in her middle years, stilled by the double blows of the sudden death of her beloved and dashing young husband and, later, the failure of her fourth play in London's West End—a play out of kilter with the new atmosphere in the theatre of that time, since epitomised by *Look Back In Anger*.

Then in 1981 she published *Good Behaviour* under her own name. It was shortlisted for the Booker Prize and she has written steadily ever since, to the enormous pleasure of a new generation of readers and indeed television viewers since *Good Behaviour* was adapted for a three part "classic" serial. The story of the emergence of Molly Keane, a delightful, witty woman in her late seventies from the ghost of the anonymous, sexless M.J. Farrell is charming and arbitrary, as so much connected with this diffident author seems to be. She wrote *Good Behaviour* in her late sixties and sent it to Sir William Collins, who had published most of her earlier works. He turned it down on the grounds that it was too black a comedy—"Couldn't I make the characters more pleasant? Imagine a black comedy with charming characters. I couldn't and wouldn't do it—the bravery—and put it away in a drawer and thought 'I'm too old. I've forgotten how to write plays and now I can't write a novel any more.'"

There the matter literally rested until Dame Peggy Ashcroft came to stay with Molly Keane in her house perched on a cliff-top in Waterford and, ill in bed with 'flu, wanted something to read. She gave her the manuscript to read and Dame Peggy loved it—her enjoyment and encouragement spurred Molly Keane to send it to André Deutsch, who found they had a new classic on their list, greeted with popular and critical acclaim. It was no new thing for Molly Keane—she had had success from her earliest days, both with her novels and with two early plays written in collaboration with John Perry, directed by John Gielgud, and, in *Spring Meeting*, introducing the inimitable Margaret Rutherford to delighted London audiences. Hugh Walpole wrote,

I think that Miss Farrell is one of the best half-dozen younger women novelists now writing in England [sic]. She has in the first place a beautiful gift of description ... She has, secondly, a real sense of drama ... Thirdly, she can create character. There is beauty here with understanding and an original mind.

The myth is that she shut herself up for a time whenever her dress allowance—some £30 a year—ran out and she herself seems to subscribe to this explanation of her artistic motivation. But her writing has no feeling of expediency, her novels are never journey-work—indeed they contain few of the ingredients necessary for writing as a commercial venture. She writes of narrow horizons, élitist occupations, the preoccupations of a moneyed, hunting, curiously dislocated class of people, floating as it were over the political, angry geographical reality that was Ireland. In *The Rising Tide* there is no mention of political turmoil though at the time in which it is set the issue of Home Rule was tearing the country apart.

In this disregard for the outside world she is akin to Jane Austen; in concentrating on the two inches of ivory of one Edwardian family, in her feeling for the minutiae of human behaviour, she gives an unforgettable picture of a vanished world, the world Home Rule was threatening. These people are sustained by an absolute sense of their own superiority, by a certainty about the appropriate social response to every crisis, including tragedy. It is a book about, among other things, heartlessness. It is also about houses, hunting and horses, her central themes.

It is remarkable in its conjuring up of the lustsome women have for hunting: literally mad for it, finding in the chase everything lacking in their ordinary lives—glamour, muscle, music, passion, thrills, admiration, spills and exhaustion. Horses were the great pursuit in Molly Keane's Ireland—that other Ireland. Everyone rode, even the most timid and shrinking of daughters. It was mandatory for acceptance in that world and in *The Rising Tide* she paints a shocking picture of the heroine Cynthia's utter belief in the "rightness" of riding.

She did not love her children but she was determined not to be ashamed of them. You had to feel ashamed and embarrassed if your children did not take keenly to blood-sports, so they must be forced into them. It was right. It was only fair to them. You could not bring a boy up properly unless he rode and fished and shot. What sort of boy was he? What sort of friends would he have?.

And was it really like that?

"When I was young" Molly Keane says, almost with disbelief "I really disapproved of people who didn't ride, it was the only thing that counted. I've had this feeling for horses all my life. It's a frightening excitement that takes the place of something else. Of course my father provided the horses I rode in my early days, but he was as distant about hunting as he was about most things. He was a beautiful horseman but never instructed us. It was all long before things like the pony club existed. Then you just were, or were not any good at it, there was no question of your being taught. It was your occupation, it was supposed to be hereditary, you just knew how."

She *did* know; she always loved and enjoyed hunting, as did all her family, save her mother who did not ride (one brother, Walter Skrine, rode in the Grand National although he had been badly injured in the war). But this mastery of the saddle never precluded her imaginative leap into the minds of her compatriots who were terrified of riding. "When I started to write there were lots of books about hunting and awful hunting romances. . . *The Queen of the Chase* and all that kind of thing. I thought it much more interesting to write about fright. . .It's natural to be frightened." She describes brilliantly the horror of children rising in the cold damp chill of a November morning, when the very hot water bottle is frozen in the bed, to drive in an ancient car to the meet, to get onto their ponies. Driven also by the fear of their parents, by the social shame of refusing.

They looked at the fields and the fences as they drove past them, seeing them with a curious relationship of fear and not fear. The fields were not ordinary fields as in summer. They were places you had to get out of, that you were inexorably carried over. That field now, with green plover waddling and pecking about on its dark, sheep-bitten turf, was a dreadfully unkind field with wire on its nice round banks and as cruel a coped stone wall across one side of it as a frightened child could face. The very young may be sick with cowardice about a fence but they are more afraid not to jump it than to jump it . . . It was not soft falls in water or bog that they dreaded, but that shameful, hurting falling off and the moments before you fell, their agony seeming to endure in interminable uncertainty before you went with a sort of sob and the ground hit you from behind, strangely like a house falling on you, not you falling on a house.

As children Molly, her sister and her three brothers were much neglected and left to their own and the servants' devices—and from her earliest days she was fired with a fierce

viii

determination to lead her own life away from the influence of her mother, who lived in an atavistic world of her own and didn't pay the least attention to her children who were educated by default. Her mother was a writer, who wrote under the pseudonym Moira O'Neill and was known as the Poet of the Seven Glens. She had great success with her "folkloric" poems which are often magical and touching although they incline to show the peasantry in a moral, amiable and trusting attitude which seems out of order with the real thing like pious children in Victorian genre-painting. "I fought her every inch of the way" Molly Keane says, "She really didn't know how to treat us. You can't think how neglected we were, by our parents. I mean they didn't do anything with us at all, they simply didn't bother. They were utterly reclusive. My mother had great taste but was totally oblivious to comfort. Life was much more stringent then, there was no such thing as hot water or central heating. There were fires but they went out and I remember the deadly cold of the school room and the blue cold coming off the wall. I never remember a fire in my father's library or in the dining room, although my father was perhaps a bit more warmth conscious." One memorable day when her father had forbidden her to ride a horse she'd been given she was discovered weeping behind a fox covert by a Major Perry who lived in a beautiful Queen Anne house, Woodrooff, in the centre of the glamorous Tipperary hunting country. She went to stay with him, his wife Dolly "the dearest woman who ever lived" and their two children Sylvia and John, who also hunted like lunatics. (In later years John Perry encouraged and helped her write her first play, Spring Meeting, and sent it to Gielgud.) Woodrooff became her home—"I almost lived there for six or seven years, mostly in the winter months, when I hunted three days a week on horses largely provided by Woodrooff, although a few others chipped in. There were so many horses in those days of the late twenties and early thirties that if you were lightweight and a moderately useful rider your fun was endless."

"My mother disapproved of Woodrooff—she was frightened by the idea of it. She belonged to the nineteenth century and didn't change, and I think I must have been a hideous worry and an anxiety to her. When she was very old she said to my sister Susan 'Oh the mistakes I made about Molly.' Rather a sad comment. I expect we all make mistakes about our children and always will. She feared that I would get into a fast set and fall into bad ways—she was as worried as a mother would be now about her child going on drugs. There was a woman there who'd been divorced and some what *she* would have called dirty talk which I didn't know a thing about, but I soon found out about and was rather good at. My mother was alarmingly prudish and old-fashioned in those ways. In fact everyone there was wonderfully kind to me. I met marvellous people, and it was only when I went to stay in London with some of the women I'd met there, one especially who was very sophisticated and on the fringe of literary and intellectual life in London and taught me what to read and to go to the theatre, that I began to be in any way educated. I was utterly ignorant."

"I remember once one of my books got into one of the bestseller lists and I was asked to a literary party at the Piccadilly Hotel and I thought 'what awful, ghastly boring people—still I'd better go'. I travelled over on the boat with this hunting gent—really rather mad and in fact deadly boring, but how I wished I was with him instead of at this dreary party. I met Elizabeth Bowen and I thought 'what a strange lady', not what I considered attractive, and she introduced me to David Cecil and I thought he was ghastly. Just shows my state of ignorance. Elizabeth Bowen became my greatest friend in life and when I met David Cecil again I realised he was the most divine person who ever breathed. But the hunting people had their own style. It was like a club with its own language and rules."

In fact her whole life belonged to a club—an exclusive club

x

called the Anglo-Irish. The meaning of the term—though most people seem to accommodate imaginatively what it means—is elusive, full of heft and emotion, and covers anything from a cool description of a class to an indictment, depending on who is using it and how they are using it. It is for a start a comparatively new term. Before the breakaway from England many of those people now described as Anglo-Irish would certainly have described themselves as Irish though, (and this is where things thicken) the native Irish would not have allowed them the privilege of their Irishness, as a kind of revenge. It is an angry refusal, perhaps the only refusal that was left to them since the Anglo-Irish were powerful and believed themselves to be socially superior. In the time when M.J. Farrell was writing—a generation before Molly Keane and a generation after *The Rising Tide*—Ireland was a place of three countries, the newly created states of Eire, Northern Ireland and this older, floating notional world of Anglo-Ireland. The "real" Irish (the peasant Catholic Irish) seem only to enter this world—and thus Molly Keane/Farrell's faithful rendering—as a sub-species, good for opening gates and giving amusing, barely subservient lip service, the words and rhythms of which were recounted as hilarious anecdotes with broguish emphasis on the Oirishness of it all. Perhaps in no other country has simply and artlessly belonging to that country been made such an inherently ridiculous thing, an object for mirth.

Indeed Oirishness was the Anglo-Irish interpretation of how the Irish who lived outside their club and class behaved and spoke: there was no question of admittance. "No-one would have thought of marrying someone not of their own class," Molly Keane said. "It would have been more than death. It simply wasn't an idea. Those things were completely part of the code." These co-existing cultures had nothing in common except their country and that extraordinary Irish climate, which as George Bernard Shaw said "will stamp an immigrant more deeply and durably in two years apparently than the English climate will in two hundred".

It worked the other way round too—even those great families who had been in Ireland for centuries and regarded themselves as more Irish than the Irish, when they "turned" Protestant for political expedient and earthly survival, became aliens to the common mass of the people, indistinguishable from the English. There is a famous story of how Oscar Browning rushed up to Tennyson and said "I am Browning" and Tennyson said "You are not." The Anglo-Irish have said over and over again "We are Irish" and the Irish have said "You are not." That the class that had endowed them with a sense of social inferiority and, as they believed, taken their land, should claim the same national identity whilst despising it in its purest form was an anathema to the mass. De Valera said that to know what the Irish people wanted he had only to examine his own heart. There was little room in his heart for the Anglo-Irish, though he could far less easily claim to be Irish than those he excluded.

There is little point to saying that all this is history and should be forgotten for, as Terence de Vere White wrote in his book on the Anglo-Irish, "The Irish mind hops back to the flood when discussing a leaking tap." In many ways the world about which Molly Keane writes is like that of the Raj in India. W.B. Yeats was once asked was Oscar Wilde a snob; "No" he said "I would say that England is a strange country to the Irish . . . to Wilde the aristocrats of England were like the nobles of Baghdad." The Anglo-Irish were like the nobles of Baghdad to the Irish people and the gradations of class within the Anglo-Irish so cunningly observed, so slyly mapped out by M.J. Farrell would certainly not have been apparent to the "common people". Many of the Anglo-Irish weren't rich or grand, but appeared so since it cost next to nothing to keep horses and a groom then. "The very rich did much more about being more English and their sons went to Eton and Oxford. Everything was part of the code . . ." Molly Keane says, and when she is talking one hears bewilderment that the thing has irrevocably gone and astonishment that it should have existed. There is none of that guilt that the native Irish hope the Anglo-Irish should suffer, if only because they had so much enjoyed the country in which they lived and from which enjoyment the natives were excluded—as Indians under the Raj suffered an acute sense of inferiority whilst serving their masters with loyalty, a loyalty which was largely a myth. But it was never a question of anything so subtle as gradations between the Irish and the Anglo-Irish. An unbridgeable chasm lay between them. "Those who know Ireland," wrote an observer about the time in which *The Rising Tide* is set, "need not be told that the feeling of the average Irish Protestant towards Roman Catholics was a repugnance, instinctive rather than reasoned, based on social and racial as much as religious antipathies."

In the South of Ireland that world shuddered to an end in the Troubles, in the same way that Edwardian England ground to a halt with the First World War and in *The Rising Tide* M.J. Farrell makes a spectacular imaginative leap back into that lost Edwardian world, that mysterious generation that has more irrevocably vanished and which just preceded her youth. *The Rising Tide* was her seventh book and one of her most accomplished: in it she shakes out the crushed memories of an age lying pleated like parchment maps at the bottom of a century's memory, and snatches back the looks and feel and textures of that time, its mixture of meanness and voluptuousness, its sumptuousness and sternness, its scent and meanings, and displays the protocol of its discretions—and indiscretions. And then she juxtaposes this world against the chic gloss of the world of the twenties and watches as they turn each other upside-down.

The title is layered with meaning, as closely lapped and integrated as feathers on a wing: for the tide that is rising engulfs not only Lady Charlotte, the old tyrant who rules Garonlea, the grand house at the centre of the book; Cynthia, her daughter-in-law and her foe who inherits the house; but

xiii

also engulfs an age, a class and that mythical country in which the Anglo-Irish lived with such apparently endless cocooned luxurious security. The tide rose silently, they seemed to hear no tocsins. "People simply didn't visualise any change coming. They believed life would go on like that for all time, and for some it did, because they were rich enough to remain insulated from everything that was happening—except of course for those who had the rude shock of seeing their houses with their entire contents burned around them."

Which is what happened to her father. And when her husband died she had to leave their beautiful house, Belleville. Her acute feeling for the secret life of houses, the mark that the years have laid on them, the turmoil, the passions, the domestic histories that have seeped into the very fabric, the way the colours of ages past have run into the spirit of a later age, all these intangibles play a particular and powerful part in her plots and especially in *The Rising Tide*. This is as much the story of the house, Garonlea, a great crenellated Gothic mansion, full of malevolence and power, lying brooding at the bottom of its secret valley as it is the story of two indomitable women pitted against each other like primeval forces.

Garonlea seems a convincingly Irish house, but in fact it is Warleigh Manor, lying in a wooded valley outside Bath. Her description is superb. Walking round the house—now a school—one gets the measure of her gift for evocation, of her extraordinary apprehension of atmosphere and spirit.

What is there that can be told about Garonlea and the evil that can be on a place through want of happiness. Or even a will towards happiness. Family tragedy is brief and sudden in comparison to this that lies like the breath of mould in old clothes on the people who live in such a place. It seems as though nothing could ever dissolve such mists and ill vapours, or only for such a little while. So inexact, so dim is such a gloom, it is hard to say whether it is the effect of place on character or character on place.

To this house comes Cynthia, the new daughter-in-law to

be presented to her mother-in-law, Lady Charlotte, its chatelaine and its evil genius. Cynthia acknowledges that both the house and its ruler are her enemies and that she must fight and defeat them, and the Old Queen, unscrupulous herself, knows well what the new pretender is like. "She took the utmost from everyone around her far more than she gave. She failed them and charmed them to her again. She leaned upon them and queened it over them at the same time."

The portrait of Cynthia is magnificently done: and what makes it so artful is that one never quite knows how mendacious Cynthia actually is, how unscrupulous, how fine. She is like a woman of one's own acquaintance whom one cannot help admiring, yet about whom one has grave doubts which are at times assuaged, at others nourished with foreboding. She is an early Superwoman, bearing children, running a house impeccably, hunting every day if possible, keeping her courtiers entranced and always looking glorious.

She removes herself to the altogether sunnier dower house across the valley, and there as liege lady she holds a permanent tournament. The forces are drawn up on the other side, and it is a formidable battle, a crash of styles and ways of living, a collision of hatred as well as a clash between two queens of indomitable will, and Molly Keane doesn't miss a trick in recording the fight to the finish. She knows whereof she writes. Lady Charlotte's genesis might lie in the nineteenth-century attitudes of Molly Keane's mother, but the character is based more closely on one of her aunts "who was far grander and far more deadly than my mother". Her every wrinkle and quirk, her every meanness and pretension is limned in with dreadful precision.

Lady Charlotte French-McGrath mounting the stairs in her daughters' wake was a shocking despot, really swollen with family conceit and a terrifying pride of race. She had a strange sense of her own power made real indeed by a life spent at Garonlea with her obedient husband, frightened children and many tenants and dependants. Here she loved and suffered and here she was supreme.

Her moral dereliction is delivered in one deadly sentence. "She was mean, although not so mean as her husband whom she had taught to be mean."

The Edwardian details are impeccable and irresistible.

Lady Charlotte rang for her maid. She then washed her hands in buttermilk soap, folded the neck of her combinations down towards the top of her corsets (those corsets which propped so conscientiously the bosoms like vast half-filled hot water bottles) and thus prepared stood while her evening dress was put upon her and sat while her hair was fiddled not redone. Her hair was never washed but it did not smell of anything but hair. The switches and curls of false hair were drier and frizzier in texture than her own.

The portrait of Cynthia too was taken from life—based on a beautiful Irish woman (a Fitzgerald) who was married to the local glamorous M.F.H. (who came from Warwickshire). "We all worshipped her," Molly Keane recalls, "thought she was marvellous. She had great chic and we tried to look like her and dress like her and felt that we, too, would like, if at all possible, to marry the same kind of man. Looking back I feel she was extraordinarily kind and generous to us younger generation. It was a little clan."

The Rising Tide did not just engulf an age, that clan, a woman and then another woman. It engulfed a way of life and in the book you watch it happen. As Molly Keane says, "A way of life that people thought would go on for ever, ended. It was another way of life and one treats it, must treat it as, in a much bigger way, people who are expelled from Poland, say, treat their exile—looking back as though it had never been. The place existed, but you can no longer return there."

It is gone, as you might say, for good. In Molly Keane's books it lives on.

Polly Devlin,
Bruton, Somerset 1983

I

WHAT don't we know about the Early Nineteen Hundreds. 1901 and 2 and 3 and up to '14 we can feel about only very dimly. Leisure and Richness and Space and Motor-veils and the bravery of those who flew in the earliest aeroplanes impress us. But we can't feel about those years really. Not in the way we feel about the War. There we are conscious.

It requires an effort to realise the necessities, pleasures, colossal bad taste, Romance, trust, suspicion, pride of those years. The War is forced on us, horror is so actual. But those years, the years of our cousins' youth, avoid us and will not be known. We almost forget how deeply that youth was influenced by the generation that got it. Influenced and prescribed for in a way we can't know about. So much and such nearly complete power was in those elder hands. Over the trivialities or fatalities of Life our cousins and aunts accepted so much and really managed it with admirable smoothness and dignity.

Pain they endured and accepted.

Endless Chaperonage.

Supervision of their correspondence.

The fact that Mother Knew Best.

That Father Says So.

That there is no more to be said on the subject, they accepted.

They accepted their leisure without boredom.

They accepted having occupations found for this leisure.

They accepted trivialities and treated them with that carefulness and detail which rounds such perfect smallness and makes it an acceptable part of life.

With all this acceptance they could preserve a death-like romantical obstinacy where their hearts were concerned—they had a true romantical outlook, infinitely less destructible than the quick love encounters we so often know. On absence their Romances throve. They were not afraid of sentimentality—they were not afraid of being thought girlish. They never needed to explain their emotions to themselves or to their friends. The indecency of knowing what it was all about would have been appalling to them; they didn't want to know—the mystery and the thrill enough and most secretly their own. Hence much rapture and much failure, and a certain dignity too. This outward smoothness of Life which at all costs they struggled to achieve was a politeness of living which we may envy them.

"Eleven o'clock—more than bedtime!" Lady Charlotte French-McGrath had four daughters, and at these words Muriel immediately folded up her work. Enid ceased tracing a picture of a stag's head into her album called Sunlight and Shadow. Violet gathered up the cards with which she and her father had been playing picquet, and only Diana, Little Diana, showed no speed in closing her book. Really, Mother might not have spoken——

"Bed-time, I think, Diana."

Diana shut her book guiltily and was the first of the four to kiss her father good-night.

"Ha," he said. "Ha-Ha. Bed-time. Bed-time, I suppose. Good-night, my dear. Candles, now, let me see, candles." He crossed the room to that small, dark table where immemorially the candlesticks were set out and lit the five candles. Giving each daughter a kiss and a candlestick and the same to his wife, he followed them with a very satisfied eye as they went out of the door, crossed the hall one behind another and mounted the stairs in the same pretty succession.

Muriel first with her fluffy brown hair, thin neck and little birdy body. Poor little Muriel—time she was finding a husband. Twenty-four and nothing satisfactory turning up yet. Enid then, with her purple eyes, deep voice and dark hair. She would have been a beauty if Violet had not come after her, and Violet was an Edwardian classic. Skin like shells and peaches, bosom like the prow of a ship, smooth thighs, features of bland and simple beauty and a head crowned by obedient golden hair and unhampered by brains. A satisfactory daughter. And then Diana—little Diana—there was not much of the Edwardian classic about Diana. Her mother could not find her very satisfactory, since she had neither the charm nor the biddable disposition of her elder sisters. And none of their beauty. Small and dark and angular and inclined even at the age of seventeen to a dark and downy growth of hair (ignored by her family, for what could be done about it?) Diana was hardly due for success in 1900.

Lady Charlotte French-McGrath mounting the stairs in her daughters' wake was a shocking despot, really swollen with family conceit and a terrifying pride of race. She had a strange sense of her own power, made real indeed by a life spent chiefly at Garonlea with her obedient husband, frightened children and many tenants and dependants. Here she had lived and suffered and here she was supreme.

Married at the age of eighteen to a man of good family

and one who owned moreover the best woodcock shoot in the west of Ireland, Lady Charlotte had borne six children in the first eight years of her married life— four daughters and two sons; one son unhappily died of convulsions when an infant. She was mean, although not so mean as her husband whom she had taught to be mean. She ran Garonlea like a court— her daughters like the ladies in waiting.

"Muriel, write my notes for me——"

"Enid, how about your little job of washing the china in my boudoir this afternoon——"

Such awful little employments—the walks and messages to the needy tenantry, bestowals of charities and reprimands, piano practising and "Lying Down," that cure for all ills.

God should have chastened Lady Charlotte with one malformed or unsatisfactory child. But they were all miracles of aristocratic good looks—inclined to anæmia perhaps, except for the divine Violet.

One by one the Lady Charlotte French-McGrath presented her daughters to their sovereign. But as far as entering the social contest and finding them husbands went, God or Garonlea and its famous woodcock shoot might do the rest. So far, whatever God might send them in that lonely countryside, the woodcock shoot produced for the most part only their father's friends and contemporaries. Determined as she was that the girls should marry men of Property and Title, Lady Charlotte did nothing at all about collecting these mythical and appropriate husbands. She showed such marked disapproval of any young friend that her son Desmond ever brought to stay, should the friend fulfil neither of these requirements, and such embarrassingly obvious tactics should he fulfil either or both that Desmond desisted in disgust,

8

for he was a charming creature and entirely free from his mother's influence. His sisters adored him and it was his firm intention to do all in his power for the girls when he should marry. Until then he looked on them as rather boring princesses set for a time in a castle beyond a wood.

Meantime it would be unfair to her not to allow that Lady Charlotte loved her daughters with a passion none the less genuine if it demanded first their unquestioning obedience, and fed itself on a profound jealousy of any interest in their lives other than those she might herself prompt or provide. She felt that her children owed to her as a mother, not as a person, love, confidence and obedience. She felt this tremendously. It was a true thing with her. Among all the travails and secret adventures of her own life both mental and physical she had endured, raising no manner of complaining, shyness as much as stoicism helping her here. She absolutely required that her children should prove a justification, as she should see it, of herself.

So they were—they were practically all that she required. Her son Desmond and Violet were the two at the top of her estimation but she trusted herself to keep this sacred maternal secret safely from the other three daughters. "I love all my children equally," she was very fond of saying. Although vaguely impressed by the proper feeling she thus displayed, the three less-favoured daughters were never slow to employ either Desmond or Violet as their intermediary if for any reason matters should be strained between themselves and their mother.

To-night at the stairhead they parted from her.

"Good-night, Mother dear."

A gold head bobbed for a kiss in the candle-light.

9

"Good-night, my child. Don't let me hear you and Muriel talking at one o'clock as I did last night on my way to—the bathroom. Please, Violet."

"Good-night, Mother dear."

"Good-night, Muriel. Now remember."

"Good-night, Mother dear."

"Good-night, Enid. Have you been taking your senna regularly? I see you have another spot on your chin."

"Oh, but I have been taking it."

"Always remember, darling, a bad skin is most unattractive to gentlemen."

Enid flushed up to her beautiful brow. Oh, the shame of those spots, the shame and the recurring horror.

"Couldn't we perhaps ask Doctor Maxwell if he knows of a cure," she had once asked her mother; but the answer, "Some things are best left to *Nature*, Enid," had quelled the ardour of her vanity.

"Good-night, Mother."

Diana as usual trying to be a little different from the rest.

"Good-night, Diana—*dear*."

The quick brush and escape of lips. Strange the lack of confidence in that child. Sad for her. A pity.

Lady Charlotte trailed the length of her oyster satin skirt down the passage to her bedroom and with the help of her maid undressed so far as those black satin corsets which had been in her trousseau. Then she slipped the fine white flannel nightgown over her head and fumbled under it for a long time before she thrust her arms into its sleeves.

In the blue-and-white bedroom at the other end of the house the three sisters were gathered solicitously round Violet, who lay on her bed in a state of pretty severe pain. Now that the long formality of the evening was over she could collapse and leave go that curious control which worked somewhere outside herself because it must.

"Let me help you with your stays, Violet dearest. You'll feel so much more comfy in your nightie."

"Oh, don't touch me, please, I'm in such pain." Violet sank her face into her pillow for a moment, then sat up bending herself together taut and convulsive with pain. The hair on her forehead and on the back of her neck was wet and sticking to her flesh. She was entirely in pain and moaned helplessly.

"I must go and tell Mother," Enid said in a frightened voice. "She'd give you a glass of ginger."

Violet signed to her desperately not to go.

Muriel was crying quietly for she adored Violet.

Diana said, "Mother ought to see how bad Violet is."

They all felt quite desperate and quite helpless as they stood round that neat brass bedstead where Violet lay suffering so horridly at the hands of Mother Nature. Each of them knew that the glass of hot water and ginger, their mother's sovereign remedy in such times of stress, was calculated rather to make the sufferer vomit than to relieve her pain. The only thing it did relieve was their mother's sense of responsibility towards sickness. That and "Lying down," were her two invariable specifics for all female ills.

Violet whispered, "I'm so dreadfully cold."

Muriel sobbed, "I'll sleep with you darling, and warm you."

This not very hygenic plan these sisters often followed, for fires and hot-water bottles alike were considered vaguely sybaritic influences and seldom appeared in either the Blue and White or the Pink and White bedroom. To-night the Blue and White room was full of October air, cold and hollow as an October mist. Between the window panes that flattened the outside night and the white curtains it was present and in the room too, circling bluely the candle flames when the girls had put down their candlesticks here and there at unequal levels and distances. They shivered a little in their low dresses and put a flannel dressing-gown tenderly over their poor sister at whom they continued to gaze in helpless concern.

"But where has Diana gone?" Enid whispered to Muriel. "To Mother's room?"

"Or do you think the bath-room?"

"Oh, dear, shall I go and see?"

"She's not in our room and she's not in the bath-room," Enid reported, important with omen. "Can she have gone to Mother?"

"Well, if she has and Mother catches you in here there'll be trouble. Oh, dear, do go to your own room."

With many a backward and pitying look at Violet, Enid retired as advised. She had plaited her hair in its two soft dark plaits and put on her frilled nightdress and blue padded silk dressing-gown before Diana came in.

Diana was so sharp and aggressive, tearing off her dress and her corsets and doing her Swedish exercises in her black silk stockings and her chemise. Really she didn't seem to mind at all . . . Enid couldn't always look. Embarrassing.

"Where did you go to?" she asked when she had poured her senna out of the window and hopped into bed. "Poor Violet, wasn't it awful!"

"If you did drink that senna you wouldn't have so many spots," Diana told her, still exercising with energy.

"Oh, but I simply can't. I would if I could. I hate

12

deceiving dear Mother. But where did you go, Diana?"

"I went down to the kitchen and got some hot milk and brandy for Violet and a hot-water bottle."

"Brandy—Diana, but what would Mother say? And a hot-water bottle. You'll catch it if she finds out."

"Why should she find out? Anyhow Violet's better now. The hot milk acted like a charm."

"The hot milk? Oh, Diana, I'm afraid it may have been the brandy." Enid said this sadly without a ray of amusement. She saw nothing either funny or comforting in her sister relaxing into a drunken stupor. The thought of such pain as she had seen assuaged hardly touched her.

"I don't care whether it was the milk or the brandy or the hot-water bottle, she's better now than if we'd left it all to Nature," Diana said this in the hard unappealing way which Enid admired while secretly feeling repelled by it. Now she said as she tested the almost damp cold of her bed with her thin blue feet:

"Oh, Diana, it is cold. Shall we sleep together?"

Diana said quickly, "Oh, no it's not cold enough for that." She had a dreadful inner feeling about sleeping with Enid and never did so if it could be avoided. Enid slept with her only for warmth as sheep sleep and huddle together, but Diana was afraid about this. Afraid only of herself. Obscurely obstinate in her avoidance of such contacts.

II

AMBROSE FRENCH-McGRATH who had begotten these daughters was a gloomy and nervous man who infinitely preferred the company of his inferiors to that of his equals by birth and station. He had suffered all his life from being the son of a man famous for his wit and renowned for his recounting of those tales of Ireland's merry peasants which found such delighted audience in those simpler and heartier days. Always as compared to his nimble-witted parent Ambrose had been accounted but a sad dog and a dreary one, indeed had it not been for the woodcock shoot Lady Charlotte's father would hardly have looked on him as much of a pretender for the hand of his daughter. However, as things turned out he made little Char a most suitable husband. Suitable indeed he was for he interfered with his wife in nothing, her moderate good sense was far more obvious to him than her complete tyranny. She looked to the running of Garonlea with a competent discretion that every one except the land agent felt to be a miracle of insight and almost supernatural power in a woman of those days. The agent knew too well how pig-headedly obstinate and reactionary Lady Charlotte could be, how unfair in her preferments and disposals. He alone could know how many awkward situations she had created and left him to deal with, but he knew too that good agencies were not too many, and as he was an old and tactful man, he was able to contain himself and agreed heartily with all those who so often said that Lady Charlotte was truly wonderful.

Ambrose her husband really thought so. He was implicit in his loyalty and belief in her and grateful indeed for the leisure her activities left him to pursue his own mild pleasures and businesses. His pleasure in the chase had been great though mild. There was no hunting now near Garonlea. It could never have been described as an active pursuit, but his own cowardice annoyed him not at all, so fox-hunting had been really a pleasure and not a scourge in his life. He was only a moderate shot, which of course was a pity, but a fine fisherman, and had, moreover, a sound knowledge of forestry which he was able to put into practice over many acres of his estates. His green felt hats were dented always in the same precise manner and each morning he could scarcely wait for the post to come in, so anxious was he to be off to the woods to grub up elders, or to the fields to wage his lifelong war, spud against thistle. He took his duties as a magistrate and a churchman seriously and discharged them with a punctiliousness which took no account of his own personal convenience. He was tremendously and rather touchingly proud of his house and his lands, touchingly because his pride was so truly that of a tenant for life of these possessions. He had inherited from so many before his father and the place would go down, he hoped, to as many beyond his son.

There were so few things really to lay hold of about Ambrose, that dim, gloomy, kind man. The man was so hidden beyond his circumstances—"Son of old Desmond McGrath—most amusing fellow that ever was." "His wife's a wonderfully able woman." "Best cock shoot in Ireland." These were the phrases used to describe Ambrose. Nothing about him as a person. Nobody knew that he had eaten boiled eggs for breakfast until his youngest child was ten, simply

15

because he fed the salty top to each child in turn at breakfast time. Nobody knew how he hated elders and loved ash trees though so much of his life was spent in uprooting one species and planting the other. Nobody knew how pure a pleasure it had given him to see hounds hunting a fox, or his setters in the heather or a young hound slipped on a hare. He had more connection with these things than with his daughters' beauty, or with his satisfactory soldier son, or with his lands. His wife had made all these things too much her own.

Garonlea where these McGraths had lived for a long time had its share in the forming and making of that sadness in their natures which so few of the family seemed entirely to escape. Now and then the sadness would miss a beat, as in the case of old Desmond and Ambrose's own son Desmond, and there was a character ready for pleasure and unvexed in mind, but the effect such owners had upon the place itself was as uncertain and as quickly dispersed as was the stamp they left on their successors who seemed the heavier for that brief shifting of gloom.

What is there that can be told about Garonlea and the evil that can be on a place through want of happiness. Or even of a will towards happiness. Family tragedy is brief and sudden in comparison to this that lies like the breath of mould in old clothes on the people who live in such a place. It seems as though nothing could ever dissolve such mists and ill vapours, or only for such a little while. So inexact, so dim is such a gloom, it is hard to say whether it is the effect of place on character or character on place. Thus was Garonlea affected beyond its native melancholy by these gloomy McGraths who had lived there such a dreadfully long time.

One side of a deep valley lay Garonlea with its rich lands and its woods of Craiga and Laphonka and Gibbets Grove, and its village of Garonlea. And on the farther side of the river that ran down the valley length, on this opposite side of the valley there is a gayer, lighter air to breathe. It is really and tangibly a better place altogether.

The house of Garonlea is built so near the river that the terraces of its garden drop down from the windows to the lush banks of the river. And above the house the comely embowering woods fulfil the act of clothing the mild valley in a manner more suited to an English manor than to a sad Irish place. The House was best described by some lady whose gifted pen wrote of it in a weekly paper as "an elegant castellated mansion." Such a house indeed was built by the McGrath who pulled down a Georgian dwelling house and built himself this habitation of glorious Gothic, out of a rich wife's money. Well, they had let themselves go and probably enjoyed the result.

But with all its vulgarity of architecture some curious eternal line of beauty remains to the house. Perhaps because its awful Gothic mass is built of the local gold-grey stone. But colour is not line. Vaguely the house is the right height for its width and has been built in the right attitude exactly for the shallow wooded height of the valley behind it. Below, the terraces dropping flight by flight, lion-guarded at each flight, towards the river, were well and elaborately cultivated. Crimson ramblers threading an intricate pergola, much bedding out of lobelia and geraniums in their proper season.

Here the girls would walk and sit and sew together and read the novels of Sir Walter Scott aloud to their mother. And if their brother Desmond was at home he would come out and have a joke with them now and then. They thought Desmond was marvellous. So daringly frivolous. So of a farther world. So brave, so sweetly scented when he kissed them in the morning. So full of jokes he might not say to them. So languorous and dreamy on some summer night when the valley was heavy in mist and white jasmine scented the air, its sprays leaden white near a dark window.

III

Iт was in November that Desmond McGrath brought
to Garonlea his love and Bride-to-be. It was her
first visit to his home. Nor had she met Lady Charlotte
before nor Desmond's father nor one of the four
sisters.

It had been one of the quick things in her life, this
engagement to Desmond, and her father saying,
"Well, you have only known him six weeks——
But the Garonlea shoot is famous, really famous.
Besides there is something I like about the boy. You
must please yourself, my pet, and remember I hate to
lose my little girl."

"You mean you hate to lose your little housekeeper,"
Cynthia had said with a practicality unusual at her
date. "You'll marry again, Daddy. You're a very
attractive man. I've had a hard time keeping off
prospective stepmothers. Much worse than you've
had with my suitors." It was the wit of the day, and
ran in rather flowing periods. Nobody resented this.

"A naughty little girl, I regret to say," he answered.

One of those admirable filial while maternal kisses
and she had gone.

At Garonlea Lady Charlotte was saying to her
husband, "Her family is all one could wish. But we
have never had anything to do with Racing. I could
have hoped that was different."

Ambrose answered, "Well, she has seen her father
lose a lot of money—what about the Cambridgeshire
when his horse started a red-hot favourite and finished
down the course."

"Let us hope the child knew nothing about the matter. Anyhow it's good blood, remember, and I was presented the same season as her mother. So really one can't help feeling dear Desmond has made a good choice."

The girls were told:

"Desmond has written to his father and to me saying he wishes to be engaged. He is coming over for the first woodcock shoot and hopes to bring his—his bride-to-be with him so that we may all get to know her and to love her."

"Mother! Do we know her?"

"Next week?"

"Oh how exciting!"

"Who is she?"

"Well, Diana, if you will give me your attention for a moment and try not to interrupt I will tell you. She is a daughter of Colonel George Holland-Mull and her mother, who was presented the same year that I was, was a Hamish, a daughter of the last Coolcullen."

"But they're all as mad as hatters."

"Di—ana?"

"Oh, but it's true. Half the Hamishes are locked up."

"My child, to repeat such foolish gossip is both vulgar and dangerous. Please never mention the subject again to any one."

"All right. But it is true."

"Diana, I don't wish to hear another word from you. The idea. Are you aware that you are being extremely impertinent to Mother?"

So Cynthia Holland-Mull (such good blood, remember) came to Garonlea for the first time one November evening when there was a high star in the sky and a light frost and the moon as clear as glass above the high hedges and faintly patterned fields and the thin distant line of mountains. She and her lover bowled along in a dashing high-wheeled dogcart behind a brisk chestnut horse. Desmond, though his unqualified happiness was almost unendurable, did not touch her hand with his once, not her gloved hand beneath that fur rug as he drove the seven miles from the station to Garonlea. After all there was a stable boy sitting with his back to them in the rear seat of the dog-cart.

" You're certain you're not cold?" he asked her every mile or so and she smiled at him through her veil, for how could she be cold in her dark green driving coat lined with fur and its three-tiered cape like a highwayman's, and her feet in their pointed glacé kid shoes were warm as toasts in a blue fur-lined foot muff. And though she would scarcely have said so, how could she feel cold in the glow and the thrill of Desmond beside her.

"Oh, no, I am deliciously warm," she said.

"We should have a good day to-morrow, they've had nearly a week's frost, Dempsey told me——" Desmond could hardly have felt happier. His Love and his Bride by his side and the prospect of two excellent days' shooting in front of him.

"Are we near Garonlea yet?" Cynthia asked.

Desmond said, "Yes, this is Garonlea now."

But they drove on for miles before they came to an avenue gate, and always down hill. Down hill with woods sloping down to the road on their left hand and dropping thickly below them down the side of the valley.

"What a long way down hill," Cynthia said brightly. Through all her insensitive happiness a faint feeling of hostility and coldness was at her heart which she could not explain. Perhaps she was a little chilly after all. Perhaps it was nerves at the thought of meeting Desmond's relations. Whatever it was it did not leave her when the dog-cart turned in at a vast and over-powering gateway, an impressive cross between the entrance to a mosque and a street lavatory, and bowled (that was what the best dog-carts did) smoothly down the smooth falling slope of the avenue.

Cynthia was not shy when she first met people. She was too certain of herself. Quite sure of her success. So that this first encounter with Desmond's relations was hardly the reason for the constricted chill that was causing her to feel so unreal to herself; on the defensive and alone when they stopped before the great wan house sprawled at the bottom of the valley with the mist rising round it off the river below. Soon, in a moment almost, the door was opened and Desmond had lifted her down and she was real and breathing easily again, feeling as well and free as she only did near him. Her head swam a little as they went together through the strange light halls and into the library where Desmond's mother and all his pretty sisters kissed her with eager embarrassed welcome. All but one kissed her so, the little dark one with a stiff white collar up to her young soft chin, she shook hands nervously and with a blushing determination that evaded graceful readiness for a sisterly salute.

"And how cold you must be!"

"Such a journey!"

"Did you have a long wait at the junction?"

"Muriel, my dear, you may take Cynthia up to her room."

"Yes, I'm rather a dirty girl, I think," said Cynthia, blinking like a cat, a gold cat in the warm light room where white chrysanthemums smelt antiseptically and a majestic silver tea service glittered on an elaborately clothed table.

"There will be some fresh tea for you and Desmond by then," Lady Charlotte passed over Cynthia's little joke as perhaps a pity. "We're all rather smutty after that journey," she added.

Cynthia, knowing she looked superb in her new green facecloth coat and skirt with a dark flat velvet cap skewered through the pale puffed wings of her hair, agreed and followed the shy eager Muriel upstairs.

She had been put into the most important bedroom —very high and papered in white and silvery white stripes with a dado of brisk pink roses. Rosebuds on the chintzes too and fresh frilled covers on all the cushions. Two brass bedsteads shrouded in starched elaborate white. A red carpet on the floor and a greataunt's faded water colours on the walls. Malmaison carnations in a silver vase on the writing table and a small coal fire in the grate. The rest of the furnishings by Mr. Maple.

Cynthia changed with speed and total disregard of cold into a mauve chiffon blouse, dislocating herself cleverly to fasten its back buttons and the nine minute hooks that fastened the wire-supported net collar, which finished in a wee Toby frill under her chin. An embroidered yoke and deep soft folds of tulle, long big sleeves gathered in ten different directions and very tight on the wrist—that was how this romantic blouse was made, and worn with a dark purple skirt and bronze kid slippers with bronze bead buckles. Cynthia tucked a bunch of silk violets into her waistband and was ready when Muriel knocked at her door again.

That was the start of the shooting party at Garonlea

23

in 1900; the party that was to make known to the county the next Mrs. French-McGrath.

Cynthia enjoyed it a great deal. She understood the organised formal entertainment perfectly and played her part as star guest with tact and an exquisitely right sense of drama.

Only Desmond knew something of her under that perfectly constructed facade towards which his mother could not deny her approval and with which his father and his sisters were soon half in love. She excited them all. He saw that and it pleased if it disturbed him. He knew she was a powerful and secret person and it delighted him profoundly that this creature should with him be moved by so strong a current that she was as helpless as a body in a smooth flood. He liked her efforts at restraint or dignity and would uphold her in them with a certain subtlety until she abandoned them because she was entirely and urgently in want of love. He was not grand about this to himself. It did not make him feel either as masterful or protective or indifferent as it might have done. As it certainly should have done according to the "never give all" theories of the date. Not that it was possible, or even thinkable, to give or take what they called "all" at such a party, but moments of practically unendurable ecstasy and severe strain were permissible and considered both romantical and seemly under the auspices of that magic word—Engaged. To such moments Cynthia brought a wild whole life and an entire lack of austerity, very touching if it had not been for the complete freedom with which she regained her balance when they were over.

I V

A DAY and a night from such a party, what were they really like? Not like the jolly reminiscencing of some countess who had tremendous success with King Edward—— "We joined the ' guns ' for luncheon in a keeper's cottage, all very jolly and informal. I remember old Lord X having five helpings of Irish stew." . . . No. Probably depressingly the same as the same shoot to-day—except that the women didn't drink so much or talk dirt. Anyhow there is no truth to be got from the queens of these past festivities. How vainly we seek it. Why can't we get hold of any truth about them ? They are defensive now—the Enids and Muriels and Cynthias. One asks them some absurd question—clothes, for instance!

Instead of saying, "My dear, you should have seen our buttoned boots, they were too nice. And you really were a dashing girl if you put black ribbon in your camisoles." Or, "How well I remember my first ball dress—White. You practically had to wear White. White satin, the bodice cut down to the bust line and my bosoms propped and supported, all most pneumatic and attractive to the gentlemen. Puff sleeves and white kid gloves turning the elbow. And such a waist, darling—twenty-three inches without going black in the face. Then a full flowing skirt (bodices and skirt were not attached, you wore a folded silk belt pointed back and front). But petticoats—there was drama for you!—Flounces and lace and insertion and ribbon bows among the lace. It all gave one such a sensation of one's own glamour. Glamour I think was what we had. Glamour was the thing——"

No. They say instead, "Well, I think our clothes weren't so very unlike what you wear now. Long skirts in the evening, you know. Really I think we were very much the same—not so very different. We used to have tremendous fun. Perhaps we wore more elaborate clothes in the afternoon."

And they were so different. Really they had everything we haven't got. Why don't they boast about it more? Why aren't they prouder of their glamour and their chastity and their dainty boots and their rich leisured lives. Why don't they see that they lived in a definite Period? Not in a moment of transition between the Victorian and the present age. Why don't they face the Edwardian Practical Jokes and insist that many of them were fine jokes, much funnier than simply breaking things?

Perhaps it is because they are too Spartan ever to face the truth. One only gets at the truth by admitting a lot of pain. By not minding being a fool for a moment. By forgetting one's natural tremendous vanity. By coming off one's poses. But they cannot speak a lessening thing of themselves, a thing that leaves them open to wounding, anything near the truth. Still we must allow them their glamour.

Breakfast time at Garonlea. The ladies were all down to breadfast—very neat. Shirts and fringes and little watches ticking on their left bosoms, pinned there by a silver, a gold or a jewelled bow. Sunlight poured in through the long windows and an enormous breakfast was on the sideboard. Undefeated by the hour, the wit of the party, Colonel Stagg (who had not missed a Garonlea shoot for ten years) made his jokes and the ladies all laughed merrily. He told Lady Charlotte what an Irishman called Pat had said, which put the table in a roar. After this he ate a dish of kedgeree, a snipe and some cold ham, and got to the lavatory first. He was a very civilised man and knew the technique of these parties well.

Lady Charlotte was having a talk about St. Bridget anemones and the new rhododendron, Pink Pearl, with his wife on her right. This was her mate for the party. Enid was sitting silently beside a young man called Poor Arthur, with whom she had surprised herself by her success the night before. "He has far more in him than I ever thought," she told Diana when they went to bed. Violet and Muriel maintained strained but bright conversation, one with her Uncle George who told her in sentences not longer than nine words how well his daughter Phyllis was getting on, and the other with Lord Jason Helvick, who only cared about Bird Life and was destined to disappoint Lady Charlotte's hopes that he might care about Muriel too. After all he was forty-eight and it was time he settled down.

Diana sat between her father and Muriel so that she need not talk. Cynthia on Ambrose's other side delighted him with details of moors he had shot over in Scotland and men he knew, but had been too shy to make friends with. She had an entirely accurate and reliable memory. Desmond sat on her other side in a live union of silence, delighted because his father was so impressed by his able young Love. Across the table Diana with frequent shyness raised her eyes to Cynthia's gold head and dropped them quickly on her plate. Puffed and back combed, braided and whorled, Cynthia's hair could not quite lose the yellow extreme softness of willow flowers—the yellow that is almost silver.

27

After breakfast the men disappeared for the morning and the ladies sat about in the drawing-room chattering amiably. They looked out through the window down the drop of the terraces and across the sleekly flooded river to the high bright rise of woods on the opposite side of the valley. The morning was damp and full of sunlight, still sweet air as soft as a cat's fur.

But inside the drawing-room the day seemed far off and hostile to the creatures and furniture and ornaments enclosed. There was a good deal of furniture in the drawing-room and the ladies, poised about on gilded chairs, their heads bent over pieces of needlework, looked like faintly dusty stuffed birds—the sun in their fuzzed hair made a dusty effect and their bosoms and padded behinds were birdlike. In the crowded groups of Dresden china the sun picked out dust in the raised wreaths of flowers and struck high lights off the smooth bosoms of those other china ladies and fat behinds of china Cupids. The lovely chandelier looked dark and sinister as dark glass can look, the chairs were slippery with sun, and the fire strove against the light till Muriel, at her mother's nod, drew down a blind.

As though she had been waiting for this, Diana jumped up and said to Cynthia:

"Wouldn't you like to come out? It's such a lovely morning."

Her words sounded distressingly prearranged, she had been rehearsing them for nearly ten minutes, and brought them out now with unnatural speed and boldness.

Lady Charlotte looked up from the note she was writing. She paused a second, raised pen in hand, and in that second in that room streaked by long moted beams of sun, she seemed to swell with strange arrogance among those swords of sunlight before she said in her voice of commanding benignancy:

"My dear, I think you and Diana will be quite tired enough by to-night without going for one of her long rambles now. Besides which, Diana"—the voice lost some of that benignancy—"you must remember Desmond might like to take Cynthia round himself."

Cynthia smiled faintly in good-humoured acquiescence. It was not till after Diana's blush of fury had died its last beneath her high collar, and the ripple of embarrassment had widened to oblivion through the room, and Lady Charlotte's pen pursued once more its dignified course, that she lifted her eyes to send Diana a look of such complete understanding that Diana's heart was stilled for a suffocating moment before it went galloping off on its pledged way. She was exquisitely, powerlessly committed to Cynthia. It was one of the most important moments in her life.

To Cynthia the incident was chiefly important as a mark for her when the faint hostility she had felt last night towards Garonlea became through that enclosing room, that quiet arrogant voice, that helpless blush of rage, a real thing which she must hide from every one except the little Diana. But most especially from Desmond.

V

THE ladies and the luncheon set off at 12.15, to meet the guns. A phaeton with curling springs and blue cushions carried most of the party. A side-car with a red crest on its back and food in its well the remainder. Gloved in tight dog-skin and neatly veiled the ladies drove along the little roads that climbed and twisted and shelved their way about the valley side of Garon-lea.

Then greetings at a keeper's cottage high above a wood of hazel and rhododendron. Chaff and laughter, always bursts and ready tinkles of laughter, and an enormous quantity of rich hot food served in the dark parlour of the cottage where pictures of Popes and stags and Jesus (with little faded crosses from the last Palm Sunday stuck in their frames) looked on at the gay and social scene.

There were more men now to pay compliments if not court the girls. Violet's smooth blush rose and fell at things that Colonels said. And Muriel's sweet rather deprecating giggle was drowned in the hearty male voices of men who were men.

Poor Arthur had been shooting well (for him) and sought Enid's company in a gay and confident manner that did not escape Lady Charlotte's notice. A pity he was staying in the house. She would just drop Enid a little hint before dinner. The agent's son. No money and socially not quite—quite, he had been asked to fill a gap at the last minute. The fact that he was rather good-looking in a pale languid way struck Lady Charlotte for the first time. Fairly presentable considering his grandfather was a Solicitor, was all she had thought before.

Huge savoury stews, game pie, and brawn and ham and mince pies and cheese; whisky and white wine and port (and water for the young ladies, but Cynthia drank half of Desmond's whisky and a glass of port, looking at him in a quick secret way and saying, "I think I'm cold"; even Lady Charlotte missed this, it was so gently and so speedily done.

Later she stood with him in a wet quiet ride where little white flies and midges were like steam and the late Autumn felt as dark with life as Spring, as they waited there for first sound of the beaters. Desmond was an awfully keen shooter so he only kissed her once a little abstractedly, for it was unthinkable that even one cock should swing across the open ride and tilt and dodge away among the trees unslain by him.

And Cynthia who was always keen for love but particularly after she had had a drink or two, restrained herself a little sullenly, but forgot about some of it soon for she was interested in shooting and in any case would have attended Desmond with fervour if his sport had been fishing for eels or shooting pike in a weir.

Soon there was tremendous popping and banging through the wood. And everywhere some lady smiled and nodded commiseration or congratulation, relieved from making silly speeches by the merciful imposition of silence that attends these woodcock *battues*. At other shoots they had to rack their brains for something to say to their " guns." When they said the wrong thing it was taken for granted. The only things that were not taken for granted were silence, or staying at home or wanting to shoot themselves.

The end of the day came at last. Lady Charlotte

31

had driven home long ago and the girls were strangely gay and comfortable without her. The last drive was over and the early dusk was running softly through the valley. The smooth river as though its course was on a map curled along below them. The whole evening felt sleek and finished. Good and indifferent dogs were highly commended. The party walked down the soft rides through the hazel groves and glossy cold leaved thickets of rhododendron, the girls gay and chattering.

"This is the wishing well."

"A real wishing well?"

"Yes, The wishing well in Craiga Wood."

"Oh, I must have a wish!"

"And so must I——"

They stooped laughing to the low icy water in the roofed well. They stood in the soft ground where springs broke up and stooped like spotted antelopes among the shining dark leaves. They drank out of their cold pink palms and wiped their wet chins with handkerchiefs. Their eyes were dark—they would never tell their wishes for love and marriage, but lied and said they wished for a new hats or diamond watches.

"A *rich* husband!" Enid said to poor Arthur with daring sauciness. A good thing Lady Charlotte did not hear her, or see her changed eyes when they met his unsmiling answering look, or know the deep-sweet change of his voice in her ears.

Back to the house in the valley then and the ladies scurried upstairs to change into smart clothes for tea. After tea a group played cards, a group leaned round the piano causing havoc among the photographs, singing softly.

Two were missing, Cynthia and Diana. They sat

by the fire in Cynthia's room, Diana talking—thirsty for this new sympathy, a little drunk with the excitement of it, the thrilling discovery of Cynthia. Their moment together was stolen, for they had no business according to the rules of such a party to absent themselves like this. One should not relax in effort; one should be beautifully, endlessly hearty and sparkle meritoriously at all hours. Yet here they sat upon the floor by Cynthia's fire, spread skirts, heads bent talking as the moments raced by. Cynthia saying yes and yes and yes. Her weight leaning on one arm, her strong hand with fingers spread propped on the floor behind her. Diana sat up straight, her voice going on and on, as emotional as wings in the dark beating on, to what end they do not know.

"But, Cynthia, I can't go on living here. I must do something. I must escape. . . . Muriel's all right. She adores Violet, and besides she never thinks anyhow. And Violet, she's sure to marry."

"Yes, and Enid?"

"Oh, I have no patience with Enid. Always some silly, rather disgusting flirtation and then a row with Mother, and tears, and everything forgotten."

"Yes, and you?"

"Oh, I hate young men nearly as much as they hate me. I only want to get away from Garonlea. It's so awful, I know, I've never confessed it to any one before, but I loathe and loathe this place. I never feel well for a moment and there's that awful depression pulling one down all the time like lead."

"Yes."

"You feel it too, Cynthia?"

"Yes, it's overpowering."

"Did you know we aren't supposed to talk about it?"

33

"How do you mean?"

"The oppression—it belongs to the house. It's a thing we aren't allowed to admit."

"This melancholy?"

"Do you know, it got so bad once, Father got a man here who was supposed to clear up horrid things in houses. But he didn't do much good. We were all sent away."

"How eerie. But the feeling I have is that no one has ever enjoyed themselves here; and if any one ever did anything wrong it's been a sad wrong, not a bit enjoyable."

"Perhaps you and Desmond will change the house. He is so much gayer than the rest of us."

"Oh, Diana, but Desmond and I will be old before we come here to live."

"It is so wicked of me to say but the thought of living here with Father and Mother for the next twenty years seems absolutely unbearable."

"You must live with us a great deal."

"That will be lovely." Her acceptance was casual because this telling was so much more important, all the luxury of first spoken grief was in it. "But Cynthia, if you only knew what it's like, always being watched and ordered about. Everything *known* about one. Even if one writes a letter to another girl—one has nothing of one's own at all. Not even a dog. Father won't let me have a dog of my own."

"My poor darling, I do so understand."

"I can't believe that two days ago I didn't know you."

"Or I you. . . . Should we go down? I'm afraid we should."

Violet was captured too with talk of clothes and bridesmaids' dresses all planned for Violet. She was easily capturable and except for her beauty unimportant. But still Cynthia meant to have her.

"This design won't suit my other big bridesmaid so well—poor Mabel, she'll need a lot of padding—but you will look so lovely in it, I think it's the only one to have. What do you think about the bouquets? . . . Yes, I think you're right there. . . . Yes, I agree about those shoes."

Then with Enid: "What a charmer that dark young man is. And he never takes his eyes off you. Are you interested in him or just amusing yourself?"

How grand it made Enid feel, how worldly and successful, as though she had dozens of beaux.

"Well, I am rather attracted. But I have to be dreadfully careful on account of Mother."

"Yes, I see. But he seems so charming. Why does she disapprove? No money, I suppose. The nice ones never have, do they? Tell me more about him."

It was sympathy that would listen even to Enid's shy rhapsodies about poor Arthur. And unscrupulousness that could sit with Lady Charlotte for an hour and agree and agree:

"I do see how difficult it is. There are very few men here, aren't there? But naturally one must put one's foot down about people of that sort. I don't want to betray a confidence but from something she said to me I think perhaps she is—just a little—— I do hope you will let them come and stay with Desmond and me. There is a charming Major Blake in the regiment. I thought of him the moment I saw Muriel. Yes, a little money and some helpful connections. One isn't a snob but you know I *do* think Family matters a lot—don't you——?

"I've no sisters so it's wonderful to find a ready-made family of them. . . . I expect you remember my

mother better than I do. I was only six . . . so it's
wonderful to find you. I know you won't mind giving
me help and advice and I shall want such a lot, shan't
I?"

Diana was discussed too. "I think you're very wise
with her. Obviously she's rather difficult. But it's
only a stage she's going through, I expect. One does,
doesn't one? I was dreadfully tiresome at eighteen but
my father was so sweet and wonderful to me."

With Ambrose too she was tremendous. She walked
out with him, visiting his young plantations, and
paused comfortably at every alder tree they met in
the woods. This was not the thistling season or she
would have had to pause at every thistle too. She asked
him all the questions he could answer about the fishing
and the shooting and whether the land would be
suitable for bloodstock. For she had a very good plan
about getting Desmond out of his dreary regiment
and—as she thought it necessary for him to have an
occupation which would interest her too—this would
be excellent. A stud farm on the other side of the valley.
Some really good mares. What a help Father would
be about getting hold of them. She saw them standing
with their foals in the deep shades of chestnut trees in
July. Next year she saw those beautifully bred and well
fed and insolent yearlings galloping and wheeling
and stopping in the strong railed fields. She saw the
prices they made at Doncaster and every one con-
gratulating Desmond on a wonderful sale.

She had seen too a big bright house on the other
side of the river. A charming house with every possibility except that it had been inhabited for the last
fifteen years by two old aunts of Desmond's, but no
doubt a more suitable little house could be found for
them when the time came.

Cynthia and Desmond had gone to tea at this house one day. They had eggs for tea in filagree silver egg-cups, and buttered toast and medlar jelly and Sally Lunn teacake, while the Aunts bustled about scolding each other and lavishing flattery and adoration on Cynthia and Desmond.

Aunt Milly had been a beauty and married an exotic Swedish Count who spent her money and shot himself. She was a little mad and enjoyed behaving as though the parlourmaid was three flunkeys in scarlet and gold braid, and generally induced a sensation of red carpets and foreign courts. Her sister Mousie who was little and brisk and loving was the real ruler of the house-hold and queen of the garden wherein was walled their pleasure and chief sport in life, their expectation, adventure and triumph.

Although the month was November, Cynthia was shown the garden. Out through the drawing-room, where old Pieces, small and perfect, were crowded and obscured by bamboo and plush furnishings, and photographs of the late Count Standoof jostled Chelsea figures and deep Worcester saucers patterned in scaled blue and flowers, as rich and thick as sweet-williams.

They trooped out through a long window and across a small sunk lawn bounded by a little nut walk, the Aunts pausing at every step.

"And in the Spring you can't see the grass for the crocus—that bank, my dear, is as blue—as blue now as china with the scyllas."

They talked like so many Irish ladies of their gener-ation with rather plummy brogues which however detracted nothing from the brisk and distinguished pronunciation of each word.

Beyond the lawn and the dark little nut walk was a

37

walled garden entered through a small green wooden door, and in here they moved from one point of excitement to another.

"That's my robin."

"No, that's *my* robin, Mousie."

"As if I didn't know my own robin."

"You must see the Christmas roses."

"Well, you can't exactly see them, dear, as I gathered them for the tea-table—seven lovely blooms, Fancy! But here's where they grow by the door of the potting shed."

"And Iris Stiloza under the wall here. The dear creature, she loves us here and Mrs. Barclay who lives a mile away can't get her to flower at all. In spite of her five men in the garden."

"And here's where our prize Auriculas will be a lovely show in the Spring. Look at all I have now, and I started with three little plants your father brought me from a big flower show. Look, Desmond— You must tell him when you go home."

And so round the empty, tidy garden which to them was alive with a reality beyond any dim sleeping promise, and back to the drawing-room where candles and a lamp that gave as much light as a goldfish in a bowl were lighting. The Aunts showed Cynthia their china, about which they were as well informed as about their flowers, even if they did obscure it with photographs. And when it was time to say good-bye they gave her a ravishing Chelsea group. A naughty musician in a braided coat bending towards a sleeping lady, thrillingly and for ever suspended in a moment before a kiss.

They would hear of no refusal which Desmond was inclined to urge, knowing their china was as much to them as their garden, and that they would mourn the piece sadly when the excitements of giving and of Cynthia were gone.

"Ah. no, Desmond, you mustn't forbid us such a pleasure."

"Our new niece and all."

"But you'll be careful of it, Child," a sudden anxiety overtook Aunt Mousie, "see, there's not a chip anywhere. And just count her petticoats—she has seven, I declare, and a different pattern on each, stripes, and flowers, and her farthingale spotted with little strawberries."

"I will, indeed I will, and thank you a thousand times."

Cynthia kissed them, making it the most important matter in the world, and set off for her walk home with Desmond, carrying the china figures preciously within her muff.

From half a mile down the road she looked back but she could no longer see the house, only a slight pale tongue of trees advancing from the solid wood at its back, coldly delicately stepping up towards a pale winter field and a pale sky.

She put her hand into Desmond's, her other hand holding the china figures inside her muff, and walked on down towards the river, exquisitely conscious of herself and of him and of a happiness so whole that it seemed impossible it should last. And if it did not, there was no further happiness to look for.

They crossed the river by a twisting cramped stone bridge, its walls niched for the safety of foot people in the coaching days, and in the middle niche Cynthia stood looking down at the river and knowing her reluctance to go back to Garonlea. A quarter of a mile distant the house rose romantically towards its woods, a pale milky mass of stone with the river

39

dark as a moat below it. The strangling sharp river breath of evening caught her and the cold remote river sounds filled her with a curious despair.

"Desmond, Desmond," she said and clung to his hand as if in a dream she saw him lost to her. She set her fur muff with its china burden down on the stone, a last formal little act, absurd beside her need for Desmond and those kisses in the chill and quiet darkness of the evening.

But when he had kissed her and after she knew with that fleeting realisation and sense of power that makes women gay that his love was even beyond her own, there came to her again as they walked back along the smooth avenue towards Garonlea, that sense of oppression that was like dying or weeping in its strength. She pressed nearer to Desmond under the dark tree, but his nearness only made her feel more sad.

VI

THE warm, full light of an August day poured liquidly into the schoolroom filling it with round generosity. At the piano with her back turned to the window, Enid sat playing; turning her music, sometimes she smiled secretly and touched the bosom of her blue dress from which came the faint but thrilling crackle of a letter from Arthur—no longer to her Poor Arthur, but the first and most beloved of men. How, she wondered, had she ever thought differently about him. How had she lived so long only half living, unloved by him. She went on playing her Chopin in the most unconsciously uxorious way, half delighted, half dreaming in the warm room.

Lady Charlotte walking briskly down the flagged path outside the window pursed her lips disagreeably. One knew without looking in that it was Enid being rather embarrassing at the piano. A pity girls didn't understand themselves more clearly. A pity one could not explain anything to them without destroying their innocence. One could only indicate and forbid. And this reminded Lady Charlotte that she must have a serious talk with her Enid. There had been yet another letter to-day from that most undesirable young man. And he was to be home on leave almost immediately. Enid had suggested with nervous indifference that he should be asked to Thursday's tennis and croquet party. To-day was Tuesday, and there she was playing the piano "like that."

"Enid! Enid!—A pity, dear. Too sentimental, don't

you think? I was looking for you to come for a little walk."

Enid blushed cruelly and sprang up from the piano with a violence that set all the photographs rattling. Desmond's wedding group in a silver frame and all the Presentation pictures were still vibrating when with sullen indignation she followed her mother towards the distant kitchen gardens. It was not entirely an auspicious opening for the little homily which Lady Charlotte was about to deliver.

Within the high brick walls all was hot and still and orderly. It was as orderly as a prison yard and Lady Charlotte had as much authority over her children as any prison Governor. She was a dispenser and an arbitrator and behind her was unquestioned power. A habit of obedience overlaid the tumultuous desires and suppressions of her young daughters. There was nothing good about that habit, and had they not been rather stupid girls they would have evaded it with subtler lies and schemings than they were able to concoct.

"——So you see, my dear," said Lady Charlotte after five minutes of uninterrupted speech——"I trust my little Enid and I appeal to her own good sense. Is it quite wise or quite kind to encourage a young man whom neither Mother or Father could ever consider seriously possible? Just write him a perfectly kind, straightforward letter by this afternoon's post saying, let me see, saying, well, perhaps you can think of what you will say. But in any case give him clearly to understand that all this silly letter-writing must cease."

Enid said in a strained, small voice, "But, Oh, Mother, you don't understand——"

"I think I do, dear," Lady Charlotte's interruption came bright and remorselessly. "Mother understands

42

a great deal, you know, about what her little girl is feeling, but she is old enough and wise enough to know what is best."

"But, Oh, Mother, you must have forgotten—don't you remember how you felt about Father?" Enid's voice faltered over this rather bold and embarrassing question.

"My dear child, that has nothing whatever to do with it." And here Lady Charlotte spoke more truly than she knew, for that seemly, unloving and fruitful union had been at no moment familiar with the heat of love. "Nor do I consider that this is a particularly pleasant or suitable matter for you to argue about like this."

Enid's face was crimson. Her breath came interruptedly so that she could not speak clearly. She was helpless to speak in this passion of rage against her mother and the quiet, controlled force of her mother's power. Tears swelled in her throat. Her fingers were stiff as little darts as she fought for the control which she had not. The most wretched and passionate young creature imaginable, she stood in the sunshine between the hot savoury-smelling hedges of lavender, with the high, warm prison walls about—walls against which delicate fruit ripened decorously in the faint shadow of its proper leaves.

"Of course, my dear, if you would rather that I wrote——" Lady Charlotte dropped the suggestion almost casually. It came as the hot garden world was spinning in a bright globe of tears before Enid's eyes and it shocked her into a realisation of more than her own present emotion. Such a letter would wound—shock her Arthur, her love, in a way she could not endure. She gathered her voice and spoke high and uncertainly, almost neighing with nervousness.

43

"No, I'll write," she said. "I see, I see what you mean." There was a moment within her mind of almost maniacal tension when she thought of all she might say. I must marry him. I adore him. You don't know how much I need him. Why shouldn't I marry him ? You could give us enough money, and with his pay we could manage. What right have you—Oh, you have no right—to do this to me!

But to hint of money or to speak even in the shyest, most romantical terms of "sex" (that then unknown and unspoken word) was beyond Enid even in the most desperate circumstances. Her heart might break as she stood there but she could not do it. She heard her mother's voice commending her good sense and obedience and then hoped to escape. But no. She was bidden to hold a basket and snip the rotten paper heads of dead sweet pea. It was not till Lady Charlotte thought those foolish tears and sniffings might attract the notice of her head gardener who came lumbering slumberously down a path towards them that she dismissed her daughter in waiting, saying:

"Go to your room and splash your eyes with cold water, dear. Then lie down for half an hour, you'll soon feel better. Yes, Williams——?"

Although too encompassed and overcome by habit and emotion to tell of her love, Enid possessed too much obstinacy, passion, caution and cowardice to let her love go. It was unthinkable that she should forgo those thrilling embracings, and lonely hours of delighted imaginings, all dependent on Arthur and her relations with him. So, although for a fortnight no more letters came in Arthur's writing, letters still came, with writing curiously disguised, and there were fevered short meetings in woods and fields and other outdoor places when the strength of their emotion delighted and terrified them both, and the mental and physical strain became quite absurdly unfair.

Not unnaturally, Lady Charlotte's suspicions soon fell on these peculiar letters. While her imagination could hardly compass the possibility of Enid's disobedience and deceit in such a matter, at the same time she could not feel quite easy in her mind. Then one unlucky day Poor Arthur, emboldened by the safe arrival of so many ardent letters, was taken with the fancy to write to his love not once but twice. Two letters. It was too much for Lady Charlotte's trust. These two peculiar letters arriving together even lowered some of the surprising conceit which forbade her mind to accept suspicion of disobedience in one of her children. Her pride at once transmuted this lessening of her vanity into a sadness. Lies and deceit besides being wicked were sad, but especially sad and wicked—useless as well—when employed by a more than foolish child against Mother or God. The tremendous urgency of a matter that could have made an Enid rebel in such a way did not occur in any just proportion to Lady Charlotte. A court was set in the library, Ambrose in so serious a matter was an unwilling lay figure of extra authority, and a message was sent for Miss Enid to attend.

Miss Enid, who for the last hour had been in that exquisite state of hot and cold impatience which each day preceded post time, arrived in the library with every nerve twittering. She felt like a tree full of starlings.

"Yes, Mother?"

Lady Charlotte came directly to the point. She handed Enid the two letters, saying, "Your father and I would like to know who your correspondent is."

Ambrose cleared his throat as if about to speak and then said nothing.

45

The summer air in the library was astonishingly still. In all the small, scattered vases of flowers not as much as a feather of asparagus fern stirred. From the walls a few pompous ancestors seemed to puff their dark cheeks, strain their bellies against their waistcoats and lean a little closer to this trouble and tension. The photograph of Violet in her court dress smiled divinely on. The stillness could not last. It was swelled to its extremity.

Enid spoke.

"I shan't tell you," she said.

The room seemed to stagger back from her words and before its force returned or Lady Charlotte could gather herself for a deadly rejoinder, Enid, terrified by her own daring and its possible consequences, had turned and run out through the door and, unseen by sisters or servants, out of the house.

Lady Charlotte's first and truest reaction was shown in her first words:

"What a pity I gave her those letters. It was my duty to read them."

Ambrose, though he suffered slightly from shock, was pleased that the matter of the letters had been taken so briskly out of the hands of proper authority. Proper Authority seemed to him at times so cruel if so necessary a weapon in dealing with the young. He thought for a second with a faint quickening of life of Enid fled from the house sitting now in some dark strip of wood, where lately he had cut the elders, where sorrel flowers were blown on the faintest air, reading her letters, her rescued letters, preposterously thrilled by the written word. . . . A pity that it was all so unsuitable. However, Charlotte must deal with it as she thought best. Charlotte was a wonderful woman.

He said, "I think, my dear, I will attack the thistles in the Long Acre this morning——" He hesitated. "If that is all?"

"Poor child," Lady Charlotte was recovering her poise. "It is most distressing. It seems to me most sad, a sad—sad pity that she should have acted like this. Yes, Ambrose, I will deal with her after luncheon."

But the luncheon gong rang in vain as far as Enid was concerned. The cold lamb and salad and raspberry tart and cheese were eaten to the accompaniment of rather strained and spasmodic conversation and the three girls stole questioning looks at each other and could scarcely wait for luncheon to be over so that they could discuss the matter in the schoolroom. But this design was astutely opposed by Lady Charlotte who took the lot with her to pay a round of calls, sending them up to their rooms separately to put on their smart hats.

The due reward of maternal tact, diplomacy and firmness awaited Lady Charlotte when, more unquiet in her mind than she would admit, she went up to her room on her return from that weary round of calls in the company of three sulking daughters. The reward was almost too wonderfully apt to be true, and through it Lady Charlotte experienced a sensation of placidity and pride at this fresh proof of the eternal rightness of her judgment.

The reward was Enid, showing extravagant signs of repentant hysteria. Lady Charlotte, who derived an unknowing and not very pretty excitement from the emotional outbursts of her children, gave Enid's sobbing apologies every encouragement.

"My child is truly sorry?"

"Yes. I am."

"Then what have you done with those two letters?"

"I tore them up. But I never want to write to him again or hear from him, or see him, I promise."

Enid was shaking all over. She had the look of one with a chill on the stomach and a fever on the mind.

"Again? Then you saw him to-day? And alone? Oh, Enid, Enid."

Enid leant her head against the end of the stiff little sofa and sobbed steadily.

"Enid?"

"He's going away to-morrow."

"*Oh!*"

"And I don't want to see him again."

"Can Mother trust you this time?"

"YES," said Enid, almost on a howl.

After this Lady Charlotte had sense enough to bestow a kiss in which forgiveness was suspended if not actually granted, before she sent her to bed and ordered a glass of Marsala to go up on Miss Enid's dinner tray.

VII

VASTLY interested with her handling of the situation and relieved if a little puzzled by Enid's sudden change of heart (accountable no doubt to the shock of such conduct as hers had been to-day) Lady Charlotte rang for her maid. She then washed her hands with buttermilk soap, folded the neck of her combinations down towards the top of her corsets (those corsets which propped so conscientiously the bosoms like vast, half-filled hot-water bottles)and thus prepared, stood while her evening dress, so like those the Queen wears, was put upon her, and sat while her hair was fiddled, not redone. Her hair was never washed but it did not smell of anything but hair. The switches and curls of false hair were drier and frizzier in texture than her own.

She opened her jewel-case with certain snapping fingers and gazed in the glass thoughtfully, many things forgotten, almost an unruled, apprehensive creature, as she put the little hooks of ear-rings through her ears, and fastened a great, sprawling diamond bird in the velvet band round her throat and a spray of diamond daisies in her bosom. She did not really dream. Only for a moment she was not quite alert or prepared.

At this time Enid was hardly fully conscious, although she had frequently-recurring moments of lively mental agony in which words like Seduced, Betrayed, Giving All, and Wicked Woman, held up her mind in a grip that allowed no other thought.

So this was where Love led you at last. Only to this embarrassing and uncomfortable experience, this unsatisfactory and disgraceful conclusion. And—fly the thought, let there be no remembrance—at the back of Enid's mind was the horrid admission that she herself more than the faint-hearted Arthur had been the one most grossly responsible for their wicked act. While I was Pure I was happy, Enid thought miserably, remembering those months of Purity when she had done everything "But," as a period of Grace foregone for ever. Sadly confused, unable to think or know anything at all clearly, she lay in her horrid disillusion, overcome by a shattering remorse, a remorse such as one might feel to-day, should one follow the impulse of beating a maddening child until it died. Quite as terrible a remorse, for to her mind her sin and shame were beyond measure, condemned by other words such as Adultery and Fornication . . . Thou shalt not. . . .

She was much too ignorant (innocent was the word preferred by Lady Charlotte) to imagine that such experiences should ever show improvement on the brief horror of this afternoon's. . . . I didn't think it would be like that. I couldn't have thought so. I thought it would be beautiful and wonderful. Oh, how do women endure being married—how can they——? Poor Enid lay in a dreadful state induced by a little ignorant incontinence in a summer wood. It was worse than that. She was shattered beyond belief. Romance was dead and she had sinned and left herself nothing, none of that vanity called self-respect. Not even her own love for another was left. All was impossibly lessened and cheapened according to every one of her standards. Everything was spoilt and laid in dust. The only moment that she could remember clearly was an hysterical sensation of the ridiculous that had overcome her when Arthur, looking woefully ashamed of himself, had mounted his bicycle and ridden away. Thank God he was joining his regiment to-morrow and perhaps they need never meet again. Never indeed, perhaps, for in two months' time his regiment was going to India. At this thought a feeling of complete desolation took entire hold of Enid's mind, an unfair hold, and beyond it the first faint stir and twitch of a fear.

There followed a week or two in which she tried to forget, with a concentration that made her all the more conscious of the unclean and awful crime that she had committed. It was terrible really, this frightful feeling of shame and self-hatred which quite demoralised her as a rational being, and she was never too steady at the best of times. And it was not so much the thing she had done (which indeed seemed to her punishment enough for its doing) but the fear of what other people would think should they guess her to have done it. She became very affectionate and emotional towards her sisters, thinking of them as pure and different creatures from herself. This only Diana found embarrassing. Muriel and Violet, calm, cordial creatures, accepted this sudden lavishing of affection without undue surprise—they knew so little about each other, a thing like that neither surprised them or weighed with them at all. They were like children, thinking, "Enid has been naughty to Mother—now she's showing how good she can be to us all." They encouraged her affectionately.

Lady Charlotte, of course, accepted all Enid's eager busyness as a proper showing of remorse for conduct magnanimously forgiven. She inquired no more into the sudden closing of this affair, beyond ascertaining the date on which Arthur rejoined his regiment, and the date on which the regiment departed for India.

But Enid, poor, foolish and most singularly unlucky Enid! The weeks (as they do) went past and while they brought her a sort of unbelieving forgetfulness of what she looked on as the most disgraceful and painful act of her life, they brought her nearer to a horrid doubt. She was indeed most unhappy, for what had it all meant to her? Nothing. Nothing but pain, embarrassment, the death of this romance and then— Nothing. A tremendous blank, a chill sense of entire failure. And now there was this suspicion. A despair that doubted towards hope once for every three times that it sank to terrifying certainty.

The terror that lived in everything then. Terror in the morning, waking early and lying still in bed while the swift, full consciousness of fear returned. She would gaze with eyes of terrible envy over at the bed where Diana lay sleeping, dark and sullen and safe from this unanswerable fear. The dread of the morning came on her then. First, breakfast-time and the question whether she should feel ill or faint. The necessity of eating or incurring her mother's comment. Then the later day and a thousand elaborately-sought reasons for solitude. Solitude in which to exercise her body—Enid's soft body that loathed activity. Now she was all eagerness to ride in these autumn days, lumping along solemnly and studiously hour after hour, clap-flop in her side saddle, short stirrup and close pummels. She could find no reasonable excuse for work of any kind though she longed to dig and cut down trees. But in the afternoons, on the pretext of a walk, she would hurry through the yellowing woods, unseeing, until she came to where there was a three-foot drop off a wet rock face, and from the top of this to the ground she would jump with horrid mechanism time after time and hour upon hour. Resting sometimes, her forehead sweating in her hands, and then again, five steps through the hazel bushes she had broken and twisted back, and spring, land, and repeat, spring, land and repeat. All no good. No good as she knew in her secret terror, running back through the wet woods to teatime and early lamplight and the long horror of the evening. All the time she felt ill and yet too frightened to mind feeling ill. She was as if looking through glass and feeling across a distance.

A week was like seven years and a fortnight a lifetime of entire despair. She never wrote to Arthur, feeling nothing but complete revulsion and a tremendous embarrassment towards him. A dreadful little letter of his more of apology than love was the last she had heard from him. He seemed now to be more outside her life than any person in the world, as day after day she took her silly measures against her certainty of pregnancy and each day her mind in its desperation grew further from normal. She had nothing. She had no hope. What did girls do? What happened to them after this? How soon would people notice what was wrong? She would stand quite still sometimes or lie taut in her bed, her whole conscious being only knowing complete fear. And then an agony of small realities would come to her until she would tremble and sweat. She did not often cry because she did not dare.

Should she write to Arthur? Should she not write? No, she could not write. Perhaps everything would still be all right. She had read in an enthralling book called, *Till The Doctor Comes*, of nerves affecting women to this extent. It was a tremendous piece of knowledge this, and it gave her rather a comforting sense of grandeur to state it to herself. It was only a very momentary comfort, when she was trying to be

53

desperately strong-minded and reasonable. But when three weeks had gone her nerve cracked utterly. She could not endure any more. The horror of life at Garonlea continuing its measured daily course overcame her. She longed so deeply to be borne once more on the even current of its going. Writing notes for her mother. Messages to the tenants. Afternoon calls. Delicious confabulations with her sisters on the endless subject of clothes. She saw that state of life as the only desirable way of being, and the state of being in it yet outside it as she now was, overcame what little sense of proportion Enid had. And about this there was no possible foundation for her having the faintest sense of proportion.

One Sunday she was overwhelmed by such a desperate feeling of faintness and sickness during the Litany that a sense of inevitable disaster caused her to touch Diana who knelt beside her on the arm and sway down the length of the aisle down past the pews so well filled by neighbours in their best clothes. A rustle of taffeta as she passed and bowed elegantly-veiled heads turned to watch her for a half-second before they bent again in devotion and possibly disapproval over their prayer-books. Then the cold air in which the beads of sweat felt like frost on her forehead and a wild dash to the back of the family vault where she was sick amongst the nettles and drew in breaths of mouldy air in sharp relief.

"Don't tell Mother I was sick, Diana, please promise me." There was so much urgency in Enid's voice, such energy, that Diana promised quickly, feeling as she usually did as though she stood outside Enid's weakness and hysteria. But to-day as she followed her half-way up the long wet avenue towards the house, Diana was aware of something fixed in Enid, something that was beyond hysteria, something that she vaguely knew was dangerous. It made her hesitate and obey when Enid begged her in a strained, urgent voice to go back to church and leave her to walk home alone. Ordinarily Diana would have played the sensible bully and ignored this appeal, but to-day she went sturdily back to the family pew, whispering to her mother that Enid was quite all right, the air had done her good, and meeting her sisters' wondering looks and stolen nods without any encouraging air of secrecy.

"Well, but, my dear child," Lady Charlotte said with great moderation and reasonable authority, "surely if Mother says she wishes the Doctor to see you, you must know she has her reasons."

This was later in the day when Enid, fulfilling her Mother's invariable prescription for any ill, was lying down. A long Sunday afternoon under her eiderdown, broken now by this new and immediate terror.

"Oh, Mother, really there is nothing the matter. Please do believe me." The dark head and lovely brow were lifted from their pillow. Those tremendous, imploring eyes dark with tears and fear.

"Surely, dear, Mother is the best judge of how her little girl is looking—and I don't want you to go and stay with Aunt Alice next week if you aren't at your best."

"But I didn't know I was going to stay with Aunt Alice."

"Yes. It's a surprise Aunt Alice and I planned for you," Lady Charlotte lied agreeably for she had not yet written to Aunt Alice on the subject—the idea having only vaguely occurred to her during the sermon that morning.

"Oh, must I go and stay with Aunt Alice? Must I, Mother? I'd rather not."

"Now, my dear, this is pure foolishness——" Lady

Charlotte felt the moment had come to be brisk. But Enid felt that the moment had come past which she could not endure. She sat up in bed in that white petticoat bodice run with so much blue ribbon and trimmed with so much lace and she wept in terrible despair.

Lady Charlotte left the room more determined than ever to summon Doctor Maxwell and compel him to agree with her that a little change was what the child needed.

Enid's sobs lessened gradually, for what was the use, what relief was there in tears for her? Presently she got out of bed and leant out of the window, her hot eyes burning in the cold autumn air, her bare arms like glass. She was conscious of the unseen stoop of the valley above and behind the house, the downward pressing of the great woods. Her eyes travelled across the wet levels of the lawn, resting on distant groups of trees with the ease that their planters had designed. She was entirely in despair and the thought of death seemed to her the only easy thought. Leaning there in the window she considered means of suicide with the detachment of a person just beyond reason.

Looking out of her window across the lawn at the bare wet walnut trees with their brown soaked circles of leaves below them, she thought of hanging herself from some easily reachable limb—you just kicked the chair away, but what sort of knot do they tie? She caught herself softly by the throat and knew she could not do this. Then there was the river, a deep, smooth-barrelled autumn flood dropping over its weir, dark alders and willow trees twisted round with the pale rubbish the flood had brought down. Enid thought of the strong water catching her, swirling under her, lifting her skirts and closing over her face, drowning her cries and choking her.

56

In personal extremity the least imaginative people see things with this awful clarity of vision. Knowing she could not hang nor drown, Enid's mind turned to the methods of more domestic if more horrid suicides. Leaning there at her window, her mind turned over these matters with less concern and excitement than had gone two months past to the planning of her new winter clothes. She thought now of chemists' shops and arsenic and of the dark toolhouse in the kitchen garden and weed killer. Again she saw the shelves of a chemist's shop and a neat little packet of Salts of Lemon marked in neat red letters, POISON, lying on the counter. It had been bought for removing stains from household linen, but she understood it to be a deadly poison. Shelves. Little dark cupboards with different deaths on their shelves. Her mind knew it could find something. In a moment remembrance would be alive in her mind. She was so afraid, she was so much afraid to remember that it came to her with dreadful ease. It was in the cupboard above Diana's washstand, hanging above the muslin splash-cover, dotted muslin over pink, frilled against the wall. Open the little cupboard and on the right-hand side you will see a dark bottle, POISON—NOT TO BE TAKEN. A bottle of black hat-dye with which Diana had intended to transform a summer hat, refraining on Enid's advice and substituting a less drastic change in the shape of a wreath of Mr. Liberty's brown silk poppy heads and assorted grasses.

So in the summer when she was happy, before any of this had come to pass, she had planned her own death. She took the filthy black bottle out of the cupboard and read the directions on the label with a mind numb to their unimportance. She took the cork out of the bottle and sniffed the thick, rather sweet, smell.

There was an oily glimmer in the full neck of the bottle and her throat closed up at the thought of swallowing the stuff. With tremendous speed her mind found a reason for postponing the moment and the terror. "I'd better wait until they are all at dinner," she said to herself, "or some one might come in and save me."

It was now five o'clock. She drank her tea when it was brought to her and passed the interval between tea-time and Diana coming in to change for dinner, emotionally, but not entirely disagreeably, in the composition of a letter to Arthur and one to her mother.

"DEAR ARTHUR,

"When you get this letter I shall be dead. You must not think of me sadly or feel that I blame you in any way, but this seems to me the only Way Out. I feel it is only fair to write and tell you I forgive you utterly and trust you will find Happiness and never let the thought of me haunt your life.

"ENID."

Then she wrote to her mother:

"MY DEAREST MOTHER,

"I have done this to save you all from pain and shame. It seems the only Way Out after having been so foolish and wicked as I have been. Remember I blame no one but myself and forgive me if you can.
                    "Your loving daughter,

"ENID."

The writing of these two letters uplifted in her an extreme consciousness of sacrifice. Now she did not feel any longer poor frightened Enid but a creature

58

able to rise beyond the torment and horror of her circumstances, able and ready to make the supreme sacrifice of Life itself. She felt keenly the pure and entire nobility of her motive. Perhaps her desperation only matched the rather desperate issues of such a situation at that date. Perhaps, had she taken it, that desperate escape would have caused her less pain and less entire spiritual shame than the life that was to follow.

For, of course, that black cup of poison was never drunk. Even if Diana had not come running back, called by some dire sense of disaster when she was half-way down stairs and badly in the wake of the dinner gong, it is hardly likely that poor Enid who had so little resolution even for the swallowing of senna would have managed more than her first sip of that burning and dreadful cup. She put it down with a little cry of horror and her body was shaken with sobs and convulsive nausea when Diana came in.

The bottle and the cup were both beside Enid and her lips were blackened and her eyes staring wildly. Diana kept her head long enough to seize both cup and bottle. Then quite suddenly she lost all hold of herself and ran screaming downstairs for her mother.

But to Enid was at least left the conviction that had it not been for this interruption she would have carried out her plan to its end in death. This conviction mercifully never left her—not even when the Doctor's verdict that twice the contents of the bottle would scarcely have proved a fatal dose was made known to her. The conviction, as a spiritual support, remained unshaken.

Tremendous inner confusion and upheaval masked by a splendid show of decorum followed the discovery of Enid's frustrated attempt at suicide. The family Doctor, called in to prescribe for nerves, was hardly allowed even to hint at the real cause of the trouble. Lady Charlotte was, of course, present during his slight examination of Enid, who entirely collapsed and in floods of tears refused to answer any leading questions. When her mother and the doctor had gone she lay with her face to the wall, quite still and completely vanquished while Spiller, her mother's maid, sat and sewed by the window in the clear autumn afternoon. She was not allowed to be alone for a moment. She had even been forbidden to lock the bathroom door. She lay like an animal waiting in a trap for her mother to come back, as she soon would. Soon she would. Then she came. The door opening and her voice saying:

"I will sit with Miss Enid for an hour, Spiller."

She would not look round to see. She could hear Spiller softly gathering up her sewing and softly going from the room. She heard her mother sit down beside her bed and felt her leaning across towards her. She looked up and saw tears falling, running down that smooth, pale face, caught on the brown shelf of bosom —almost rebounding off its firm and matronly contours. The padded shoulders ringed with braid were leaning over Enid, and nearer still the pale face, the puffed grey hair.

"Oh, Enid, Enid, my poor little girl—tell Mother all about it. Mother will see to everything. It will be all right. Don't be frightened, my darling."

Ah, the easing sweep of such words. The comfort. The kisses. The tears. Enid's head was laid upon that maternal bosom. Her tears soaked into its brown silk. Her cheek, as in childhood, took the impression of its knotted braid. She breathed the faintly stuffy smell that was her mother. She knew complete relief and presently her tale was told.

VIII

ONE cannot deny that the days of maternal omnipotence had their moments. There is something to be said surely for the tremendous ease with which the young could fling themselves upon the mercy of omnipotence.

But the end was not in that hour of maternal consolation and spiritual ease. The end was a long way further off. Enid indeed, never quite saw the end.

"My darling, tell Mother, it will be all right—I promise you——" And the tale was told and Enid's whole life was taken out of Enid's keeping, indeed, she did not wish to keep or order her life, she had no plan for it. She had ended her present life as surely as if she had died and now Lady Charlotte like God, must give her a new one. Really, there was nothing else to be done except the things that Lady Charlotte did and she did them with wrath and speed and efficiency and throughout showed an unflinching social front.

There was a visit to Arthur's parents during which nothing but money matters was discussed. Womanly delicacy alone prevented her from seeing Arthur and telling him what she thought of his past conduct and how little she hoped for his future happiness. It was with real regret that she abandoned this hour to Ambrose and maintained herself only an icy politeness towards the culprit. It was lucky for Ambrose that she never knew how miserably he had faltered even over the opening lines of his speech, "*You are a Cad, Sir*——" and had with pitiable weakness abandoned the rest,

61

saying only, "I should rather not discuss your conduct," and proceeded at once to the matter of settlements. Perhaps, as well. For Arthur, being an emotional young man, was very near tears as it was.

As for Enid, she was not allowed to see Arthur alone for a moment during that unspeakable fortnight which preceded that nightmare day when, heavily veiled in Brussels lace and garlanded stupendously with orange blossom, she wavered sobbing up the aisle on her father's arm, followed by her sisters, shivering in muslin gowns and weeping in sympathy.

During the fortnight between her confession and her wedding she was not quite fully conscious except at mercifully brief intervals when the truth of what was happening to her closed over her body and her spirit, drowning her in an agony of shame and revulsion. But the round of occupation found for every day and every second of every day by her mother left her so exhausted that she felt only numb when left in peace though never alone. She was borne up and onwards on this current of ceaseless things that had to be done, on towards the last dreadful necessity of marriage beyond which she would not look.

Daily she wrote notes of thanks for wedding presents and stood for hours while calico shapes were pinned and unpinned upon her before being sent off to a London dressmaker. The gowns which came daily from different shops were fitted and altered by Spiller—enthusiastic but perhaps not very apt. And Enid, who loved clothes with passion and excitement, would stand in a clearing among new tissue paper and half-unpacked boxes, insentient now to the thrill of lace flounces and the sharp whisper of taffeta, the gleam of gold tissue and the mists of tulle on her shoulders, the feather boas and all the hats.

"Oh, Enid, how happy you must be. All these lovely, lovely clothes, and Arthur is really quite nice," exclaimed Violet one day, from the bottom of her heart.

Enid smiled wanly, taking what refuge she might in the mystery and dignity of an engaged young lady.

Lady Charlotte left nothing undone to make this hurried wedding appear a desired and successful event. She could hardly have turned a braver face towards her world. There were parties at Garonlea for luncheon, tea and dinner, at which Enid appeared pallid (but she was always pale) and with a smile pinned on her face to receive the congratulations of the countryside. These were very hearty, for Lady Charlotte was not too popular among the local mothers and they were not displeased in consequence that the first of her daughters to be married should make a match that the most generous-minded could scarcely look on as brilliant.

Towards Enid, Lady Charlotte maintained a demeanour of rather stern solicitude. There were no more tears, there were no more confidences, but there were no recriminations. Enid made only one flutter towards escape. When she was told that the date of her wedding was fixed she grew pitifully red and said with nervous effort:

"Mother—don't make me marry Arthur."

Lady Charlotte replied, "My dear Enid, you have left very little choice in the matter either to me or yourself." And so the subject was closed. That faint shaft of sarcasm left Enid silent and powerless. The horror of acceptance was less than the horror of explanation. Perhaps it was as well that Lady Charlotte discussed the matter no further for, however clearly Enid had been able to explain her present fear and dislike of Arthur, the situation would in the end have remained unaltered.

There was one moment of which Lady Charlotte felt herself unfairly defrauded by the unfortunate incontinence of her daughter. But it was a moment she was to fulfil gloriously a few years later when, twenty minutes before Violet departed among showers of rice and confetti for her honeymoon her mother told her (with perhaps more delicacy than exactitude) what she might expect in Married Life.——"The poor child was really upset," she told a very intimate friend later, "although I veiled it all as much as possible."

The intimate girl-friend replied with forgivable maternal pride, "When I told Little Mabel I saw to it that she had a good breakfast first, but even so she cried so dreadfully, I thought we should never get her dressed or to church. Such innocence seems very beautiful to me."

"Wonderful," agreed Lady Charlotte, "and especially in a girl of thirty-two."

"Perhaps. Mabel was twenty-nine when she married."

"Really. I thought I remembered her toddling about the winter before Desmond was born."

"Twenty-nine," replied Mabel's mother, solidly refusing to be drawn into the question of dates, "and as innocent as a child."

Only Diana was particularly conscious of Garonlea as a place during this time of bustle and confusion, new clothes and parties, solemn conclaves in the library, Muriel's and Violet's excitement by day and Enid's tears at night.

Garonlea was the house and the reason for this dreadful thing that was being done to Enid, Diana thought quite unfairly. No ugly scandal must touch a Miss French-McGrath of Garonlea. No vaguest clouding of the rich Protestant chastity of that valley. The Family, the Place, the Other Girls, Enid's Good Name, everything but Enid's happiness and Enid's freedom to live. Diana was necessarily a little vague as to what she herself would have done for Enid under the circumstances but she was really bitter over her parents' line of action. Night after night to hear Enid crying—Enid cried very easily, it was true, but not with this hidden insistent despair. Diana would pretend to be asleep for she could not possibly face the scene that must follow if she should show herself entirely aware of the trouble that encompassed Enid. Secretly she was disgusted by the real cause of this trouble. It was a sort of fulfilment of her dislike of Enid's lack of control. It was a slap at her own extreme repression too. She, only, knew what she had found Enid doing. She had not told her sisters, taking in this reserve a sort of defence against the self who had run downstairs that night calling, "Mother, Mother"—and put the whole matter at once into the power of Lady Charlotte and Garonlea. She had not even paused in her acceptance of the real powers in her life. Violet or Muriel who had no resentment towards these things could hardly have acted in a more girlishly conventional way.

Garonlea, the place and the house armoured in all its sham magnificence of Gothic, terrified and overcame her by its inviolability. It was more than usually the placid, ordered house she had always known, with its many chimneys and its stable yard with four fat horses and many sheeted, elegant carriages. It all overcame her. All of it! The slope and rotundity of the valley; the kitchens and many fat, clean servants; the echoing, icy dairies; those passages and pantries and dark little courtyards; the clock tower; the wet, well-kept gardens and dank lawns; and all the paths through the nearer woods swept and raked on Saturdays; the hot greenhouses; the orchid house where the orchids did not thrive too well in that hot breath and unseen dripping of water; the fat voluptuous stable cats; in all these places was that inexact, familiar sadness. You knew it all too well. Nothing lovely, nothing exciting, would ever happen here. The level of sadness and propriety was so secure. There would never be a break or a change in this. No matter what happened to the McGraths who lived at Garonlea —what sadness overtook them, happiness, adventure or heart-break, all was finally subdued to the pattern of Garonlea.

Now it was to be the same. This crisis in Enid's life was hushed and blotted out and drained of its power in the ruthless benignancy of Garonlea and all that Garonlea stood for. It would always be the same, it always had been.

IX

On the Saturday afternoon before Enid's wedding, Muriel, Violet and Diana fitted their bridesmaid's dresses for the last time. They put them on in their icy bedrooms with Spiller running from one to another with pins and suggestions. Violet wore her dress in that hushed rapture in which new clothes invested her; Muriel shyly, with little tinkling laughs; and Diana looked like a rebellious little policeman in her confection.

They paraded before Lady Charlotte in the library. Lady Charlotte, busy at her writing-table; very busy, affecting extra preoccupation as the chatter she had heard on the stairs hushed at the door and Muriel came in blushing, and Violet followed her, a ravishing and satisfactory daughter, and then Diana, sturdy and irritable, picking up a paper and reading it as she stood there, all to show how little she minded whether her dress was approved or not.

Lady Charlotte gave the dresses a businesslike attention which excluded any possible hint of admiration for the daughters inside them. Towards Diana, indeed, this was no affectation, but she showed herself her maternal impartiality and at the same time gratified her resentment of Diana's dark independence by making Spiller practically refit her dress, altering the position of each pin not once but twenty times.

Diana spent the rest of the afternoon in the woods in a fret of rebellion and disgust. Only one thing stood out for her, Desmond and Cynthia were coming that evening. The thought of seeing Cynthia was like a hot ripple of excitement, making her feel stormy and uncertain. Half of her fury at her mother's quiet bullying had been caused by this unrest. Now, as she walked through the woods, there came to her their undefeated certainty of life to be, the strange strength of woods in winter-time, their arrogant loneliness and sense of power from within. Sitting on a fallen tree that had seeped itself wet and rotten and almost back into the wood's life, Diana gave herself over to the warmth and comforting thought of Cynthia's presence and sympathy. Shyly dramatising their meeting one moment and the next realising ruefully how little able she would be to make any such smart and interesting remarks when it came to the point. A passionate creature, she sat on there in the wood, all her dramas and theories so true to her, there she sat in her green serge, tailor-made, with stuffed shoulders and tight sleeves and a high, starched collar cutting severely into her soft neck. She had a god and waited there alone, for an hour of worship was near.

Cynthia arrived. She was perfect with every one. An enormous pale-blue feather boa foaming round her shoulders—you kissed her within its scented, fluttering depth. Soft wings of hair under a monstrously romantic hat and a carnation flush in her cheeks, when she lifted her veil for kisses.

"I hope you're not quite worn out——" for Lady Charlotte, and a speaking look of sympathy combined with congratulation.

"Dear child." Lady Charlotte felt warmly satisfied with her daughter-in-law.

"Popsie, darling," and she embraced Ambrose, "I have the naughtiest story to tell you—Oh, you'll turn me out of the house." She managed it so that Lady Charlotte missed this and only Ambrose got his kick.

"Popsie darling"—why was it none of his own children could show such confidence in him? He almost blushed with pleasure.

Then Enid was kissed and congratulated so that for a fleeting moment she thought herself almost an enviable creature. And Muriel—"Darling, what an enchanting blouse—you look like the sweetest baby. I must buy one——" Muriel, in her lace and bébé ribbon, fluttered a delighted kiss. And Violet—"My dear, so lovely just to look at you again." For Diana—"Little one," and a closer kiss. But later by the schoolroom fire, between six and seven, they had an hour together.

A great deal of sewing and excitement had gone on in the schoolroom lately with Violet and Muriel stitching at flounces and threading miles of narrow blue and pink ribbons, ribbons that pulled everything into frills. The Empire tops of nainsook nightgowns, the legs of knickers (below the knee), the gentle tops of camisoles and their foaming laces were all run with blue and pink by Violet's clever, languorous fingers and Muriel's, bird-like and eager. In the air of the schoolroom their thrill was faint and vibrant still.

Old photographs of the girls—taken and framed and carefully preserved since childhood's earliest days up to the big moment when three feathers nodded and the photographer did his utmost, sparing no balustrade where a girl might lean with grace, or any joke that might evoke a smile—stood on every available inch of space, and hung upon the walls too, jostling dark-brown reproductions of the works of Mr. Watts, Mr. Burne Jones, and Mr. Rosetti. The carpet was faded and the pale chintz more friendly from careless use than the covers in any other part of the house. The bookshelves were still full of schoolroom stories—

romances of the Upper Fourth, or the Lower Sixth, and adventures of gorgeous young girls and gorgeous young Brigands, Hunters, Trappers, Sailors and Explorers. They were fine books, sometimes three hundred pages in length, yet no matter how intimate the circumstance of adventure, never once on one of the three hundred pages did sex ever show its hideous head. Violet and Muriel read them still, with keen excitement and really felt more moved by them than by some of the novels which Diana and Enid read in privacy and hid behind those virtuous and friendly red and blue backs on the schoolroom shelves.

"Is Enid happy about this, do you think?" Cynthia sat on the white fur hearthrug. Her lovely hat was gone and her hair seemed as pale as white broom, not glancing or golden in the firelight.

"Cynthia, she's miserable. I think it's such a terrible thing that's being done to her. I suppose it's her own fault, but is it? After all, if Mother had been human to her about Arthur. But Enid's always so frightened and then does something wild and uncomfortable for everybody."

"My dear, what *do* you mean?" Cynthia was alive with curiosity.

Diana told her what she meant.

"But Lady Charlotte can't possibly do anything else," Cynthia said soberly. She entirely accepted this fact and her sympathies were directly with Lady Charlotte and her condemnation for Enid. She was very hard. She did not condemn, she dismissed. She who knew love only at its utmost best, seemed isolated by this very fact from sympathy with love that had gone astray. Sordid was the word for it then. Her own heat and passion were justified sacred mysteries, ennobled by marriage and suitability. Without any pretence she

70

despised Enid and sympathised entirely with Lady Charlotte.

"I know it has to go on," Diana sighed. "There's really no way out."

"No. There's no way out."

"I think it's so unfair," Diana spoke bitterly.

"Well—unfair? But weren't they insanely stupid? What did they expect?" This was not really the way a young married woman ought to talk to a young girl, Cynthia knew. But she knew, too, how flattered Diana would be by this assumption of knowledge and equality.

She was right. Diana valued it more highly than she had ever dreamed of valuing a relationship. She fought on to explain her reaction about Enid's marriage.

"You see, it's for us and Garonlea and the family name, it's for everything but for Enid's own sake that they are making her marry him."

"But where would she be if they didn't? And if they had let her marry him three months ago you'd all have been delighted and said how right, wouldn't you?"

"Yes, perhaps. Yes, we would. But now you see, the awful thing is that she knows what it's all like and she doesn't want to. Is it always like that for every one?"

"No, no, you've got it all wrong!" In a flash, Cynthia was the clear, passionate creature that bound others to her. For half an hour she talked to Diana with simplicity and no embarrassment, telling Diana all the things that she would never need to know. It was in times like these, natural crises, that Cynthia was really unafraid and almost great. And it was by such moments that Diana saw her and by such stray acts that she was blinded and lost to the lesser things in Cynthia.

71

Cynthia was the greatest help through Enid's wedding. Much more beautiful than she had been, she was a live and present example of what marriage should mean. She was most efficient about helping Lady Charlotte without once taking the responsibility for anything. She comforted Ambrose simply by being herself. She walked out with him and sowed the seeds of her stud farm plan most cunningly in his mind; slightly dramatic, impressively businesslike, not too ambitious: "Just a few well-bred mares." And she knew what she was talking about.

She could have been of great help to Enid but Enid shied so desperately away from all near contact that Cynthia simply could not take the trouble, or embarrass herself sufficiently to get through Enid's defences. After all, Enid was neither attractive to her nor useful, so she let her be.

And so Enid was married to Arthur, Arthur who had so lately changed from a lover into a frightened stranger, and was to change from that into a bullying and selfish stranger, but never back into a lover. She went away to India with him and wrote to her sisters by every mail until the following April, when one week there was no letter from Enid, but a cable for Lady Charlotte, and the girls were told how sad it was that Enid's little baby had been born dead. And while they put away the clothes they had made for it very sadly and wrote long letters of sympathy to Enid, Lady Charlotte sighed with relief. It was astonishing how Providence was always on her side. A dead, premature baby was so much simpler to explain to her friends than a hearty live one. And poor little Enid had lots of time before her.

X

In 1910 Lady Charlotte and Ambrose still reigned at
Garonlea. Ambrose was a great deal frailer than in
1900, but he still kept up a systematic if enfeebled war
against the elders and thistles on the place, and never
faltered in devoted deference to his wife, although he
differed from her wordlessly in those sturdier wars
which she waged against that Rebel Queen, that
Cynthia, whom she had loved and trusted so un-
fortunately.

It would be impossible to say when Lady Charlotte
first realised that Cynthia, while she asked for advice
in the sweetest way, took none but her own counsel.
It was from this discovery that the declaration of war
dated.

There was a grievance when Cynthia's son and
Garonlea's heir was born in a nursing home in London
and not at Garonlea, as Cynthia had agreed it should
be, and as Lady Charlotte had told all her friends it
would be.

A tremendous stand was made over Desmond's
leaving the army, but again Cynthia won, helped by
guile and patience and a fate that ordered his regiment
to an impossible place at the critical moment in the
struggle. Aunt Milly's opportune death helped her
here too, for it was much easier to remove one sad but
unprotesting old lady from the house you wanted
than two sad and perhaps, from mutual support,
determined ones. So Aunt Mousie and all her parcels
of plants (for she took a very small piece of almost

73

everything in the garden with her) went to the nice, suitable little house nearer the village. And there, surprisingly enough, for she was old for changes, she found new life and interest in making another garden and in improving the suitable little house. Cynthia never failed to send her game and fish and *The Illustrated London News*, and was her most regular and popular visitor. In spite of all Lady Charlotte's efforts to enlighten Aunt Mousie on the methods by which Cynthia had caused her removal from the house where she had spent so many years, she remained unshaken in her allegiance.

There were a thousand other matters of variance too. There were the hounds which Desmond produced to hunt a country from which the chase had been too long absent. Through these hounds he became almost entirely lost in a peculiar, myth-like glow of popularity. He was adored where Ambrose was mildly liked and respected, and his house of Rathglass had an importance far beyond that of Garonlea and its shoots. Whoever was young and gay in Ireland came to Rathglass, and strange and rather grand English visitors came too. And were they all explained to Lady Charlotte and was she asked to meet them? Almost never. Worse, there were many parties full of possible husbands at Rathglass to which dear Muriel, growing each year a little thinner and a little more uncertain and eager to please was not bidden. Where now were all Cynthia's plans and promises for the marital advancement of the girls? It had been in no way due to Cynthia that Violet had married Lord Jason Helvick, who had once been thought of as only suitable for little Muriel. But when Violet was twenty-four and still unmarried the outlook seemed gloomy enough to justify the acceptance of the gentle ornithologist's slightly abstracted suit.

74

And like Aunt Mousie, Violet seemed unexpectedly happy in her life. She liked to bully Jason and enjoyed being just a little grand and married towards Muriel when she had her to stay. Aside from vague yearnings for the dignity of the married state, she had been happy at Garonlea, and now, that state achieved, she found all that she knew how to expect, and was untroubled by any vague yearnings in any direction. Certainly she was the most satisfactory product of Lady Charlotte's upbringing. She was in fact, the exact material that such an upbringing demanded.

But past all such grievances as these, and in a different sort from the small ones (as, for instance, the ridiculous way the children's hair was cut, the absurd clothes they wore and the useless and expensive dentist who attended to their crooked teeth) there was always the constant itch and grievance of Diana's happy escape from Garonlea to Rathglass. More and more of her time was spent there, losing, as Lady Charlotte saw but could not explain, more of herself each year and growing to find all her happiness in being Cynthia's slave and shadow.

It was strange that Lady Charlotte was able to see so clearly exactly what Cynthia's form of friendship for Diana meant. All her own life she had been Queen and had ruled her children sometimes by main force, sometimes by emotional appeal, but always behind these things had been, for her at least, a right and a reason why she should demand obedience. There had been no absence of principle, however tortured the principle. She herself was self-sufficient, she was beyond those whose lives she ordered and commanded. But Cynthia was of their lives and in their lives. She took the utmost from them, far more than she gave. She failed them and charmed them to her again. She leaned upon them and queened it over them at the same time.

Lady Charlotte grew always more bitterly jealous and resentful of her, dreading the time when Cynthia would take her place at Garonlea; watching Ambrose's health with a fostering eye for this as much as for any other reason; making long lists of china and silver and linen that were her own and to go with her out of Garonlea. She took a tremendous interest in all that happened at Rathglass although she pretended to none at all. In reality the children could not have stomach-ache or a kitchen maid be sent away that she did not hear of it and derive satisfaction from the smallest disaster. Of course such major calamities as the July when they lost their yearling in a thunderstorm or the time that Desmond had six hounds poisoned—were a sort of gloomy heaven to her, even if they were offset by a successful sale at Doncaster or by the felicitations of some old friend on her superbly able daughter-in-law. None of her friends really knew of the distrust and jealousy of Cynthia which were like aching and hidden corns in Lady Charlotte's soul.

Only Diana guessed the strength and the depth of that dislike. She could feel it in her mother's changed breathing if Cynthia's name was mentioned, in the faint excitement and desire to quell which held the air close to her. Then if Diana felt in form for argument was the moment for her to produce a remark about some horse at Rathglass, or some exotic rhododendron lately flowered with success, or even some story of what the child Simon had said to, or of, the infant Susan. As surely as it woke in Ambrose a curiosity and pleased interest, quite as surely it called forth a sort of muffled virulence in her mother.

Suppose Diana said, "Simon has a hen sitting on ducks' eggs. He doesn't know how to wait for them to hatch." The reply might be, "I wonder when Cynthia is going to get that child's adenoids attended to. If she leaves them in much longer he'll be quite idiotic."

Ambrose would say, "Idiotic? Brightest little chap I've ever seen. Dearest little chap in the world."

And Lady Charlotte would swallow back her hot feeling against Cynthia, it was like a dark web within her, a fibrous tangle like the roots of plants in too small a pot. It would have been too contrary to her idea of dignity to have said openly to Ambrose or anybody else all that she knew and felt about Cynthia. But on each contact she made with anything done or said by Cynthia she cast a curiously lessening shade. And always when she could in any way compass it she prevented Diana's being at Rathglass.

Although Diana was twenty-eight and Muriel thirty-six, they were still treated much as they had been at eighteen and twenty-six. They were the daughters at home. They had no fixed allowance beyond a small amount to cover such expenses as stockings, gloves and stamps. Their clothes and their journeys were paid for and they were still told what to put on and where to go. True their clothes were bought from the best shops and they travelled first-class but for all that it was an absurdly unfair system, making Muriel so entirely dependent as to be nearly half-wit, and making Diana entirely rebellious, souring and closing her spirit in all directions except towards Cynthia, the one towards whom it flamed unquenchably, towards whom it must for its own sake refuse all disillusion. For there is no romantic creature living who will be entirely thwarted of Romance.

77

Rathglass in these days was like a court, a small and fashionable court well filled with courtiers and ladies-in-waiting, and of these ladies-in-waiting Diana was the chief. Behind her came perhaps a dozen younger ladies to whom Cynthia sold her horses, sometimes gave her old clothes, often gave confidence and advice and criticism. She told them what to eat and what to drink, what to wear and what to think, and she was never bored by their continual worship. On the contrary she was always thrilled by it and it called out at moments a dramatic feeling of goodness and humanity in her, rather an imitation sensation perhaps and one that never lasted long enough to cause her any serious personal inconvenience. Besides the girls there were their mothers, with whom she was more than wonderful and who only rarely mistrusted her, blaming their own foolish daughters if they could not ride the horses Cynthia sold them or caused them to buy.

Sympathy was the chief thing Cynthia gave to her train. She gave them sympathy for the hardships of home, the tyranny of parents, the shortness of money, the waywardness and backwardness of lovers—sympathy and a tremendously personal interest.

"Don't let him maul you about, child, you're much too nice."

"Never let me see you in that dreadful little hat again. It quite hurts me."

"I wouldn't let everybody ride this horse, but I always say you have quite exceptional hands."

"Blue, dear? *Not* your colour. I think I see you in rather a sweet shade of mauve."

It required a certain amount of concentration never to let one of them go and to make each feel that she was the superlative one, but Cynthia had immense physical strength and was almost never caught at a moment when she felt too tired or too ill to contend with every aspect of life. She was always hard at work or play, and her court had to work and play (but especially work) with her.

There were in those days lots of boys for the girls to play with, for Ireland was full of soldiers who hurried willingly to such houses as Rathglass to shoot and hunt and do reverence to Cynthia, while they flirted with and sometimes married into her Court. It was really rather an exciting and powerful position for Cynthia; not that she was unique in having soldiers eager to go to her house, but she was almost unique in the way she could always secure the ones she wanted and if she planned a match she often succeeded in making it.

No wonder that the mothers of the county were eager for her patronage for their daughters. No wonder that they encouraged them to hunt with Desmond's hounds, however cowardly and indifferent they might feel about the chase, and endured with patience the long tales of Rathglass and its doings which were almost the only subjects the girls could talk about. It was amazing how Cynthia filled Rathglass with a sort of glamour that was real and thrilling, a thing no one could escape, intoxicating to any ardent young Miss of her train.

Another curious thing about the Cynthia worship was the unbridled spirit of imitation which it engendered, so that soon even the moderately independent girls tried to dress like Cynthia, use the same soap and face cream, ride like her, and do their hair for hunting like her. Beyond this, they even tried to talk like her, copying faithfully those little words and phrases which each person has peculiar to themselves.

What did the train talk about then? They talked about Cynthia and her clothes and their own clothes. They talked about her dogs and their dogs. They talked in an ignorant and excited way about hunting and endlessly about how their horses jumped and who was behind who in the chase, and who was closest to Cynthia. Where the hounds were hardly mattered in comparison. They also vied with one another in the collection and life-like delivery of funny stories about the Irish, disasters recounted by cooks and grooms having a special vogue. But no peasant could really open his mouth without saying something they wished to remember and repeat. A good Irish story went with an easy swing in those days even when told by an English soldier.

Nothing is so revealing about people than the aura or influence they put forth round themselves. They cannot be strong enough to maintain it if it is unreal. It is not, unless it breathes of the very life of the person it surrounds. And this romantic excitement which was of the very air round Cynthia was a true reflection of her life at this time. She was tremendously happy and immensely painstaking in her happiness. The first and truest thing about her was that she was still in love with Desmond and needed him with as wild a longing as she had ever done. Perhaps this was the core of her romantic appeal. Then life was not a thing settled and over, it was vividly of the moment. She had Desmond, yet because she loved him so she had him not. This put the keenest edge to her vitality in living. It lent a glow to all effort. It was for her a matchless thing to have in life.

True, Desmond had never shown the remotest desire to stray from his domestic felicity, but this was not quite the point. Not only must there be no faintest thought of straying, but life together must be beyond solid domestic felicity, and here she was a winner—through ceaseless elaborate, tireless effort she never let Romance quite out of sight. In a thousand hard-working ways she gave herself leisure for this glamour, setting her whole life so that Love might be first.

Her house was lovely. It was comfortable in a way not as usual in 1910 as it is to-day. For instance, there were several bathrooms, invariably provided with delicious essences for softening and scenting the water which was always hot. The beds were soft and sheeted with the finest linen. She often changed the decoration of her drawing-room but she never changed her cook, who was an artist with an imagination of divine versatility.

In the garden where Aunt Mousie and Millie had grown their favourite flowers in nooks and patches, she made sweeping and exciting alterations. Round the house where the ghosts of walks and paths had threaded their way for years through dark tangles of Portugal laurel, she cut down and opened out and planted with azaleas and rhododendrons and rings of fuchsia, putting rustic seats in all the places where people might sit down for conversation or for Love. She did not really mind about gardens, and had an unfair way of achieving success with them, using flowers as decorative furniture.

It was in her garden that she made great use of her court. She would give a young man a day's hunting on a young horse she wanted well schooled and the following day he was made to sweat and toil cutting down laurels and rhododendron. It was rather a good plan and really the young men liked it, especially as their girl of the moment was so often sent out at the same time with the bulb planter and a few hundred bulbs. Of course they complained a lot in a comical spirit, for gardening was not then the fashionable excitememt which it is now.

Only Diana, who had never thought of gardening at Garonlea, indeed it would have been rather a silly and embarrassing occupation under the amused patronage of Lady Charlotte and Williams, took to it now with a real passion and delighted excitement. The ideas were generally Cynthia's but their successful fulfilment were more often than not due to Diana's streak of gardening intelligence and hard work. For good sweeping ideas don't make gardens really grow, although they sound so assertive and unanswerable that they seem bound to lead to a "blaze" here and a "mass of colour" somewhere else, the disheartening thing about them is that the blaze is so often the meanest flicker and the mass of colour fails to appear at all.

However, between Cynthia and Diana and the court workers and two able-bodied men, Cynthia's garden five years after she had gone to live at Rathglass, was a lovely and romantic garden and quite as successful as the rest of her life.

XI

ON a quiet exciting afternoon in March 1910, Diana left the Gothic towers and battlements of Garonlea behind her and set out on her bicycle for Rathglass. She looked exactly the same as she did in 1900. Everything was still shut up inside her. Her mind still registered the same protests, except towards Cynthia she had not expanded in any way. Garonlea still held her prisoner, depressing her health and her spirits unnaturally. It cannot be good for a person to live in a place towards which they have as strong a dislike as Diana had for Garonlea. But where else should she live? Was not Garonlea her home. And girls should love their homes although they must be willing enough to leave them when Mister Right comes along.

It was one of those March days when there is the first strong feeling towards life in the year. The end of winter, a false end because it does not really end here at all. For a moment of great sweetness and drama you see a deep red in the blackness of the hedges and the distances are like smoke, honey and irises. The fields that were white as bones and dry as meal, although there is as yet no growth about the grass, look kinder and more bosomy. Afar off on a turn of the river a fisher stood, his ghillie squatting, an attentive blot, on the bank near him. There were hazel catkins, hanging straight and architectural curtains up the flights of the woods, nothing whimsey or faëry about them ; they had on the contrary an exotic and orchid-like effect in the absence of other flowers.

Diana bicycled through the day feeling separately pleased by all these things in the detached and finished way that people can who have never confused the spring weather with their emotions. Connect such a day with a memory or with a hope about love and it loses its edges and that sharp ring which such days as these have for the very young. Diana had kept this quality of seeing days as days entire and unconfused.

At Rathglass Cynthia's baby, Susan, was asleep in her perambulator in the shelter of the bank where Aunt Millie's scyllas flowed down towards the little lawn and spread in brilliant flat pools across the grass. Cynthia had planted a thousand more each year and ordained that her child should sleep there covered in a blue blanket. She took great trouble and pleasure in an effect of this sort, for it is not easy to buy a blanket the colour of scyllas or to have a child as beautiful and healthy as Susan.

Diana took a look at her niece and a longer look at the scyllas. The house was empty, with cross little terriers lying in patches of sun on the steps and window sills. A red japonica, very correctly pruned and trained against the wall, held its first flowers stiffly on stems thick with buds. There was a rich, trim air about the house. The rooms inside would be warm and full of flowers. There would be a very delicious tea when Cynthia and Desmond came in from hunting.

Diana went off to weed the rock garden. She felt quite silly with delight, the day was so fine and she would see Cynthia soon. Then the purple primroses she had planted caught the afternoon sun and made her wild with pleasure. The shaft of sun went through them as though they were a bottle of port.

At five o'clock Cynthia came back from hunting

in their tall motor car. She wore a check tweed coat with a velvet collar over the new fashioned safety habit that Lady Charlotte thought so indecent. She wore a silk hat and a veil and a bunch of violets, now limp and dark and very sweet from being worn all day. She stood in the hall looking at the post with her arm absently through Diana's. The post is always of curious importance when people come in from hunting it brings them back with a sudden turn into the other excitements of life.

"Only a catalogue from Stevenson and a letter from Mrs. Walls to say the chestnut mare ran away for three miles down a road with that tiresome Mabel. I thought she might do that. I'd better take her back and let them have Silver Tip. He won't run far, he's too crippled. I think I'll have a bath now and tea afterwards. Desmond's feeding his hounds, we may as well wait for him. Well, darling, I'm sorry you weren't out to-day. We had a nice little hunt. You'd have enjoyed it. Come and help Cynthia have a bath."

On their way to Cynthia's room they looked in at the nursery where Simon sat with his smooth round young head, olive blond as a linnet's wing, bent over his plate. Susan dragged and tramped her way up and down her railed cot.

Simon who had been lost in the stupor of nursery dullness came to life with a flash.

"Mummy, Mummy, did you kill anything?"

"Not a thing. Those silly old hounds of your silly old Daddy's couldn't catch a fox. They can come down in half an hour, Nurse. Well, Susan, old lady. See you soon, Simon."

"*Yes*," Simon shouted.

Cynthia was rather impersonal about the children. If they had not had decorative value and if they had not excited Desmond so much, she would have had very little to do with them. Perhaps when they were older and started riding they would be more interesting. But Desmond wouldn't let Simon ride yet although he was five and it was quite time he began. Cynthia was always seeing ponies that would be the very thing for him.

Cynthia's bedroom was very good of its period. It was pink and silver with a pale grey carpet and a pink satin eiderdown. Pink and silver brocade curtains and a dressing-table covered in stiff white dotted muslin over pink calico, with all Cynthia's silver-backed hair brushes on it and a vase of pink carnations and on the writing table a silver bowl of violets. It was a nice setting for a gorgeous blonde.

Cynthia undressed in the fine graceful way she did everything, pulling off her rather pointed boots with a nice gesture; laying herself at last in her deep warm bath and only giving Diana her attention when her first exquisite shudder of delighted relaxation was quite over.

"So Mother said I was to drive to Barretstown as she and Muriel were going in for Muriel to see the dentist. And what, I said, do you intend me to do? Wait for an hour at the Ladies' Club looking at the Punches? As a matter of fact I didn't say that. I said (quite quietly) 'As a matter of fact I happen to be going to tea with Cynthia!' She said, how curious it was how I always kept my movements quite secret, and might she ask, if it wasn't probing too far, whether I was doing anything with Cynthia next Thursday as she would like me to go with them to lunch at Summertown. 'Next Thursday' I said, 'let me see. No I think Wednesday's a hunting day next week.' "

Cynthia vaguely knew that it did Diana good to

report these almost fictional and extremely boring conversations with Lady Charlotte. Whether or not she had ever been so calm and balanced as her version of the contest invariably showed her to have been, when she had told the tale she thought she had and this did her great good.

Cynthia was turning a piece of purple soap round in her hands and then slowly lathering her long fat arms. She said, entirely without malice, "What a horrible old woman she is." And then, "I think you're wonderful to stand her at all. Only an angel would."

"What else can I do, child?" It made Diana feel a little grand to call Cynthia "Child." Grand and easy.

Cynthia always wanted to say, "Come and live with us," because Diana would be so useful and work without ceasing and praise without ceasing from morning till night. But she could not. It would have involved too bitter an argument between Desmond and his mother. And she saw the stupidity of that. Diana dimly saw it too, but she was always waiting for Cynthia to say this as people when they have a long hopeless affair feel that the only important words their lover can really say are, "Will you marry me?" Even when they know he can't or know that they would not if he could. Still it seems the touchstone of all meaning.

Cynthia slid down into her bath, saying instead, "I do call that a pretty tweed. Mine that he made is horrid." It did nearly as well but not quite she knew, so she added, "The hat I had made to match doesn't suit me either. I wish I'd thought of giving it to you two days ago. I've sent it away to be altered now and perhaps it will be all right. If not you can have it."

"How sweet of you, dear. But you mustn't——"

Diana took off her own hat and fiddled with her dark hair which would have curled if it had not been so heavy. However, it was the date when the great thing to be able to do with your hair was to sit on it and if you could do this, never mind how it looked under a hat it was still a boast and a beauty. So Diana need not be pitied because of her hair at any rate. She could easily sit on it.

Possibly it did lend a certain heavy air of seclusion to the face below, this massed quantity of hair. The face was like a little bird's pale egg, one had to look for whatever it had near beauty. Every woman could not by cunning barbering and painting be compelled to look her best all the time.

XII

CYNTHIA came down to tea in a mauve dress with a good deal of silk fringe attached to it. She put on her rings too: opals and diamonds and emeralds on her warm hands. She made tea in a slow way, heavily as if she had been captured. Desmond was looking at her. He seemed cold and independent in the hot fragrant room full of cyclamens and freesias sending out wreaths of scent, but he was not.

They were all hungry and ate a quantity of very good food without talking much. Desmond could hardly be very interested in Diana. He asked her a few questions about Garonlea, rather as though she were still a little girl. They were not all at familiar. He thought she ought to try and marry, or else be more like Muriel who was at least an apologetic failure. He simply did not try to understand anything about Diana. Although he had a warm and quick imagination where Cynthia was concerned or his children, he could give no more than acceptance to Muriel and Diana. He saw Diana's infatuation for Cynthia with a faintly contemptuous indulgence. He accepted it as he accepted without notice the respectful adoration of all young men for Cynthia. He knew without a shadow of question that she never had a flicker about one of them. He and she were two people apart. Really apart from others. It was a very strong thing of which to be so aware.

He was pleased when the children came down. He and Cynthia played with them, throwing cards into a hat. Cynthia said—"Dash!"—that rather modern slang word when she missed the hat. They both preferred playing with their father which did not annoy Cynthia at all. She would have liked Simon better if he had been sturdy and curly like Susan, instead of being rather long and thin with soft straight hair. And she would have liked Susan better if she had been another boy. Susan was enormous, she burst out of her white dress when she laughed. Cynthia kept buttoning it up again behind but the buttonhole was too large for the button. "Terrible figure the girl has," she said in a detached way.

"Oh, she has a lot of improvement in her," Desmond said.

Simon was looking at a book.

Cynthia said, "I hope that child's not going to turn out clever."

"It's all right. It's only a hunting book."

"Simon, old boy, stop reading and come and tell Mummy what you saw on your walk to-day."

"I was reading."

"Yes, but what did you see?"

"Didn't see anything."

"Oh, nonsense darling. Where did you go?"

"Down the Green Lane."

"And you didn't see a thing?"

"I saw some rabbits," said Simon, driven to rather obvious invention.

"Pity Daddy's hound Grampion wasn't there, he's very good at catching rabbits."

"Daddy's hounds catch *Foxes*" Simon knew this much. And the remark was so successful that he was allowed to go back to his book.

Presently the children were fetched away to bed and Nurse was told about the back of Susan's dress. The curtains were drawn and the scent of freesias redoubled in the room. Desmond finished writing endless lists of which of his hounds had done what, that day and came back to the fire where Cynthia and Diana were drinking sweet brown sherry. One of the pleasant things about Rathglass was that Cynthia was much ahead of her day in providing drink when it was needed between meals. She liked a nice drink herself and saw no reason why her girl friends should not have one too. She managed to invest this drinking with a sort of sacramental quality, for then women did not drink between meals and at meals hardly enough to do them any good.

Here it was warm and there was a feeling of intense life. Diana, just the faintest degree drunk, stared into her sherry glass. There was wine and confidence here and the dearest thing in life. Diana was thrilled by Cynthia's life in the way she had been thrilled when she first read Mr. Kipling. Forbidden moments with *Plain Tales from the Hills*. This could not be better, with *Puck of Pook's Hill*. Complete romantic illusion with the Brushwood Boy. It was touching that for reality of comparison she had to go from the lives of others to reading of the lives of others. She had no criterion of happiness in herself. Seeing Cynthia and Desmond and Susan and Simon it was as if she read a thrilling story about them. Now she had come to the end of a chapter. Now she had to go. She looked round the room putting it once more in her memory—the deep soft reflections in the polished faces of bureaus—the breathing flowers stirring in the warm stillness—the solid turns of heliotrope cushions. Cynthia silent a little tired, her mauve dress agreeing mildly with the cyclamens.

Now she must go.

"Wednesday, Thursday, let me see—— I'm going into Barretstown on Friday. I could pick you up. If it's not a frightful day, could you be on the bridge at three? Or I'll pick you up at Garonlea if you'd rather."

"Cynthia, lovely! I'll be on the bridge. Good-bye, darling."

"Good-bye, darling. Thank you for all your work in the garden. Oh, one moment; shall I give you the pattern of that dress Muriel was going to make for Susan? Tell her to make it a bit bigger for the monster."

Then Diana went away, riding her bicycle carefully along in the last of the dusky peach light. The evening was utterly quiet and the turning reaches of the river untruthfully apricot under the sky, and the woods were heavy like smoke against it. The edges of old fields were enfolded mysteriously in the wood's earlier darkness and the hazel catkins in their heights and lines were only little hanging ghosts. The slope of a newly ploughed field looked rich and promising. Presently she passed Aunt Mousie's house and saw a faint twist of smoke from a bonfire in her garden and a brilliant ring of these same blue scyllas low round a tree stump near the gate. So like Aunt Mousie to decorate a tree stump instead of grubbing it up. A light in the window of the post office and another in the shop that sold everything. The pink and white sugar-stick and bunches of bootlaces and packets of starch behind the square small panes of its window front looked quite sophisticated and urban, so illuminated. Diana felt rather gay looking at them. But when she crossed the bridge at the valley foot the feeling of loss came through her like a draught, thin and penetrating. An air blowing from the other side of life. Not the other side really, but her own side to which she belonged. This was her own Life from which she could not escape, and the warmth and beauty at Rathglass the fantasy. This was the real she, this rather soured and flattened creature wheeling her bicycle into its shed, taking off her gloves among the stubby little suits of armour in the hall, and blinking in the lamplit library where her mother and father and Muriel looked up at her from the world where they belonged and she belonged.

"A little late, perhaps, Diana, for bicycling round the countryside?" Lady Charlotte suggested. The atmosphere was full of acid and broken glass. Yes, the other life was the fantasy.

"It was quite light till I crossed the bridge and came through the woods," Diana said in rather a Russian way.

"Curious. It was dark here at least an hour ago."

"Oh, nonsense, Mother."

"Thank you, Diana. Thank you very much indeed. Since when may I ask have I been in the habit of talking nonsense? And since when have I allowed one of my children to speak to me as you have just done?"

Diana looked at her darkly and sat down. "Children?" was all she said.

But they all knew what she meant. Poor little Muriel blushed hotly, she could never get over the shame of her age and single state. Ambrose looked as discomposed as though some one had talked about adultery. Lady Charlotte's grand bosoms shook like jellies with rage. No one in this house ever got even into the shadow of reality, so to say "children?" like that was more daring than it sounds.

"I never expect you to be particularly civil on your

93

return from Rathglass," Lady Charlotte was really trembling with rage. "The place seems to affect you in a most unfortunate way, doesn't it? Doesn't it? Well? Can't you answer? Can't you find an answer?"

The room was too full of hidden grief and helplessness and power misused and grown weak and wicked. No stir in the air of past love or pleasure. No remembrance of indulgence for foolishness. No jokes or good honest quarrels.

Ambrose turned his paper miserably inside out and Muriel bent her head in diligent absorption over the jersey she was knitting for Enid's Ambrose. She minded so much and felt violently towards Diana for this breach through her pretence of contentment, in being the invaluable daughter at home. The pretence which her vanity demanded was only too necessary to her. And all Diana had said was "children?" It was appalling that one word spoken like that should mean so much and cause such devastation of spirit.

Lady Charlotte's demand for an answer was purely rhetorical. She expected neither answer nor retort, and would have been still further incensed if either had been forthcoming. Diana knew this perfectly well and she had neither the wish nor the will to provoke any further trouble. The sense of nausea and desolation that these scenes left in her, while it did not quite stop her provoking them, was still too powerful to allow her to come to any real issue. Now she could feel the twittering apprehension of Ambrose and Muriel, small birds frightened in their cages, saying to her, "Please stop. Oh, please, no more." And her mother's heavy swelling anger. What was the use of protest? One had no power. And what have I done, Diana thought with despairing resentment, what have I done beyond spending an afternoon weeding in a garden and having tea with Cynthia and Desmond? It's too ridiculous, too humiliating, that it should lead to this. It's so cruel and so unfair.

But she knew how much more than this she had done. She knew how tremendous was her escape from this atmosphere and place to Rathglass. In moments like this the contrast was so dramatic that she could not find herself believing in either one place or the other. Two extremes, met, leaving her somewhere suspended in a sort of mental mid-air, from which in a moment she would fall sickeningly into the complete reality of Garonlea.

XIII

MURIEL came into her room before dinner.

"I wonder if you would just fasten this for me."

Diana stopped the intricate work of coiling her hair round and round layers of hair inside which was her head. She was fond of Muriel though often exasperated by her and she was strangely jealous of Muriel's pretences about happiness. Muriel could fill her life so full of small importances and interests that unless it was cruelly brought home to her, the indelicate subject of her real unhappiness need hardly ever be faced. Besides through all her rather simplehearted pretences she arrived at some unexpected points of joy. She maintained her interest in clothes as keenly as ever. She had far more success than Diana ever did with her nephews and nieces, taking immense trouble to find them interesting toys and to tell them interminable serial stories about a family of frogs. Violet and Enid really enjoyed having her to stay with them, she was so flattered by confidence and uncritical in comment, whereas Diana was a defiant and embarrassing kind of sister who obviously knew in a silly, theoretical sort of way, far more than an unmarried girl had any business to know.

Now Diana stooped, peering and hooking her way up from Muriel's narrow hips to her neat bird's neck. Her clothes were always exquisitely fresh and neat, every smallest frill stood out primly separate from its fellows, and there was complete absence of scent about her, only a feeling as fresh and smooth as a little bird's body caught in between your hands.

96

"Thank you so much, Diana."

"Did you have a bad time with the dentist? I forgot to ask."

"Oh, not too bad. It's never very pleasant, is it?"

"No, horrible."

"How were Simon and Susan?"

"Very well. Cynthia sent you the pattern for Susan's dress."

"Oh splendid! I found a delicious piece of stuff to-day—a sort of duck's egg blue."

"How sweet."

"Unless Cynthia would rather keep her in white."

"I don't suppose she minds."

"Wasn't it a lovely afternoon?"

"Yes, wasn't it. Is that the gong?"

"My dear, do hurry! I suppose I'd better fly down. One of us ought to be in time."

"Oh do wait, Muriel. If you're late too, it won't matter so much."

In her old green velvet gown Diana looked like a greasy little middle-aged toad compared to Muriel. She had none of Muriel's gifts for the smaller pleasures of life. That trivial little chirp of conversation just now had been typical of any sort of communication with Muriel. Diana went heavily and as slowly as she dared behind Muriel's fluttering, skipping rush down stairs. They both paused outside the library door and looked at each other like naughty little girls who are late for prayers again. Diana was ashamed of the reality of moments like this. Having been caught by herself and Muriel feeling like a silly little girl, she felt angry and unbalanced and summoning a sort of sulky dignity she walked unto the library as boldly as she could. And at this time Diana was twenty-eight and Muriel thirty-five years of age.

But then neither of them was married or ever likely to achieve that state of bliss and dignity. They had no caste. They were the girls at home.

They escaped reproof—beyond that which was conveyed by Lady Charlotte's dignified, "Well, shall we now go in to dinner?"

In to dinner they went, Lady Charlotte on Ambrose's arm, as she did every night if there was no other lady present. Muriel pattering and Diana striding solidly down the hall behind them.

All the leaves had been taken out of the dining-room table and it was now a very small square in the centre of the room. A long way from the dark indifferent pictures of ancestors swallowed in the gloom of red wallpaper. A long, long way from the screened door, through which the butler and his satellite brought course after course of dull food and cleared it away again.

Ambrose was not unnaturally more interested in his food than in his daughters, who could hardly be said to sparkle as they sat one on his either hand.

"What's this, Coulthwaite, what's this?" he would ask impatiently at every course, for he was too blind to read the menu written on a little china slate propped in front of him, and too forgetful to remember it though it had been read to him once by Muriel and once in a loud, defiant voice by Diana.

"Delicious soup, sir," Coulthwaite would say in a reverent and at the same time indulgent voice. He managed to invest the most horrible food with a quality and rarity it never possessed.

"The fish? Grilled salmon, I think, sir. No, sir. I'm mistaken. A nice piece of cod from Cork."

"Spring chicken, sir."

Ambrose chewing away at a fowl that had seen

many an active springtime would have liked to meet somebody's eye and wink, but there was no such possible person, so he felt slightly cross and grieved instead.

"What sort of day did Desmond have? What's this pudding? What is it, Coulthwaite?"

"Some farinaceous substance, sir." So did Coulthwaite elaborately disguise his master's pet aversion, sago.

"Sago? No. No thank you, take it away."

"Just a spoonful, sir—very nourishing. Would you try a spoonful of black currant jelly with it?" Coulthwaite's posture was such that one imagined he only just refrained from patting Ambrose on the back like a coaxing nurse. His stoop was a respectful benediction.

"What sort of day did you say Desmond had?"

"Good, I think."

"Where did he have a hunt from?"

"Oh, I don't know. They just said they had a nice hunt."

"Dear me, why didn't you ask, child? Well, where was the meet?"

"I forget, Father."

He tried Muriel next.

"And who did you see in Barrettstown?"

"No one, Father."

"No one? It must have been pretty deserted. Diana, remind me to tell Desmond there are badgers using that earth in Gibbetsgrove again."

"Yes, Father."

Two plates of shrivelled apples, their varieties labelled, provided a useful subject of conversation when the labels had been read aloud.

"You can't beat Cox's Orange, *I* always say."

"I feel sure these labels are muddled," Lady Charlotte announced with decisive asperity. "This apple is certainly off the unnamed russet near the well."

"Yes, I think so too, Mother," said Muriel quickly.

"What do you think, Diana?"

"I haven't had an apple, Father."

"Try a piece of this. I'm sure I'm right. It's a funny thing if I'm mistaken in the flavour of a Cox's Orange."

"I really don't think I want an apple, Father."

"It is too much to ask you to do as your father suggests for once?"

Diana silently cleared her finger-bowl and its lace mat off her dessert plate. Her hands shook and her mouth quivered ominously. It was all too much. Even being bullied about a beastly piece of apple. Had one no right of one's own? Not even the right to refuse to eat a withered quarter of apple?

Across the table over the six tiny packed vases of snowdrops arranged by Coulthwaite Muriel gazed fearfully at Diana, her eyes wide and startled, her hands clinging together on her knees, so that her knuckle bones felt so enormous she thought she would never unclasp them. For Diana was going to cry. Muriel knew it as surely as anything. Knew it in Diana's silence as she took and slowly cut into little pieces her slice of apple, knew it from her head bent as though it were twice its proper weight, knew it again from her long struggling silence.

Lady Charlotte knew it too. She bent forwards, her great bosoms pressing upwards, a deep clefted shadow between them, as she bent, staring down the table, her eyes bright yet calm with satisfaction.

"Well, Diana, and what's your opinion? Is it a Cox or a Russet?" Her voice was almost persuasive as though she wanted to prolong a delicious moment. She peered eagerly in the light of the candles. She shifted one branched candlestick a little as though greedy for more light on this unhappy moment. Muriel drew in her breath quickly, slightly, sharply.

"Well, speak up, Diana? Surely you have some idea. If you were at Rathglass I dare say you could find your voice, eh Miss? But not much left to say when you come home, have you?"

Diana broke down, sobbing into her hands, tears running through her fingers over her plate and apple and silver knife and fork.

Ambrose looked on pityingly, making little ticking noises with his tongue, and Lady Charlotte sat back in her chair, very quiet, in a sort of horrid repose after ecstasy. Muriel went on choking down small pieces of apple and sipping water.

Presently Lady Charlotte said:

"Muriel and I saw the first primroses to-day. Quite extraordinary late—aren't they?"

Diana's dreadful tears were not, because she chose to ignore them. It was entirely typical of her attitude towards her children.

Ambrose was fumbling with the decanter of port, pushing a glassful towards Diana, saying, "There child, that will do you good. Drink it."

Diana shook her head violently. It was a last indignity that all her just grievances should be looked on as no more than a wave of hysteria to be cured by a glass of port. She could not and would not drink it. The glass stood there half-way between Ambrose's place and hers, and he still nodded and murmured and pushed it towards her a little more.

"Well," Lady Charlotte said presently, "when Diana has finished her port, shall we——?"

Muriel jumped up. There was a white sick look about her.

"——I said *when* Diana has finished her port, Muriel."

Muriel sat down again. They waited. Lady Charlotte sat with her hands folded calmly on the table in front of her. Sometimes she looked down at her hands. Then she would raise her head and look down the table towards Diana. Now her face showed nothing but calm impassioned disapproval, a kind of patient resignation.

Poor Ambrose who had precipitated this new crisis sat like an old mouse now. They waited for more than five minutes. Then Diana put out her hand, picked up the wineglass and drank her port at last, choking it down in three quick gulps. She was not crying any more but she looked rather wild and strained with her face blotched blue and white. It seemed unnatural too to see such a square little person trembling so violently.

Lady Charlotte, still watching, drew her breath regretfully in and out through her teeth.

XIV

It was November 1915 and the War had been going on for a year and four months, when Cynthia heard the news that Desmond had been killed. She had never really expected him not to be killed. She had felt quite fatally certain about it from the first. Before he went to France and during his short leaves she had been infinitely various in love and wildly living in the moment. They had each known quite well and each tried quite futilely to hide from the other the foreknowledge that this was going to happen.

It must all have been very much as it would be if it happened again now. All the patriotism and memorial services and kind letters from brother Officers which comforted mothers and sisters, can't have been of the smallest value to lovers. They had endured those horrible brave good-byes, and those other moments when neither could find the other and the time was all too short, flying along. There were moments when Cynthia could hardly endure Desmond's spending so many of her brief hours with the children. It was because there was no strain with them, they were entirely uninvolved and untouched by all the pain. They were calm.

Can one know about things like this? What can one think of the deaths of silent young men like Desmond who are as much part of the place they live in as any field is such a part.

Cynthia had made herself hard over this so often that when she read the telegram and said, "There's no answer," she only felt a sort of hot dizziness.

She had been rushing about after an early breadfast because it was a hunting morning and she had a quantity of things to see to before she rode on to the meet with the hounds. Her mind was on this level and it seemed stuck there, buzzing like a small overthrown machine. Part of her felt furiously angry. She went from one window to another. She could not keep still. Walking about in this most familiar room was like walking about in a photograph. Everything was only like a picture of a thing. Nothing had solidity or four sides or reason any more. Out of a window she saw Susan going out with that untidy and tiresome Belgian refugee governess to feed her rabbits. She must go; she must certainly go. Quite useless.

Then she remembered what had been annoying her so much, what she was looking for before the wire came—the list of groceries that must be sent off by to-day's post. Then she would be ready. She was still searching for it blindly, turning over envelopes on her writing table, when she heard the Garonlea car coming up the road.

"I can't stand this," Cynthia thought in a crazed panic. She flew out through the hall, collected her gloves and whip and ran as fast as she could in her hunting boots down the kitchen passages and out through the back door.

She was determined to go out hunting. She was not thinking, as she easily and truly might have done: Desmond would have hated nothing more than for people to come to the meet and find no hounds there because of him. She only thought that the important and sensible thing to do was to hunt.

She wondered if Lady Charlotte would hear the hounds clamour as they came out of the kennels and down the slope of field to where her horse and the huntsman's horse stood together in this strange day from nowhere. But the high toppling looking car did not appear. They rode on unmolested. They talked about the business of the day and the hounds.

There was old Tarquin, he should be knocked by rights, but the master was so fond of him perhaps they'd better leave him till he came back.

"No, you may as well put him down," Cynthia said absently.

"Well, he only meant to keep him up to the end of cub-hunting really, didn't he?"

"Yes. That's all."

At a wide cross-roads Lady Charlotte overtook them. Cynthia always remembered what it looked like: the flatness of a pond, the common ducks that splashed shrieking across it away from the hounds. The three dirty cottages that the hounds would have investigated thoroughly for twopence. The wet November leaves in the road and a full ditch of brown watercress. Lady Charlotte sitting in the back of her car like a sad and outraged toad—Lady Charlotte climbing out with her chauffeur's help.

"Cynthia, my poor child, you haven't heard——?"

"Yes, I've heard."

Cynthia seemed a thousand miles away from Lady Charlotte, sitting up there on Desmond's horse among Desmond's hounds. She called out the name of one of them that was looking towards the cottage door, in a harsh important voice.

The whole group, Cynthia, Richit, the bright horses and hounds, was outside Lady Charlotte's power or keeping. The whole drama of sorrowing mother comforting the tearless widow was taken from her by this strong, dangerous creature who said:

"I'm afraid we must be getting on now; we're a bit late," and looked at her watch.

Lady Charlotte was very pale, her fat hands in black gloves made futile extravagant gestures.

"You can't do this, Cynthia," she said. The hounds fussing round her and Cynthia fidgeting to be off made her furious and hasty: "It's indecent—it's an insult. To Desmond and to Garonlea and to us all. Wait. Listen——" She was distracted and angry.

Cynthia looked down as if she would like to spit on Lady Charlotte from all that height above her. She gathered up her reins and nodded to Richit.

"Perhaps I'm the best judge of how Desmond would feel about hunting," she said. They rode away and Lady Charlotte turned blindly round in the road as though she could not see where the car was. The chauffeur put her in and shut the door on her, when he had tucked in the blue fur-lined rug.

The powerful excitement of her meeting with Cynthia was over. It had buoyed her spirit up for hours. Now it was over. Her hate for Cynthia and her bitter sorrow for Desmond were of equal and cruel importance. As she was driven slowly back to Garonlea she mumbled to herself plans of revenge and broken troubled words.

"Oh, Madam," Richit said, he was in tears, "I'm that sorry, Madam. Oh, excuse me, but no one will want to hunt to-day."

"I want to hunt, Richit," Cynthia said. She rode on in front of the hounds that went so gaily and proudly down the road round Richit's horse. The day was still like a very glazed photograph to her. Nothing real had happened in it yet.

Every one at the meet—where the news had travelled in the peculiar way it does—was deeply shocked and embarrassed by Cynthia's appearance with the hounds. This quite truly surprised her when she took it in. She said to a young soldier, whose last day's leave it was:

"I'd have hated for you to be done out of a day's hunting, Johnny," and this soon got about and rehabilitated her in that atmosphere of starred romance. Even Johnny, who was rather nervous and unenthusiastic about the chase, felt hallowed and important.

Saying things like that did not disgust or annoy Cynthia at all. She had hardly said them before she believed them.

It is difficult for people who don't bother about hunting to make any sense of Cynthia's strong desire and insistence on hunting this day and causing such unnecessary distress and embarrassment. There are people, and Cynthia was one of them, to whom the mental and physical excitement of hunting are both a religion and a drug. At the moment of happening, at the moment of danger, at the moment of decision or fear, and in waiting for these moments there is not time to suffer or know about one's other life. The brain is tremendously independent of the body in the excitement of hunting, and that excitement fulfilled, the body is curiously independent of the brain. One is filled with either excitement, fear, or content; never, as it were, in slack water.

Then there was the semi-fanatic "must hunt" attitude which is often stronger in women than in men. Cynthia had it very strongly developed, especially since Desmond had gone to the war, and she had done so much of the work for this pleasure, it was a flame that was part of herself.

It is difficult to understand why people with enough money and leisure to lie in the sun for the winter months should prefer to hunt, but it has to be accepted that thousands of them do, and with less reason and passion for the sport than Cynthia possessed. To-day and during the months that followed she hunted because she loved it as well as for the sake of oblivion. For hours she found this, though not always exhaustion enough to compel sleep because her body was particularly strong.

To-day she did not once feel entirely conscious about Desmond because mercifully they were hunting nearly all day, and when she and Richit rode home with the hounds it was quite late in the November evening. She was tired with that complete weariness which sets in on a long ride home after hunting. Poor Richit was far more aware than Cynthia was of the desolate and dramatic sight they presented when they said Good-night to the small field and rode away together with the hounds. It was the sort of emotional drama that Cynthia either consciously or unconsciously was always staging through her life. Desmond and Cynthia had always been alone and at a distance together. Now she was alone without him and his hounds and his servant were dearer and of more importance to her than any person.

XV

THE evening was quite dark when they got back to the kennels. A quarter of a mile down the road Richit blew his horn in warning of their coming and for some reason the sound of his horn in the darkness seemed to catch sadly at the still air. Sound shapes like wreaths for coffins. All that had been, all that would never be again, made Cynthia bow her head and her cold face nearer her tired horse's neck for comfort. But there was no comfort, no help in being near anything or any one forever again.

From the kennels to the yard she rode by herself, under the beeches, up the narrow back avenue. The air was very soft and full under the trees and there was with her so true a ghost that she half-turned in her saddle to speak, as she had so often done at this place and time before. But she was by herself, whispering alone to prove her love.

Diana was waiting for her when she came in.

Cynthia slipped her arm into Diana's and went over to the table to look at the letters lying under the lamp. "You'll stay with me, won't you?" She was sorting the letters, putting Desmond's in one heap and her own in another and suddenly stopping and putting them all together. "A bath, I think, and then tea—— Come and help me."

On their way they looked into the schoolroom where Mademoiselle sprang off her chair and seized both Cynthia's hands with unspeakable looks of sympathy, and where Susan dropped the toffee she had been busy making into the fire and said with becoming drama:

"Oh, Mummy, it's not true, is it?"

"Who told you, darling?"

"Granny."

Cynthia's first feeling of relief that she did not have to do the telling changed to one of perhaps justifiable annoyance at Lady Charlotte's action. Even now she did not know what to say. There ought to be a formula. She never knew what to say to these children. Was it fair that they should mean so little to her? She stood there tired and stiff in her habit and said nothing except:

"I'm sorry, darling. I am so sorry," behaving quite truly as though Desmond belonged more to Susan than he did to her. Susan looked terribly embarrassed. Inside she was saying:

"Daddy's dead, it's so awful, Daddy's dead," and trying very hard not to laugh. But the desire to laugh was uppermost. It had been all she could do not to laugh when Granny sent for her to the drawing-room this morning and told her. However, she had enjoyed the pomp of the day, with Mademoiselle allowing her to do just as she liked. No French. She needn't ride her pony in the afternoon—indeed no, your grandmother would enrage herself. They did history instead of geography and had a wonderful tea. She was indulged with a gloomy importance that pleased her very much. And now how quickly it all dropped into a deadly dreary reality with Mummy saying, "I'm sorry." A feeling of suffocating desolation like the first morning after the holidays, with Simon really gone back to school. The beginning of a term was as long as forever. Ah, now she saw what it would be. At last she had a comparison. Tears slowly stiffened her throat and the wish to laugh was over.

Cynthia in her room (which had been changed from pink and silver to cream and delphinium blue) sat down by the fire and leant her face against her hand. She looked defeated but very alive behind all the shock and fatigue.

"Do you suppose your mother sent a wire to Simon's school too?" she asked.

Diana said, "Probably," and gave her a drink that she had brought up from the dining-room and went off to turn on the bath.

"I don't think I'll have a bath after all," Cynthia called out suddenly, "I haven't fed the dogs and I forgot to tell them something in the yard." She went off again in a determined sort of way, flying about the house, feeding all the dogs, out to the yard and back to the house again, still in her habit and stiff dirty boots.

Diana stayed with her, trotting about silently. Holding this. Fetching that. She did not talk. She was like a cosy little black bitch, silent and loving. She said nothing about going back to Garonlea and it was not till bedtime that Cynthia said:

"Gracious, darling, are you staying the night? I forgot to tell them to get a room ready for you. Or perhaps you could sleep in my bed and I'll sleep in Desmond's. I would like that, I think, it's lonely enough when he's just away." She was sitting at her writing table getting through a pile of hunt correspondence, claims and stopping cards and lists of meets.

At about eleven o'clock the Garonlea car appeared to take Diana back, but Cynthia sent a message to say that she was staying the night. Cynthia sent the message out in a quite unconcerned way, but she said to Diana, not with displeasure:

"There is sure to be trouble at your staying—isn't there?"

"Hardly. I mean I suppose there is."

Cynthia said, "Well, they may as well face the fact that you're going to live with me now, mayn't they?" She did not even pause in writing out the card she was doing as she said this, glancing from the book of addresses back to the card under her hand.

Diana sitting by the fire felt a constriction of happiness that almost hurt her heart before it let it go in pure delight. Yet when you have what is in your dream, you have no dream. Your dream is in your poor hands to bruise in ignorance and lose in confusion. It is the moment before the moment that really counts whether the matter is love or hanging.

Cynthia would not go to bed till very late. She thought of a million things to do and when they were done and she couldn't think of anything else she turned to Diana her face of shocking despair—despair beyond exhaustion and all spending—and said they had better go to bed.

Diana was so tired that her sadness and her delight had both fallen long ago into a complete gulf of fatigue, but each time in the night that she woke she knew Cynthia had not gone to sleep yet.

Simon in his bed at school did not sleep either for what seemed to him a long time. He kept turning and turning and what he kept thinking was, "Did Daddy tell her I needn't ride Mitty at Christmas. He said to me I needn't. He knew I couldn't stop her. Oh, I wonder if he told her." In his mind he could see Mitty's piggish pony's eye. Mitty knew who was boss. He could feel her now taking all his power away, making him feel sick and despairing, and Mummy's voice saying to some one, "She does rather take charge, but she's such a perfect jumper," he had heard her say that one day when all his secret wish had been to see Mitty boiled up for the hounds and know that he would never have to ride her again. Now all his thoughts about Desmond were focused and centred in this. He knew he would never be able to tell Cynthia that he was afraid to ride Mitty. Had he remembered to tell her? If he had forgotten now there was nobody left to trust. Next day poor Simon looked pinched and miserable, they all thought the little boy was taking it terribly to heart, but really he was thinking more about Mitty than Desmond. And about Desmond only that there was no one you could depend on now.

XVI

Soon Lady Charlotte had everything she could possibly require to complain about. There was no horizon or limit to Cynthia's monstrous and cruel behaviour towards them all and towards what she insisted on calling "Desmond's memory." There was simply nothing she did not do, from making them change the day of Desmond's Memorial Service so that it did not clash with hunting, to selling two of his horses for troopers. Lady Charlotte discussed her actions with the sort of fervour that belonged to religion in the days that religious people burnt one another. And she was always hearing of some new thing that Cynthia had done. How she had locked away or destroyed every possible thing at Rathglass that was his, sold some of his saddlery and given even his clothes away to any of his friends or her friends who could wear them. Always she came back to the question of the Memorial Service and Cynthia's rage that they had chosen a Wednesday. How she had flown into a temper and insisted on the day being changed because she would not go unless they changed it. How all the farmers and horse copers and vagabonds in the countryside came to Rathglass to sympathise and would stay there half the day or half the night drinking. One night Lady Charlotte heard they had played cards. Again she heard of a party. And this was not a month after Desmond's death. She sent for Diana; if Cynthia could entertain the countryside she did not want company. But Diana made excuses and would not come back. Lady Charlotte did a thing she had forsworn. She went to Rathglass once more, grieved and bitter beyond measure, and demanded to see her daughter. They said she was out. Lady Charlotte said she would wait. But she waited in vain, for Cynthia had taken the precaution—knowing Diana's vulnerable nature—of locking her up in the straw-house. Lady Charlotte had to drive away without seeing Diana and next morning there was a letter for Ambrose saying that Diana thought she would stay with Cynthia indefinitely as she was needed far more at Rathglass than at home. It was quite a reasonable letter and quite a reasonable idea. The consequent ferment that boiled up at Garonlea was out of all sane proportion. Lady Charlotte made poor old Ambrose (not herself) quite ill with her emotional and half religious attitude towards the matter. Now she would mourn for a lost child—two lost children, in fact—then she would abuse Cynthia by the hour with a sort of false justice and acute perception of all her worst side.

Ambrose, who was brokenhearted by Desmond's death and devoted to Cynthia and her children, had a miserable time of it. His chief pleasure in life was taken from him—there was nothing he enjoyed more than toddling round Rathglass with Cynthia, seeing all the horses and the hounds, advising her about shrubs, and doing a bit of pruning. He got the same sort of life at Rathglass as any of Cynthia's girl-friends. And she was so sweet to him.

"You must come and look at the Teneriffe colt—you were right about him and I was wrong."

"Look at that shrub you cut back so savagely—isn't it good? And I thought you'd certainly killed it."

She showed genius in treating him as a contemporary. She never compelled him to see his grandchildren or expected him to like them. Simon and Susan liked him. He had not much more to say to them than he had had to say to his own children, but he never put his thumb and forefinger into his waistcoat pocket without bringing out sixpence or a cough lozenge, and now and then—Oh unbearable suspense, will it be now!—what he called half a sovereign and they called ten bob.

Much as he loved Garonlea it was a sort of traditional affection, and his passionate interest in Rathglass was that of an older woman for a young lover. It was as alive as that. It was no wonder that he suffered and failed in health after Desmond's death and this now open hostility with Cynthia. He gave in to Lady Charlotte over it all, of course, he was not strong enough in mind or body for any sort of contest. But he changed his will a little, leaving Diana more money than she would have had in her mother's lifetime. During the winter what sap there was in his life seemed to run out. They said his arteries were hard and his heart was tired. They said he must have no worries. One faintly warm day he pottered out to slash at his young enemies the elders; he had been forbidden to grub, but he found one so lightly rooted in a sandy bank that he believed he could manage to pull it out. They found him dead in the shelter and sun at the edge of his wood. He had defeated the young brute of an elder first and settled himself quite composedly against the bank.

Cynthia's hounds did not hunt till the funeral was over.

Lady Charlotte, who had never given more thought to her own death than was warranted by her assurance in perpetual and respectable comfort hereafter, now began to dread it very much indeed. And her fear and angry resistance were due to her horror of the idea of Cynthia succeeding her as mistress of Garonlea.

The thought upset her so much that she would tremble and feel sick when it was in her mind. She was convinced that Cynthia was only waiting and watching for the moment when she should step in to Garonlea and overset the thoughtful ordered train of its present state, outcome of so many years of economy and right living and dignified hospitality.

She felt that Ambrose had behaved a little traitorously in pulling up that elder and dying without an effort under his bank of celandines. If she had been there she would not have let him die. And she found it hard to forgive his ample provision for Diana. It was a cowardly undermining of a possible time when the poor child might have been brought back to reason and Garonlea again . . . with Cynthia married perhaps . . . if she had had no money or less money, Diana would have been forced back to Garonlea. Lady Charlotte thought that Ambrose should at least have discussed the possibility with her.

The first result of her fear of death was the quite practical plan of going to bed if her finger ached or if she sneezed. This was hard on Muriel who grew thinner and more twittering than ever as she ran in fifty directions to do the bidding of the muffled old queen in her bed upstairs. There were all sorts of wartime economies that required perpetual supervision. Though there was abundance of food of every sort in Ireland, patriotism gave Lady Charlotte a fine opportunity for meanness in many directions. She could hardly trust the cook to divide the tea into small enough packages or to issue bacon and butter to the household in strict enough portions. Lady Charlotte had made a great many discoveries about food which she tried hard to convince every one were particularly delicious. Barley meal and saccharine

117

and margarine. There was no end to the substitutes she found for food which was really there in profusion. Cutting down expenses became her greatest interest, justified by the war and by her determination to save all the Garonlea money she could for Muriel and Enid. She was to live at Garonlea till her death, or till Simon came of age, and somehow Simon's coming of age seemed to her much nearer than her own death. To her, more than to most old women, her age was simply an illusion of other people's. She could not let go in any direction.

Muriel with all her birdlike busyness and sweet temper found the days at Garonlea very long in the year that followed Desmond's death.

Breakfast by herself in the schoolroom—for the dining-room and drawing-room were both shut up. Perhaps an egg, perhaps not, if Lady Charlotte wished to send four dozen into the town instead of three dozen and eleven. Barley scones and margarine and jam. The room was heated by a black stove that burnt sawdust, but the heat it gave out was so negligible as to be almost an insult.

After breakfast Muriel would go briskly into her mother's room which was even colder than the schoolroom, but Lady Charlotte, with a white Shetland shawl over her head and two hot-water bottles early provided by Spiller, did not feel the cold.

"Good-morning, Muriel dear," she mumbled, her lips for a moment near Muriel's pale cheek, and her hands in white mittens rustled the letters that the post had brought her.

"We seem to have a busy day in front of us. Quite a busy day. My tonic, dear, on the wash-hand stand. Yes, Muriel, it must be there. No, not that bottle. It's the new tonic."

"Won't Spiller know where it is, Mother?"

"Perhaps, dear, but Spiller has gone down to her breakfast and I want to take this immediately after food. Perhaps the parcel from the chemist is on my writing table in the library. Just run and see."

Muriel ran obediently down the passages and the long stairs and the hall and back again, shaking her head.

"I have a letter I want you to answer—it's all right, dear, Spiller had left it on my tray. The letter is from Mrs. Barclay saying she would like to come to tea on Thursday. Say I should be delighted. Then there's a letter from Enid——"

"Oh, from Enid?"

"Yes, to say the children have had whooping cough and may she bring them here for a change."

"Oh, Mother, how lovely!"

"Really, Muriel, I hardly think we can manage it. We have a minimum of servants in the house—Enid seems to imagine that there is unlimited food and luxury here. She forgets that we do our little bit to help to win the war too, and I really can't have the heater for the bath-water going any oftener than I do."

"Oh Mother, do let them come. The poor little things, they do love being at Garonlea."

"Trust me to know what is best for us all, Muriel. Then, will you write to Roche and say only seven of the egg boxes were returned and what has he done with the other one. I expect a brisk walk would do you good, so trot off to the church and collect the holders for Sunday's wreaths. And walk, Muriel, remember, don't take your bicycle."

They had luncheon together, a carefully served and rather nasty meal.

Muriel had a little news:

"I met young Byrne and he told me they had a good hunt on Wednesday and Diana had a nasty fall."

"Hurt?"

"No."

"Oh."

"He said poor Simon cried at the meet and Cynthia shouldn't let him ride the pony."

"My dear, should you discuss Cynthia with young Byrne?"

"I didn't. He just told me."

"I pity those poor children. Did he tell you anything else?"

"No. I think that was all."

After luncheon they might drive round the place in a round pony trap, Lady Charlotte delivering herself of admonishments and charity. She was extremely popular with all the people in the place and never spared time or trouble to help them. Then back to tea and the long hours before and after dinner when Muriel knitted socks and read the war news aloud. Till the war is over life will be like this. Muriel looked towards the end of the war as a sort of term. When it was over she did not quite know what she would do, but she hoped vaguely that life might be different.

News from Rathglass came through Spiller as often as not, for she had struck up a friendship with the Belgian Mademoiselle who had somehow survived at Rathglass. Spiller would tell Muriel who listened with thirsty excitement, and sometimes she would impart little pieces of information to her Ladyship, who longed to hear more but was by principle entirely cut off from listening to any servants' gossip. Principle, however, did not go so far as forbidding Muriel to hear all that Spiller could tell.

"Oh, Miss Muriel, there's no margarine in the

servants' hall at Rathglass, heaps of butter and bacon and Mrs. McGrath doesn't keep them to the rations at all—— Mademoiselle says it's terrible the way those children are made to ride their ponies every day and the poor little things would rather be reading books or off on their bicycles some place——

"Miss Diana is forever working, work! she never stops, Mademoiselle says. Exercising the horses and digging in the garden, yes, and feeding the chickens and pigs——

"Oh, Miss Muriel, such a thing Mademoiselle told me to-day. Mrs. McGrath has bought Miss Diana a pair of breeches and boots like one of these Land Girls in the *Daily Mail*. Whatever would her Ladyship say if she could see her? And Mademoiselle says she hardly ever takes them off but goes striding about in them like a real little man. Mademoiselle says she doesn't think it's suitable at all.

"There was a party at Rathglass last night, Miss Muriel. Fancy, Miss Muriel, and poor Mr. Desmond as you might say—— All out hunting all day and back they came without a word to the cook at seven o'clock in the evening. Six hot baths and bacon and eggs and champagne and the gramophone playing till three o'clock in the morning. Three gentlemen home on leave it was, and two young ladies. And at three o'clock, Miss, out they went hunting rats in the stable yard. Yes, and Mrs. McGrath in a beautiful black satin dress with a sequin tunic and the fish-tail skirt and her mink—imagine that gorgeous coat—thrown over that and out with lanterns and torches through all the dirt.

"Well, I did hear a thing to-day you won't believe. Miss Diana has bobbed her hair. Yes, really, and Mademoiselle says she looks ten years younger. She saw her the other night—don't pass this on to her Ladyship for I think she'd have a stroke, if you'll pardon the expression—in a pair of blue silk pyjamas and her bobbed hair and she smoking a cigarette and drinking a glass of whisky (and now Confidence, Miss Muriel), down in the drawing-room in that turn-out talking to a gentleman. Yes, fancy, imagine. And Mademoiselle said it gave her quite a nasty feeling and at the same time she said Miss Diana looked charming you wouldn't believe.

"And they had poor Miss Mousie McGrath up there one night and giving her champagne and a kidney omelette till she went on quite undignified. Yes, Mrs. McGrath wouldn't let her go home though it's only down the road as you know, but a bed had to be made up for her and a fire lit at ten o'clock at night in the blue bedroom, and Mrs. McGrath put her to bed herself in one of her own pink satin nighties and a pink Shetland coat. Really, I think it would have looked sort of pagan on an old lady.

"And hunting, out hunting every day in the week and Bob Richit up in the drawing-room after tea and a big glass of whisky for him and talking of the hounds and the horses and the gallops they had till near dinner-time. It's a wonder, Mademoiselle says, sometimes she wouldn't keep him to dinner. She'd sooner talk to him than to any of the nice young gentlemen she has there."

Spiller's accounts of life at Rathglass were fairly truthful. All the events she described with delighted horror and popping eyes really happened but with less forced and pagan joviality than appeared in her accounts of them. At the same time, Life at Rathglass was—in times of sore tragedy as well as in times of happiness—a terrifying contrast to life at Garonlea.

XVII

SINCE the news had come of Desmond's being killed, Cynthia was like a person wilfully keeping herself half-anæsthetised. The final reality of being without him was more than she could endure. Also she was a person to whom the present was of more importance than what had been or what would be. If she could fill the present moment so that she need not look before or behind it, she found that she had some ease and quietness of mind. Hunting she thought was best, but what really made her nearest to forgetting was her perpetual and indefeatable success with the men. It did not do her any good but it seemed to stop that gap of loneliness sometimes and it gave her a sort of wild satisfaction too, continually denying the love she could have had. In every possible way that was hard and stupid and unkind she laid Desmond's ghost, but though she denied him, trying to save herself from pain, he was still so real to her that she dared not think of him. She was really afraid, in the strength of so much sorrow and took any means to put it away from her and exhaust her mind and body towards forgetting.

Life without Desmond seemed to kill all the warmth and kindness that had ever been in her and leave bare a sharp wolfish twist that looked for satisfaction in different ways. And found it. She found it in exciting men about her and denying them love. In their need and unhappiness she felt less alone. She found it in a sort of wild, hard gaiety, in those silly parties that Mademoiselle chronicled so faithfully to Spiller. The only people to whom she was a little kind were her dogs and Diana. The amazing change in Diana amused her a lot and gave her a fine sense of victory over Lady Charlotte. She was never so pleased as when, having persuaded Diana to ride astride, as her side-saddle was always giving sore backs, they met Lady Charlotte and Muriel driving the fat pony in a narrow lane-way and Lady Charlotte was compelled to maintain a glacial front for nearly five minutes while Cynthia pretended that she could not persuade her horse to pass them. This gave her the keenest amusement and even Diana was able to treat it with a sort of swagger. Such was her escape from the old power at Garonlea, that she did not even feel sympathy for what this meeting meant to Muriel—Muriel beating the fat pony, blushing up to her eyes and bravely saying, "Hullo, Cynthia! Hullo, Diana!" Diana had nearly forgotten what this must cost in effort at the time and in trouble with Lady Charlotte afterwards.

At this time Diana was deeply and entirely happy. She was not tiresome or jealous in her love for Cynthia. She worked for her because she liked working—not in romantical slavishness. All the new excitements like cutting off your hair, and drinking whisky, and dancing to the gramophone (she and Cynthia would practise tricky steps together because dancing well really did matter in those late war years and after) satisfied her desire for pleasure and excitement, even her sense of being entirely daring was gratified by the constant thought of that tremendous shadow of displeasure across the valley.

The knowledge that she was at last of real value to Cynthia made her in a dim, unknowing way, grateful for Cynthia's wild and driven unhappiness. Although she could not by any standards measure the loss, she knew something of the despair that Cynthia fled in that grasping at life which so scandalised Garonlea.

She saw another thing too, which she put out of her mind because it frightened her a little, and that was the vein of cruelty in Cynthia's relationship with Simon and Susan. She called it by other names. She called it "Cynthia making Simon hardy." She said Cynthia was so wonderful about not spoiling Susan. How good it was for Susan to be teased. How well Simon rode and how Cynthia would stand no nonsense from him about not liking his pony, or from Susan either for that matter. Let them fall off, she always said, that's the way they'll learn that falls don't hurt. They must shoot and fish, too, and swim and play tennis seriously in between. Cynthia was wonderful about Simon's holidays. She never let anything interfere with hunting, or riding in children's classes at shows, or with his shooting or fishing or any other manly sport in which she wished him to be proficient.

Those were all the things Diana said to herself and to other people about Cynthia's ways with Simon and Susan, but secretly she could not help a creeping feeling of dismay and fear at the hardness of Cynthia's ways with them.

Since those first holidays after Desmond was killed, when Cynthia had passed over Simon's one small, desperate effort about not riding Mitty, he had gone uncomplainingly through the sort of martyrdom nervous children endure through being compelled to ride their ponies and take part in the chase.

Susan, who rode much better than Simon, disliked hunting very much, too. It frightened and bored her, even if she didn't have quite so many distressing falls. When they were older and discussed the matter without shame or passion, they could not think why they had not admitted their fears to one another at the time. Those evenings in the schoolroom, with the meet at

Drumbeg next day, and the first fence away from the first covert a stone wall with a dirty, unseating drop the other side, were quick with unadmitted cowardice.

"Ah, Simon, do stop playing scales; I can't read my book beyond it," Susan was a pale, overgrown creature with long arms sleeved in blue velvet. She had a face short and blunt as a cat's, but more irregular, and shy, stripey eyes.

Simon stopped obligingly. His heart was not in his playing to-night. He came to lean over her shoulders at the scarred table.

"You aren't reading, Sue, you were at that page an hour ago." He moved away to the window, an elegant, soft-looking creature. He opened it, leaning out: "Still freezing. Hope it won't be too hard to hunt to-morrow."

"Hope not. But it won't be."

"No, it's only the second night's frost." Simon's voice was thin with pretence. He dropped the curtains and went fiddling over to the fireplace.

"If it *was* too hard to hunt to-morrow," he said, "what would you like best to do?"

Susan said, "I'd rather hunt than anything."

"Yes, of course. But if we really couldn't."

The pupils of Susan's eyes expanded as they always did when she imagined hard, growing so dark that they spread across her eyes. "I'd like to stay in bed with my favourite book and my favourite rabbit and have all my favourite food for breakfast and lunch and tea."

The contrast between such a day of luxurious idleness and the stern reality of the real to-morrow was almost too much for Simon.

He said, angrily, "I hope that beastly Dolly Bryant isn't out. She always shoves me out of my place, and Mummy always seems to know when I'm last in the hunt."

"Last in the hunt"—that shameful position.

"How does she always *know*?" They were a little closer to truth and sympathy.

"And she never even noticed when I jumped that high wall on Wednesday behind Richit."

"I saw you. I jumped it on your left as a matter of fact." Susan was a little grand. Then she caught Simon's eye and added, because obviously he knew, "where some one had knocked a big hole."

Susan was a shade more sophisticated about being cowardly than Simon. Once, in her very young days—before Cynthia had given up persuasion and taken to more arbitrary methods—she had wasted about twenty minutes trying to induce her daughter and her daughter's refusing pony to leap some bushes in a gap.

"Look at that little boy, wouldn't you like to ride like him?" She indicated a tough child who drove his pony at the place with commendable bravery and energy. Brave and enviable as he was, he unhappily flew off as his pony leaped, landing first in the next field, much more hurt and frightened than he was allowed to admit. "You see," Susan said, "that's the sort of thing that puts me off huntin'. . . ."

Of course, it was not too hard to hunt next day. Just not too hard. They went into Cynthia's room after breakfast to have their stocks tied. Their noses were pink, like half-ripe strawberries in their pale faces, their stomachs were queasy and unsteady and not much breakfast in them.

"Turn round, darling. Safety-pin? Safety-pin? Turn round. Too tight? Never mind, it's very tidy. Now, Simon. It's time you learnt to do this for yourself. You might try on Friday."

"Am I hunting on Friday?" Simon's face was

faintly greener. He hooked at the tight white-linen stock with his finger.

"Yes. Now I've let the cat out. It was to be a surprise. I've got Myer's grey cob for you again. It's too far to send you on your pony."

"Yes, that's what I thought," said Simon faintly, "thank you so much."

"Poor old Sue will have to go round with the terriers."

"Or couldn't I ride the grey cob half the day?" Susan asked, impelled by the force of despair that she knew was loosed in Simon. He was the only person who hated Myer's hot, grey cob (such a perfect jumper if a bit quick on her fences), more than Susan did.

"Well, we'll see, darling. Run along now and let me get dressed. And Simon, for heaven's sake fasten your leggings inside your shin bone, not round the back of your calf."

Nearly an hour with nothing to do. An hour feeling quite cold with rather a nasty taste in your mouth before Mummy came down, Mummy in her iron-dark habit and little tight pieces of hair like flat, netted coins under her velvet cap, Mummy, so brisk and hard and clean, picking up her white gloves and her whip in the hall and shouting for the terrier that was to go in the car with them, on the edge of being very angry if he had gone off rabbiting. But Diana had shut him in the car already so that he couldn't. They were glad she was hunting to-day. She often helped them when they were in trouble and never told if she saw them avoiding a stone wall.

Simon ran stiffly across the gravel, its little knobs frozen solid under his feet, to open the gate with a wreath of ice on its bars and latch. Crouching under rugs in the back of the car, he shared with Susan a period that was blank except for that slight, persistent feeling of nausea. They did not seem to belong to their own bodies at all. Those large hands in string gloves were strange people's hands. They crossed and uncrossed their legs clumsily as if they were wooden legs. They did not mind about each other, each feeling that the other was better equipped to contend with its beastly pony. Susan remembered that Simon's Dinty was much easier to sit on over a wall than her own Mouse, and Simon remembered that Susan was much more adhesive over any sort of fly fence than he was. Each felt that the other was less to be pitied and each longed for the end of the day with an ardour which saw such ease a month away at least.

They looked at the fields and the fences as they drove past them, seeing them with a curious relationship of fear and not fear. The fields were not ordinary fields as in summer. They were places you had to get out of, that you were inexorably carried over. That field now, with green plover waddling and pecking about on its dark, sheep-bitten turf, was a dreadfully unkind field with wire on its nice round banks and as cruel a coped stone wall across one side of it as a frightened child could face. The very young may be sick with cowardice about a fence but they are more afraid not to jump it than to jump it. Then there might be a wide, benignant field with an open gateway in a corner, or a ditch full of dark, cold water, but only a low bank in front of it, very heartening. It was not soft falls in water or bog that they dreaded, but that shameful, hurting, falling off and the moments before you fell, their agony seeming to endure in interminable uncertainty before you went with a sort of sob and the ground hit you from behind, strangely like a house falling on you, not you falling on a house.

XVIII

THEIR ponies were waiting for them at the meet, looking hard and unkind and as if they would gallop and jump for weeks without ever being tired or ceasing to pull like bulls in those round, smooth snaffles. Cynthia liked the children's ponies to look fit and well and they were beautifully turned out, their tails pulled to the last hair and their manes plaited up. They eyed them for a moment with hatred from the car before they remembered to get out and fuss over them as keen, sporting children should.

"Thought we should hardly hunt coming along," Richit said; his face looked red and blue and his eyes were as pale as a jackdaw's under the peak of his cap. You could not possibly have mistaken his mouth for the mouth of any one but a hunt servant.

"We'll hunt, all right," Cynthia stood among the hounds, digging the heel of her boot into the grass at the side of the road. The smell of the hounds' bodies was like a warm, low cloud round her. She looked at the list of hounds Richit handed to her, and when he said, "The north side of the fences will be like iron," she did not answer.

"I shall have some lame hounds coming home to-night," he said after a pause. The fact was, Ricket was scarcely more anxious to hunt to-day than Simon and Susan. He hated his first horse and his piles had been giving him great trouble. Cynthia guessed about the horse though not about the piles. She went over to the public-house at the cross-roads and sent him out a double Irish whisky. She and Diana drank a glass of disgusting port each.

"Isn't it filthy?" Cynthia said, "I suppose I'd better have another."

The children visited a field before they mounted their ponies. When they had mounted they wished to visit the field again but hardly liked to. Their insides were most unsteady. Presently they were on the steep hill beside the covert, with that wall standing up very dark and tall at the foot of the hill. The covert was on the left-hand side of the field. They could only see the very edge of it. There was a steep lime-kiln, grey and white like the sky, and the gorse bushes appeared to be navy blue in the cold morning.

Their ponies fiddled about and tore up mouthfuls of grass and smelt other horses and screamed and then stood very still, galvanically still, with their heads up, gazing into the blue gorse bushes as though longing to see a fox. Once a hound came out under Dinty's tail and was kicked. Cynthia was on the other side of the covert and they hoped she did not hear the hideous noise it made. They were supposed to know most of the hounds and they wished they could remember the name of this one but they could not. A man they did not know said, "Do the brute good." He looked at them in a friendly way and said, "She's all right, you hardly touched her. Cowardly, that's what it is. So am I." They found this rather an embarrassing remark so did not answer. They did not have time really, for at that moment one of those hunting cries that are supposed to excite hounds and horsemen to a perfect fever pitch of determination and endeavour split the cold air with awful clarity. They gathered up their reins and looked wildly down towards the stone wall.

Their ponies stood like trembling rocks about to hurl themselves over the edge of an abyss.

Then the strange man who had been looking up over the hill did a queer thing. He turned his horse round and galloped up the hill and away from the wall. Simon and Susan looked at each other. He couldn't be right. Foxes always went away at the bottom of the covert. The field always had to jump the wall. But still they whirled their ponies round and hurried up the hill after the cowardly stranger. He had jumped a little bank into the top corner of the covert, squeezed through a gorse-filled corner and was out in the field beyond. Screaming to each other to get out of the way, they followed.

From your point of view when you are a child a hunt is purely a question of obstacles and not falling off. It is a good hunt for Irish children if there are no high walls or pieces of timber and if you are not quite last in the chase, and if straggling hounds keep out of your pony's way, because in any case you can't stop. Susan and Simon were often borne along for miles with tears pouring down their faces, and every one said how much they were enjoying themselves and how well they went for children of their age. And it is the best sort of hunt of all if it is short, with a long dig at the end of it.

To-day that breathless moment of cowardice which had given them determination enough to turn their backs on the stone wall and follow the strange man out through the top of the covert put them in a surprisingly commanding position in the hunt, for any one who knew the covert was of the same opinion as they had been, as to the direction in which foxes usually left it. So for some time the stranger, the first whip and Simon and Susan clattered over the country in rather grand isolation with the hounds.

Susan's pony elected to follow the whip's horse. As his horse changed feet on the bank, Mouse took off and sprang up behind him, arriving in the next field just a second late and just mathematically without a collision. The first whip was an unimaginative boy and riding a steady and solid cob, he did not mind. But it was another matter for the stranger, who was riding a sketchy sort of hireling, to have Simon just missing the small of his back at every leap. He tried saying "Not so close, old man," and "Take a pull, child," but he soon saw that no admonition could have any effect, and at each mistake his hireling made he resigned himself to the worst and was mildly surprised not to find himself on the ground with Simon and his pony and the hireling all on top of him together.

In the end it was one of those tiresome, straggling hounds that caused all the trouble. The stranger, with misplaced consideration and *ésprit de chasse*, waited for it to scramble over a fence and the delay was just too long for Simon's pony. As the now rather weary hireling leaped, so did he, they met with a tremendous impact, and the hireling, without making the smallest effort to reassemble its forces, fell out on its head in the next field. Simon's pony staggered, recovered himself and jumped off the bank straight on top of the stranger whom he kicked in the head and clouted in the ribs before he galloped away in pursuit of Susan and the first whip. Simon, in the confusion and shock, had fallen off.

Cynthia was very upset about it, although pleased that Simon had been going well enough to knock David Colebrook off a fence and jump on him, and concuss him. She knew the stranger better by reputation than her children did or they might have faced the wall in preference to pursuing him through the country. As it was, he was put into the car and driven back to Rathglass and put to bed. The blinds were pulled down and his ribs were strapped up by the doctor.

The children were told they could only stay out to see one more covert drawn as they would have to hack home. Owing to their carelessness in nearly killing a famous jockey and spoiling Mummy's day's hunting, there was not room for them in the car. They expressed suitable regret and then how they prayed that the covert might be blank. They prayed like anything. Their prayer was granted, too, because Richit was not very keen about hunting to-day either, so when they got back to a road they were able to turn their ponies' heads towards home almost before two o'clock.

That was a good day. They stopped at the pub and bought themselves ginger biscuits and ginger beer. Their insides felt marvellously steady and glowing again. It was not like one of those dreadful evenings when a court of inquiry was held over their failures as they sat in the back of the car and Cynthia shot questions at them over her shoulder all the way home: questions that always caught you out somewhere.

"Susan, how did your pony jump the wall near Lara Wood?"

Susan cast wildly about in her mind, how had she been so fortunate as to escape that wall?

"Jumped it well," she might say.

"And didn't shift you?"

"No, I was all right."

"And how did you get on, Simon?"

Simon said cautiously, "I almost fell off."

"But not quite? I see. Well, I think it's a pity you

should tell lies as well as being little funks because I saw you both going through a gate."

They felt ill with shame.

Then there were the Bad Scenting Days when she got behind them and beat their ponies over places when they stopped, knowing exactly where their riders' hearts were. And whether they fell off or did not fall off, they were certain they were going to, which is acute mental strain and agony.

Cynthia, too, minded dreadfully that they should be such pale, uncourageous children, these children of hers and Desmond's. Why could they not love hunting and dogs and ratting and badger digging and their ponies, as all right-minded children should, instead of having to be compelled and encouraged to take their parts in these sports and pleasures? The moments when she said to people, "Simon? I think he's digging out a rat in the wood," or, "schooling his pony for the gymkhana," or "looking for a snipe's nest," and all the time knew that he was playing the piano in the school-room or drawing one of those hideous, left-handed pictures, so unspeakably like Susan or Diana or the sewing-maid were really bitter moments for her. She did not love her children but she was determined not to be ashamed of them. You had to feel ashamed and embarrassed if your children did not take keenly to blood-sports, so they must be forced into them. It was right. It was only fair to them. You could not bring a boy up properly unless he rode and fished and shot. What sort of boy was he? What sort of friends would he have? Besides, Simon was to live at Garonlea.

Since Garonlea was so soon to belong to her son the place had achieved an importance with Cynthia that it had never held when she lived so delightedly with Desmond. But now she had lost Desmond with the most cruel completeness. She had lost the feel of his hands. She had lost the look of his hands. She could not imagine the sound of his voice now. She had lost him entirely. Without him the importances that had only been the outside of her life before became all the life she had. She took them eagerly, driving herself into hunting and parties and hard work of all sorts. She was striving to forget. Soon she had forgotten. She could not realise the danger of that thirsty, unsatisfied part of her life that had been so entirely complete when she lived with Desmond. She did not know that she gave herself a masochistic pleasure in her treatment of his children. She denied this satisfaction to herself and had a thousand reasons which entirely justified her in her own mind. It never occurred to her that she bullied them and drilled and ordered and tortured the miserable little lives out of them because she wanted to, because she did not love them, and needed to hurt them. If the whole import-ance and love of her own life had not been swept from her she would at any rate have left them alone. But as it was she could not leave them alone. They were another importance to fill that blank and solitary place.

Of course, what Cynthia needed was love with another man. But although men's praise was the breath of life to her and she lived for their admiration and their company, she had a romantically obstinate pose at this time about her faithfulness to Desmond's memory, Desmond whom she had struggled to tear out of her consciousness. Desmond, whom she missed in the flesh so atrociously that she must exhaust herself before she could sleep because of the hopeless cruelty of nights and days and weeks and months without him. She had that extra mould as of glass upon her which people who are physically very brave and very strong too, can maintain uncracked. It shivers very soon with weaker people, leaving them soft and vulnerable. It did not shiver and splinter away with Cynthia, and because of it no one ever got really close to her. Inside her glass mould she would act and go on and produce effects which came through distorted and dramatised and with very little relation to the pain or the savagery that was behind it all.

Another thing was that no one ever criticised Cynthia. This left her more alone. She could not even tell when she was being absurd. The criticism from Garonlea of course, was so far-fetched and fantastic that it cancelled out on itself. Beyond that she was one of those popular Queens who don't meet the people who think them either comic or boring or vulgar or selfish, or any of the things which they so often are.

XIX

THE day that she drove David Colebrook, very shaken and definitely concussed, back to Rathglass, Cynthia took into her house a man who never really minded what he said to people and was not inclined to be impressed by anything he had heard of them. He had knocked about the racecourses of England for some years before the war, and he knew how to look after himself. He was quick and hardy and very tidy in his ways of riding a race, or telling a story, or wearing his clothes, or making love. Being rude to people was rather a pose with him really. But it was a pose he got away with nine times out of ten. Especially with women.

On the way back to Rathglass he came out of his trance of stupidity to say to Cynthia:

"Pretty silly thing. Child riding a pony like that. Couldn't begin to stop him. How would we like hunting out of control all day? Tiring. Frightening. Terrible thing. So dam' silly."

Cynthia felt furious before she remembered that he was concussed and didn't know what he was talking about.

But ten days later when he was still at Rathglass (he had a genius for prolonging a visit if a house suited him, he could compel even people who loathed him to beg him to stay on indefinitely) and made almost the same observations to her, as together they watched Simon's and Susan's unwilling progression round the riding school, she felt really cross. If he hadn't once ridden the winner of the National she could have turned on him and told him he didn't know what he was talking about.

"Their ponies are nappy little—oh wells, too. Some one ought to set about them. God, what beasts children's ponies are."

"Those are two of the *most* beautifully bred ponies you could find and perfect jumpers," Cynthia said coldly, and then added in a voice thin with disappointment, "It's the children that want hotting up, I'm afraid."

"Hotting up? Poor little—oh wells. Their ponies want civilising and a diet of hay and turnips. Civilising. Look here—you and I will clout them round those little fences and give them who began it."

"We're too heavy for them," Cynthia began. She felt for once a hot little wave of fright go through her. She really hated jumping the smallest fence astride, and on one of those refusing little eels of ponies and with Susan and Simon looking on, it was preposterous. But before she could possibly think of an excuse that did not include saying, I'm afraid of falling off one of these perfect ponies over that tiny wall, the children had been called up and dismounted, Susan's leathers were lengthened and she was sitting perilously with apparently nothing in front of her and a great deal of strong and obstinate pony behind her. And there was David bouncing about, feeling for Simon's stirrups.

"You make these children ride far too long," he said, and beat the perfect pony heavily. It thought once about refusing the wall, but thought again very quickly and leaped with zeal.

Cynthia's pony, coming after him, refused, whirling round and stopping just as it so often did with poor Susan. Flame in her cheeks, fire in her eye, but misgiving in her heart, Cynthia presented it at the wall once more.

"I'll beat him for you, Mummy," Susan said. She felt quite stilled by the rapture of this moment. This exquisite reversal. It was almost embarrassing. She danced about between the wings of the fence, screaming at her pony and her mother and Simon. David, who had gone on to jump the little bush fence on Simon's pony came back to look gravely at the drama in progress. After a full minute he gave Simon his pony to hold and dealt with Cynthia's solemnly and very severely from behind. It sprang over the wall at last and scuttled away towards the next fence. Cynthia, who had lost an iron and only got back into her saddle by a miracle, found him not too easy to stop. At the bushes there was another refusal and the children panted up and threw small sods and stones and shrieked advice, emboldened by their mother's second failure.

"You see," David said to her an hour later as they walked into lunch, "you do put them throught it, poor little devils."

"You should be ashamed of yourself, shouldn't you?" Cynthia gave the matter one of those flashing twists—"putting me to shame like that before my children. Don't you think it was a bit hard?"

Instead of turning to her that look of penitence and romantic promise that any admission of failure from her surely called for, he said:

"You did look pretty silly. Frightened too, weren't you? Do you good. Makes rather a change, doesn't it? You aren't often frightened, are you?"

Cynthia said No. This tough young man was no older than she was, but he made her feel years younger. She was afraid that he could fool her and frighten her if he felt like it, and rather respected him in consequence.

But he spent most of his time with the children, giving them arbitrary riding instruction, getting twisted snaffles, quite sharp ones, sewn into their ponies' bridles, shortening their leathers and making them lift their little bottoms out of their saddles when they jumped walls. Silencing all Cynthia's protests and giving the children brief, illuminating counsels— "You set about that pony—give him a good job in the mouth as soon as you get up on him. Let him know who's boss—all right—Children never like their ponies till they can bully them."

He went away quite suddenly one day after he had stayed for more than a fortnight. Diana fell over his suitcases in the hall and told Cynthia who only said that with such a tough and peculiar man they ought to count the spoons before he left. She was feeling rather sour about him since the evening before when he had told her that he thought she drank too much and also he thought her stud groom was robbing her —two absolutely shattering insults. But when he had gone she had to work very hard to keep herself free again from her terror of loneliness. Anyhow, it gave her something to do getting the children out of all the bad riding habits he had got them into.

A person who succeeded in hurting Cynthia and getting under her vanity got dangerously near her and found her both vulnerable and uncertain as vain and lonely people so often are. David had gone through her glamour and seen three true things, not very pretty things either. A woman who is unkind to her children, who is robbed by her stud groom, and who drinks is cruel and foolish and weak. If one of Cynthia's idolising train had suddenly turned and told her these things about herself the impression caused would not have been half so deep or so secret. It was in the shock of her failure to impress a stranger that remembrance lived. She did not see David again for about three years—when he came to stay with them at Garonlea.

XX

LADY CHARLOTTE was dying. Her blood pressure had got the better of her at last and two slight strokes had left her "a dream of what she was, a breath, a bubble," a poor, silly, muttering old woman with the last tyrannies possible to her taken out of her power. She hated her nurse because she could not bully her and tried hard to cling to Spiller's meeker ministrations. But the nurse was firmly established by Enid and Violet after the second stroke and before their mother recovered enough of herself to frighten Muriel into dismissing her. Lady Charlotte whined about it a great deal. She had turned into a very old woman now—pathetic, repetitive, futile. All the narrow dignity of her mind had become as the mind of a not very attractive child. Her wits were soft and blunt. She was greedy as a pig about her food. Sometimes there was a flash of her as she used to be, an order given to Muriel about the garden or house or a quick, backward thrust of memory over some quite complicated matter to do with Garonlea. A word to Enid that sent her spinning back to the helpless, dependent creature she had been twenty years before, a commendation for dear little Muriel that made her feel indeed but the solemn little elder sister of four pinafored children and one fat little boy in a sailor suit.

Violet and Enid took it in turns to stay with Muriel at Garonlea during the last year of their mother's life and in a way it was a vague, comfortable year for Muriel at Garonlea. It was fun to have the sisters

there and fuss after their comfort as they hardly did
over hers when she stayed with them. There was a
feeling of luxury and power about ordering more fires
to be lit and better food to be cooked and more frequent
bottles to come up from the cellar. The soothing lies
she told her mother about all these things spun a thread
of independence through her—her confabulations
with doctors and agents and gardeners strengthened
the thread and gave her for the first time in her life the
thrill of being a person held accountable, a real person
with responsibility.

Enid and Violet were very sensible about leaving
things to Muriel and not fussing her in any way. They
encouraged her to see Cynthia and Diana too, and this
secret coming together with Rathglass and especially
with Simon and Susan gave her tremendous pleasure.
Cynthia was very sweet and gentle with Muriel.
Indeed, she had never been anything but charming to
her, for she would rather have even Muriel like her
than dislike her.

Lady Charlotte did not ask to see Diana, only
saying, "bad! naughty!" as one speaks of a dog, when
she was asked whether she would care to see her. For
her part, Diana had not the smallest wish to see her
mother, or the woolly, futile shadow of her mother.
She did not feel the least emotional about her. But
what did upset her so that she could scarcely think of it
was the day, uncertain but possibly near, when she
must go back to Garonlea.

Cynthia was forty now. Desmond had been killed
when she was thirty-six. Four years she had been
without him. She had quenched that terrible reality
of a ghost that was no ghost. Never again could she
let herself suffer as on that first evening when she had
heard he was killed, when he had ridden home with her,

nearer than in any perishable fever of love. She had done with that time. She had got away from the closeness of his love that had pursued her and filled life full again. Hunting, children, friends, parties, gaiety—sordid, silly, rather desperate gaiety—and tremendous, unassailable popularity. Her position was so strong that she could have done what she pleased in that countryside with rich or poor. And now, very soon now, she was to leave Rathglass and go to live at Garonlea. She looked forward to this as another battle and occupation and excitement for her life. She had not forgotten her dislike and mistrust of Garonlea, but she had such tremendous self-confidence at this time, she felt the oldest, most inward character of a place must yield to her if she should determine to change it. And she was defiant about changing Garonlea.

"Cynthia, couldn't you let the place?" Thus Diana, emboldened by a glass or two of sherry. It was lunchtime in September. The sweet, hot sun was in the room. Her eyes were occupied fondly with a great rich decoration of autumn flowers that she had put on the table. Flowers she had grown, gold and purple flowers and spotted lilies—a bowl for Ceres. She was thinking of the red-walled dining-room at Garonlea and of Mr. Price-Harcourt-Price, a picture that a grandmother had brought to Garonlea, and all the other pictures, cold and dark and not very valuable. She looked out at the little hot lawn. The scyllas got half-way across it now in the spring. Just a few down the bank in Aunt Milly's and Mousie's day, a short spring flood when Susan was a baby, and now a lake bluer than any possible water. "Surely you could find a tenant, darling, couldn't you? I mean, with the fishing and shooting and everything."

144

Cynthia looked sadly down at her ringed hands. In this as in everything, she was going to take her own way without abandoning the pretence that it was at the cost of enormous self-sacrifice.

"Tenants? Fishing tenants? Shooting tenants? My dear, what sort of state do you think the house would be in when Simon is twenty-one? You won't mind so very much coming back with me? I couldn't get on without you possibly. I've forgotten how to. And darling, we're going to change it so enormously. Pull the whole place up by the roots—cut its hair, paint its face, give it some royal parties. Oh, we'll lay the ghosts."

"I don't think you'll ever change it," Diana said, quite gravely. "You'll only break your heart trying to."

Cynthia made a face.

"Reassuring little thing, aren't you? Never mind, I'm going to try, and you've got to help me. We've got—how long? Six years till Simon comes of age. It will be a gay house then—you'll see, darling. And when Simon marries some lovely girl, you and I will come back here and end our days like Milly and Mousie. You'll survive me and Simon's children will whirl you into a cottage like we did to Aunt Mousie."

Cynthia laughed her rich, sweet laugh at the absurdity of it all. She was blind to the possibility of failure or age or sickness, except in the most practical ways. She looked after her skin seriously and kept her body fit and hardy. She would easily have passed for a woman in her very early thirties, except perhaps for a slight heaviness and thickening through shoulders and hips. Her clothes, that she used to wear with a breath of strange romance, seemed rather more full of solid flesh and bones now. But she was lovely to look at still, her skin had neither withered nor coarsened and her hair, cut short now, was almost as good a colour as it had been. And yet there was a look about hair and skin and body of being skilfully and indomitably preserved, a certain rigidity. She was a beautiful woman still, people said. They forgot what they missed. It was that look as of a young river, which had lasted excitingly past her earlier youth and her children's births and had passed from her when Desmond was killed.

Susan had this changing, fluid look. It was the only thing about her that was at all like Cynthia. She was thirteen now, sulking in a fashionable girls' school in the south of England. Simon, who had surprisingly good taste for his age, was almost the only person who admired her. Cynthia certainly did not admire either her daughter or her son at this time. She found their pale-green skins and pale lips most unattractive. Susan's hair was inclined to curl, that was the best that could be said for it since it had turned from its promise of Cynthia's true gold to become almost the same olive colour as Simon's. With their faces she could not be very pleased, but their figures were all right. Long thin creatures like the thin green shadows of a poplar's bones in winter. Another thing that pleased her and proved her right about them was that they both now rode well, no longer apparently afraid, they no longer fell off or made their ponies refuse at stone walls, no longer were sick on hunting mornings. So while they managed to conceal their distressing and disgraceful boredom with the chase they did her due credit among her hunting friends. She was very much afraid that a terrible day would come when they would admit and even boast of it. So far as she knew, even to Diana they had not done this, but she feared that they would.

Simon and Susan told Diana a great many things and she confided in them too, although her confidences were distressingly abridged by her terrific loyalty to Cynthia. Not so much loyalty as faith, for loyalty implies criticism and Diana's love had never taught her to look closer and see what her idol's feet were made of.

Even now, in this matter of Garonlea, though she felt miserably unhappy and apprehensive, she accepted all Cynthia's reasons for leaving Rathglass and did not see as far as that chief tremendous motive of vanity which impelled Cynthia to scour the very shadow of Lady Charlotte as swiftly and brutally as possible from the place where she had imposed her will for so long.

With all her schemes and plans for Garonlea, Cynthia could scarcely wait for the news of Lady Charlotte's death to come across the river. The drawing-room at Rathglass was stuffed with parcels of patterns for hangings and chintzes, Cynthia was itching to get estimates for this and that—Light and central-heating, painting and new baths.

When at last an incoherent note came one afternoon from Muriel saying that Mother was almost dead and anyhow, quite unconscious, so would they come over as it could not possibly upset her now, the doctor said, and it would be better for the family to be together. Diana felt that Rathglass was now so permeated with the idea of Garonlea that she would be glad to see Garonlea as a real and separate place again. She could not bear its importance so flowing into Rathglass.

It was the most perfect and quiet autumn afternoon when they walked over to Garonlea. A clearness like a bell's note hung in the air, if days and sounds were interchangeable. In the village, children's voices were loud but rather sweet, Hydrangeas were shockingly blue in a cottage garden and apples on branches as definite as a story that starts about an apple tree. Birds were flying so low over the river that their dark wings seemed to pierce its smoothness. The shadows under the arches of the bridge were black still. In the change succeeding summer the distances were unfamiliar, heights and levels seemed altered. You saw a little valley within the summer valley, the form behind the accomplished shape of things was briefly obvious.

Then they came to the Garonlea woods across the river and the day's clearness and purpose were submerged and lost for Diana in that stillness and pressure of woods; in the dark reek of laurel and rhododendron that masked the very stems of trees, leaving visible only confused worlds of branches, blocking all distance, shoving close round the turn of paths and walls, eager with rankness and strong life.

Cynthia's chin was up and her eyes shining as she walked through the woods. She gave herself no room or time for melancholy.

"You see, darling, we'll clear out all this smelly jungle of laurel."

"Woodcock like laurel," Diana said dispiritedly.

"They don't want all this laurel. Anyhow I shall clear and cut some marvellous vistas."

"You will have to mine the valley before you find a vista."

"I can see you're going to be an enormous help to me." Cynthia had good reason to feel irritated with Diana who was fiddling along behind her in an absent-minded, dreary sort of way and making disheartening answers in a manner very different from her usual thrilled acquiescence and delighted elaboration of any plan of Cynthia's.

148

So far it was not dramatic, this return, although it had every element of drama: the old queen dying: a change at hand: a house waiting its new possessor—a house muffled in history and tradition about to be stripped and woken. The coming of a new, angry Queen through the woods did not change their calm by a breath, her strength would use itself against Garonlea in hopeless endeavour. The house was calm too, confident and unafraid. The afternoon sun lay on its face as if on the face of a cat, a yellow, fat cat, tigerishly striped and blotched—autumn creepers gorgeous on the walls, red geraniums splendid in the sun. They walked in at the door, the sunlight mounting the four steps and lying flatter than water on the floor, and beyond in the dark hall a smell of coolness, a reserved and musty breath. Their feet made a faint clatter on the diamonded, tiled floor, coldly noisy between rugs. Pots of blue lilies were scattered here and there among the little suits of armour. ("How typical! Why not a group?" Cynthia's mind busily criticised.) There was a basket of earthy-looking green apples on a table outside the library door with a pair of worn gloves curling from the use of hands beside it. In the room the dead ashes of a wood fire lay white and cold in the sun.

There was nobody in the library, only the dead fire and the empty hush. Diana stood on the white curly fur hearthrug, apart, Cynthia was no help or protector to her now. Again there swept through her that feeling which in four years she had almost forgotten, the feeling of helplessness and depression that she would never escape at Garonlea. Standing there in the library she felt as if her life had already begun to drain and trickle away from her. She was changing already, slipping back into the real she, that sad creature of vague despairs and rebellions. The room was so unchanged since she had last been in it that a night and its dreams only might have lain between her going and her return. There is something strange about a room staying just the same after a long time even if one has been happy there. As it was, Diana shivered under the memory, brought so much too near, of Lady Charlotte sitting in that chair exactly at the writing-table, a vase of flowers in its usual place at her elbow, the silver inkpot and paper-knife shining still. The three different sorts of notepaper still there: one grey-blue with *Garonlea, Co. Westcommon, Ireland*, stamped on it in black letters. The thin white sheets on which letters to shops were written and the address here:

From: The Lady Charlotte French-McGrath, written on top. And the small thin sheets with no stamping that she used economically for notes and lists and writing to the children, they were all there with their appropriate envelopes in the divisions of that upright, red leather box. The chairs and sofas were in their same positions to an inch, and on all the tables the same small vases held the same tremulous little bouquets, dim and unoffending but a little sickening in their silliness and failure to decorate. Everything in life seemed less real to Diana than the terrible sameness of this room. Already Garonlea was soaking up what power there was in her. She felt herself slipping into its dangerous strength, absorbed and half-languorous in the melancholy.

Cynthia was outside its power still. She had no hag-ridden memories, and the rebellion she brought was fresh and strong within her. Her mouth was taut and her eyes half-closed now as she took in the room, concentrating on its possibilities. Calculating, condemning, wondering, changing her plans every moment and fully conscious of her power.

To-day she was wearing a soft yellow silk shirt and a short brown skirt. She leant back in a corner of the sofa facing the room. Her strong thin legs were crossed. Her short hair was bright with health and her thick smooth skin faintly brown. She looked invincible and eager and amazingly young. Diana, who thought that her own terror of Garonlea had been understood by Cynthia and a real thing to her, saw that she had been wrong. Cynthia did not understand anything about fear connected with Garonlea. It had only been her wonderful faculty for sympathy, that gift of hers, that had misled Diana. But Diana was not quite right. Once Cynthia had been afraid of Garonlea.

Presently Muriel came in, a little figure, stooping together and crying sadly, with Enid on one side of her, looking rather quiet, and Violet, fat and lovely and rather flustered because she was not crying too, on the other.

They sat Muriel down in the middle of a sofa and then sat down themselves one on each side of her, patting at her and nodding and grimacing the tidings of death towards Cynthia and Diana. None of them could say, "Mother is dead"—"Gone"—"Passed away." Why are there no simple words for poor, ordinary people to use about death. They can only translate their emotion into words that pervert all meaning and embarrass any natural truth.

Presently Muriel looked up with streaming eyes.

"Darling Mother's gone," she said.

Diana said "Yes." It sounded unloving and aggressive but it didn't mean anything.

Cynthia said, "My poor darling, you must be com-

pletely worn out——" When had she said that before?
In this room? Yes, to Lady Charlotte at the time of
Enid's wedding. She was bending towards Muriel,
her eyes full of sympathy, her arm lying with ease
along the back of the sofa. Diana could remember that
other time as she could remember so much about
Cynthia . . . the scented, plumey pale blue feather
boa, the ease of speech and movement. And now she
was bending towards Muriel, her eyes full of sympathy,
her voice deep with kindness, her arm lying with the
ease and strength of flowing water along the back of
the sofa.

"How long have you been here, Cynthia?" Enid
asked in a whispering voice as though she were in
church.

"How long, Diana?"

"About half an hour."

"About half an hour, Enid."

Muriel looked up with changed eyes although they
still swam in tears.

"Then you *were* here when she—Passed."

"I expect so, darling."

"Oh, I'm so glad. It makes a difference, doesn't it?
Anyhow, we were all together at Garonlea. She would
have liked that if she had been herself."

"Yes, of course she would." Violet and Enid echoed
politely and Cynthia and Diana bowed their heads in
agreement. Though all four of them knew perfectly
well that had Lady Charlotte indeed been herself it
was the last situation she would have countenanced.
But this immediate romantical and wilful falsifying
of a dead person's character was both natural and
comforting to Muriel and less embarrassing to the
rest than candour can be at such a moment.

Presently Diana said, "Cynthia shall we go? I have

fourteen clocking hens to let out and—and—a lot of things."

Immediately she saw that Cynthia was displeased, and when Muriel said, "Oh, do wait and have some tea and after tea nurse says we can see dearest Mother again," she looked pleased and even a trifle eager. She wanted to renew her mind with the upstairs possibilities of Garonlea. Neither was she at all averse to the idea of taking a look at her old adversary lying dead. It was not a girlish desire, but Cynthia was a strangely natural person and had no recoil about death or birth.

Diana was afraid of all three. She got very red and then, very white and said, "Oh, Muriel, I think I won't. I don't think I need, need I, Cynthia?"

"Of course not darling. Much, much better not. You go quietly back to Rathglass now and I'll be after you in no time at all."

Diana stood about for another minute, uncertain whether to kiss her sisters and go, or go without kissing her sisters. It seemed rather extravagant to kiss them and yet just to walk off seemed as if it was going to be rather a bald departure. Cynthia helped her again, saying:

"Tell them I won't be back to tea," and on this note Diana smiled at the three on the sofa uncertainly and left the room.

"You did understand my encouraging her to go," Cynthia said with soft persistence. "Anything like *that* upsets her for days. I've known her not to sleep after a badger dig."

They all nodded mournfully but agreeably at Cynthia, accepting without question some obscure link between a badger dig and their mother's deathbed.

XXI

In fact, Cynthia was curiously but absolutely right. It was death that made Diana shrink and shrivel as though spiritually she had eaten a lemon and caught a chill on her liver both in the same hour. She hurried back to Rathglass now, and when she was over the bridge took deep breaths of village air and avenue air and sweet, airy breath of flowers in the hall. She stood breathing it in, waiting for Rathglass to heal the sickness of Garonlea within her. Very slowly she felt the first thin returning tide drawn through her, drawn by her as though she was the moon. It came slowly, curling, falling small waves where sands had dried and bleached again in the sun that afternoon. Sands that had been covered for four years.

She waited another long moment, almost as though in an embrace, as if this was a lover's breath, this warm, light smell of flowers and air. Then she went out of the hall and down the tidy warren of passage towards the kitchen. The warren was blowing with the delicious and intoxicating fragrance of boiling jam—such a warm and reassuring odour. Smiling quite certainly now, Diana opened the kitchen door to ask for tea and to say Cynthia would not be back.

In the kitchen the cook (a handsome, fat young woman with flat blocks of hair, to whom Diana was greatly attached) had just whipped a bowl of cream and was stirring strong coffee into its smooth thickness. Blackberries were boiling on the fire for jelly and bottles of whole, rosy-looking plums stirred about in a black pot of bubbling water. There was a heap of tiny plum stalks lying in the sun on the window sill.

"I'm sorry to hear of her Ladyship's death, Miss," the cook said. Diana was pleased with the detached way she spoke—as though her Ladyship had died in Arabia years before. And no doubt she was burning with curiosity over what changes this might mean for them all. Diana went down the steps to the scullery—a cold, clean place, smelling of earth—to see if her chickens' food was ready. The kitchen-maid was startled to see her, a toothless, stupid creature, older than that kind and able cook, she jumped inside her blue-flowered pinafore. She was pathetically full of another idea, cabbage and small green marrows in her hands. Oh, yes, the chickens' food was ready, Miss, and she was so sorry to hear of the trouble at Garonlea. Again the Trouble at Garonlea had been disconnected from the life at Rathglass. Comforted and set to rights, Diana went back to the drawing-room to drink her little brown pot of Indian tea which she liked so much better than Cynthia's scented Chinese brew. Strong kitchen tea with a little cream lining its surface was what Diana liked, and that sweet cook had made a delicious Sally Lunn tea-cake, thinking they would return in need of her restoring art. Presently she went out to her chickens, and at about seven o'clock, since Cynthia had not yet come back, she took one of those aimless but enthralling evening wanders in the garden.

It was one of those curious autumn evenings, perfect completion of the clear day. There was a light and particular distance and glamour over near and familiar things, as though one looked down through sea-water into the end of the day.

In her garden, Diana came to a group of lilies in half a drift of faint smoke, a mist of pale apples on boughs behind them. Their thrilling animal scent was blown across the faint smell of burning weeds.

She thought that forever this scent would haunt her with her present fear and unhappiness. How deeply exciting she should have found it. She could see it all so sharply, but she could not feel it. She could not be quite conscious, she was looking through glass or through water. She went out of her garden and would not go back because she was so afraid.

XXII

"Susan, my darling, you look perfectly beautiful. Really. Show me the back. If I wasn't Simon I'd choose you to-night. Do you think any of Mamma's smart friends will choose me and my gardenia and my smart coat?"

"Oh, Simon, don't be chosen or I shall have no one to talk to or dance with."

"Nonsense! Our kind mother has asked several suitable young natives of both sexes so that we shan't feel out of it with her ' crowd.'"

"I'm such an awkward age for her," Susan said despairingly, "an old fifteen. But if she would have her dance in the Easter holidays——"

"We mustn't blame her for that. She wanted the magnolia and the cherry trees."

"And she's so lucky—she's not even going to have a smart hail-storm."

"To-night might be July."

"Without any thunder."

"I like your green ribbons. Couldn't you put a bow in your hair? And why must girls of your age have their dresses just down to the calves of their legs? Such a trying length. You should wear either a long dress or a Grecian tunic."

"Or a leopard-skin, or a crinoline. I follow you, Simon." It was so like Simon to say just how lovely you looked and then little by little undeceive you, calling attention first to the fact that your hair was wrong and would be improved by a ribbon. And then to the unalterable ugliness of the misse's party frock. Better get it all over. "You haven't admired my new shoes either. Enormously long, pale-gold canoes," she held one foot that seemed a yard long, out to him. "Pretty, aren't they?"

Simon sighed. "If only I could dress you. Of course, I shall be able to by the time it matters." They both brightened up at this.

Simon leaned over Susan's shoulder, peering into the mirror. He flicked nothing off the shoulder of his coat and drew his gardenia farther down in his buttonhole. At eighteen he wore his clothes with exactitude, elegance and forgetfulness. Except when he was looking over Susan's shoulder and admiring himself quite naturally in a glass. He was charming and distinguished-looking, with soft, near-fair hair and dark, apostolic eyes. But the lower part of his face did something (besides not having a beard) that spoilt him for being an apostle and tried to make him look like a monkey, but gave that up too. It was an attractive failure. He had lovely though rather faint hands, no hips and long narrow feet like Susan's. He was just but only just as tall as she was.

Susan's face was still a blunt cat's or frog's face with a hole in her chin and a full mouth and green and brown striped eyes, and another untidy sort of hole near one cheek-bone. She was not fat any more, but much too tall and thin, although she avoided the Alice Wondering look by just a little, perhaps because she moved well, slithering through her life with hips almost as narrow as Simon's. Her preposterous white dress had a V-neck and elbow-length sleeves and she wore a locket of turquoises and pearls in a short, stout chain round her neck and about three silver-wire bangles. She liked a nice bit of jewellery, whatever Simon might say.

Her bedroom at Garonlea was not the one Enid and Diana had shared, nor was it the one still known as Muriel's and Violet's. No. Among greater changes at Garonlea, the children's rooms were established where Lady Charlotte had only lodged her favourite visitors. Their windows looked up a strange new distance of the valley where trees had been cut down and a new prospect discovered. A little unmellowed and afraid of itself still, this newly opened world, now vain of its daring, now shrinking and refusing to show off—like a new, unsoftened girl needing only time to be sure and beautiful.

Inside and outside, Garonlea had been pulled about and improved (undeniably improved) and changed beyond all knowing. What Cynthia with her enormous grasp of affairs had done in two years in the way of cajoling trustees and carrying out her plans and spending money when she needed to was astounding and beyond belief. And all done in the name of her love and enthusiasm for Simon. "How wonderful you are," her friends said to her, "really, you are wonderful." "Oh, no, it's been such fun for me," Cynthia would say, "though I can't deny it is a bit of a contest at times, and rather exhausting, you know. But then, so tremendously worth while. And I *think* Simon's going to like it."

And by a strange chance, Simon adored Garonlea. He loved it beyond any fret at his mother's hackings and hewings and paintings and trimmings, in which he had no smallest voice nor opinion. In fact he approved them nearly all. He drew Susan with him in his strange quests and discoveries at Garonlea. They had both begun to be happy, discovering happiness by thrilling moments and disconnected pieces as children who have been battered about in early days do chance delightedly on the possibilities of life—suddenly finding themselves unafraid to touch, unafraid to refuse, unafraid to laugh or find the jokes they should respect quite unamusing. Simon had, of course, gone further in this than Susan but he brought her with him because he was so fond of her. She seemed to him the dearest creature in the world, and as he liked all beautiful things he was glad that she was going to be so exciting to look at, or so he believed.

To-night he was determined that she should enjoy herself and with him. Susan danced very well, she was the person he enjoyed dancing with beyond any one. In 1922 dancing was an enthusiasm that one had to share with one person to get the utmost enjoyment. Simon had taught Susan to dance all those complicated steps which really seemed to matter then. So to see her wasting herself, dribbling about the room with one of the young natives asked by Cynthia to be her partners, when together they could make those intricate fluid, delightful patterns to music annoyed him unspeakably.

They leant out of Susan's window when she was dressed, watching cars come twisting towards the house down the opened length of valley, watching women in fur coats with scarfs on their heads bundle out and if they spoke, their voices were sharp with the uncertain sort of anguish that precedes parties. Their men put their cars on the far side of the gravel sweep and came strolling towards the house, white scarfs round their necks and black trousers under their overcoats. They did not mind whether they were a success or not and took the party easily. Cynthia's dances would certainly be good and the drink wonderful.

Below the house there was a white vaporous mass of cherry blossom, it seemed less solid than the mist from the river, coming like a crowd in blue cloaks through the stems of the trees and lying heavy already on the lowest terrace. Where Susan and Simon were leaning out they looked down into green fish-like leaves and slumberous white flesh cups of one of the magnolias for which Garonlea was famous. They grew against the house in great white crosses and there was one on the lawn that looked as strange and dramatic as though it was the tree of the knowledge of good and evil.

They drew their heads in at last from the disturbed quietness of the evening and decided it was time to go downstairs. Susan looked sadly round her room before she left it. That sensation of horror which preceded social intercourse for her made her wish that she was now bundling into bed in her blue and white striped pyjamas and finding her hot water bottle with her feet and placing it on her stomach before she opened one of the books that Simon gave her to read—books which so soon sent her to sleep among all the delightful pictures of horses and hunting by "Snaffles" and Mr. Lionel Edwards which Cynthia generously gave her children on Christmas and Birthdays. The cream walls of Susan's room were covered with them, and the bright expensive chintz of the curtains and chair covers was gay with an ever repeated pattern of red coats and pied hounds and bright bay horses. Over the mantelpiece was a sort of shrine in which were hung a fox's mask mounted on a wooden shield, two foxes' brushes and below them a row of three little dark pads, all trophies of prowess in the chase which Cynthia desired her daughter to preserve and respect. There was a blue carpet on the floor and a blue eiderdown on the bed and a delicious woollen dressing-gown as soft as a little fawn folded on the back of a really good arm-chair. The room was entirely Cynthia's doing. She could not possibly have taken more pains to make her children comfortable. It was a constant echo of the time when Susan's blue blanket had been chosen to match the scyllas. That part of Cynthia had entirely survived.

Simon waited for Susan and followed her in a reserved and dignified way down the wide staircase to the hall where Cynthia was saying "how do you do" to her guests. He realised at once that they had made one of their idle, stupid mistakes again. They should have gone down the back stairs. Now they were bound to make an entrance.

Cynthia saw to it that they did. She could not have been more pleased than she was to watch their unhurrying descent. Pride in Simon had only come to her as self assurance had come to him. She had taste enough to find Susan's reserve and possibility of beauty enthralling.

It was not a pretty staircase at Garonlea but it had width and a wide pallid air, with its new extravagant pale carpet and the white creamy walls from which red paper and Victorian progenitors had been stripped and only one enormous decorative but boring portrait of Laetita, wife of a Desmond French-McGrath, remained. Her creamy lace and silks and ribbons and fluffy dog were moony and romantic with no further contrast than the milky walls. She was not at all like either Simon or Susan as they came past her and turned the wide corner to the last short flight.

"Hullo, Angels!" Cynthia said. "You know Captain and Mrs. Church, don't you? Simon, darling, you must see that Sue goes to bed at one and don't let her get drunk. The champagne cup has rather a kick in it I'm afraid."

They let this pass though they knew that she knew that Susan never and Simon hardly ever drank anything except water. It was the same thing as jokes about their smoking which they were not very fond of either. Simon put her in good humour in the most able manner in the world by saying, "Can I have a dance with you, Mamma, some time? Or are you quite full up?" She looked so young to-night in her spring and summer lilac gown. She would want to show off with him in his new coat. He would have to, so he might as well do it properly.

"Yes, Simon, of course we must. Before supper. No. 9. Find yourselves programmes, children. You aren't to dance together all night."

"Oh, I can remember No. 9," Simon said and moved away. He was glad it was to be before supper as he was just beginning to realise that he disliked being near his mother when she was slightly drunk. Before supper was best. He must have one with Diana too.

"Simon, I shall be so busy with these cocktails," she said. Cynthia had made her mistress of the cocktail bar and she felt pretty grand about it though a little confused and inclined to mix them far stronger than necessary. Also the smell was beginning to make her feel odd already. She was looking rather smart in

162

a sort of white linen bar-man's coat which happily concealed most of the old black satin gown which had been Cynthia's and altered to fit, though hardly to become, Diana's solid little figure. But the coat had a real flick about it and looked gay with her trim dark head, its short bird's-wings of grey brushed back across her ears.

"One-third Cointreau, one-third gin," Diana muttered distractedly, too taken up with the responsibility of her post to spare even one wondering or incredulous thought to the improbability of a cocktail bar in the library of Garonlea.

"Don't make them too strong," Simon advised, "or every one will be drunk and drunks are often sick and I do hate that in my house. Good-bye for now, I see you won't dance with me or listen to me. Where's my Sue? Will you dance with me my darling?"

So far only the band was in the drawing-room. It was vast and empty and at one end Diana had excelled herself in the construction of an exotic and impossible tree decoration of cherry blossom and white lilac. It had taken a long time and much skill and patience and wire but its large and beautiful result against the water-green walls was most exciting. The windows were open to the floor, so that you could walk out towards the other cherry trees and the nearer brooms and lilacs and thousands of tulips, with which Cynthia and Diana had planted the terraces. The room was as full as a full tide with the river and the garden and the evening. A strange dark man in the expensive band smiled at Susan and Simon and although it was the wrong tune for the start of a jolly evening he played such a waltz for them as he thought the night and the lovely empty room and their empty youth demanded. Susan and Simon waited a moment half shivering with

163

pleasure before they went swirling and sweeping round the pale cavernous room full of music. Together they danced with such skill and accord, it was as if each danced alone.

In the hall some one was saying to Cynthia, "Look, Cynthia—we've brought an extra man. You do know him? Do you mind? He would come."

Cynthia was saying, "How lovely to see you again," to David Colebrook. He spoke to her as if he had not come with his party at all but straight from Africa to be in time for her dance. He looked brown like all sea-voyagers do and spoke in a detached way and looked at her as though she was not a Queen by right, but he was not sure that he would not think she was, which would settle the matter beyond argument.

Cynthia in all her two years' tremendous business over Garonlea, her terrific occupation with every sort of affair—from distemper at the kennels to the discovery and successful proving of a Gainsborough at Garonlea—had not quite escaped her memory of David. He was the preposterous young man who had made her feel absurd and afraid and told her she drank too much and would ruin her skin. He had gone out of her life for three years. Now here he was back again, and once more she was conscious of that chill air of reality, a draught between her skin and herself, that she had known before when he had roused her interest and hurt her rudely and gone away for three years. Now here he was back again on a night when she only looked for praise and comfort and worship. She would not let herself be upset or disturbed by him . . . and yet she wanted him to know that she had not spoilt her skin by drinking; that every one thought her the most wonderful woman in Ireland; that this lovely house and party were all of her making and that

164

she was desirable and inviolable beyond any man's wish. She wanted him to know all these things because he had once dared to hurt her.

Before David had said anything to her, for he always took his time before he spoke, some other arrival called for her attention, and when she thought about him again he had gone. He had not even waited to ask her to dance with him. Perhaps rather a crude way of keeping her attention on him. But this was not his reason, he had gone because he wanted a drink and he wanted to think. He did want to dance with Cynthia. He wanted to spend as much of the night as possible dancing with her. He would leave her alone till the right moment and then he would step in. He was an extraordinary good judge of pace both in love and racing. He never lost a race through winning it three times over and his methods with the women he wanted were rather the same.

Three years ago he had been excited by Cynthia right enough, but at the time he had been feeling too sick and muddled from his concussion to pursue the matter with any venom and since he had left her his life had been pretty busy. He had not thought of her in any way that really counted or disturbed him. It was hardly likely that he should. But now and then he felt alive about her and remembered what a brute she was to those children, and how he had got home on her by finding out that somebody robbed her, because obviously she was eaten up by a sense of her own infallibility. And then the thing about drinking— that got under her guard too, past all that beauty and dignity she was so fond of parading. Yes, what a brute she was to those children—and how grand she looked on a nice quality horse, as though she had been blown straight into the middle of her saddle.

Beautiful horse-woman she was . . . and how shame-
lessly she worked that little black-haired companion.
Diana had had a birthday when David was at Rathglass
and he had been enormously tickled and impressed by
the fact that Cynthia had given her a new spade for
a birthday present. . . . Not that she was afraid of
work herself. Then that morning when she had
worked a cross cut saw with him, and with a simple
skill that made endurance look silly. A ravishing
creature and as strong as a bull. . . . He was glad he
had put her through it that time over the children's
ponies. David was an experienced and successful
jockey before he became a successful trainer so he
knew what it was like to feel extremely frightened
quite often. For him it had been a question of his
livelihood, but he never quite saw why children should
endure the same sort of thing over a matter that was
presumably for their pleasure.

David watched Diana for a little making her cocktails; then he said, "You'll have everybody blind in
half an hour. Some of them are swaying now." He
stepped in behind the bar without being asked and set
her going on different lines, doing it all in an impressively expert and absent minded sort of way. Diana
did not resent his interference at all. She felt rather
flattered by his presence, and in her slightly fuddled
state she liked having some one she could rely on.

He stayed with her for nearly an hour, until the
party had really become itself and arrived. A lovely
supper-party it became with every one enjoying themselves a little wildly. There was a great deal of dancing
to the expensive band, which persuaded people to come
in from their love-making under the smoky ghosts
of the cherry trees; to abandon the elaborate refuges
Cynthia had constructed all over the house; to set

166

down their drinks, wet glasses on any table, and extinguish their cigarettes in the nearest and easiest way—in fact to do practically everything except spit on the floor.

There was not one corner of Garonlea where you could escape from the excessive success of this party. It swept and surged through the house and through all the people who took part in it. There was a gorgeous untramelled atmosphere about it, in which the least forward girl found success and the more forward became daring and romantic to a degree. The heartiest people blew hunting horns (rather an unnecessary trumpeting perhaps in the spring of the year) and slid down the banisters and threw méringues and rolls of bread at their jolly girl friends.

And such a night for love as it was. Not only under the cherry trees couples were embraced, but wherever you went it seemed to Simon impossible to find a place where you could talk to Susan with dignified composure. He thought it was not right for a young girl to see so much love-making. He had the forethought before he took her up to bed at one o'clock to go and see if her room was empty. It was not.

"I am terribly sorry to interrupt your talk," Simon said in clear childlike tones, "but Mamma has sent Susan to bed and this is her room."

He watched their embarrassment without any pity—this unyouthfulness belonged with his previous momentary affectation of childishness. There was harboured within Simon some of the chill horror that his grandmother might have felt at this debauch and rioting. Cynthia would never lay the last ghost at Garonlea because its lodging was in the blood and bones of the McGraths themselves.

Simon locked Susan into her room and put the key

in his pocket. "I will let you out when Mother's last guest has gone," he said.

"And if they set the house on fire I can climb down the magnolia, I suppose," Susan answered. But she was really pleased to be protected from the savage horde below.

Simon, rather detached from human intercourse now that Susan was safe in bed, met David, also alone, in the hall. A dance was in progress. There was not so much love lying about.

David said, "Remember trying to kill me?"

Simon did. He said, "You forgave me that a long time ago."

David thought, "Like his mother. Just the same twist. But he's too sober for her party. Nice boy." He said, "Enjoying yourself to-night?"

"Not more than I enjoyed jumping stone walls when you saw me last."

David grinned and yawned. "You should. It's a wonderful party and you're the right age for it."

"No, I'm too young. Are you liking it?"

"No, I'm too old. But I hope it's going to improve soon."

Simon said, blushing rather, because he knew David was rather a grand man, "Are you in Ireland for long? Do come and stay with us if you can manage it."

"Yes, I'd like to. I could come over to-morrow."

"Yes, do that."

XXIII

CYNTHIA came out of the dining-room. She had
nobody with her. She had just been seeing how things
like food and drink were going on and given a few
brisk simple orders to the servants, who were rushing
and muddling about as the best servants do at dances.
Obviously she thought the hall was empty when she
came in. She stood a moment collecting her forces
and then went over to a mirror and taking a little
comb out of her bag began combing out the short
soft bits of her hair.

David and Simon stood very still because they
were both taken aback by the reflection of her face
which they could see in the mirror. It looked grotesque
with her pretty hair and her strong assured shoulders
coming out of her beautiful lilac and pink dress.
Perhaps it was only the reflection, Simon thought,
distorted in the glass. But was that haunted, hungry
face the real Cynthia, or the smooth bare back and
strong pretty neck and quick able hands more like
her? After all the figure was real, the face was only
seen in a glass. Still in the looking-glass they saw her
shut her eyes quickly, shutting them hard as a child
shuts out sight and sticking her fingers in her ears
venomously, as though all the tumult and music and
hunting cries and lover's whisperings of this party
were hateful and terrible to her. Then she opened her
eyes again, frightened. And with a sort of wrench,
a tremendous effort and change, her face in the glass
became smooth, as bland as her back, almost, and she
picked up her bag and went running very light on

her feet, as though she chased the party spirit itself down the hall towards the drawing-room door from which the music came so sweetly.

Before she reached the door David had caught her up. Simon saw them dancing together that dance and the next and after that he did not see them. He felt a little sorry that he had asked David to stay. He expected to see him entranced and captured and cast away just as he had seen others in the same process. Sometimes he had thought that they were hurt unfairly and unnecessarily. He did not really mind about them. His mother's beaux seemed to him peculiarly boring and unperceiving people, well deserving of their courted distress. But about David he felt rather differently. Already he had some understanding of the cowardly and highly strung children he and Susan had been and he thought a man who had done so much and so quickly to help such children must be a very nice person. With a nice twist of humour too, Simon thought, a little wave of remembrance breaking in his mind as he remembered Cynthia, angry and insecure, on Sue's pony. No. That sort of person should have more sense than to hurt himself unnecessarily. He should certainly have more sense.

When David had caught Cynthia up at the door of the drawing-room he had not said anything. Nothing like, "Marvellous party!" or, "May I dance with you?" Or anything at all. He put his arm round her and moved in among the dancers without a word. When they had danced once round the room, still in silence, Cynthia said:

"I hope you've been enjoying yourself to-night."

David said, "Not much really. I only came here to see you and I've been wondering why you look so damned unhappy."

Cynthia, the Life and Soul. Cynthia, the Wonderful Hostess. The Successful Mother. The adored Chatelaine of Garonlea, accused of the indecency of looking unhappy. Unhappiness was an attribute of failure. It was even uncivil to one's guests to dare to look unhappy at such a party. One should never let go for a moment. Besides she was not unhappy. Only once during the long carnival of the evening, ghosts had nibbled at her heart, for a brief distracted moment at the height of this brilliant success. She had been delighted with this night of her making, with ordinary parts of it:—such as the delicious food and drink, the flowers, the band. And with stranger parts of it:—her destruction and recreation of Garonlea, Simon's poise and finish, Susan's soon to be beauty; all, her house, her creatures, her doing, praising her. Then for a moment all this splendid sense had died in her, died like wine in a drunken woman, leaving her alone, sick with her hopeless necessity for love that she had never taken. She truly believed it was only Desmond that she needed with such anguish then. Desmond to sleep with and wake with and eat with and talk to. All the rest of her life was a dangerous shell of pretence, a thin shell against her ear full of screaming whispers.

Now she said, "My dear man what a cracked thing to say." This was in her worst sort of smooth voice.

He said, "I'm the only person who is ever likely to talk sense to you or tell you the truth ever."

"How touchingly interesting."

"Yes. But stop defending yourself. No use."

"I find you rather boring—— Or should a hostess say that?"

"Perhaps. To a guest she hasn't invited. Or if he says outrageous things. Perhaps then she may."

171

"No. But I don't like your saying I'm unhappy," Cynthia wanted to touch this subject again. It gave her a strange vibration of fear and pleasure. Like touching a spiral wire within herself.

"But I often think I know when people are unhappy —or frightened. I'm often wrong."

"Frightened too? What am I frightened of?"

"Of your age. Of Love. Of losing your success. Perhaps of your children. They were of you once. It will soon be your turn."

"*Oh*," Cynthia said. "What a ridiculous, boring conversation we are having. Please shall we stop?"

"Are you bored? You know you're not." David stopped dancing when they got to an open window. He put his arm through Cynthia's and took her out with him on to the warm flagged path that ran outside the windows above the terrace.

"Of your age," he repeated to the night, "or Love. I don't know which frightens you most."

"No," Cynthia said, "I think I'm most afraid of losing my nerve."

"Your riding nerve? But you don't have to jump fences if you don't want to. You can ride about on a nice mannerly horse and talk to your friends. That's my ideal of an enjoyable day's hunting."

"You don't understand about it."

"Yes I do. I've been frightened all my life. I was delighted when I couldn't compete with my weight any more. But do we have to talk about horses all the time?"

"What about then?"

"About unhappiness. Or love, perhaps."

They were walking down the first flight of terrace steps, Cynthia silenced, her head bowed and the silvered panniers of her dress making a hushed rasping sound on the stone beside her and behind her. The cherry trees were blanched unearthly wreaths of flowers below and the sliding and turning of the river beyond and below again was insistently audible in the night. Cynthia went to the left at the foot of the steps, walking on in silence between a thousand faint uncoloured globes of tulips. They stopped and leant together in an outward curve of the Gothic balustrading, brooms and lilacs, their flowers drenched and bloomed with mist directly beneath them, and then the river, always turning and repeating its sounds in darkness.

Cynthia felt terrifyingly languid and capturable. Of Love and Unhappiness, he had said. Of love and unhappiness, she heard it in the river sounds and walled and muffled in the mist it assailed her spirit. From her garden and from her lighted house above, again the desolation renewed its power. She was alone. She had been too long alone—too long peerless, un-questioned and lonely. She would have liked to put her face in her hands and lean weeping for comfort on the high half curved rail of stone. But she did not cry. It was too foreign to her. She did not say a word more. And when David spoke again it was to ask her a question about the fishing. Then they had a long conversation about Blood-stock. After that they went back to the house and danced again, more sympathetically than the first time. Then they ate oysters and drank stout and champagne, and David had a long brisk conver-sation about racing with a man he put right several times. But in spite of talking to other people he kept Cynthia with him. She was oddly in his power already. The tears she had not shed and the wine made her feel a little shaky and emotional. She did not want to go. She wanted to be near for her own sake. She liked eating and drinking and being with him. It was important. It was something close to contentment. Something uncertain and alive with excitement.

Soon everybody was going home and coming to say good-bye.

"Good-bye, Cynthia, thank you for the most lovely party——" a woman in a black satin gown, very short in front and short behind and long at each side and dashing black gloves turning the elbow.

"Good-bye, Mrs. McGrath. I have enjoyed myself so terribly . . ." a rather tousled young girl with one of those new permanent waves that made hair look like hay.

"Cynthia, you surpassed yourself. Bless you, my dear . . ." an old admirer slightly romanticised by wine.

"Good-bye . . . Wonderful . . . adored it . . . darling. The most marvellous show . . . thank you . . . thank you . . . thank you . . ." As always the incense of praise and gratitude enraptured Cynthia. She accepted thanks and good-byes, wonderful to every one and particularly sweet to the people who did not matter.

David came by himself. Instead of good-bye, he said, "Simon has asked me to stay. I think I'll come to-morrow."

"Yes, come to-morrow," He went away and after that she was a shade more absent over the last leave takings.

She was left with Simon and Diana, both rather pale and cross. The thought of their exhaustion did not come within an inch of her consciousness.

"It's been a tremendous success, hasn't it? You were marvellous in your bar, dear, and you looked so original in your little white coat. That was a good idea of mine."

Simon yawned. "It was my idea," he said. "I thought it would be a good plan to cover up those rattling old sequins. Diana, you must buy yourself a new dress if Mamma is going to give many of these routs. And Mamma, you must buy Sue something more becoming."

"Oh, her dress is quite suitable. It's *such* a mistake to dress up girls of her age. Anyhow I must go to bed. Simon, you asked that Colebrook man to stay?"

"I don't suppose he'll remember to come. He seems casual."

"Well, perhaps he won't. Good-night, child. You looked extremely smart."

"So did you, Mamma."

"Good-night, Diana, darling. Just have a tiny look to see there aren't any burning cigarettes about. Will you be so sweet?"

"Go to bed, darling. You're exhausted. Of course I will."

"I *am*, just a tiny bit."

Cynthia went upstairs holding her panniers in either hand. She was not at all tired really. But her heart was full of a sort of murmuring excitement. Alone in her room she sighed and trembled and looked at herself contentedly in the glass before she undressed and got into bed. She slept till very late the next morning—a lovely sleep, all the time she felt as if she was sliding between glass and water.

XXIV

SIMON and Diana sent the servants to bed and prowled about wearily, tipping ash trays into buckets of water, recoiling from the more nauseating horror and disorder, putting out lights and closing shutters against the approaching light. In the drawing-room Diana's tree was slack and wilted, an anæmic drooping object. No one could have imagined how lovely it had been.

Diana went about her work with quickness and ability and a sort of grim satisfaction in the disgusting shambles to which the house had been reduced by the party. She did everything that really needed to be done but not a thing more. She spoke to Simon quite sharply when he loitered behind her, examining with disgusted fury the mark a cigarette had made, laid down on the corner of the marble mantelpiece in the drawing-room. There were lots of little things like that as well as grosser signs of misbehaviour on the part of his mother's guests.

They heated some soup in the kitchen and drank it sitting on the kitchen table before they went up to bed. Simon looked about him with satisfaction.

"It seems to be the only room in the house that hasn't been sullied and polluted," he said grandly. "I'm going to bed in a minute and I'm not going to let myself wake up for four days. Then perhaps my house will have been put right for me, though I don't think I shall ever feel the same towards it after the hideous sights we've seen."

Diana glanced round the kitchen restlessly. She didn't care if Garonlea had been set on fire and burnt to the ground. She rather wished it had.

"What about the man you asked to stay? What is he to do while you are sleeping off your mother's party?"

"I don't expect to see much of him in any case," Simon looked at Diana, his eyebrows raised into flying lines of unspoken comment. "Mother seems interested." He got off the kitchen table and went over to the door, waiting with his hand on the light switch till Diana joined him. Then he switched out the light, bringing down a mammoth and startling gloom. The tables and dressers and armoury of copper pots and pans, the two shining ranges, were all obliterated entirely for a moment before their outlines took pallid form and unearthly depth of shadow in the green sickly light of very early day.

When Diana took off her crisp white coat it was rather as if she took off a mask. All the swagger and impudent line was gone, leaving behind a tired but tough small body in a black dress too big for it in the wrong places. The slack dress came off in a moment and after that a great many underclothes. She got herself into the red silk pyjamas Susan and Simon had given her, slapped the expensive cream ordained (but not paid for) by Cynthia on to her face and tumbled into bed.

In the same way that Cynthia had planned Susan's bedroom to be a constant reminder of the chase she ought to love, she had in Diana's gone back constantly on the garden motif which seemed to her so suitable and right in connection with Diana. So there was a delightful chintz covered in rich polyanthus primroses, pictures of well cultivated and luxuriant gardens on the walls, a shelf full of gardening books and a great, great many photographs of Cynthia to remind Diana to whose garden her energies should be directed. Her room was her father's old dressing-room and opened off Cynthia's, who had taken great pleasure in making Lady Charlotte's bedroom into one of which the most expensive French tart might have felt proud.

It was a pity that all these changes at Garonlea altered it so little for Diana. To her Garonlea was more itself than it had been before Cynthia had torn down its red wall papers and hurled the unwanted ancestors into attics with their faces to the wall, accompanied forlornly by the Dresden china black boys (life size) in white socks, who had so long been torch bearers in the drawing-room, and other objects upon which she looked with contempt and nausea. In all these locked, out-of-the-way places—bedrooms still waiting their sack and purification, cupboards where old hoards of rubbish had not yet been dealt with mercilessly, trunks of photographs fading in their expensive silver frames, corners of the shrubberies and old airless parts of woods—the spirit and power of Garonlea still lived with a tenfold strength. It was as if it stored and reserved its power for a future day. Quite literally the breath of such places, the strong camphor-filled breath, on the still laden air of an outdoor place thick with old childish memories filled Diana with hatred and a tremendous consciousness of things as they had been at Garonlea all her life till now.

For Cynthia's sake she had fought hard to get rid of this feeling. But it was too strong and could not be defeated. She had given her mind faithfully to the garden, but she had no quiet and secret thrill out of it, such as she had at Rathglass. She only saw its successes and failures. She did not feel them. She knew Cynthia felt her blankness if not hostility to-

178

wards all her plans and changes and she tried to get round this and deny it by giving Cynthia almost all her income to spend on Garonlea or on what she pleased. Cynthia spent it cheerfully and gave Diana her old clothes and new tools on birthdays and Christmas. Not only spades but pruning scissors and forks and trowls and iron dibbles and many other useful things. She also gave her a horse whenever she wanted to go out hunting, which was not often now, as she felt so rotten and without energy living at Garonlea.

She had, besides her unwavering faith in Cynthia and her love for her, two other chief excitements and pleasures in life. Real pleasures about which she schemed and planned and in which her enjoyment was satisfactory, not a shadow and illusive enjoyment bolstered up by the imagination. One of these was her friendship with Simon and Susan which was a deep and true pleasure, and the other was her unfailing care of the garden at Rathglass. Her feeling about this was comparable to the thrill of making a wild garden when one is a child—an adventure and an excitement beyond any satisfaction to be got from the garden plot supervised and interfered with by kind Authority. Or the thrill of making a house in a wood that nobody knows of yet.

Of course Cynthia knew about Diana's pre-occupations with Rathglass but she had quite enough sense not to bully her on the subject. So long as she gave enough time and work to the garden at Garonlea, Cynthia managed not to grudge her her adoring ventures at Rathglass. Materially it was not at all a bad thing that the garden should still enjoy Diana's skill and imagination. Some day, sometime, no doubt they would return to live in the closed house again. But the date seemed as vague to Cynthia and as far off as Lady Charlotte's death had ever seemed to her.

Meanwhile Rathglass was let to fishing tenants in the fishing season and it was always Diana's chief dread that permanent tenants would be found, tenants (insufferable thought) with ideas of their own about gardens. So far, however, it was only the rich, middle-aged fishing men in their lovat tweeds and mackintosh deer-stalker's hats who came in March and left in May and those of them who understood about gardening gave her praise and interesting comment. She had nothing against the fishers. She would go over to Rathglass in the long spring days when the fishers were in possession, days like those when Desmond and Cynthia lived there and Susan lay in her perambulator among the scyllas, and work in the garden, making plans with the man whom she was busily turning into a useful gardener, weeding in her rockery, her hands busy among the little Iris, their roots like little hairless paws pressing faintly warm against her hands. And when she went back to Garonlea the colour of the purple primroses would get into the dark and into her sleep for that night.

Some day Diana knew they would return to Rathglass to live, and Simon promised often that he would never, not even to make room for Susan and her husband and their children, turn her out before she was carried out in a coffin. Diana indeed believed him and was more than grateful, for she knew that she would never be as brave and gracious as Aunt Mousie had been when she was moved to the suitable little house.

XXV

THE day after the dance Cynthia was in a stormy mood. She soon lost the peace in which she woke from her long lovely sleep and started rushing about, scolding and apologising to people by turn.

Simon and Susan stayed in bed, Susan because Simon had forgotten to unlock her door and she was not going to have him woken to produce the key, or scolded for her incarceration. So she feigned exhaustion and stoically denied the pangs of hunger. Simon slept and woke determined not to sicken himself further by looking at the house by daylight.

Diana alone was caught and buffeted about in the whirlwind of Cynthia's unease. She could not account for it entirely by attributing it all to the after effects of the party. These did not explain her hasty questioning looks when a note or a telegram was brought to her. The uncertainty and changeableness of her orders were foreign to her too, and so was the show of temper when they were misunderstood or carried out wrongly. She was really much too sure and capable a creature not to foresee and allow for the stupidity of others. But to-day this seemed to enrage her. Nothing could be done quickly enough. Nothing could be done just as she wanted it done. She cursed and stormed over the ignorant savagery of the friends she had asked to her house when she discovered things like the mark on the mantelpiece burned by a cigarette. She sent Diana flying about to arrange flowers when a room was restored to its normal state and then criticised her decorations and pulled bits out and stuck them in again and then said, "Oh, Darling, you must forgive me, I've absolutely ruined it. What made me touch it I can't think. Put it right again, Diana, and I won't do it any more."

And Diana, who had been almost angry, was mollified and touched by the sacrifice of such an apology, and strengthened by a drink and an anchovy on a biscuit at exactly the moment in the morning when she felt she could do no more. That was typical of Cynthia too.

It was a deliciously hot spring day—a day when there is both sun and crispness in the air and flowers look young and well groomed and dewy, not swooning and languid. And beech leaves are light as spring muslins, not black-green shrouds as later they come to be. Cynthia took her drink and Diana's out into the sun and they sat on the hot low stone balustrade of the flagged walk round the house, looking down into the hot, widened cups of tulips on the terrace below. Cynthia grew more placid as she drank and sat in the sun, wine and sun always had the most superb effect on her, and began talking to Diana about the beauty and success of the party, and stopped raging at the awful things people had done. She was wearing a soft, blue wool skirt and jersey, with a black belt low down on the hips, and her bosom strapped in as flat as possible as was then the fashion. Her hair was short and sleek and really gold in the sunshine. She did not look the least exhausted by the party—only as though she had caught a slight fever.

They were sitting there, the benefit of wine still attaining its full capture of the moment, when David came round the corner of the house and down the long path towards them. Then Diana, with that flash towards conclusion that comes sometimes when a person is slightly in wine, was able to answer with a single reply all the questions about Cynthia that had puzzled her during the morning. Cynthia was in love.

Diana's immediate reaction to this was a feeling of excited pleasure. Her thought sprang at once from Love to Marriage. No man could love Cynthia without wanting to marry her. Diana's head swam a little. What with wine and the thought of Cynthia happy and the possibility of leaving Garonlea, she looked on David as a saviour and a saviour who would have her unqualified support. She had nothing to go on in her excited acceptance of Cynthia in love beyond her own interpreting of Cynthia's look and silence. But in this she trusted herself entirely and looked for no further confirmation. Though she had not seen this heavy, half-sheltering half-asking look about Cynthia since Desmond's death she could never fail to know it again. It struck her with a blinder force because she had not seen it. "Mother seems interested," Simon had said to her the night before. He had only meant that Cynthia was out to capture another man as they had seen her yoke so many to her. But Diana knew that this time Cynthia herself was in the weighted nets of love, caught and struggling.

It was only the truth that Diana saw so promptly and clearly. Cynthia was really captured. She was in the power of an imaginative man who was also quite as hard and in a way unscrupulous as any one need be. David wanted Cynthia. He wanted her as his mistress and he was going to have her entirely on his own terms. He knew she was not clever and she had no defence once one got inside her pose and vanity.

183

She was really one of those super conventional women on whom an almost brutal hardness has a wonderful effect. David sat beside her in the sun for an hour drinking her wine and talking about his wife and child. By lunch time Cynthia for the first time was consciously out to wreck a marriage if she could. Heretofore all the marriages that she had upset had been upset without any further plan and left at that. Now there was a purpose and drive about what she was doing. She was determined to do this. But she was unsure. She was afraid. She was in a panic that he knew she was in love. She was afraid he did not realise it. She was at once in delight and in despair. Desmond, Garonlea, everything was passing for her at this moment. Realities became only a background for her present self and her present want.

And things went against Cynthia. For instance, the weather. Even the dreadful month of May betrayed its inconstancy by a week of days as lovely as this morning; days as gay and shining and delicate as the tulips and cherry blossom; days when each child you met on the road in the mornings carried a bunch of bright flowers to school; days when the thorn trees leant their branches every hour more heavily towards the fields under their thick loads of flowers; days when creatures like foals and young ducks and hound puppies flourished exorbitantly.

During these days Diana saw that Cynthia became more troubled and enamoured. It worried her a good deal as she knew now about David's wife, and goodness knows why she had not known before. She felt sorry about it, but she hardly supposed it would stop him if he really wanted to marry Cynthia. As he surely must. Surely he must. She could not understand his indefiniteness, his lack of response to Cynthia. By responding to Cynthia, Diana meant that people should lay themselves humbly down and wait for her to walk on them.

All through those bright days when they worked and played—sometimes fishing, sometimes fiddling about at the kennels, getting puppies out to their walks or standing looking and listening and seeing an incinerator being built, or watching the mares and foals, or starting early for a distant race meeting, David seemed quite as much inclined for Diana's company or the children's as for Cynthia's. He was quite easy whether he was with her or not, although now and then he kept her with him for no special purpose when he happened to know that she thought of being somewhere else. And now and then he would make tortuous little speeches that excited her while they did not give him away so much as an inch.

"I don't know why I stay here, I'm only upsetting myself." . . . "What do you think? Do you think one ought to take what one wants always and disregard the consequences?" . . . "You're the most disturbing person; I wonder where Simon is." . . . "I was right about Simon and Susan, they'll soon bully you. What you need is a tough and virile man to help you keep them down." . . . "Shall you mind if I tell you something? Are you sure you won't mind? Promise me? Well then—I think that Sesame colt you admire so much has weak, nasty-looking hocks. I wouldn't like them at all, and I'm not sure but I *think* there's a curb forming on one of them already."

That sort of thing went on for days till Cynthia's sleep left her and she looked old and cross and hollow eyed and all this energy and imagination that she had expended on Garonlea brought her in no return now. The results were there but they were no good to her at all. She thought no more about the house or the garden, she felt exasperated and repulsed by it all at this time. All the things that mattered to her—the hounds and the horses and food and clothes and the friends she had taught to make ceaseless demands on her, even their endless feeding of her love of power and her love of praise lost grip and hold on her consciousness. These things were much less support to her now than they had been when Desmond was killed. Then she had absolutely required their importance. Now all importance seemed to hinge for her on the one fact of her success or failure over this love. In the space of a week there had been nearly as great a revolution in her life as Desmond's death had caused. She had loved Desmond really and tremendously. It was the only way she knew how to love. She had not kept in practice all these years. She had not grown less selfishly romantic. She demanded exactly the same return for her love as she had known before. In fact she demanded to have twice what only one woman in fifty has once in her lifetime. She looked for the same thing. She thought it must be the same. She had no possible sense of proportion. She looked for disappointment.

One evening after dinner they went down to the river to fish for trout. Susan and Simon went off, a rod between them and determined not to exert themselves over much or near their mother. David and Cynthia shared the other rod. First one would fish a rise and then they would move to another spot and the other would have a turn. They hardly spoke, the evening was so quiet after a hot day. The turns of the river were olive under the willows. The mountains, high beyond the last bend of water and the woods, were nearer rose than blue and more smoke than opal. The sky had the bloom of fruit. There was lilac somewhere. The river air was washed distantly in its pale billowing scent. The plumey sweet stuff leant far out from the edge of a dark wood towards the bluebells, their first hyacinth colour spread sparsely down the slope of the field, more like smoke than flowers. In an hour's time the lilac was as white as a sea-bird and the bluebells a cold dead grey. The river was black where it had been olive and had caught the first quarter of the moon between three dark stones. The mountains had changed to the exact blue of speedwells and the chill in the air was like a constant infinitely small shudder.

Cynthia said, "We'll go back now. It's too late to fish any more." She turned back along the river bank. She said bleakly, "I wonder what those beastly trout were feeding on? Nothing we've got."

"Wouldn't it be much quicker to go back through the wood?" David said.

"No, it wouldn't. It would be far longer."

"Would it matter?" He took the rod away from her and put his arm through hers. In the wood they kissed. Cynthia kissed like one who has found what matters to her most after long waiting. It was sleep after an endless night of waking. It was as needful as that. But it was like drinking wine to quench thirst. It was lovely but it did not quench her thirst.

David found what he had known he would find if he waited just long enough. But beyond this acceptance of things and himself as they actually were he was moved more deeply than he had thought. He knew that now he would hate to hurt Cynthia. There was something disarmingly and inescapably young, unquestioning and untricked about her loving and kissing. In love she was that same divine and unspoilt creature she had been years past at Garonlea before she was married to Desmond.

They slept together that night. Cynthia was deeply delighted and comforted. She said so to herself the next day, accepting the fact of things as they were with entire simplicity. "It was such a comfort to me," she said tranquilly to David, and this was no more nor less than the truth.

He did not say anything. He was not very good at talking about love, either past, present or future, as Cynthia soon knew. But especially about future love he was disquietingly vague. Cynthia was so captured by him, so held by her newly recovered delight and peace, that for the present she would not risk provoking any discussion that might, in its unsatisfactory outcome, prejudice her happiness. She was shy too, with that shyness which especially hampers vain people. Like most of them, Cynthia could not ask for anything she wanted directly, a refusal would have shamed and angered her too much. And now that she had put herself where she had no terms to make, she was forced to keep up with herself a new pretence that the position was of her own choosing—that the present was enough—that she preferred to leave the future undefined—that (most useful of all phrases) *the whole thing was too difficult*. His wife was a Catholic. One could not expect her to do anything rational. Soon it became that for the children's sake Cynthia would rather Leave It Alone.

All these things were said to Diana and at the end of a month when David went away Diana knew quite clearly that there would be no divorce, no new marriage, no leaving Garonlea. None of the things she had thought David would mean had come true. Not one. And yet she could not dislike him or grudge

188

him his victory. She liked him personally so very much. He was almost dear to her with his unaffected thoughtfulness and interest in her and in Simon and Susan. She could not have believed that she would ever like and respect Cynthia's lover so much. She helped Cynthia to bolster up all her pretences about the impossibility of anything further being done. She underpinned her vanity and extreme happiness, a loyal loving prop to both. It was wonderful to see Cynthia so happy, good-tempered and laughing and with something of her old rich gentleness coming back. She was more free and careless too, less distressed about detail. Daily the change became plainer to Diana.

XXVI

ALL that month while Cynthia and David were making love there seemed to be a kind of skin of ease and tranquility over Garonlea. Even Diana felt momentarily at peace with the house and the place. As one lovely day followed another she was aware of a sort of blooming on the new Garonlea of Cynthia's making. The rooms became more real to her and less as if they had only been painted on top of the rooms she had always known. It was as though Cynthia had really and at last won the house over from all its dismal hauntings. Those pale light rooms opening out of one another, full of bright chintzes and spring flowers—tulips and broom and irises and rhododendron—were at last really different from the old rooms with their shut and curtained doors, red carpets and rich dark covers and tiny scattered vases of flowers.

Outside too, the new rides and clearings and vistas in the woods had covered their scars. The woods no longer screamed to one another and to those who looked at them, "My wound that was a T is now an H." The battle was over. The dead were gone and the living throve without them.

In the garden Diana felt a surprised thrill of pleasure in the success of the schemes she had worked out with so little enthusiasm.

The children seemed well affected by the weather and the air of happiness too. They were particularly gay. Delighted to find Cynthia daily in better humour, they pursued their own concerns without having to fight any of those exhausting battles against her plans for their entertainment or improvement. They were very sweet to Diana, keeping her with them all day if they went racing so that she might not feel a bore to Cynthia and would not have to wander about by herself in the crowd, which she hated doing although she tried to be very independent about it at the times when Cynthia did not want her. It always surprised Diana that Susan should appear quite unmoved when loosed off by herself at race-meetings and point-to-points. She would wander about all day talking to all sorts of queer people on the cheap stand (for Cynthia often economised and let the young race cheaply), or on the course and watch a race with a sort of airy and actual observance and intelligence for her age. She seemed quite detached from any feeling of loneliness or self-consciousness in a crowd. She and Simon had been taken racing by Cynthia since they were quite small. Susan had always enjoyed it the better of the two, though she would not have been acutely distressed if she had heard she was not to see a racecourse or a racehorse again. Simon's lack of intelligent interest was maddening to Cynthia. Even now when she felt so happy she complained about it once to David.

"And do you know," she finished, "he doesn't even *quite* always read the racing news."

David was sitting in her room while she changed for dinner.

"No," he said. Obviously he was not attending. Cynthia was doing things to her face in the heavy-handed, absent-minded way that produced such a good result. She paused, stared into the glass, and did something slowly.

"You don't think it's important?" she said when she had done it. "I do think it's rather terrible in a boy of his age."

"Well, Cynthia, why should you bother him about it if he's not interested. Leave him alone."

"Isn't that rather what you said about their riding when they were small? And you see I didn't pay any attention to your advice and now they ride so well."

He saw her completely satisfied smile in the glass, a beautifully shaped smile, sure and a little smug. He remembered the reflection he and Simon had seen on the night of the dance. It was because of that he was here now with his back to the magnolia flowers and the soft evening outside the window. At the moment Simon really meant nothing. He was looking at Cynthia's long, bending, fat arms and strong, clean shoulders and thinking inevitably of the magnolia outside the window.

"He'll be all right in time," he said. "Everything takes time. Boys, horses, yes, everything."

Cynthia made a little face to herself in the glass.

"You're a genius for taking a good long view," she said.

"Did you say I was a genius for taking a long view?"

"Oh, it doesn't matter."

"Kiss?"

"Yes. . . . Now it really doesn't matter."

"All the same I know what you mean."

"You do talk so much. I wish I didn't mind about you so much, David. Isn't it a mistake?"

"You shouldn't criticise your lover. You should simply be delighted by him."

"Yes, I am, I think. But don't talk so much."

"Well, I think it's a good plan to keep talking at times . . . especially when it's nearly dinner-time."

"Well then, darling, please go away and talk to yourself severely."

Diana heard their low laughter. It took the air very quietly and seemed to be a necessary part of the gentle glory of the evening. It was not insultingly secret and apart as lovers' laughter can be, but like a smooth stone thrown in a smooth pool, its rings widened out and out through all the changes in the house. It was part of a whole. Perhaps Garonlea had never seen a love affair like this one. If so, the place took to it most indulgently.

On the day David said to Diana, "I'm going away on Wednesday, I think."

She said, meaning a great deal more, "And when are you coming back?"

"I don't know quite when, but I hope very often."

She knew she would get nothing more definite out of him, and in a way she was content with this. There was no reason why she should be easy in her mind about the continuance of his relationship with Cynthia but she did feel confident about it. She saw Cynthia's happiness and she believed in Cynthia's hold over any person she wanted. In this way she thought Cynthia entirely indefeatable. But here she was not a very sound judge for she had only seen Cynthia holding one man, Desmond, who had loved her romantically and singly and quite as deeply as she had loved him. And at that time she had been at the very summit of her beauty and her mind had been imaginatively sharpened to keep her love. Sharp and yet elastic because she was younger then and the years of complete power and success had not become as solid behind her as they were now. Of all the other men who had courted Cynthia she had not wanted one for loving, or if she had, her vanity had denied her flesh such indulgence. They were no more than courtiers and escorts. She had charmed them and hurt them and sent them about their business and whistled them back again when she wanted them without shame and without difficulty, because she did not mind about them.

But with David it was disastrously different. She was defeated and delighted and undone and uncertain and for all these reasons she loved him the more. But because he had defeated her and seen through her vanity and got closer to her than any one else, he had himself destroyed that very quality of strength and hardness and intense unhappiness in her which had first made him love her. For him it was now no more. Instead of this woman he now had one the more intensely dependent and wildly loving because she had depended so little and loved not at all for so long. It was like capturing a wild-looking white town on a Spanish hill and then discovering that its streets and houses are as only a Surrey garden-city, orderly and complete with every modern convenience and houses with "Tivoli" and "Mon Repos" written on their gates.

There were hours when he found her enthralling and his domination of her pleased his vanity and he felt fond and indulgent and romantical, times such as that when he watched her using her beautiful heavy arms sitting in front of her glass and thought of the thick skin of magnolia flowers so near in the evening. And there were times when his complete power over her exhausted and disgusted him. She was so much a less interesting person than he had thought. And still he could not escape from that feeling he had had on the first evening when he kissed her in the wood, the feelin; of her unquestioning confidence in love that had disarmed him of any unkindness towards her. He had known that he could never expect from her that hard and reasonable acceptance of a love affair as a passing thing which is the simplest expression of disillusion and absence of real success with so many women.

It was quite true that he could not without the exercise of tremendous and cruel determination have compelled his wife to divorce him, and he did not even distantly contemplate taking so unkind a step. He was fond of his wife and it was Cynthia's happiness which must take its chance. But he would not hurt her more than he could help in either her love or her vanity. And most skilfully he did not. He parried the openings she gave him for any suggestion of permanency in their love with assurances so vague that a girl of sixteen could not have founded any hopes on them. And though sometimes he implied that Cynthia was the one unattainable never really to be and so never really to end romance of his life—he must leave her for a little. He must go back to England and his horses and his catholic, unrelenting wife and his one tough, ugly, witty little daughter. But soon he would be at Garonlea again. Soon and often, with her at Garonlea. It must not be too long before he came there again. He would have to see her soon. He was only happy with her and at Garonlea.

194

His touch was very light. He was so uncaring and apart, for all his understanding and kindness, that even such promises became unduly weighty. Cynthia could not reasonably keep him now. And it was beyond her vanity to look for any definite assurance. But on the night before he went she whispered for hours with desperate earnestness that need for his love to continue . . . Do you? . . . Are you sure? . . . Will you always? . . . Do you still? . . . Ah, I know you don't. . . . There were tears and kisses and love and deep sleep and a feeling of safety and peace that lasted for some time after he had gone away.

Soon after that, Simon and Susan went back to the schools they found such a heart-breaking bore, and Diana and Cynthia were left alone again at Garonlea. Cynthia had more plans than usual for that summer. She had asked the people she most wished to impress with her skill and success over Garonlea to come and stay in a continuous succession. She had what she thought an undefeatable show-horse which she had intended to take round to all the agricultural shows during June and July, ending up with a big triumph in the Dublin Horse Show in August and the right size cheque from the right sort of American going home to Garonlea instead of him. Cynthia liked riding in shows and did the thing to perfection.

Then a month after David had gone, Cynthia was abandoning all her plans, all the summer procedure that she had set herself. Putting off the visitors (except poor little Muriel whom Diana could look after), finding some one to ride her horse in all the shows except Dublin. Yes, she neglected Garonlea, her proper setting, and went to England for the summer and bought herself a great many lovely clothes and was a trifle importunate altogether.

Tactically, of course, it was a great mistake. If she had really wanted David and desired no more than to keep his love, she should, as it were, have remained in her tower. At Garonlea, which was both Cynthia's tower and kingdom, her love with David had taken its course with ease and dignity, or as possible a measure of both as the circumstances allowed. The worst small, furtive aspects of an intrigue at least were absent, the time and the place had been so right for love.

But that summer in England, things went very differently. A word from him had brought her flying over for a Newmarket meeting. They stayed together in a friend's house. He had wanted to see her then badly and it was all a great success, worthy of any attendant difficulties. David had never seriously considered Cynthia as necessary to him, but he kept on rediscovering that he minded about her far more than he wanted to. Her loveliness and eagerness and success with other men and her full, perfect and sufficient love for him made her very dear and exciting. If after that week she had gone back to Garonlea she would have gone near to reversing the question of power in the matter.

XXVII

But Cynthia did not go back to Garonlea. It was beyond her power and beyond her imagination to do so. She spent the summer in England, staying with her friends and seeing David in their houses and in London. She saw far too much of him under the circumstances which were bound to be wearing and difficult. He was quite enough in love with her to make tremendous efforts to see her and be with her, and the necessity for secrecy and intrigue soon more than equalled the good he got of the affair. Soon there was not so much secrecy as intrigue about it. All this can be very exhausting. It came to be so with Cynthia who, used to being supreme and unquestioned, was inclined to conduct the affair like an importunate ostrich. She must see David. It was necessary to her happiness and well-being, and if she chose to presume that none of her friends suspected the truth, that was enough. She did not allow herself to think they suspected it.

It was enough for Cynthia but it was not really much help to David when his wife's closest friends took him aside and tried to have long confidential talks on the subject. He realised, if Cynthia did not choose to do so, that people, especially people who liked his wife, were no longer very keen to fall in with plans for parties that included Cynthia as well as him. In fact, they became remarkably cool and tiresome about it in a short time.

But would Cynthia see the growing difficulties? No. She continued to make plans for weeks ahead, writing down dates in an inexorable way in her little engagement book. She looked happier and more beautiful than she had done for years. If tiresome people would not have her to stay on the week-ends when she wanted to be with them, she found other less tiresome people who were only too enchanted to have her and David together. She failed to see that the matter was becoming obvious to others and trying to him. She just went on and on, ignoring the fact that the affair could be recognisable to any one.

The situation became every day more difficult for David to contend with. Since the situation was difficult, Cynthia became difficult too. He still wanted her, but he wanted her far more to go back to Garonlea and wait there for him to pay those frequent romantic visits he had promised her and himself. That English summer, with his wife being rather sour and silent and dignified, and his friends obviously disapproving (though, of course, Old Boy, it was none of their business), was as unfortunate a way of spoiling the possibility of happiness as Cynthia could have found and insisted on. She was asking for failure, while she presumed with imperturbable confidence that this love could develop and endure as that earlier love in her life had done.

At last she went back to Garonlea. She had a most sensible reason for returning—she wished to ride her show-horse conscientiously during the fortnight before Dublin. Even in love she did not leave an important matter like the sale of a horse to chance. She told David it was almost more than she could endure, saying good-bye to him but, after all, it was only for a fort-night. He would be over for the show and would come down to Garonlea afterwards. Another plan was made and David agreed to it. He would have consented to anything then, he so wished Cynthia would leave him in peace to recover some of his wife's esteem and attend to his business of training horses to which she had been a grave interruption.

He did not come over for the show. Cynthia was amazed and angry when she understood that he was not coming. But when she told Diana she elaborated all his excuses . . . Goodwood . . . his wife . . . he couldn't leave the horses . . . to such an extent that she believed in their reality, and only Diana was left in grieved surprise and doubtfulness.

XXVIII

THAT Horse Show was like every other Dublin Horse Show. In spite of the fact that Ireland was at the time in a state of war, the Horse Show was its usual and inevitable social and business success. Triumph and failure, disappointment and disaster rode round the rings together. The whole of Ireland went there. Women in grey flannel coats and skirts, awful hats and brown suede shoes sat on shooting-sticks round the rings and gossiped and criticised and sometimes admired. There were busy men in clean breeches and boots without a moment to spare for anybody, and less-busy men in suits and bowler hats who had lots of time for a drink with anybody who would pay for it.

There were Indian princes in Jodhpurs that zipped down their legs in all directions, and every one in Ireland with a horse to sell coveted their acquaintance. Old ladies coming to see the flower show jostled foreign soldiers in Belgian blue and French grey who would ride their horses in the jumping during the afternoons. It was comic to hear horse-talk going on in French:

"Mais c'est effrayant." A gunner, now, would take longer to say just why he didn't like the dreadful horse.

There were lovely girls from England who made the lovely girls in Ireland look nothing. They wore their clothes so much less briskly and painted their faces with less-advanced skill and determination.

And last and first and all the time and through everything there were horses. Horses in the rings. Rows and rows and dormitories of stabled horses.

Horses led and ridden about wherever anybody wanted to sit and have a chat. Never in any place are horses so thick upon the ground as in Ballsbridge at this time. After all, in apology for the nuisance they are, it has to be remembered that this is the greatest horse-show and fair in the world, and it is natural that the warm, close smell of horses and their bedding and their leather accoutrements and their attendants should be heavier on the air than July dust under chestnut trees, as one pushes through the turnstiles to the show grounds, each morning a little later and a little more wearily as the week goes on.

Cynthia was there at ten every morning. Brisk and beautiful in her blue habit, no matter how late she had been to bed the night before, and she was rampantly gay that week, drinking too much, dancing too much, making (had she not been Cynthia) rather a fool of herself for her age. Still, she was able to attend most effectively to business. Her horse won in his class, won the light-weight Challenge Cup, was runner-up for the championship of the show and sold for a vast sum to a fabulously wealthy American. She accomplished what she had set out to do with her usual royal success and among the applause of her friends.

Diana should have felt happier about her than she did. Everything had gone wonderfully and there were six different men at every moment eager to fill the blank left by David's absence. Diana should certainly have felt happier than she did on the Thursday of the show when she and Cynthia made their way down through the main hall, full of rather jaded-looking stall-holders, towards the place where her horse was stabled.

Diana felt absolutely exhausted and sickened by the show, by the sight and sound and smell of horses and the people who got their living or their pleasure by them. She felt if another man with trim legs and tired eyes and a bowler hat tilted over one of them stopped Cynthia and asked her to come and have a drink with him, she would like to scream and spend the day in a stall of Irish lace or nosing round the already wilting flower show, abandoning her job as chief attendant and messenger to any one who chose to take it on.

Cynthia was slightly strung up. The championship was judged in the jumping enclosure where horses could really gallop and her horse took a bit of a hold. She exasperated Diana by stopping to converse with every acquaintance she met on her way to the stabling. Telling each one of them in exactly the same words how cowardly one of the judges was and how she was sure he wouldn't begin to give her horse a ride, and at the same time how a child could ride the horse. All round, the air was crossed and recrossed by broken currents of horse-talk; people standing still, people walking on, people with nothing to do and people in a hurry, all talking and murmuring about horses, their soundness and unsoundness, their slowness and their speed, their stupidity and skill in leaping, their strange inability to walk, trot or gallop as those who bought them wished them to do, and those who sold them upheld they could do.

Cynthia fiddled about her beautiful horse for a long time, talking to her groom and telling every one who passed how cowardly the judge was. She sent Diana on two messages and then went away to keep a drinking appointment with her prospective buyer. Diana had twenty minutes before the class went in. She hustled along to the flower show. Here, too, she was only conscious of the horrid oppressiveness of a crowd. Her mind refused to act about the flowers. She forgot

what it was she had come to see and inquire about.
She was jostled and overcome by people who wandered
about, ignorant and unseeing, filling in time with no
intention of buying or growing any of the flowers
exhibited. Their talk, too, made one hate everything
connected with a garden, just as the talk outside
reduced horses to a plane of extreme boredom——
"My dear, don't you call that wonderful——"
"*There's* an unusual colour——" "Now, Elsie, we must
make a plan. You see, I can come by the Dalkey train
if you can meet me. Shan't have a lot of luggage—just
a light valise——" "Yes, dear. Pretty, isn't it? But
I like the salmon pink best myself——" "Darling,
those *quilled* puce carnations—*too* lovely——" "Now,
how much money have I got left? Well, how much
did you spend at this stall? I don't know. Well, ask
him. Ask the man who took the order. Oh, could
you tell me—I'm so sorry to interrupt you—but could
you tell me how much I've spent——?"

Diana nearly ran out of the flower show, hurrying
past the monster rainbow bouquets of carnations and
the pale, airy-blue spires of delphiniums, past the rich
artificiality of gladioli and dahlia, back into the horse-
world again. She was very nearly late to put a hairpin
straight in the back of Cynthia's veil and watch her
mount, superbly confident after her drink, and ride
insolently, easy and magnificent as she always was,
through the crowded rings towards the jumping
enclosure.

The judging of the championship went on for hours
and hours and hours. Diana sat in the stewards' box
with her chin in her hand and Cynthia's handbag and
her own on her knee and watched in the mist of
invincible ignorance about horses' shapes (through
which she had never actually learnt to see the good

203

from the bad or the better from the best) the long-drawn-out process of Cynthia's defeat. She saw the noble throng of horses moving at different speeds round the great oval of green grass. Rather a lovely sight, really, especially when they laid themselves down to gallop in the shining, morning sunlight. She saw Cynthia among others called in to the centre of the ring while many horses looking to her much the same, sadly left the gay picture. Then followed a period when the judges judged and judged and horses had their saddles buttoned and unbuttoned and their riders ran them up and down and then fidgeted with them ceaselessly in case they went lame standing still.

All Ireland and England that could squeeze into the stewards' box had done so. They sat in tiers and gossiped loudly about the horses and people whose sisters or lovers or cousins were bound to be sitting within twenty yards of them at the most.

"Oh, I think he's a horrible horse. Look—he can't begin to gallop——"

"Forty, my dear, and she looks twenty-five. One can't get away from it, and I hope quite suddenly she'll just break up."

"Johnny gave Madeline's horse a shocking ride. Didn't you think so——?"

"Yes, I've had mine out, but oh, it was horrible. I shall never forget going into that nursing home. . . . Waving good-bye to every one, I was almost in tears; I thought they were all *too* unkind to want to cut poor little Lila up. . . ."

"Now I call that a lovely horse. I've always liked him. I wanted to buy him as a two-year-old and Robin wouldn't let me. He's never been allowed to forget it either. . . ."

"You know I'm not a prude but last night really I

thought every one went too far. I don't know what the man on the lift thought about us. . . ."

The Judges were riding the horses now. Diana could not make out which was the cowardly one. She was so hopelessly vague about the people Cynthia knew well and she could not tell by just looking. They both seemed to her to be decorative and able horsemen. And in this she happened to be quite right. Cynthia's horse did not begin to frighten either of the judges. He was beaten because they liked another horse more and, as usual, many people found reason to say they were ignorant and prejudiced and cowardly, and without a doubt about it, Cynthia's horse should have been Champion of the Show.

Cynthia was disappointed but not actively vindictive. She had done more than well and her horse was even better-sold than she had hoped, and her hopes had been high enough, for she never under-rated herself or her possessions. She went back to Garonlea with an enormous cheque in her handbag. And at her heart a less-hungry, wildly-defensive feeling about David than she had known was there and denied to herself when he failed to come. In fact, she felt rather bold and grand and entirely less vulnerable about him because during the week she was in Dublin without him and surrounded by other men she had discovered in her escape from consciousness about David a new spark of attraction and interest towards some one else. She did not tell herself this because she did not know or guess what it might mean. She had no idea of the emancipation that had come on her since her affair with David. But she felt a stronger current of emotional excitement than she had ever experienced with vague, inactual worshippers that had succeeded Desmond and preceded David in her life.

It was tragic if perhaps natural that Cynthia should come off her spiritual pedestal, cease being an unattainable ideal and become a vulnerable creature almost at the last possible moment in her life. With ignorance and vanity and unhappiness she had cloistered herself in the years after Desmond's death, when she could have had one man or all men. Now, in ignorance and vanity she made her belated experiments in love. She was not too old if she had had a more elastic temperament. But she was too set. She had been a queen too long, and the tide of her beauty was too surely on the turn. All her power over men and women was of a very temporal kind, lying in her looks and her bravery, and their admiration for these qualities. Not in any nearness of spirit or sympathy she might have with them. In a way her popularity was a cheap and public sort of thing. Although she had bought it dear enough and kept it so long, it was as unstable and as dependent on her own constant effort and upkeep as such popularity by its very quality must be.

XXIX

JUST as the Horse Show marks a division in the
Irish year between definite summer with horses at
grass and hunting forgotten and indefinite winter
with cub-hunting in view, and fat, preposterous horses
to be caught up and timidly mounted, so this particular
Horse Show became for Diana an ever-fixed mark of
that time when Cynthia's whole life slipped on its
decline. She dated it all from that first week in August
and their return to Garonlea with Gerald Turnbull,
the huge and charming American with the gentlest
voice and the most unquenchable thirst for whisky.

On and off he spent most of that winter at Garonlea.
He was enraptured by the place and the house and the
hounds and the horses and he enjoyed making love to
Cynthia, and when she was faintly drunk she did not
talk quite so much nonsense about love spoiling their
friendship as she did when she was sober.

David had come back to Garonlea in the autumn to
find Gerald almost installed and rather inclined to
show him round. Cynthia was on the defensive. She
had Gerald there on purpose. She produced his best
American jokes and showed him off to David. But it
was no use. David was only amused and politely
ironical. Cynthia had to explain without being asked
that Gerald was not her lover and David said it was
perhaps a pity, a fine, able man like that who knew so
many good stories too. In a week Cynthia was
recaptured, a bird between his hands, and Gerald had
been sent off. But in another week David went away

and did not come back. Gerald came back with new stories to tell in his soft voice and all the money possible to spend on any horse Cynthia told him to buy, or on any present he imagined or she let him know that she wanted. David had given her little pieces of jade and some handbags. Gerald gave her diamonds and a mink coat. She could have married Gerald that winter if she had wanted to. But she did not want to. She felt idle about it and she was always hoping that one day she would win David back to her. She could not know that in each day that passed she grew further away from that hurt, secret creature she had been when for a little while he had found her enthralling.

That winter Garonlea was strangely isolated from the near world of neighbours. A civil war was going on in Ireland, much to the inconvenience of social life. Cynthia and her hounds were so popular that there was never any difficulty over the hunting, but motor-cars were commandeered and bridges were blown up and houses burnt and people frightened away from the country. It was not possible to be out late at night, where neighbours dined, there they must sleep. Because of this, no one thought very much of the matter if Gerald, whose hotel was five miles from Garonlea, should lie five nights out of the seven at Garonlea. The crested wave of Cynthia's popularity had not yet turned. She did so many things that people admired. She swam her horse and her hounds and her unwilling hunt-servants across rivers when the bridges on her road to meets were broken. She compelled her rich American to buy horses from her friends. She had poker parties and lovely food and drink and soft beds for her guests to lie on when they had lost or won. An occasional decorous evening's bridge and a deliciously-planned dinner for the elders of the country kept them still just where she wanted them to be. She was wonderful, they all said. She went her way with all classes. There was a meal and a drink for any man on the run at Garonlea. Or a bed and no questions asked. Yet miraculously the house escaped burning by either party. Cynthia was really loved by the Irish people who knew her. She would have done anything for any of them or they for her. She was closer to them than to her own kind and class. Most of the people on and near the place knew, deplored and accepted her relations with the big American. They looked on her as too great to marry a man they truly thought common and beneath her, and the women would shed tears and spend prayers for the frailty of one not of their blood or religion.

Cynthia felt closed in and contented that winter at Garonlea. In January the thought of David was infrequent and not important. She had never had a better season's hunting. She liked having Gerald for a lover. All through, her spirit and her body felt of a smooth, thick texture. She was possessed of a happiness that seemed inviolable. The atmosphere of Garonlea grew ever richer and easier. It had become a house in which the true luxurious spirit prevailed. It seemed as though Cynthia's victory over Garonlea and the unhappiness bred there was complete. She had sustained without bitterness the loss of her first lover, and established her happiness with another. She had imposed her will of the flesh and the spirit on Garonlea, refusing the draw of its dark, established currents. Not to be happy was unnatural to her. It seemed as though now the years when she had gone struggling and hungry, held by Desmond's memory and her own faithful vanity, were over.

XXX

NEARLY dinner-time at Garonlea. A quarter-past eight on a January evening. Cynthia was down first, trailing about the library in a black velvet dress, one of the soon to be inevitable chokers of big, blatantly-pink pearls casting fat shadows behind their circle on her long, full neck. She poured herself out a cocktail (Gerald's special) and sat down away from the huge fire. The whole room was as equally and agreeably warm as a bath full of water. Groups of freesias and papery sweet narcissi and violets set about in silver mugs gave out their delicious evasive chorus of scent. A little terrier rose from its dark nest and leaped neatly as a robin on to her knee, turning its eyes away from the shaded light behind her. Cynthia looked at it distantly for a moment, enjoying the exquisitely clear and delicate lines of its throat and neck, the bird's poise of its head, before her hand went down to it in a slow, adequate caress. She was tired after a long, successful day's hunting, but not so tired that she did not look with pleasure towards the lovely meal about to be. How right she had been to order champagne to-night. A necessity. Really the only thing.

Gerald came in. Enormous. Heavy shouldered. Carefully shaved. Most attractive in that red velvet dinner-jacket made by a London tailor. He took her glass and filled it again for himself, giving her a new drink. It was a simple sort of love token, rather like a mink coat, but cheaper. Then he lit a cigarette and stood with his back to the fire.

"Cynthia, you're looking very wonderful," he said.

She sent him a look as slow as her hand had been going out to the dog.

"And didn't that horse of mine carry you well to-day?" He swallowed half his drink. "You may say it gives me a big, big thrill to see you ride to hounds on my horse. Certainly it gives me a thrill. You bet your life. I want to see you ride that horse in Leicestershire."

"He's a tiresome sort of horse," Cynthia said thoughtfully. "But once you find out how to ride him he's grand. He's not your horse though, Gerald. For one thing, he's not really up to your weight."

"I bought that horse, Honey, before I ever met you. And listen, sweetie, if you like him and get on with him—he's yours."

"What's yours now, Mamma?" Simon asked. He had just come in. He tipped up the cocktail-shaker and looked from the teaspoonful of drink in the bottom of a glass towards his mother and her friend in a way they could hardly mistake, before he poured himself out a glass of sherry. His grace and assurance had improved. Gerald thought he had a disgusting amount of confidence for a boy of twenty and often told Cynthia that what he wanted was a Father's Authority.

Cynthia said, "Simon, how mean of us. We've drunk it all. Gerald is very sweetly trying to give me Klondyke, the horse I rode to-day."

"I named that horse Klondyke, you see, because I hoped he'd prove a gold mine." Gerald adored naming his horses and explaining about their names.

"Yes, I thought that must be why you named him Klondyke. Yes. I expect he will be a gold mine to Mamma."

"I haven't accepted him yet," Cynthia said with dignity and without humour.

"You don't want to make me mad now, do you?" Gerald gazed across at her, Simon forgotten. "You know I'm crazy for you to have this horse."

"*Pas devant les domestiques*," Simon murmured to himself in governess French.

Cynthia respected Simon now, though she found him trying. She caught back her answering look and said, "We'll think about it, I promise. You must ride him again and if you really don't like him——"

Gerald, who, until Cynthia had told him so, had been unaware of how much he disliked his best horse, nodded wordless agreement.

"How tiresome and late Sue is," Cynthia had no more to drink. "And Diana. I'm so hungry."

"The one good thing about hunting is its lovely hunger, don't you think so?" Simon asked Gerald.

"I'm afraid I hunt for love of the sport itself," Gerald replied ponderously, and could not understand why Simon looked so delighted. He did not know Simon and Susan's game of drawing Bromides from him.

Sue came in. She was wearing a fancy dress that Simon had copied for her from the portrait of an ancestress, green brocade and a quilling of net drawn on a string round the square neck opening. She had a little white dog, a silky, plumey little cur that she sometimes led about on a ribbon if she wished to annoy her mother.

"So sorry, Mamma."

Only Gerald sympathised with Cynthia when she said she wished her children would call her "Cynthia" or "Mum." "Mamma," so ethereal and unhearty and old.

"But Diana's behind me. Oo Simon—just one sip."

"I don't approve of young girls drinking. They don't require any artificial stimulation. But here you are, sweetie, just the same. Why? Gee, because I love you, honey."

Another thing was to talk as they fancied Gerald might do in emotional and unbridled moments.

"Delicious sherry wine to keep out winter chills. Thank you, Simon."

Diana came in then in a spruce little dinner-jacket. Her short hair brushed and pomaded and charmingly grey at the temples. Her finger-nails trimmed squarely. A blue lapis signet-ring. Simon helped her to dress like that. Although he was at Cambridge now, he scarcely realised the implications. In 1922 a great many people did not. Especially in Ireland. He and Susan had bought the lapis ring out of their small allowances and great love for Diana. There was never any difficulty about the names they called her. She had always been Diana and other fond little names.

"Diana, we're rather hungry, darling. But you did have some lunch to-day and we didn't."

"Cynthia, I'm sorry——"

"Don't you be sorry, Diana. You're ten minutes late because you've fed the puppy that has distemper, listened to Mamma boasting in her bath, sewn on a button for me, made Sue almost be in time and after all that you look as tricky as possible."

"If Simon would stop talking we might go in to dinner," Cynthia gave Diana a private smile. Simon was used to do all the forgiving.

Gerald, who enjoyed food and wine and love with elaborate greed, opened the door, courtesy elaborate too. The one thing Simon really liked about Gerald was his knowingness about food and wine.

Strengthened by the soup of extreme strength and clarity they began to talk about their day's hunting again. There was a conscientious preamble about the

213

chase itself: what the Fox had done; what that young hound Tarquin had done; why old Venus must die. But soon they got to the really enthralling part: what Cynthia had done; what Gerald had done; what other cowardly or mistaken people had left undone.

"I did a remarkably foolish thing to-day——" This was Cynthia helping herself to sole in a sauce that just tipped the edge of heaven. "Really one would think a woman of my age would have had more sense."

Gerald said, "You scare me blue, the fences you take on."

"But four foot of timber and into a tarred road. I should have had more sense, shouldn't I?"

"You certainly should."

"But I was in a hurry and I was riding your horse, Gerald. I knew it would be all right."

"Where was it?" Gerald couldn't bear to think he had missed leaping an ugly fence. He would almost go back at the end of a hunt to jump anything he thought might cause his horse to fall or himself to suffer injury. It was a fetish with him.

"Leaving Gramore. I got a little left on the far side of the covert and they ran like smoke for almost a mile."

"Oh, yes, honey. I remember missing that blue back in front of me away from the covert side. Then you appeared from nowhere and none of us could catch you."

"That horse flies."

"I wouldn't mount you on a slow horse, now, would I? Would I be likely to? But, honest, Cynthia, I'd like to have seen his answer to a question I asked my old Foxglove, going away from the covert. The field were all going for a gate——"

("That's US," Susan and Simon said.)

214

"I dare say you were correct," he accepted their admission kindly. "Well, that was when I pulled out left-handed down a steep slope all rock and bog and bushes and asked old Foxglove to jump the highest stone-faced bank I've seen in this country. Yes Sir, and the ground sloping into it—— Cocked his old ears——"

("I knew he would," Susan and Simon said.)

"—and went right bang to the top. That was his answer."

Susan and Simon took their blessed refuge in an exchange of looks, silent communion from the further side of laughter. Then they devoted their attention to woodcock, a Spanish sauce and a surprising salad. The wine had drifted their fatigue afar. They remembered their day's hunting with enjoyment made clear and understandable at this short space of time from its happening.

Simon and Susan felt very emotional about hunting. There was nothing hearty or commonplace in their enjoyment of it. They refused to talk about it like Gerald or a *Tatler* correspondent. It keyed them up on a higher pitch of imaginative excitement. They loved the emotion they had from it; the thrill going beyond fear. They did not deny the fear. Now they endured it, saying to each other, We have so much imagination, that's why our stomachs are so queasy——

People who like hunting in this way are not tremendously sane but they do experience a great emotion, the contrast between danger and safety, heat and cold, a hungry stomach and a full one, thirst and its assuaging are some of the things that take this sharp importance.

For Simon and Susan there had been to-day a wait beside a dark grove of hazels associated with all the fears of their childhood. The wall that had loomed so

cruelly was not a bogey now. But the feeling of inevitable danger was still there as the hounds, heavy, bright
creatures, filled the grove with their voices. Filling the
little aisle between the close-grown spears of hazel and
the secret fox-ways, pale bents and brambles where
little foxes ran and turned and ran on again with the
noise of their hunting. The air of the day was lost in
the clamour. Hot or cold or fair or stormy, it was a
void now, hollow but for the overture to danger. They
felt sick. Their horses were like lions beneath them;
they were enveloped in the terrible music and the
waiting was like waiting for death. There was no
other importance in the fields and fences and rivers
and unfamiliar distance beyond the necessity of crossing
them. Their other reasons stood beyond this. The
mountains and the receding day were as distant to the
moment as houses seen on the way to a scaffold might
be.

Then at the unbearable moment of tension the scene
changed. A voice, shrill and surprising as a bird at
night-time, telling the fox was gone. Wild and in-
human as a hound's voice this call for pursuing. Then
the horn blown and blown again and the hounds' bodies
no more bright and heavy and separate but creatures
light as fire, hurrying and flying together like fire in a
wind, settling heavy as bees an instant then gone as if
winged.

Pursue them. Pursuit through the hour that has no
time, over fields that have no name, a spirit purged of
itself pursues. A horse that was a lion is now a dove,
a part of self, but braver and more skilled for the brave
time. Green fields, dark fences, bogs that had no
meaning yesterday, dark alders and bright willows
let us through. Oh, kind little gap, be thanked. White
seagulls following the plough slip behind, forgotten.

Little arrowy snipe darting from white grasses, what is it to a mind and body so hotly set forward?

Before the chase is over the lightness and the thrill are suspended by moments of fear and heaviness and lack of quick choice. Fatigue of spirit and body weigh despairingly. A tired horse, staggering and recovering, is more sickening than a fall. The wild feeling of conquest is gone and yet the pursuit goes on. The hounds pursue, fearless, merciless, tied to their intention, untiring. They must be followed, with tremendous effort, vast expense of energy, absurd endeavouring. It is the phase of unhappiness which endures till fear is strangely purged again from the spirit. Thrill is passed and fear is passed and a period of reality survives in which the most jealous rider will take grateful advantage of another's decision, throw shillings to the gate-opener and desire only to endure until the end, not to surpass in brilliance and bravery his fellows.

An insufferable thing, a treatise, a homily on hunting. No, but a day in the spirit of those two who feared and loved it, Susan and Simon, would be like that. Composed of sickness and wild love and the real pain of fear and, that cast out, content to suffer or enjoy and then at the conclusion again exhilaration. Relief? Physical pride in endurance? The held memory of lovely things seen from a strange angle? The heron that rose from its fishing, the little fox escaping. The swiftly flying beauty of a pack of hounds, that dream-like quality they possess, the quality that goes behind the horns' notes too like ghosts of crowns on the air. A magnificence, a royal tradition, lies behind all hunting.

But such a day was done. They sat together in the changed dining-room of Garonlea. Diana for one could never overmaster the feeling of drama which possessed her at Cynthia's conquest of this room. Now she sat where Lady Charlotte had kept her place for so long, but the change, it was too far-fetched, again too dramatic to endure.

Lady Charlotte in jet and mauve satin, diamonds sprawling on her great square bosom, possibly an aigrette pinned in her dignified puffed and greasy hair, directing such conversation as there was. The first primroses. The Kaiser must be hanged. Surely I know a Cox's Orange pippin. Well, Diana, have you nothing to tell us? Nothing? And I think you spent the day at that enchanting house, Rathglass?

"And Ambrose: What's this Coulthwaite? What's this—Sago? *Really*, I cannot eat sago. . . . Where is the meet on Thursday? You didn't find out? No, it's not a Cox's Orange, I'm convinced it's not—Diana, try a piece—— One of those terrible nights of tears and unknowing frustration came back to Diana. How cruelly, sharply, the past can live even in contentment. Her eyes went down the table to find Cynthia and all reassurance in the warmth and beauty she had made. In the delicacy and plenty of the food, in the luminously pale room, and in the glow of wine. Cynthia in Lady Charlotte's chair, her black velvet dress with its great sleeves was winged and shadowy. It melted into the gloom the coarser fullness and thickness of her body. She seemed melodiously calm. Satisfied. Still beautiful. More beautiful because her lover found her divine.

Divine was what Gerald actually found her. Beyond him. Goddess of the chase he loved so much. He could not give her enough or love her enough, and he was generous and wholly loving. He had lived with Cynthia for three months now and his whole being was centred in his desire for marriage with her. To make her his own so that she could not escape him. He was very simple in his possessiveness. He wanted her—his love—to keep. He was not unsure as David was unsure. Artistically selfish, living only for the moment, holding his life and his love at a distance, powerful in his refusal to sacrifice himself. Uncertain, unpractical, romantic, full of understanding yet hard as steel.

Could nothing tell Cynthia that this was her hour, her last hour, her day was ending, her power would soon be past, and here, giving into her hand, was the super conventional happy ending that her life demanded?

She could not perceive the truth of this. Always beyond her physical contentment with Gerald were the wraith-like, uncertain memories of her affair with David. The uncertainty and delight of those days of last spring, the joy and laughter and delight of her love with him. Other things, Simon and Susan's pleasure in his company remained with her. She compared their attitude to Gerald, half-scoffing, half-pitying, to this and it almost caught her to the same attitude. The laughter of the young is such a sincere belittling. Again, David's almost cruel independence contrasted with Gerald's heavy reliance on her will and choice in all matters. He was too trusting. Too generous. Too loving. Too loving was the worst offence. The pity of the mistakes people must make when they love sincerely. But it was not through too much loving that Cynthia made her mistakes.

Simon said:

"How lovely these peaches are, yours, Gerald? Sue, ah, Honey, try one. Just to please me. They really are very delicious."

"They're marvellous, Gerald," Cynthia said. She felt almost as earnest and unimaginative as he seemed

219

in the light of the children's quick mockery. His peaches and his orchids and his carnations came just too often. Not that it mattered. Other things about him really mattered far more. She poured out another glass of cointreau. On top of champagne, too. But nothing ever made her feel ill to-morrow.

Sue was sitting, affectedly enough, beneath the portrait of that ancestress whose dress Simon had copied. She was giggling a good deal and wiping her enormous eyes, sometimes on her napkin sometimes, on her handkerchief. Even a sip of wine made her like this. Anyhow, she always giggled for hours before she made a joke—"My jokes are so poor, people must have time to prepare their laughs."

Now she leant back her head and pointed to the portrait of her dress with an upflung hand, not looking.

"Pearls, darling. Not that I want to fuss or complain. But isn't it strange there are no Garonlea pearls? There ought to be, shouldn't there? Where have they all gone?"

"I can't tell you that, Sweetie, but I know where they ought to be and know where they will be, next time you and I make Bond Street together——"

Sue yawned, her laughter all gone before the joke was over.

"We're so unkind," she said to Simon, and then to Gerald:

"Dear Gerald, let me ride your lovely mare, 'Kiss Me To-night,' on Tuesday. And why did you call her that?"

"You certainly shall, Sue. She's a perfect performer. Beautiful mouth. Beautiful manners. Yes, I called her 'Kiss me To-night' because she was by Presto out of a mare called Gipsy Love by Poets' Corner out of Spanish Lass. See? It all fits in as neat as pie."

"Oh, it certainly does, Gerald."

"——How does she endure him at all, really, Simon. Tell me——" Sue said to Simon. She was sitting up in bed, the collar of her pink, quilted dressing-gown turned up like a shell round the back of her round head and little neck. Her lovely frog's or cat's face was polished and clean. Simon liked to see her turned back purely into young, virgin woman. There is something exciting about this sudden stripping of artificiality. It is each night a stranger's pale oval of real face. Pale lips that were red. Pale lashes that were dark. Wax flesh. Smooth hair that curled. "Will she marry him, Simon?"

"Oh what a disgusting thought. Is he to be always with us? Saying, Honey. Saying, I want you to know. Eating in that French-American way with his mouth half open. Did you hear him say his horse had very good ' gaits '? Action, he meant. It's a word."

"We shouldn't listen to what he says about his horses. It would make us give up our good food."

"He's clever about food."

"Will Mamma marry him?"

Marriage. Simon always remembered that love meant marriage to Sue still. Their mother's friends all wanted to marry her, of course.

"Perhaps she will, Sweetie. Do we want her to?"

"And us to live alone here with Diana? Oh, yes, Simon."

"It would be nice. But how soon would you marry and leave me?"

"Never, Simon, never. I have no need of Love and chaps when I have you."

"I think Diana would stay with Mamma."

"Oh, no, we must have her."

"I don't think we shall get her."

"How tired I am. Please put my dressing-gown away and open the window as little as possible. My horse did frighten me to-day, and oh, it was exquisite. Good-night, dearest Simon. Give me my little dog to keep me hot. Good-night."

Simon knew she was asleep before he was half-way down the wide staircase. She was the most complete creature.

That staircase was the wrong background entirely for Simon. He was too olive and oblique for its space and clarity. He required a background of red wall-paper and too many pictures. He was wrongly cast for his part in Cynthia's new Garonlea.

In the library he read the paper. The atmosphere of the room which he had broken left him feeling acid and miserable. His mother's idleness and silence, her palpable mood of waiting were obvious to him. So was the fact that she had, quite gracefully, had too much to drink. Gerald he hardly regarded. For him he only felt an absurd, enveloping contempt.

Active anger stirred in him towards Cynthia. He thought of Susan and he thought of Garonlea and he was furious that she should so slight the importances of either by this greedy intrigue. Simon was a person who would soon be very fully conscious. Even now, although he went to bed soon, muttering pleasurably to himself, "call you his mouse—or paddling in your neck with his damned fingers——"—he was completely aware that for his mother's sake he did not care two-pence who called her what or who paddled where.

XXXI

A WINTER's morning. A sky like a dirty old slate. Trees untidy, lead-coloured brushes against it. The air full of snow and rain and the hour full of the absurd necessity of going out hunting. At such a moment there is one thing impossible and that is to see a summer's day. White flowers in the evening seem the only terms in which it can become remotely visible. Say, stephanotis in darkness.

Ten-fifteen at Garonlea on such a morning. Every one felt cross and unnatural and a little late with everything they had to do before they faced the outdoor day.

Sue could not master her hair or her stomach. Her hands were cold. She nearly cried.

Simon complained about his new boots and the bitter, bitter, unfair weather.

Diana had to hunt to-day because it suited Cynthia to provide her with a horse on Tuesdays. She had no complaints to make except that her hat gave her great pain.

Gerald, standing by the fire in a coat with a fur lining and a fur collar and boots beyond all dreams of brightness, was the only really comfortable person. He was drinking a large portion of port and brandy.

In a moment Cynthia would be drinking too and feeling better. Up till now she had been flying noisily about in her boots and writing out stopping cards to catch that day's post. In the snowlight her face, under the peak of her velvet cap, looked old and faintly sagged and terribly preoccupied.

Susan did not drink, of course. Simon would not have allowed it. And Simon did not drink, nor Diana. They stood round the fire, looking unspeakably sullen, their minds tortured with their own immediate problems. They could not have felt less genial or looked more dreary.

Cynthia came across the room, a bunch of cards in her hand. She took her drink from Gerald and swallowed half of it. Better already. Definitely better.

"Almost time to start," she said. "Don't I hear the car coming round?"

"I left the car at the door twenty minutes ago," Simon said.

"Oh, then who is it, I wonder."

It was David. He walked in among them—through them—past them. Coming to Cynthia. There was a faint colour of dismay and delight in her cheeks. She made a tremendous effort to appear casual.

"Why didn't you let us know you were coming? We'd have found something for you to ride."

"It's all right. I came over to try a horse of John Hearn's."

"Oh, I see. Would you like a drink?"

"No, thank you, Cynthia. A little early for me."

Cynthia and Gerald had another glass of port each, just to uphold each other.

"Well, hadn't we better start?"

It was all so broken off, so without meaning in that horrid hour. It was the sort of awkward moment David would choose to return, inconvenient, un-romantical. Putting himself into his old position of ascendancy with this not telling, hardly caring. Riding a dreadful horse of John Hearn's when Cynthia's perfect hunters were at his wish. Contradicting all his uncaring by coming twenty miles out of his

224

road to see her, not for a drink nor any convenience of time or place. But to see her, though he claimed nothing, wanted nothing——

She did not ask him to drive on to the meet with her. He took his own car and Susan and Simon and Diana in it. Cynthia and Gerald drove together. At the back of the ease after her drink she felt bored and rather squalid with him. All her content was gone. But she was nearer to tears than to happiness in seeing David again.

She said to Gerald:

"Do you know David well, Gerald?"

He said:

"Quite, Honey. He's not the type of man I care about. I'm sorry he's a friend of yours."

Cynthia felt as unaccountably angry as she had done on the day when, she having complained at great length of Simon's tiresome and affected ways, Gerald remarked weightily, "I'm afraid he's just a great big Cissy."

Both Simon and David were really so much beyond Gerald's praising or blaming. It was a gross impertinence from him even to agree with her own complaints or condemnations of either. Now she was furious. She kept an elaborate silence and lit a cigarette for herself.

"Please?" Gerald said.

"Yes?"

"Cigarette please, sweetie."

"Oh."

She lit one for him.

"You're not mad with me for what I said about your friend? I know he's not your type either."

Oh, God. Really, what an uncivilised man. What a way to speak. What a pity simple people ever try to

225

put their emotions into words. They so destroy any effect they might have just as emotions. Looking at him, Cynthia saw how deeply troubled he was. If he had not spoken she might not have had her pity made impotent by irritation.

"I really didn't pay much attention, I'm afraid. I'm wondering if it would be better to draw Lara Wood first or go straight to that little wild gorse where we found the last day."

Gerald, who had a simple and uncomplex temper, did not answer her. He sulked like a bear all day and jumped the most preposterous fences on the faintest provocation. That evening he got very drunk and was insultingly possessive with Cynthia.

She was clever about this, affecting a lightness and tolerance to hide her furious displeasure.

People came to dinner and stayed for the night. It was one of those parties where every one talks a very great deal, conscious of difficult currents in the atmosphere. The food, the wine, the warmth, the flowers and colours of Cynthia's Garonlea endured. But behind the outward ambience it was as though feet stirred and rustled in an old darkness. In trouble there was something behind—something more powerful than Cynthia's new Garonlea. Contentment and happiness were necessary to her house. To-night there was a faintly mask-like importance on her decoration of Garonlea—a little ghastly, as masks are.

Part of the mask was in her friends who really loved her and lent themselves now unconsciously to tide across this dangerous moment. Although, like Cynthia, they all preferred David, they were sweet to Gerald, indulgent to his drunken reminiscencing over his horses. Perceiving, as who would not, the trouble in the air, they talked to Gerald so that he should not

226

quarrel with David, and never let David alone for a moment so that he should not be disastrously and pertinently rude to Gerald, as he seemed on the edge of being all that long evening.

Beyond anybody, Diana felt the alarm and the quiet possessiveness of the unhappy past creeping back through all the kindness of people and the rich and fluid ease of present life at Garonlea. It had happened and she was helpless. Unhappiness was here again. She could not say to David, Go away now at once. Say no more. Never come back again—— He had come back and it was too late. Dear David whom they all loved. She herself and Simon and Susan were nearly as much in his power as Cynthia was. He was back again—tuning them each to a curious pitch, unenduring for its very level. He did not wish his influence to endure. He wished for nothing beyond the moment, and for him the moment could not be fragile enough or short enough. Too selfish, too romantical, he would not see his moments endure and grow worn and sordid with use and time. To him there were no such words as dear or accustomed—the gentlest Pirates do not know such words.

XXXII

Simon saw what would happen too, and Diana knew that he was excited and pleased far within at the idea of Cynthia's mistake and disaster. She knew it as she had known how it satisfied Cynthia long ago to rule and frighten Susan and Simon when they were pale and cowardly children.

Susan did not know what was happening or mind. It was lovely to have David back, that was all. And cruel fun to see old Gerald sweat about it. Susan did not play cards to-night. She hardly ever did, or smoke or drink. She had a work-bag as big as a sack, full of pieces of tapestry which she had worked at now and then through the evening. She was very partial to green tulips and then paler green tulips in her designs. She was never cross and liverish from doing nothing. If she thought about anything, she thought about birds or Simon or how terrifying and lovely hunting was, or she might wonder if her stomach would ever allow her to ride in a race. She thought not.

"David, you're not going away to-morrow, surely?"

No one had said anything about his going or staying. It was a cry of sudden pain from her distance and wilderness of green tulips.

Simon felt so pleased. What drama the child called forth, sitting a sort of Sabrina among her cool tulips away from the men and women and wine and falling cards.

"No, Susan, of course I'm not going. I want to stay for weeks."

"You will stay here with us, dearest David. It will be lovely. Like in the Spring."

"Yes, I would like to. Last Spring was lovely, wasn't it? We were all so good-tempered and we thought of such good jokes."

"It was lovely."

"And do you remember——"

Across Sue's thin netting of talk, clear behind its meshes, Gerald, spoilt and simple and exhausted with the heavy pain of the evening, was staring at Cynthia, a little drunk, saying silently, clearly, with all his heart and strength, "You must not ask him. You can't have him here. Hell! am I to share you? I love you so. I love you so much. Honey, believe me, darling, I'd give you the earth."

And Cynthia, looking at her cards, knowing each word in Gerald's mind, looking at no one, hard, considering, eager, greedy, helplessly enthralled to David, made her choice and her mistake, thinking, "I can have David now. I can have Gerald back again."

She lifted her head and gave Gerald a long, strange look, surprise in it and dismay for his bad taste. A slow withdrawal of her eyes and herself. It was a piercingly cruel and stupid thing to do. Stupidity and impatience and greed were in that dismissal.

They ran riot in the ugly scene that was bound to follow it.

"But I don't understand, Cynthia. I may be dumb. Say I'm a big boob if you like. But you loved me, you said so. Isn't it so? Did you say so?"

Still the library, but changed. Much later. The hint of very early morning behind the close curtains and the low fire and the scent of flowers reasserted in a room empty for an hour.

There was no wish in Cynthia to keep Gerald, even

229

his future return was not weighing with her now. She accepted it as entirely probable. Now there was no kindness in her towards him.

"I may have said so. But does anything I said account for your curious behaviour this evening?"

"Behaviour? Hell, I just want you. That's all."

"It's embarrassingly obvious."

"What is?"

"What you want. The only thing you do want."

At least Gerald did not want mink coats and rich jewels and horses as well. She thought it safer to hurry on.

"You'll admit it's embarrassing for me."

"Cynthia, listen——"

"Simon and Susan. All these people——"

"Ah, listen now."

"You pull yourself together and listen to me. I simply hate saying so, but this sort of thing is quite beyond me. It just ruins everything. One can't compete with it."

"You make it out pretty rough, don't you? And what have you got on me? Tell me, because I don't understand. I'm no different to-night from what I was last night."

"You rather sickened me to-night."

"I sickened you?"

"Flinging everything about like you did."

"I don't see your viewpoint. The folk here to-night, they knew last week I loved you. I'm proud to love you. Your friends know it. To-night didn't show them any different."

"If you'd had rather less to drink, Gerald, you might be able to see some difference."

"I was drunk too?"

"I said, 'If you'd had rather less to drink.'"

"Well, let that be. I've been drunk before and I will be again. You can't pick on me for that, can you? Considering how you drink yourself, don't you?"

Cynthia was rigid with fury, stammering for words which she could not find.

"That's all right, Cynthia. I don't quarrel with you for that. Forget I said it, but it's true, remember."

"Thank you."

"And listen."

"I'm getting rather bored with all this listening. I'd be rather glad if you'd say what you have to say in one minute and if possible leave the house before I come down in the morning."

"But you keep interrupting me, Cynthia. You make me feel kinda mad with you. Child, you've got to know how much I love you. Of course you know. You don't forget Tuesday, nor Sunday, nor that lovely week in London. I know you don't. You can't. Then what is it? What's got you to-day and to-night? What have I done to you? What's happened to us? You loved me."

"I've told you. If you don't mind, I'm going to bed now. Good-bye."

"It's not Good-bye and you've not told me. Listen——"

"Oh, God, if you say ' Listen ' again—Let me go!"

"It's the way I act and the way I talk now. No, I'm not letting you go."

He had pushed her down in the sofa by her shoulders and leaned over her, amorous, animal, nervously, desperately in pain. His eyes and his mouth out of his control—he was asking to be hurt. He could not see the pain that was coming to him. It would be pain beyond consoling.

"You think I'm dumb. Certainly you must think I'm slow if I can't see what's happened to-day. You

231

changed to me. Yes, I felt it the minute David walked in at the door. Didn't you now? Are you in love with him? No. You can't be. Not when I think of yesterday. Excited maybe? What's the good? He's no use to you. I know David better than I said to you this morning."

"You do?"

"I do. You're not his type. Believe me, it's so. His wife holds him. She's a clever woman. Do you know her? Like Sue. Sue reminds me of her, I can't tell you why. That coldness they have. That's what he likes."

"Really? Perhaps now I might go to bed."

"Cynthia, don't move. Don't make me bully you. I would. I've got to talk this out with you."

Cynthia leant back, pinned in her corner of the sofa behind all this heavy talk and heavy shadow of love. Where was all her wish for him that yesterday had warmed and soothed her? Now her body felt like a wire cage against him. Her arms fleshless as wire. Her eyes looking on him, cold. Back and forwards through her mind through all the truth of his talking, walked the poisonous word against her vanity—"You drink too much. I don't quarrel with you for it." Cynthia could not think how to hurt him enough for that moderate and deadly thrust. It was so true, so much more true than it had been years ago when David said it, as true now as his assumption, his knowledge of her desirousness. . . . "Like Sue—She reminds me of Sue—that coldness——" It was insufferable. She could never hurt him enough.

"—This is what I want to say. I want you to marry me. My darling, realise things. You do love me. Perhaps not to-night? Yesterday and to-morrow though! Ah, Cynthia, we could do so much together. Everything you wanted I'd get for you, Honey—— Everything I could."

That was all he said about his money. This was Gerald, simple and very kind. Speaking of his love, asking his mistress to marry him as ardently, as gravely as though theirs had been the most austere courtship imaginable. And this was Gerald really, beyond his talk of horses and his smart, dirty stories. This was the man whom Cynthia beyond any one should have known after these months of love.

She was too blind. Blinded by her vanity and by her greed and her pathetic lack of imagination. She was going to hurt him so that he must be forever lost to her. She was not very quick of tongue or very clever, so the words she chose were blunt, heavy, bruising words, strung together in short, plain sentences, easy to follow.

"——Do you realise quite what a crashing bore you are? How you think any woman would have the nerve to live with you for the rest of her life—— Did you really think I would? Poor Gerald, you did? Well, I'm awfully sorry—— Rather touching, I thought, trying to reclaim me from drink. I'm not sure when I've seen you entirely sober. Or have I ever? Not that I mind. But it dulls the brain a bit, doesn't it? You find it difficult to see when people simply have had enough of you, don't you? When they've heard *all* your dirty stories and all about your horses and all the fences you've jumped five times each week."

Gerald got up very slowly from the sofa and stood looking down at her from the great distance of his height.

"One thing I never thought I'd do, Cynthia," all the possible weight and simplicity in him behind the words—He stopped and then spoke, "I never thought in this world to despise you as much as I do now. For what you've said." He went away.

It was an answer she did not expect. She was left

233

alone, still flattened back in her corner of the sofa. All the words she had said, ungoverned, cruel words, were clear and loud in her mind for a moment, their meaning now trebled from what it had been in her angry mind. She felt frightened and ashamed and minded curiously that Gerald should have spoken so finally. She wanted reassurance terribly. Through and through she felt shaken. Reassurance? She crossed the room to a glass and looked in it, moving away a little wildly. Again she had been shaken—tired, that's all, only tired. It was never age looking back from the shadows. What had she said? What had she done? I can't be left alone. I must discuss this with some one. Diana, she understands. Diana loves me. Should I have a drink just to steady myself? Nor fair to Diana to wake her up and go on like a nervous wreck. I suppose I ought to have one. Yes, I will, it may do me good——Ah, better—already much better. And a tiny one for while I talk. I've had so much talk to-night. It's so exhausting.

XXXIII

CYNTHIA went upstairs a little awkwardly with a glass in one hand and the front of her dress caught up so that she could not stumble. The picture of Lætitia, wife of Desmond McGarth, seemed withheld in a wintry isolation from her successor. All that Cynthia had done for her importance made the division clearer. Cold, honeyed mouth; hands preposterously unlifelike, inamorous as sea-shells. Oyster-pale dress. Powdered hair, and a crisp posy of white, moss-rose buds and tiny, dripping fuschias—such sanitary flowers to pin between those reserved and symmetrical breasts. Cynthia, groping a little stupidly for the light switch at the top of the stairs, was remotely aware of a chill breath between that piece of lovely decoration and herself.

Diana was curled in bed like a little dog, absolutely fast asleep. How strange that always she should have slept like this by herself. I can't think why it doesn't make more difference between us, Cynthia thought. She felt a surge of trust and gratefulness go through her as she put her hand gently down on Diana's shoulder.

"Diana, darling, I'm so sorry to wake you. Listen, I've had such an awful time——" Cynthia began to laugh. She certainly was not very steady.

"What is it? Sit down, Cynthia." Diana had woken in the quick, untroubled way children do. "Mind, darling, give me that whisky. You're spilling it all over your dress."

"Don't give a damn about this dress. Never suited me. I'll give it to you, Diana."

"No, darling."

"Yes, darling. You deserve it. You're such a comfort to me. Give me my drink and I'll tell you about it all."

Diana looked at her mistrustfully, but she handed over the drink. One could not argue with Cynthia at this hour.

"What an evening! Do you agree with me that Gerald was behaving shocking—preposterously, or am I wrong? I don't want to be unfair. But it wasn't fair to me, the way he was going on, was it? Or to you or Simon or Susan or anybody. Was it?"

"Cynthia, darling, I think you ought to go to bed and discuss it in the morning."

"No. Now. I came to tell you now." Cynthia seemed to gather herself for a moment out of her absurd drunken importance. "I've been simply brutal to him, Diana. The things I've said." Then she relapsed again. "Can't have it, I said, think of Susan, I'm always thinking of what she may think. I said, you must go away, Gerald. Stop boring us all about your horses. He said, I love you. I want to marry you. Give you anything, he said. All men are the same, Diana, about me, aren't they? Look at David. Back again."

"For how long?"

"I don't know what you mean. David's come back to me. Then he said I was drinking. Pulled me up for drinking. He did. I don't think that was fair, do you? That made me very angry. Wouldn't you have been? I do so hate unfairness."

"I suppose you refused to marry him?"

"Yes, David's come back. Wasn't I right?"

"How can I tell what you should do. Oh, darling, I wish you'd go to bed."

"Don't you want to talk to me? I want to tell you about this. You see, I've been very unkind to poor Gerald. He's off—he'll come back though."

"Probably."

"But I took a tremendously strong line. I thought it was only fair—don't you know, Diana? Finished, I said. Two months with you enough for any girl."

"I'm worried, Cynthia. He's been so good to you. He's so absurdly generous. How unkind were you?"

"I was very. I couldn't help myself, Diana. To have him here going on so unfairly like to-night when David came back—what could I do? I ask myself, I do really."

"Is he going away?"

"To-morrow, I think. That's to-day."

"Finally?"

"I hope so. Do you know he dared to say to me he despised me—— Oh, what *am* I saying? But he did say so. Fancy Gerald saying so! It's almost funny. I could only tell you."

"You must have been very very unkind."

"Yes, I think I was. Was it very cruel of me?"

"What are you going to do about all his presents! You'll have to charter a whole train to take them away."

"I forgot them. I like people for themselves. Not because of what they give me. You know what I mean. You see how I quite forgot his presents. Isn't it funny?"

"What are you going to do about them?"

"I can't pack up that horse and send it back."

"I thought you hadn't quite accepted that."

"Yes I had. And I may be unkind but I couldn't hurt him as much as to send back the horse he gave me, could I?"

"And the mink coat?"

"It wouldn't be fair on him to give that back. What could he do with it?"

"And all the diamonds?"

"Oh, the vulgarity of those diamonds! Poor Gerald. I can't throw them in his face. There are limits, and honestly, would it be fair to him?"

Diana got out of bed and tied the cord of a blue dressing-gown firmly round her waist. She looked very tired suddenly. Her hair and her face seemed faded and sad.

"Cynthia. Bed for you, my dear. Come on, I'll help you to undress and tuck you up. To-morrow we'll talk about it all."

Half an hour later Diana got back into bed. She slid down between the chilled sheets without resentment. She was curiously detached from the comforts of the flesh, enjoying them as presents, not as rights. Now she lay very straight, curled no longer like a warm little dog, while thoughts and speculation chased each other in her brain and she turned things backwards and forwards, puzzling and aching over the problems they presented. Cynthia, her dearest, whom she so loved, how was it in her power to help her? Could any one help and steady her now? This year had done so strangely by Cynthia. In it she had broken the abracadabra of her faithfulness to Desmond. She had found delight and disaster and content. She had loosed her hold on content, to grasp at stars again; and what now? But it was not like that in Diana's mind. It was not a stated situation. It was all in half-spoken thoughts, in condemnation caught back for love's sake, in old gratitudes and memories of the glamour and tragedy and drama of Cynthia's life that had so strongly caught her own into its flow. There were new thoughts too—thoughts the depth and truth of which she had hardly learned to own—thoughts in which fear and pity for Cynthia were equal. To her it was as if Cynthia had suddenly lost hold of herself and of integrity towards others. She could not see that this year of yielding and greed was only the outcome of all the long years when she herself and all who touched her life had deified Cynthia beyond reality. Cynthia in their eyes and twice magnified in her own eyes could not suffer change by what she did. Contempt was the one thing not alive in the world towards her, and could it now be coming to her? Contempt from the lovers she took too easily. From the friends towards whom her charm broke and failed. From Susan and Simon whom she had tortured yet cherished. Children who had made her ashamed and who filled her now with a sort of pride and distant respect. There was a pathetic nascent awe in her relations with them.

To-night Cynthia's cowardly refusal to give back those too rich presents of Gerald's had filled Diana with real dismay. Static little codes like that, of which she had read in books, were very true to Diana. She detached it from all she had known of Cynthia's tremendous power of taking. It seemed to her a real loss of integrity. Part of the year's undoing of Cynthia. Part of the lessening of Cynthia's self as Diana knew her.

Another question which tormented her about Cynthia, a question which she avoided in her own mind because she found it so unanswerable, was the problem of her drinking. Since Diana had known Cynthia first she drank far more than other women, but she did it in a virtuous, necessitous sort of way—a duty towards herself and others, almost as if she was going to communion oftener than others (and in this matter too she had for years been the parson's pride and pleasure). Diana had grown so used to seeing Cynthia always drinking a good deal with a great air of moderation that she could not have told when it was that it had first come home to her that there was nothing moderate about the way Cynthia drank. That it was a complete necessity to her. There had been a time, in that first wonderful freedom from Garonlea, when her life changed in the anguish and joyfulness of Rathglass, when Diana had attacked whisky (that was her drink) with defiant vigour. But this was only as a testament to freedom. The phase did not endure. She did not really like whisky.

Perhaps it was through Simon that she had grown to realise the extent to which Cynthia's drinking had developed. He seemed so sharply aware of it.

Coming home from hunting, "Oh, let's go the other road—Mamma will sit for hours if we pass Carney's Pub."

Cynthia's changed face of disappointment and her hurried search for an answer:

"No, we must go by Carney's. I want to give the men a drink. They're soaking wet."

It was Simon's quick look of contemptuous dislike, his restraint from argument, that Diana remembered. And the brazen furtiveness of Cynthia's excuse.

Of course she could have brought drink out in the car on hunting days, but she preferred to sit for hours in the gloom of one of her favourite bars, warming her feet at the low fire, her fur coat open, her face lost in the darkness of walls and early evening outside. Drinking bad whisky, slowly, contentedly. Buying drinks for any one who came in. Often, and so accurately, putting a name to the faces that were only a pale glimmer in the half darkness and half silence of those little public houses. At such times she was truly great, a great personage whose people were her friends. She would sit there, not making conversation, not condescending, but with them. They would drink her health gravely and she would nod back, raising her glass to the eyes outside the circle of firelight. She would blow up the fire and stretch her ringed hands to its heat while she listened to long stories of foxes and their whereabouts. She never showed her friends the discourtesy of hastiness. Often when she rose to go she would sit down again, held as it seemed by her wish for their company. And at last she would step forth reluctantly into the winter evening and drive away in her powerful, gloomy-looking car. . . . How many of those hours had Diana seen before Cynthia's need of them and Simon's hate of them were known to her? She had looked on them as part of Cynthia's being a Master of Hounds, not as part of Cynthia herself. She had often endured, uncomplaining, hours with cold feet and wet clothes while these royal drinking parties were in progress, because she understood they were so important.

When Simon and Susan were younger they used to eat biscuits and drink ginger beer contentedly in the back of the car. Now they restrained their more educated appetites till tea time and sat wrapped in coats and rugs, a complete accord of disagreeable condemnation between them. Refusing to be young and hearty, or even slumberously royal like Cynthia. Just lately they had shocked Cynthia very deeply and quite disgusted Gerald by bringing books with them which they read when they did not wish to talk to each other.

"That must be an enthralling book, Simon. You

couldn't wait till you got home to finish it, I suppose."

"No. Do you mind me reading while you drink?"

"It keeps our minds off our hot baths," Susan said. She read a little more with easy insolence before she shut her book.

Cynthia was not able for them. Whenever possible she sent two cars out hunting or arranged, which indeed they did not mind, that they should ride home.

All this Diana knew. She knew the tenuous strength of the discord that existed between Cynthia and her children. Nothing could bridge it—nothing solid and actual that Cynthia did for them, and she did a great deal, could overcome that familiar loathing for the poses they knew in her so long. The poses they had seen through so long ago. The poses they knew she could get away with over and over again. They could not possibly look on her detachedly. They could never forget, and they were too young to understand, her cruelty to them as children. They did not thank her because this very cruelty in its strongest manifestations had given them so much that they now had, their great and passionate pleasure in the chase. They thanked her for nothing. Not for all that she had at Garonlea. Not for their physical well-being to which she had attended so scrupulously. In everything she had done for them, in everything she still did, they could only see reflected back her own will towards power, or a further uprolling of that sickening full-sized cloud of glamour behind which they knew her for what she was. Or for what she was to them. How did they know what she was? And by what right of sorrow could they understand how terribly she had suffered and changed?

Diana could not understand it. She was far more

242

childlike in mind than they were. She only saw the danger of their bitterness towards Cynthia. She felt as though some wheel in life was coming slowly round. As in a dream she could not see the wheel or the circle it made, but she knew. She had been told before. She had the dream fever of panic and impotence in all her thoughts of Cynthia and the children.

How quickly they had become such entire and dangerous creatures, these two children. How flattered she was now by their love. And was this new, or had it always been so? Even in that other world, that strange dark young world of make-believe and escape, world of vast extremes in which she had been their friend? Now she remembered a shop they had once in a dark loft—their own loft. Their very gentle small hands, animal gentle, as they caught her hand to bring her and show her. Simon's simple embrace turned at the last moment into an effort to see if he could lift her. The elaborate mounting of a ladder. Then the telephone. Shut down the trap-door so that you can *only* hear by telephone. Speak softly. You will really hear. The exciting unreality of it—thinking of different things to say to each. Their pleased, eager replies. Her wonder. Then—the shop. Melted boiled sweets in little pots. A mouth-organ. Book markers— paper cat's heads. We can make you more *easily*. Tiny lavender bags squeezed into tight little stomachs. A tooth paste carton. Post cards. Look, isn't that funny? "LOVE FROM THE WHOLE D—— FAMILY." A frieze of postcards and cut out pictures running round the wall of the loft. But these are not for sale. The elaborate descent of the ladder. A pale donkey below. *How* do you jump up on her. It's quite easy now, but first I tried and tried and tried the whole summer through. The thing was that she still felt with them as she had then. To her their present world was as full of fantasy and sustained pretence as the time of that shop had been. It was as real to them and she was as much outside it as she had been then. Although she could not understand she respected the reality of their attitude. She did not ask to have it explained any more than she would have asked them to explain to her the use and sense of that telephone. She was entirely detached from them and because of this there was no bitter familiarity between them. She was content to love and fear them a little.

Dear Cynthia—beloved creature. . . . Diana turned in her bed to face the open window opposite, and the full dark, most despairing hour of winter and morning. In her thought of Cynthia tears came piercingly behind her eyes, rolling their shaped and definite course down her cheeks. . . . Ah, but these tears are pearl that thy love sheds and they are rich and ransom all ill deeds. . . . The pain of such tears if they can be shed for another, the helpless fear for which they spring and fall, the darkness they accept, the love they spend as on the idlest air, from this, their very quality of selflessness, they must go uncomforted, their pain unrequited.

XXXIV

THERE was to be a party at Garonlea for Simon's coming of age. Cynthia was far more excited about it than either Simon or Susan. Simon froze quite still and cold and then turned hot and fluttering inside at the thought of making speeches, this in spite of all his grand airs of detachment and toleration. But this could hardly be called excitement. When Susan thought of her cousins Nancy and Cecily who were coming to stay (they were Enid's daughters) and of the smart young men that Cynthia would ask, she felt quite despairing.

It was curious how easily the young were overcome. Now the thought of Muriel and Violet and Enid and their husbands all being at Garonlea for nearly a week did not trouble Cynthia at all.

Then Simon gave the party a sudden kick that landed it in Drama. He opened a telegram that was brought to him in the library after tea, and read its clear delightful message to himself through and across all the fragments of talk that were going on round him.

"——Yes, I'll give you his address, Muriel. He makes up one's own tweed for five guineas——"

"——I do think Simon has such a look of Mother sometimes——"

"——A delightful little place. Quite unspoilt——"

"——Of course the exchange was in your favour——"

"——The waiter was so thoughtful. 'This cream bun *can't* hurt, Madam,' he said——"

245

"——I followed him through some long grass. It was ticklish work. Now and then you'd see a spot of dried blood on a leaf, or a pile of fresh dung——"

"——Give me a mashie, I said. Not that club, you fool——"

"——It's worth knowing, if you ever strain a riding muscle, you cross the handkerchief like this, knot it and go once round your leg and once round your waist——"

"——These *lavages* are tremendously important, he says, so I go to this woman twice a week. Unpleasant yes—but not really painful——"

"Look, Sue," Simon said, showing her the wire.

"Oh, Simon, what a lovely saviour."

Simon said to Cynthia, "My friend Sylvester Browne would like to come and stay."

It was exactly as if he had said, my friend John Gielgud or my friend Noel Coward would like to come and stay. It was all very well for Sylvester's intimates in London to call him old Sylvester and say between themselves that the poor old thing could be a bit embarrassing at times. Or, "We *can't* be very pleased with Sylvester for that." But they did not deny his moments in which the acidity and spark of life, the depth and the laughter and the truth and sentimentality that were in his plays and in himself went beyond even the most ungenerous praise. So when Simon said in that after tea hour, "Sylvester Browne is coming to stay," reactions of all sorts went rippling round the room.

Cynthia thought, "How old is he? Quite old enough —thirty-seven? Thirty-eight? I'll have that lovely brandy up. Wouldn't have wasted it on Arthur. My white dress with the hood—pearls."

Simon was quite stilled with pleasure. He had

always wanted to have Sylvester at Garonlea, and now in this early autumn seemed the very best time. He had not asked him either. He had never thought he knew him enough.

Sue thought, "Perfect! How lovely for Simon and me."

The others talked.

Uncle Arthur said, "I went to a play of his once. Cecily took me. Thought it would be a suitable play for Father. Never was so bored in my life. I like a good musical show. Nothing highbrow. What was this about, Cecil?"

Cecily was furious. Sylvester was one of her shrines and she had very few. She said loudly, "Incest and adultery. Don't you remember?"

Quickly quickly Violet, the trained and gracious lady, said, "It always seems to me such a pity all these unpleasant plays. And why do they write them, I wonder, when a good clean play runs for ever."

"But we went to a charming play of his together, Violet. All about the Tyrol." Muriel spoke up for her shrine.

Simon said, "When a faded lady found love among the Eidelweiss. I always thought that was rather naughty of Sylvester."

And Cecily's play had been about a horsey outdoor girl and her romance with a French Vicomte. Cecily and Nancy kept a riding school near Cheltenham where they had been to school. So they were all busy making little arrangements in their own minds about how they would impress Sylvester and how they would see themselves one day in his plays. Every one except Sue and Diana. Well, Sylvester was used to it and anyhow Simon had not asked him to come to this dreadful party.

He arrived by train because he hated driving his car. Simon and Sue did not go out cub-hunting because they both wanted to meet him at the station. They were not a bit shy or compressed in their greetings and roared with laughter when it appeared that he had no idea there was a party of this sort going on at Garonlea.

"We thought you came to help with the speeches to the faithful tenantry," Sue said.

"No," Sylvester said, "I really came more to escape from my cousin, Piggy Brown, than for anything else. I thought you would make a nice change," he said to Simon.

"Yes. But there are lots of cousins here."

"We won't have to contend with them. I want to see your house."

"The house itself isn't good, but all round is nice," Simon said vaguely. "Isn't good" was the worst abuse he could bear to level at Garonlea's spread of battlements and turretings.

"The house is heaven by me," Sylvester said when he saw it. "It's my architecture of the moment. I hope the inside décor is in keeping."

"Well, no, Mamma has made that rather comfortable and modern."

"Oh no. Cream distemper and Flower Pieces and hunting prints and vellum lamp-shades by Lionel Edwards and trays for drinks?"

"Very nearly."

"Tweed sofa covers, or gay chintzes?"

"Still gay chintz."

"I expect you have black floating bowls with two roses and frog on the dining-room table."

"No, that's wrong. Diana makes nice plans about the flowers."

"Would she be a cousin too?"

248

"No. An aunt who lives with us."

"The only thing against her is that she thinks Mamma is too superb."

"Does she really, Sue? Or does she just try to defend her from you?"

"No, it's always been like that, hasn't it, Simon?"

"Yes, but we don't mind. Mamma is her romance in life."

"This is lovely," Sylvester said, "I could sit here for ever in the sun surveying this gorgeous piece of well-cared-for Gothic."

They had stopped opposite the hall door but none of them showed the smallest intention of getting out of the car.

XXXV

IT was the same sort of afternoon as that on which Cynthia had come to see Lady Charlotte dying or dead and to make her first act of possession at Garonlea. Now the house seemed fatter and sleeker. Its mullions and turrets more tigerishly striped and spread with red creepers. The falling terraces below richer far with flowers. Behind the windows and within the open door there was a great feeling of opulent and spacious occupation. On that long past day the trees and laurels and rhododendrons had pressed dark and close round the house. Now they had been cleared back and back—cut down and entirely subdued from forest. Near the house sunlight poured on flat grass and on groups of blue hydrangeas and thickets of red-hot pokers. It lay the length of the opened bank of valley as hotly as in July. Black cattle standing close together in a ring of chestnut trees looked as if they were all carved from the same block and not yet unjoined from it. There was a shaken air of blue where the half turned bracken and the woods sloped down and up.

"Sumptuous—that's what it is," Sylvester said. "Your Mamma must be a remarkable woman. I came here once, you know, in old Lady Charlotte's time."

"You never told us that."

"But I was too young to enjoy it properly. I wish now I could remember."

"Perhaps it will come back to you."

"I don't think somehow there will be very much to suggest the house as it was then."

"We don't remember. We were too small."

"We lived at Rathglass across the river."

"Nice?"

"Very nice, I think, but we were such dreadfully unhappy children."

"Always sick."

"Always diarrhœa."

"Hated our ponies."

"Hopeless with our dogs."

"Starved our rabbits."

"Obeyed our governesses."

"Implicitly."

"I was a queasy sort of child myself. I don't think it counts. Look what lovely people we grow to be."

"I suppose we must face going in some time."

"Sometime always comes."

Sue sang:

> "I shall never forget when the big ship was ready,
>   The time drew near for my love to depart.
> I cried like a coney and said Good-bye, Teddy,
>   A tear in my eye and a stone in my heart."

"Yes, sometimes always comes," Sylvester said when the song was over. "Well, shall we?"

They went into the library full of a quantity of things. Pink lilies arranged with a shrub that grew pink marabout brushes. The smell of beastly Turkish cigarettes. The smell of expensive hair stuff. The smell of new *Tatlers* and *Bystanders* and *Sketches*, (for it was a Wednesday), and, to forget smells for a moment, the presences of Violet and Enid and Arthur and Lord Jason Helvick.

251

"Yes, really rather wonderful, five guineas to make up your own tweed——"

"——Twice a week. Unpleasant of course, but *not* really painful."

Violet and Enid were going on again about their little men who made up tweed and their little women who did unspeakable things to you twice a week, unpleasant but not really painful.

Arthur was telling Jason about a mahseer he caught in a river in India. Jason was far away in mind thinking about the habits of the lesser Plaitabils and of a photograph he had once almost succeeded in taking of the parent bird at feeding time. Everybody else was having a late meal after cub-hunting.

Violet began very capably to Sylvester about people they knew. Arthur went on at the top of his voice with his story about the mahseer, hoping the actor johnny would somehow be a little impressed.

Sue said, "Uncle Jason, you aren't listening to one word Uncle Arthur's saying to you." Lady Charlotte could not have spoilt poor Arthur's anecdote more completely.

Presently Cecil and Nancy and two indefensibly smart young men called Acres, John and Tony Acres, second cousins of Cynthia's, came in—still very much in their breeches and boots. They were introduced to Sylvester and at once began to read the *Tatler* and *Sketch* and the *Bystander* to show they weren't gaping at Fame or being unduly impressed. Cecil was particularly casual. She was a romantic secret young creature behind her extreme love of dogs and horses. Quite as passionate as Enid had been in youth, but with more possibilities of sublimation. She had Enid's pretty forehead and her eyes but mercifully none of those unhappy spots.

Into the extreme heart of this room came Cynthia. Her life and distance from these older peaceful women, fulfilled with their acceptance of triviality, satisfied by their small concerns, and from those two younger ones, choice examples as they were of England's out-door girlhood, and full of rather pathetic striving toward a complacency they had not achieved, was at once real and remarkable to Sylvester. Compared to them it was as if a ring of fire burned round Cynthia, so complete was the division. Then she was more swift and easy and vague in speech. Unlike those girls, she had found time to change after hunting. Her hair superbly waved, the expensive flattering clothes—so far from the natty things the little men ran up for five guineas—emphasised all this difference. Besides she had had a couple of drinks and been kissed in a wood this morning by a daring and common man who had come from Yorkshire to buy horses. "I'm absolutely on the bit this morning, that's how I feel," he said. Cynthia gave him a sort of hard detached encouragement, agreeing with herself almost imper-sonally that he was most attractive, that was how she had grown about men now. She had other lovers since David had really left her, but at least she did not often romanticize her relationships with them.

——Simon might say sourly, "Mamma's admirers scarcely improve, do they? I mean I really am rather a snob at heart and I do mind."

But Sylvester said, "In a way, you know, I think it's rather royal of her. She could so easily stick to her own class."

"But I do mind," Simon said again. "Has she made passes at you yet?"

"You embarrass me, Simon. How could I compete with a gorgeous horsey creature like that?"

It was the evening of the second day of Sylvester's visit. He and Simon were walking over to Rathglass to meeet Diana who had been gardening. Over the river they were in that different air of Rathglass. Here the autumn seemed less opulent, of a thinner quality than at Garonlea. It was a slight shock to see trees taking shape again. A group of ash trees posing their new nakedness in an extremity of grace and affectation against a still dark wood. Limbs turned divinely. So much, so far too much has been written about the autumn. Fur and flesh. Ducks and shrivelled leaves. Level winds as flat as ribbons. Seagulls sitting on little fields—domestic inland birds heavy as pigeons. New grass, greener than spring time grass. Food and death for fat little birds. All these curious autumnal contrasts were in the evening as Sylvester and Simon walked on together towards Rathglass.

They did not talk any more about Cynthia. Sylvester guessed that Simon was thinking if he said any more he would become over confidential and perhaps a little embarrassing. Sylvester was feeling his way about Cynthia. He thought she would perhaps be good in one of his plays but he was terrified of encouraging any of her advances. Already she had made what Simon called a pass. A pass for sympathy it had been. A sort of Queen Lear pose about Simon and Garonlea. He could see that Simon was going to have hell if he wanted Cynthia out of Garonlea. If he wanted her to take herself and her horrible boy friends and that perfect dear Diana off to Rathglass and leave him and Sue to live together at Garonlea, marriage was really his only chance of avoiding unbearable scenes and woundings. But Sylvester did not think Simon or Susan would marry for a long time. They seemed to him as sexless as two jade doves swung in two silver wire rings. He wondered how much Susan understood about Cynthia's really rather skilfully decorous rioting with her lovers. Almost as much, he supposed, as Simon could understand the agony of potency in an old woman. Old? Not old. But however smooth and full the skin and restrained the figure, forty-five to fifty is old, horribly old to go looking for love—to have still unfulfilled that fever in the blood and through it to encourage the advances of tough men like this present admirer whose name Sylvester could not quite recall. How many like this had Simon seen? Just how arid and revolting did it all appear to him? Knowing a little of his feeling for Garonlea and for Sue, Sylvester realised that Cynthia would be quite beyond his pity.

They had a nice walk back to Garonlea with Diana who was particularly satisfied after such a time at Rathglass, warm and companionable. Talking to her and looking at her thin happy face Sylvester felt very glad that there were women in the world who found such contentment in things and places. Among the happy old maids he found some of the people he liked best in life. There was an unspent sweetness, an ungiven power of loving in Diana that was not sad and ingrown but within and about her, a thing both romantic and attractive. She had none of that sourness so often evident in those who lead unselfish lives. She had dignity and balance and no affectation. He was not surprised that Susan and Simon should be so fond of her. And he thought her devotion to Cynthia both natural and uncomplicated by any curious inhibitions.

In the course of his career as a playwright and player, Sylvester had seen many women fall for him. In the way old women worship doctors, he would say; a *little* difficult, he would say. But he was not often as unkind to them as he sounded. Impelled possibly by his morbidly simple sense of humour, partly by curiosity and by his perpetual discovery or fabrification of drama, he was given to the collection of rare and rich and if possible, eccentric old women. He would dine with them and listen unwearied to their stories of dead loves, dead injuries, unforgotten spites, old wills. He revelled in their rich clothes and food and wine.

And to his old ladies naturally he was the luxury of romance personified. They idolised him, went to all his first nights, struggled to understand what his plays were about, and never told him how much they preferred a nice costume piece. But all this he knew and would put the right words about his work into their hesitating praise, and if he took them to the theatre, would select one of their favourite dramas in which the gentlemen in the cast could be relied on to wear tights and the ladies to have bosoms. He was very valuable to them and it was only fair in return that he should be able to entertain his friends by the faithful repetition of their shattering aphorisms and the curious fetishes they would discover to him when a little in wine.

Such ladies he could contend with and enjoy. But the Cynthias were in another category. Try as he might he could not find them very amusing. Even as copy for some reason seldom useful. It was the more distressing to him that Cynthia with all her obvious and shockingly frequent moods for love should have about her that spark of reality, that undeniable fire of life which compelled his attention. He could not avoid his own interest in her. She captured his imagination. And he felt the pity for her that Simon obviously would never feel. He profoundly admired her attitude towards Simon's loyal tenantry and all the men at Garonlea of whom, what with servants' balls and presentations, they saw a good deal those days. Her quite royal absence of graciousness or any Lady of the Manor tricks, seemed to him most estimable. He thought, seeing the strength and dark good looks of some of the young retainers, that it was perhaps a pity that the *droit du seigneur* could not be recalled and reversed in this instance. It was a curiously wild thought but he imagined with Cynthia such a situation might have tremendous simplicity and success. . . . Possibly his inspiration came from the lovely brandy, or from the showery falling fireworks in the still first cold of the hollow autumn skies, from the bonfires and barrels of stout, from all the feeling of inheritance and forgotten powers that Cynthia seemed to personify so much more really than Simon.

XXXVI

THE festivities exhausted Simon and made him feel taut and nervous, so that in the intervals he took no ease and found his uncles and aunts and cousins quite hateful, and his mother's friend, Reuben Hill (he was staying at Garonlea now so they had been forced to know his name at last) beyond his endurance. It seemed to him past anything. That she had not been able to resist having this man here now was the crown and summit of the reality and unreality of her queenship at Garonlea. The superb insolence to Garonlea and its two assembled generations. The superb success of the insolence, for the Uncles and Aunts thought him charming and those two girls of Enid's and the smart chaps talked to him ceaselessly about their horses and had lots of jokes with him all the time. He was easier than Sylvester. None of them had begun to get near enough to Sylvester to bore or aggravate him.

But it all got tremendously on Simon's nerves.

So many things at Garonlea happened in the Library. Now the room was full of easiness to such an extent that the air was squalid with it. Everybody said what they liked there after they had had a drink or two. Cynthia arranged so that even Muriel should drink up a little before dinner. Trembling inside her silvery velvet, Muriel grew daring enough to say to Sylvester, "Of all your plays I think perhaps I like best 'Grey Morning.'"

"Ah, did you?" he said. Then finding geniality, for

258

it did seem a shame to distress her, "I'm so glad. Very few people really enjoyed it. I liked it myself quite a lot——" ——What was he saying? That awful unmeaning bit of success.

"Indeed I did. It seemed so kind and so true."

To the women who have little flats in big buildings? To the women who have had no love at all? Yes, they had been a good and paying public. And this gentle creature who had been turned away from everything all her life thanked him for them. Sylvester felt rather ashamed. Perhaps a little crucifixion would do his soul good.

"Tell me which of my other plays you liked," he said gently.

Cecil, the one in blue taffeta—a girl is always safe in blue if she has blue eyes—was trying to talk to Simon. She could only talk about horses so far as she had gone in life, and now she was saying, "I'm not really a good judge of a horse in the rough."

"Aren't you?" Simon said. Behind all such nonsense the room was full of the scent of lilies, heavy yet coming sharply. He tried to keep himself sensible of it.

"That was a pretty gay tie you wore to-day," she said. He didn't realise she was trying desperately for something to say.

"Yes, isn't it amusing? It's a ballet colour." That will put her off. Her and her nasty rough horses, he thought viciously. He was right, it left her with nothing to say, mute in her blue taffeta.

Enid, who was telling somebody about the only efficient electric toaster, saw her child's embarrassment with Simon. As across the world the ghost of a sensation came back to her. Raging impotence to make oneself understood in this room. "Yes, I'll give you the address, it really is worth knowing. One just pops the slice of bread in and it's really such *fun*——" but the draught from elsewhere had chilled her warm and ordered preservation of content. She called across several people to Cecil:

"Darling, did you like that horse you rode to-day?"

Cecil shot a furious look across the room. They never allowed their mother to talk about horses. There was hardly a subject in life in which they did not find her ignorant, confused and tiresome, but about horses most of all.

"So next season you are to be presented, Susan? Won't that be thrilling?" Violet's placid voice would have made an expedition to Tibet sound tame. The pomp of courts was as nothing. Of them all she who had least suffered in that room seemed the one most steeped in its past air. "I was so excited when Granny presented me. Queen Alexandra looked so beautiful and she gave me quite a little smile, I remember. And I smiled back, which Granny said was rather a little breach of etiquette."

"And did you go to a lovely party afterwards?"

"Oh, no, dear. We went home to bed. I was quite tired out by the excitement."

"Simon and Sylvester are going to take me out," Susan said grandly.

Simon heard this and smiled to her. "And Diana too," he said, "she's to have a new dress, the smartest model in London."

Diana went over to him, and Sue, thinking that Aunt Violet had deadened her enough, came and sat on the other arm of his chair and sipped his sherry. The three of them made rather an insolent and secret looking group.

Cynthia came in late, partly to make a little stir,

partly because she was the person behind all the smooth running of this party and these celebrations. Her evident beauty and evident content seemed very strong in comparison to Muriel's pathetic tinkling vicarious ways of talking or living.

"I'm terribly late. I must be forgiven. It's not really my fault. You see, people come to me to arrange everything," she said to Sylvester. "Something had gone wrong about the fireworks."

"Are we having more fireworks? How delicious!"

"Oh, of course that was last night. No, it wasn't the fireworks, but they make plans and then when they are failures I have to do it all."

Extraordinary the illusion of youth and helplessness that she maintained with all that efficiency. And boasted efficiency. She was wearing a white satin dress with a sort of hood at the back and lots of pearls. Her face was painted so smoothly, it looked as clean as ice. Her vitality made all the people in the room seem less than they were. Because she only wanted to speak to Sylvester he felt quite alone with her. That frightened him of her strength. And she was so interesting.

"May I ask you something, Sylvester?" she said.

"Please."

"I have wanted to ask you so much how this house seems to you?"

"It seems just like you."

"You knew it before?"

"It was just like Lady Charlotte, I think. But I was so very ignorant and young."

"I'm terribly interested to know how it feels to you now."

Praise, that was what she was looking for. Only praise. Should he say, "It feels like an expensive country club?" He said instead, "It's the Ritz for comfort."

That was enough. She didn't see much beyond that.

"Shall I tell you what it was like when Diana and I came here? No lighting or heating. Tepid bath water at the best. All the wall-paper dark green or dark red. Festoons of red velvet curtains, tassels, fringes. In this room seventeen 'occasional' tables besides big ones and a vase of flowers on each one."

"Fancy!" Sylvester felt that his exclamation was conjured from that same past. An emanation from the ghost of an asparagus fern.

"That was what it was like. Really. And the atmosphere, I can't tell you."

"Mutton chop whiskers, family prayers, dead wishes." He gave her the three rather obviously.

"It stank of all that. And unhappiness." For a minute she became less boastful and sank her voice down so that they seemed more alone. "They were all so unhappy. They could not escape from it—Muriel and Enid and Diana."

"They seem easy enough now."

"Yes, you see that? There was triumph. She had partly made and partly been given her point. "And because the house is changed. I said I could do it and even Diana said it was impossible."

"Diana hated it most, I expect."

"I took her away from here. It nearly broke her heart making her come back."

"And now, even Diana?"

"Even Diana—yes. Even Diana is happy."

"To change a place—a whole world of tradition! Weren't you afraid of so much power?"

"You see I did it when I was too unhappy to be afraid of anything," Cynthia said.

And he had thought she only minded about the comfort and efficiency of it all. The warmth and endless bath water and soft beds, flowers, wine and cream distemper. But there was more than that. It had been a spiritual contest. She had not been unconscious of the animosity walled and closed in Garonlea.

"Why did you want to change it so much?"

"For Simon and Susan, you know. I couldn't endure for them to grow up in the house as it was."

"Really for them you wanted to change it so completely?"

"Well, I hadn't much other reason, had I? Not much left then——"

She moved away from him on that unemphasized note and took up the thread of a joke with Reuben Hill—a good joke probably. What a victory hers had been over Garonlea. Really rather superb.

XXXVII

At dinner time he sat beside Diana.

"Cynthia has been telling me how you first came back here,' he said. "I'm enthralled. I want to get hold of it all. I've never seen any one so completely at the top of success as she is."

Diana said, "You know I adore Cynthia, but I'm going to say something too extraordinary. I'm more frightened for her than I've ever been."

"Frightened?" He looked up and down the long table in the warm emptied room. He saw everything of her making; space, warmth, delicate and luxurious food; the party she had called into being sitting round contented and well entertained; her children, interesting and decorative. Last he saw herself. She seemed a long way off at the head of the table. She had gathered that white hood round the back of her head. It was a sort of nimbus behind her strong, her pathetically endless beauty. That was it. If only she could end her beauty, and the life behind it, she might come to some sort of peace. As it was she could never put the power of living behind her.

"Why are you so frightened for her? You must tell me."

"Because I think she's done everything. I think she's come to an end."

"You must tell me more."

"I can't now. You're the only person I've ever wanted to discuss it with."

"Would I be any use?"

264

"Oh, I think so."

Diana did not say any more then. Once or twice during dinner he thought she looked across the table at Reuben Hill with an expression of fear and dislike. Probably that was how she had doubted and disliked all Cynthia's lovers. There of course he was wrong.

Later in the evening he listened to a curious three-sided argument which took place between Cynthia and Reuben and Enid's Cecil.

Cecil and Reuben were having one of those dreary arguments about whether women should or should not ride in point-to-points, other than in Ladies' races. Reuben was hotly against it and Cecil spoke up for it as though it was her only creed or idea of value in living. He had not observed that spark and determination about her before, only that she was a pale lengthy creature with dark hair and rather surprising blue eyes, whom he avoided because he knew how endlessly she talked about horses. Horses in sickness and in health, their bits, bridles and accoutrements, their habits and peculiarities, engaging and otherwise. He did not wish to speak to her himself but he did not mind listening to any passionate discourse addressed to some one else. Another thing he observed, that Reuben's arguments were produced and upheld only to spur this furious child towards further self-revealings. It was when things were going really well that Cynthia joined in, sounding her lazy queen-like note of authority on Reuben's side of the argument.

"But, darling, aren't you a tiny bit talking nonsense? I mean really it's a question of sheer physical strength."

"No, not entirely, Aunt Cynthia. I mean, were all the good jockeys you've known strong men?"

"I maintain you girls mustn't ride against us boys

racing. Because you might defeat us and that would be bad." Reuben lit a cigarette and Cynthia went on:

"Really darling, I think, jokes aside, we must leave the chaps their racing. We can't compete."

"I don't see a bit why not."

"Perhaps when you've had more experience——"

"How much experience of riding point-to-points did you have, Aunt Cynthia, before you knew you were no good?"

It was an extraordingary rude little speech but delivered with so much earnestness, a direct question to Authority and to the Past, that it was stripped of insolence. It was simply cruel. Sylvester saw Cynthia grow very slowly red—an old and unbecoming red— before she said:

"In my day we found hunting five days a week just about all we wanted."

Then he realised that Cynthia had never competed in a race of any sort and, most strange most pitiful fact, was ashamed of this. And was it necessary for Simon to slip himself lazily into the conversation to ask:

"How many delicious Ladies' Races have you won, Cecil? Dozens, haven't you?"

"No, only seven."

"Well, that's seven more than most of us. But apparently not enough to prove to you you're silly to try."

Reuben looked at Cecil quickly. "You sly little devil," he said, "I didn't know you were an expert."

It was a slight matter enough to bring that look of complete animal fear across Cynthia's face. Sylvester thought that never before had he seen fear of what must be written so desolatingly on a face. That and a blind refusal and lack of understanding or acceptance.

266

Was this the sort of catastrophe that Diana feared? Had she heard? Had she seen? Did she know those other lines, "Lady, the bright day is done and we are for the dark——"

Diana had seen. She had seen what she had been watching for all that day, ever since a blush and a giggling whisper of Cecil's had set her wondering. She had seen what for years she had known must one day happen. Cynthia would lose a man to youth. She would be defeated by that lost thing strong and present in another.

"Why hasn't it happened before?" she said to Sylvester.

"Are you sure we aren't wildly exaggerating?"

"Of course it is a trival thing, looked at coldly."

"But who's looking at it coldly? If you look at it at all it's a shattering thing. Don't say excusing things like 'looked at coldly,' they mean nothing at all, do they?"

"I was only trying to be moderate."

"Need you be moderate with me?"

They were in the old schoolroom, the room where so many thousands of years ago Enid's drama with poor Arthur had filled the air surging full. The little piano (not even its ghost left here) had shaken to her vibrations. The air had stilled and frozen about her while they fitted that trousseau on her unresistant body, locking all the desperate doors in her mind. Everything was changed. There was no single object to recall the room as it had been. Not a book of girlish adventure—not a photograph of Violet in her Court feathers. There were now low, long chairs and a sofa on which you almost lay upon the floor, pale grey walls and one large and lovely flower piece in a white frame. There was an urn-like vase of different purple flowers of contrasting textures, the feathers of Michaelmas daisies, the flesh of dahlias, a well-shaped decoration.

Diana said:

"It's very curious your being here now to help me. I've never had any help about Cynthia before."

"I've gathered so little from Simon. I think he feels rather violently about her."

"You see she was so cruel to them when they were little. I must speak the truth about her."

"Yes. If I'm to be the smallest good."

Diana leaned forward, looking into Sylvester's face, who sat in the low chair opposite to her. He seemed longer even than its length allowed for, leaning back and stooping his head forward towards his eternally long fingers, fish bones picked by sea-birds they suggested. His face was very gentle and interested. She knew that it would be completely safe for her to abuse Cynthia to him without apology. He knew and understood enough of her love.

"It seems simple enough to me now," Diana said, "though I couldn't see it as it happened. When Desmond was killed she had nothing left. She simply was in a desert—salt water to drink. She had the hounds. She always has been marvellous about that, but what I am saying——"

"You said, 'she had the hounds.' I thought it sounded rather a far-fetched substitute."

"Yes, but it was occupation, exhausting occupation."

"Ah, yes."

"Of course, she should have married again. But really, she couldn't then. No, it wasn't all vanity and thinking herself a queen. Not then."

"I do easily see that."

"And having the children so unlike her or Desmond

268

was somehow terrible to her. I think almost as if they were a little monstrous. Can you understand that, Sylvester?"

"She had to torture them into some sort of likeness of the children she wanted for Desmond."

"The poor little things. They were so frightened. I used to feel ill myself I was so sorry for them. And the best I could do was to do nothing."

"And outside that—all the time her queendom kept swelling and growing?"

"It was—it is—extraordinary how people do really worship her."

"And when she got here at last—was it interest or only revenge, all she has done here?"

"First one, then the other. She could not work herself hard enough for both. She just went on in a way that would have killed any one with less strength and vitality."

"And she won?"

"In an outward sort of way, yes, I think she won. She imposed her will on the place, and it's the strongest will that has ever ruled here, except perhaps my mother's."

"Do you ever feel, Diana, that there's still a sort of contest going on between them? Between Cynthia and your mother?—Child, don't look so terrified."

"I'm not frightened really. I'm so used to the idea. It's always behind everything. And the tremendous will of the place against her too. I do know about that because all my life I've known it and hated it."

"But what a victory! One can't get away from it. And she has been happy here with other men, I gather. And avoided fatalities?"

"I don't know. I think the first—David—she really minded about. But he was so hopeless and uncertain."

"Did you like him?"

"I couldn't have liked him more. The children were devoted to him too. He could have made Cynthia's life all right again. But he just didn't want to enough. He simply left her. Once she recovered from that. I thought the—what was the word you said?—the fatality of Garonlea would get her down over that. But it didn't. Quite soon she was happy with some one else, or seemed content. She'd have stayed content enough if David hadn't come back. Then her vanity got the better of her; she thought she could have everything her own way. But David didn't last and her American never came back. She'd hurt him too much, I expect."

"Since then?"

"Since then she's been just hard and silly and terribly vulgar. *How* she gets away with it!"

"Doing things like having that present fancy here with Violet and Muriel."

"Hundreds of things like that. And always thinks she can't be detected or defeated."

"It's a distressing situation. Ageing beauty. Sad enough when cold. Terrific when incontinent. Can no one tell her how unattractive and hopeless it all is? But of course not. She's very beautiful really and as strong as a horse."

"I think before long Simon will tell her," Diana's voice was strained and small when she said this.

"You'd like to spare her that if possible."

"You may think me altogether too romantic, but, you see, Cynthia has given me all the happiness I ever had in life. Really she has. I'd like to spare her that if there was any way I could."

The fire in the little room had died down long ago.

270

It was cold with the weak, enveloping chill of very early day.

"What would you say she feared most, Diana? Could anything make her see herself truly? Even for a moment?"

"She's afraid of age and she's afraid of defeat."

"If the possibility—the certainty of both, were brought home to her once, really cruelly and consciously, what would she do?"

"Immediately, I don't know. Presently I think she and I would go and live at Rathglass again."

"Rathglass again." Obviously Diana had no truer idea of happiness. He understood it and envied her. It was strangely moving to find a person capable of almost hysterical love for a place. Blessed in its air and earth. At peace in its service.

"Oh, I do believe, Sylvester, if I could get Cynthia away from Garonlea, that even Simon might like her better."

"Yes, it's possible. And Susan?"

"Susan is simply in Simon's hands."

"I think those two have a queer story in front of them, you know. And Sue is ravishing—or going to be. No, is."

"Simon reminds me of Mother. Sometimes—about Sue——"

"How dangerous."

"Dangerous! If you knew Garonlea half as well as I do, you'd know there was danger round every corner and behind every shut door in the house. And not asleep either. Look! This room—goodness knows it is changed from what it was when we were young, nothing the same. But Enid came in here to-day and she couldn't stay in here—even Enid—it's too full of her own unhappiness and despair."

Enid and her electric toasters and her wonderful little men, had she ever despaired? It must be so or Diana would not have spoken as savagely of such a time. Sylvester thought if he had ever seen truth unstrained and unexaggerated it was in Diana. She seemed to him to be altogether truthful and sane.

XXXVIII

But it is the wet afternoons in life that are responsible for so much with their interminable dangerous leisure. It rained at Garonlea on the day after Sylvester and Diana had talked so long. It rained and stormed and blew quite preposterously. Swollen leaves as big as birds and birds as big as boats were flung along the wind across a sky full of rain. There could be no question of going out of doors. Every one sat about, growing more cross and liverish with each paper they read, and each hour that passed. Those who could have a nice drink now and then were the only people who had anything to look forward to. Those who forbade themselves this relaxation from principle or because they didn't like drinking or its effect, grew waspish as well as liverish. In the hour succeeding luncheon, the library was full of edgy people, stuffed with food and inclined for either sleep or argument, but not for pleasant intercourse with their friends.

Only Violet and poor Arthur seemed to be enjoying themselves. They were playing a game they both understood—its point lay in looking up people in *Debrett* or *Who's Who*, that they did not think could possibly be there. Violet stitched away placidly at her tapestry, for it was a long game and required some such occupation. —"Look up so and so. Can't you find him? Isn't that rather odd?"

"How old is her eldest daughter? Look her up. She's sure to be in it. Really not?—How very funny."

"I must look up old Johnny Hood—dearest chap—

don't you know him?—Now that really is odd, isn't it?"

Simon said presently, "For two such awful snobs it is surprising how many common people you know. Are none of your friends socially O.K.?"

Enid's Cecil was writing a letter. She said to Reuben Hill, "But how shall I ask him?"

"Write and ask him nicely."

"How do you mean—'nicely'?"

"Well, you might say, 'I'm coming to stay with you.'"

"Is that nice?"

"I'd think so."

"Who minds what you think?"

Sue was telling one of her stories about a party: "He took me out to dine at Boddinino's and as it was Sunday they shut down too soon. So he collected a party to go on to a night-club. There was the Pro dancer and the dancer in the cabaret whom he was in love with, and her partner—a Russian peasant—and the head waiter and a man who was in love with the dancer in the cabaret too. They were the most boring possible collection of people. I had no latch-key so I had to wait for him to want to come home."

Cecily's sister Nancy was telling Simon a long, long story about a horse and the queer things she did to its hocks.

"Where are its hocks?" he said at last, as if he said, "Whereabouts is Bokhara?"

"Oh, those things with knobs. Yes, yes, I know. We ought to have dummies really that we could talk to about our horses and bore as much as we liked."

"Simon," Sylvester said, "you do keep this party in a roar, don't you?"

"Very well, I will," Simon said, "then every one will

hate me more than they do now. Listen! Who votes for a nice game of Hide and Seek?"

Sylvester said, "I do. I feel wonderfully light on my feet." Some words of Diana's, spoken the night before, came flying into his mind—Danger. Behind every shut door in the house . . . and not asleep either. Where so well as in the course of such a game could one see and feel the atmosphere in unused rooms and stuffed, airless attics? The very fact of being fugitive, or seeking, hunting or pursued, lent an antic isolation to such a spying out, such a ghost-smelling as this might be.

Other people thought it might be fun too. Cecil's eyes sparkled with old memories of turret-rooms and little dark staircases known to her as a child. Reuben Hill was as keen as a kite for any hearty games. Arthur was delighted that the young should be removed as there were at least three picture-papers he hadn't been able to see. The two smart young men said it would be exercise. Sue said it was the most boring, awful game possible, but she knew an attic with a good key that was full of old *Punches*, "and there's a very nice book there, too, I often read," she said, "called *Till the Doctor comes*."

Enid did not raise her eyes from the rather daring novel she was reading, neither for nearly ten minutes did she turn a page.

There was one person who wished with raging impotence that the game had not been thought of— Cynthia. She was not going to go bouncing and screaming about the attics. That was not her type of youthfulness. At the same time, she was not going to be out of things. "Well, I thought a nice game of bridge," she said. She put out her cigarette and considered the party without haste. "You'll play,

275

Reuben, of course. And Arthur? Violet, would you care for a game?"

It was so little. It was so much. A tremendous misjudgment. A gross imposition of will. Or simply the slightest demand of a hostess to a guest whom she knew to be her best and readiest bridge-player. But Sylvester thought she looked rather tight about the lips as she went across the room. She opened the lid of a big lacquer box and stood staring into it for longer than was necessary to take out cards and bridge markers. He was quite right. She was shaken and hardly knew what she was doing.

The rest of the party trailed rather drearily out of the room. Soon the game was in full swing, which is to say that those who had not locked themselves, nicely provided with books and cigarettes, into bathrooms and other places, were sitting in Sue's attic, taking it turn about to read aloud, *Till the Doctor comes*.

All but Sylvester who, filled now with delight now, with horror, now by a collector's frenzy for possession, took his fill of prowling in and out of those rooms, strange, full and silent, that harboured the abandoned furnishings of Garonlea. They were indeed like harbours full of old ships and ghost-ships—those rooms. Dark harbours where the sun did not shine nor the winds blow, and old ships rotted and mouldered in excruciating quietness. Once Sylvester had seen the saddest possible sight—a boat lying on its side in a shallow green estuary, its sides rotted away. He could see the water flowing through its staves like open windows. But here there was no water—only time, to rot and make an end.

But how right Cynthia had been. How terribly just and right to strip and change the house as she had done. The air of melancholy in these abandoned places seemed to him to crawl even in his hair. He sat on red plush sofas and smoked cigarettes. He counted a thousand little tables. He touched mouldered piles of velvet that gave him the recoil that the sudden touching of a still but living bat might give. He saw things that others before Cynthia must have cast away. Some gorgeous and unfaded wax fruits beneath a glass dome which he coveted. They seemed so seemly and bright here. An astrakhan cloak, moving with moths and their worms. An unbelievably elaborate and ornate bird-cage hung rusting on a wall, with all that it meant of prisoner and dead prisoner too.

And at last—it was Diana who found him—still with horror and inspiration, standing spellbound before two life-size black boys in Saxon porcelain. They wore curious, bustling sort of pale-blue kilts and white boots with tassels. They carried torches. They stood on tiptoes on heavy, elaborate pedestals.

"Diana," he said, "tell me all you know about these superb pieces. I stand simply abashed before such marvels of Rococo. At the same time I want to giggle a lot."

Diana said, "Aren't they hideous? My grandfather brought them back from Germany, I think."

"My dear, he must have had the strangest fancies."

"I don't quite follow. I think he just had very bad taste."

"Yes, of course. Exactly."

"They were almost the first things Cynthia whirled out of the library."

"Naturally. They would be. Diana, you haven't forgotten our talk last night?"

"Well, could I?"

"You may think me fantastic and mad. You may

think my idea cruel and dangerous and useless as well—
perhaps you would rather I left you out of it?"

"No, I wouldn't. I'll play." Diana sitting down on a
rigidly-curved, back-to-back sofa, its plush buttoned
a thousand times over, looked strangely weakened, as
if in this room she felt the strength of old currents
almost beyond her.

"Play-acting, Play-producing, those black boys—I
don't know what gave it to me—but this is my idea——"

"Those black boys? Oh, no, Sylvester. Don't say
things like that in dark attics—people will begin to
talk." It was Simon. He came in and sat down beside
Diana. "But what is your idea? And what have you
been doing for the last hour or so to make my party
go with a swing? Nothing. Not one merry call of
'cuckoo.' It's a shame. You're not pulling your
weight."

"Well, I've thought of something all the same. A
very good idea—for a Good Time to be had by all."

"With those two boys? Sylvester, I'm not sure
they're not pretty marvellous really. They give me
the same feeling of complete vulgarity that one has
from looking at Delysia. I'm glad they're in your idea.
Look at their boots. I think they're swell."

"Well, listen——" Sylvester spoke, and as he told his
plan the after-storm light coming so ekeingly through
the narrow mullioned windows grew less, fumbling
its way out of the unshuttered room where in the
dusk the monstrous, cluttered shapes of furniture
loomed and leaned, swelling infamously, dirty and
bubble-like, stinking feebly of moth-balls and corrup-
tion. The two black boys in their petticoats leered
unpleasingly, the last light catching an oily glimmer
on their cheek-bones and on their fat, springing calves.

Diana, from her corner of the sofa into which she

seemed to have shrunk small and brittle as a bird's bones, said:

"I think it's a terrifying idea, Sylvester. Don't let's."

"Simon, what do you think? After all, it's your house, though we do keep forgetting."

Simon was shaking a little with excitement. "I think it's wonderful," he said. "It couldn't be more exciting. Of course we'll do it. And we'll ask everybody. On Friday night—would that give us time?"

XXXIX

"——But, Simon, what can we do about our hair?"

"What about our bosoms?"

"What about our behinds?"

"We have no corsets——"

"We have no bosoms——"

"Wear hats, girls. Pad yourselves into womanhood. Use your imaginations. Have a look at those bound copies of the *Lady*."

Not a doubt about it, Simon's idea (for it had come to be called Simon's), had caught on.

—— A Period Party. '95 to '07. Come as yourselves, your Uncles or your Aunts. Dancing 10.30——

The countryside ransacked their cupboards, delved in domed boxes, fought out bitter contests for the first services of the Little Women Round the Corners. They were all coming to the party at Garonlea. Simon's party.

Yes. It was entirely Simon's party. It was some time before Cynthia took it in. Before the, "No, you mustn't bother, Mamma"—"We've seen to that"—"no. I've had a marvellous plan with Mrs. Bryant about the food"—"I won't tell you, it's to be a surprise for you too"—"Sylvester won't hunt on Friday, and we want to keep Diana"—really got home to her. When she did realise that in this scheme not only was she unwanted but unnecessary she was left with a feeling of strange disorientation and more of wonder than of bitterness. It was so long since anything at Garonlea had been carried out except by her direction and inspiration that she felt now almost as in a dream, voiceless, purposeless, but terribly resistant. Yet through it all she kept up the magnificent pretence of everything being done according to her own wish.

"Violet, Darling, shall you mind terribly if we sit in the billiard-room and schoolroom on Friday? These awful children and their mysterious decorations, you know."

"I know you don't mind, Enid. You see, I've always encouraged them so tremendously to look on the house as a place for enjoyment—not as a sort of museum in trust. I mean, if they want to break the china, let them break the china——" She was, perhaps, the only person to whom the idea of Susan and Simon breaking china did not seem a little grotesque.

"Muriel, dear, I know you don't mind."

Nobody minded. They had all caught the fever of Simon's party and thought only of the impressions they were going to make of their youth and prime.

The importance of all that was happening at Garonlea was dwarfed in Cynthia's understanding by that other terrifying thing that was happening to her at this time—the thing she fought with every powerful yet futile weapon at her command. While she refused with desperate obstinacy to admit to herself any matter for contest, no other woman could have used with less conscience her power to keep Reuben Hill and Cecil apart.

It was not that her love was involved in the matter. She had been attracted, that was all. There had been an amusing prelude to a possibly satisfying love affair with an ardent and common young man. Cynthia's world was full of such. This defence and battle were for herself alone. She could not dare to admit defeat at the hands of a girlish and earnest young creature. She fought a whole generation. She might as well have quarrelled with the tides or argued her needs out with the' winds. But from all her life there was no reason why she should be able to see this.

It was an ordinary enough little flirtation, Reuben's and Cecil's, and might have made its small progress and died its small death of inaction had it been let alone, or even encouraged. But, alas for Cynthia! she thwarted these two rather simple people at every turn and so blew up absurd fires between them. They had to make plans to meet and kiss. They knew a common enemy. Cecil giggled a little about Cynthia's age. Reuben, who was a great deal more sophisticated, did not think this so preposterous. If he had seen just a very little more of Cecil, this weapon might have turned dangerously in her silly young hand. There was in Cecil as much of that romantic incontinence as might be looked for in Enid's daughter.

After such times as that enforced game of bridge, there was terrific excitement in eyes meeting and falling across a drink at six o'clock, in small and precious plots and schemes for the evening, for the next day. Simon's party was a godsend, a milestone, a beacon in the week towards which they looked with disproportionate eagerness.

It was curious how excited everybody was over this party, as if a suddenly loosed power in the house had caught them all. Even the entirely phlegmatic Violet kept regretting that she had not brought her Madame Pompadour fancy dress with her, although everybody explained to her that she had got hold of the wrong idea. "Can't you remember what you wore in 1900, Aunt Violet? You can't have gone round as Madame Pompadour."

"Well, I don't know. I think we wore much the same sort of clothes as you do now."

"I thought you wore tea-gowns for tea."

"I don't think anybody wore tea-gowns unless they were *enceinte*." She used the word in the most delicately indecent way.

Enid said, "We always carried a fan for dances and wore gold shoes, of course, and gloves turning the elbow."

"Oh, Aunt Enid, how daring it sounds."

"Daring? I don't know. We were much the same, really, as you are now. Long skirts in the evening, you know."

"I would like to come to Simon's party in some very high corsets, to make me some bosoms, and a really tricky pair of white nainsook knickers run with black ribbon and frilled at the knees. Pads for my hair, and black silk stockings. I know I'd have the success of my life."

"I think it would be very unfunny, Sue," Simon said.

"Well, I won't, Simon. But I could have called myself a postcard from Paris. And do you remember the first bicyclists, Aunt Enid?"

"No, I don't," said Enid, sharply. Why should it appear grotesque to any one—that time of youth? These clothes that had looked so right in their own romantic period! All there seemed to say in their defence now was that they were not unlike the clothes of to-day. You could not say, "We looked lovely in those clothes. We had bosoms which attracted the gentlemen and beliefs to which we clung, we were not rude and unhappy and flat-breasted like our children." Not unhappy? The denial too was true to type and period.

Only Cynthia who had been beautiful and enor-

283

mously happy then, felt a real reluctance towards this one evening stepping back into the past. She took it all seriously and rather childishly, saying, "It's an absurd idea—it's not long enough ago." She was frightened of the travesty this would be of what she was. She would have avoided it by any means, but the general will was too strong for her.

ENID and Violet and Muriel got together about
clothes and really enjoyed themselves at last, turning
out cupboards and trunks and putting every possible
garment into an empty bedroom. Soon the bed was
up to the ceiling with its load of gored skirts and boned
and frilly bodices. There were clutches of rolled silk
stockings on the tables, black and openwork. There
were boxes of gloves, and fans in boxes, and plumes
from old hats and lovely hat wreaths of frail pink silk
roses and forget-me-nots. There were petticoats with
tapes at the waist and finely-worked nainsook knickers
(the kind Sue wanted to wear) still gathered into a
frill at the knee by a faint and quite rotten piece of blue
ribbon. There was a terrifying engineering work in the
shape of a pair of black satin corsets. "Darling, darling
Mother's, don't you remember?" Muriel put them
sacredly back in their encoffering cardboard box.

For a day they were extraordinarily excited and happy
among those clothes so carefully put away by careful
maids, so old and clean and fustily sweet, so complete
and elaborate. With flushed cheeks and sparkling eyes
they shook out skirts and held them up, marvelling
politely at the size of each other's waists. It was not a
new thing with these three. They had always been
sympathetic and sweet to each other, but this was a sort
of autumnal reflowering. Roses in the brief heats and
chilled dews of October, seeing the June before in a
heavy, luscious haze.

"Violet, you remember the Viceregal lodge party

when you wore that hat? Those pink roses and the white feather boa——"

"Muriel, darling, these must have been yours. You had tinier feet than any of us. But these seem too ridiculous."

"Your blue, Enid, surely. You always wore blue at night. It would have been a crime to wear anything else with your eyes."

Cecil and Nancy and Sue came in. They were for a moment awed and intrigued by the breath from the past that swirled and filled the room like wreaths of roses and whorls of braid, as though invisible parasols, long-handled, had flirted open, and dexterous fans swayed coyly in the air, stirring the close scent of old sachets and of stuffs long ago grown brittle in their folds. They felt a little shy of their aunts' and mothers' gay memories.

"Thank God we girls don't have to unhook each other," Sue said, picking up a gold tissue bodice veiled and ruched and frilled by an apricot and diaphanous cloud. "I'll have this, I think. Or shall I? Oh, my nainsook drawers! I suppose Simon wouldn't be very pleased if I wore them. But I could, underneath. A nice bit of atmosphere. I'll have these anyhow."

Cecil said, "What a curiously cruel shade of blue. Truly electric."

"Not by lamplight," Enid faltered a little.

"With her eyes it was quite your mother's colour," Muriel's feathers, like an angry wren's, rose and buzzed.

They took off their skirts and walked about in their slick knickers, green and pink and red. They whirled skirts off the bed and struggled into them, unashamed of the vast contrast between theirs and their mothers' waists. Only on Sue would any of them meet. Her long frame was so very narrow. Even the folded belts, pointed behind and buckled in front, she could just with a deep breath, clasp. They took their pick of all the clothes and ran down the passage to the sewing-room, their arms foaming and full of strange anachronisms, as any of the three left behind could have told them if they had been asked.

"*Deep* blue, I call it. Not *Electric*," Enid said in a wounded voice, gazing at that blue gown of '04 which had not then seemed such a cruel and persistent shade.

Violet laughed, not quite so calmly as usual. "The wreath of my garden party hat," she said, "has gone with a mauve ball dress. When do they think we wore them, do you suppose?"

Muriel said forlornly, "They haven't chosen any of my clothes."

Diana had been very firm. She would not exhume anything from her past wardrobe. Nothing, she said, had escaped from jumble sales.

"I'll have my dress made," she said, "I'll be myself by night."

Excitement ran high. Enid and Violet and Muriel recovered their setback by Youth and plotted and planned and praised each other busily. The girls, seeing their own shoulders suddenly from new angles, and curves where curves had never been before, grew enthralled by the change in their bodies and quite anxious to impress the gentlemen with their new selves. Sue even becoming something of a purist, abandoned her apricot ruchings and held grave consultations with Sylvester.

"But I'll look awful, Sylvester," she wailed, when he had given his verdict.

"No, you'll look most amusing."

"That always means wildly unbecoming. Don't I know."

287

Behind locked doors mysterious and noisy doings went on in the library and drawing-room. Sylvester and Simon, the carpenter and many helpers were there all day. Diana slipped in for half an hour when she could do so unobserved, and came out looking as if she had walked five miles in July. She lied to Cynthia about this too.

"I don't know what they're doing, Darling, but whatever it is, it won't be permanent."

"They seem to have ordered practically nothing to eat beyond fruit jellies," Cynthia said, "and I do so like my parties to be well fed."

"I think you're being very good about it."

"But it's just what I want," Cynthia said angrily. "You know I adore them to be independent. All the same, I shall see there's a good supply of bacon and eggs and sausages laid in."

"Have you decided about your dress yet?"

"No, I haven't. I haven't thought about it. It's a bit putting off the way those silly old things keep on about theirs. Rather pathetic when you've once let your face and your figure go completely."

For the last two days, as Diana guessed, Cynthia had thought of nothing else but her dress for the party. She had made plans and abandoned them for one reason or another as fast as they were made. She was feverishly anxious to look her best and to look different from those silly old things, her contemporaries.

In the passage outside Cynthia's room there stood a very long cupboard. Locked in it were all the clothes of half a lifetime, which she had thought when discarded too good to be given away. With all her sweepings and clearing of other people's hoards and rubbish, she had never found it possible to dispose finally of her own. She had always loved her clothes, buying them with vision and extravagance, wearing them with immoderate success, and cherishing them beyond any useful purpose. Because they had been part of herself, part of her beauty and glamour and powerfulness, there was a lonely and jealous force in her guarding of them. She would have been desperately angry had any attempt been made on that locked wardrobe of ghosts and memories. All the dresses were hers, her very life. Not a vague, general past. They had decorated her, been warm and light, part of her hours of love and dreadful loneliness and quickened content. There were dresses hanging there that she had worn before her wedding-dress which hung still like a Spanish queen's in isolated perfection. Not as much as a knot of orange blossom unpicked to fit it for lesser moments. Inviolate, unaltered it hung, a shapely thing in the darkness, its sleeves puffed still, as by the breath of romance, its sweeping white line a gorgeous full memorial to ripe virginity.

Often during the last two days Cynthia, suddenly and completely relieved of her responsibilities as hostess and entertainer by the occupation and interest found by all her guests in their preparations for Simon's party, had looked into this cupboard, comparing, wondering, strangely touched and plucked at by the past which she would deny and ignore and pretend to forget while keeping so many of its ghosts for torment and delight to feed on.

All her life had seemed so near her till now. Not ten and twenty and twenty-five years past. But yesterday, and to-morrow, and a thousand things done and to do. Troubles to surmount victoriously. Difficulties to smooth away. Sorrow to forget. Love to have again. Always horses and hunting to excite and anæsthetise. Always a drink if one felt low. Never an empty time in which to see fatigue or triviality or purposelessness in anything. Life for her never ceased to be a competition in which you won and won. You must never lose, never entirely let go your hold even for a moment. That was the way of desolation.

Now in her most triumphant hour was uncertainty to shake her? Was there to be a foreshadow of defeat? A week ago all tributes had been her right, everything had combined for her praising. There was truth in all the flattery.

As on Reuben's first day: "Cynthia, how can one believe that Simon is twenty-one. Seeing you together it just doesn't seem possible."

Those dramatic entrances and moments with the people on the place. She had felt a sort of wild power in her popularity. Simon was only a doll. She moved him about. The rejoicings were for her really. She knew it.

Even Enid saying, "I can never quite get used to being entirely comfortable at Garonlea. The contrast is too big—though we've known it for years."

And Violet, "How *do* you compel your hydrangeas to be so divinely blue, dear? We try everything in turn and it's no use. It seems so unfair because they never used to be blue here."

All nonsense, all ambrosial food, earned and merited by her years of unrelenting efforts and triumphs. It was true she was a greater and more lovely person than others. It was all true. She could not fail.

When did the draught of doubt first blow on her? Was it on that classical, that too nearly perfect autumn morning, when she had ridden on with her hounds for three miles between coverts expecting each sun-mellow minute to be overtaken? And Reuben had failed to overtake her.

Since then there had been other more obvious escapes, but she denied their reality with a fierce and terrified obstinacy, pinning all faith on a future moment when her beauty and her skill in loving should sweep him back to her for so long as she might wish. At this party of Simon's—that was another window into the unknown. The idea of it troubled her. It was strangely disturbing not to know precisely what was going on in Garonlea. To be in ignorance and too vain to pry and ask servants who must know of some of the doings afoot: to restrain herself from giving advice: to show the right balance of tolerance and amusement towards the unknown thing in store: to yield this shade of her authority for the first time: all seemed beyond her. But it would have been more cruel if she could have seen where the trend of it all led. Here her assurance and vanity for the moment were her saviours.

At six o'clock on the evening of Simon's party a maid was sent to summons Diana to Cynthia's room. There was something in the girl's quiet decorous face that sent Diana flying, her hands wet and iced by the arrangement of a quantity of floral decorations. A vast quantity.

"Darling, you wanted me? Cynthia, what is it?"

A fire burned in Cynthia's room. The air was warm and sweet. A big vase of malmaison carnations stood on the dressing-table beside Desmond's photograph. This morning Diana had put them there. The shaded lights lit wan ivory and gleamed in dark woods. But they lit the looking-glass as truly and baldly as mirror can be lit. The clever photographs of Susan and Simon and a hundred of Cynthia on her show horses or her best hunters stood low and high, on dwarfed tables and tallboys round the room. Light caught the superb curves of the smooth rich bed. Over every chair except the one where Cynthia sat, there hung a dress, many dresses. They kicked their frothed skirts on the floor too.

Cynthia's naked and most beautiful arms hung straight and dropped over the chair arm where she sat. She held a glass, her fingers pointing downwards round its rim. The bottom of the glass just did not touch the floor. Her head was bowed. She was pretty drunk, Diana feared.

"Lock door," Cynthia said with pompous brevity. Then she added, "Darling, please."

Diana came over to her, small and dark. Harsh with anxiety and real loving.

"What is it, Cynthia?"

"I'm not feeling too good. I'm not feeling well. Had to have a drink. Hate drinking between meals as you know. So bad for the figure. Never do it."

"You've broken out for once, haven't you?"

"What d'you mean?"

"I mean, aren't you rather drunk, Cynthia?"

Cynthia dropped her glass (it was empty) and put her hands up to her face. She was not crying. Diana had never heard or seen her crying. She put down her hands and said:

"Help me, darling—in despair. I've been trying on my old frocks and—oh, God, Diana—Oh, God, Diana——"

She did not say any more. Her appeal for help was so royal, so defenceless. It was almost more than Diana could bear.

Cynthia said harshly, "I look a joke in them. I needn't be made to look a joke, need I? Do help me about it."

"Darling, are you sure you can't wear any of them?

292

Couldn't you put some on and let me see. How can I judge?"

"There's nothing I can wear," Cynthia said fiercely. "Don't I know about clothes? Don't I know what they do to people?"

"Yes, you do know. I expect it's your short hair that makes you feel queer in them."

"Thanks, darling. Perhaps."

She seemed to have gathered herself up a bit. She was infinitely more sober and more unhappy. She looked slowly round at all the clothes tumbled about her room—all the lovely clothes that she had worn once. She, herself. Diana could not bear to think of her trying them on alone, flinging them off in despair, tearing at hooks and fastenings, perhaps crying. Alone, Diana thought she sometimes cried. Drinking herself stupid and sending to Diana for help. It was terrible to Diana to think she had entered into any plan that could bring Cynthia to this pass.

She was shivering now in this warm room. Chill and half-way to death, like a person coming-to after an anæsthetic.

"I give you too much bother, darling," she said. "I don't know how you can help me."

"I'm always here to help you. You know that, Cynthia."

Cynthia's eyes went hunting round the room again. Shifting from one thing to another.

"You know what they say about drowning? You know, seeing all your past life? I think these clothes make me feel like that. Perhaps I'd better have another drink, Diana. It might steady me up."

"No, darling, please. Isn't it silly?"

"Oh, *must* you be so tiresome?" the impatient demand, helpless, determined. "I'm not coming down to this party in any case. I'm feeling terrible. Let them see how they get on without me. I haven't a thing to wear."

"But you must come down, Cynthia, they'll be shattered." Unconvincing because perhaps this would be her last escape, her only escape. Then—Save her from this plan made in the first place for her salvation? This plan that seemed to outrun itself, already its effect was so overwhelming.

"Cynthia, you can't not come down. Or—have dinner up here and come down for the party. That might be best." How many drinks had she had before these two? How many would she have before dinner? Drinking alone in her bedroom in that horrid, reasonable way as though each drink was something she owed herself, these lolling, empty shadows from the past clustered thickly about her, her strong present hold on life had slipped. She was not trying to defend or strengthen herself in any way.

Diana said helplessly, "I'll be back soon." She must finish those filthy flowers for Simon.

Cynthia nodded. She seemed more contented and quite vague now as to why she had asked Diana to come to her.

"Why not lie down and take some aspirin?"

To her surprise the suggestion was accepted. Cynthia moved over to her bed, rather slack and ponderous, pulling on her soft pink dressing-gown.

"Put out the lights, Diana." Her voice was almost drowsy before Diana got to the door. She left her half-sleeping, half-stupid in the firelight.

XLI

SIMON heard with some pleasure which he mildly tried to conceal that his mother would not be down to dinner.

"Sue, you won't be late," he made her swear it.

She came down punctually at a quarter to eight and found him waiting for her in the hall. He took out a watch, cabled across his stomach on a gold chain, glanced at it and at the clock—gave her arm a little pat. "Splendid, my dear."

Sue giggled weakly. "Must we keep it up alone? What do you think of me, darling? Don't I look awful—you do—or I don't know. Perhaps not."

Sue was wearing a smart afternoon dress of stiff brown silk faintly but steadily striped, it dragged back from her stomach and puffed hugely over her behind; just above the puffs a little coat of the same material flirted its tail like an amorous robin. Its shoulders were tremendously stuffed, its sleeves long and tight and rocky with braid. On a foreign and glorious shelf of bosom gold and turquoise chains and lockets lay almost as on a table. A gold and heavily-padlocked cable ornamented one wrist. She wore buttoned brown kid gloves, three lines of braid like heavy starfish on their bursting backs, and buttoned brown kid boots. She had washed all the make-up off her face, divided her hair in the centre and plastered a quantity on the nape of her neck inside a netting bag. Secured by an elastic to this anchorage and further safeguarded by long pins with butterflies trembling on spirals at their heads was a small and curly brimmed hat in which feathers and flowers fought for supremacy. A hideous and wicked little hat, frightful to wear and frightful to behold.

Simon wore an almost parma violet suit with a striped green and purple waistcoat, a colossally high white collar which forced his chin into a position of unnatural arrogance and round which was tied a tight, small tie, very low down at the base of the collar, with a tiny knot and a big pearl pin. His trousers were tight to the leg and he wore patent leather boots with pale cloth tops. He carried dogskin gloves and a narrow, curly-brimmed bowler hat. He had contrived the slightest of side whiskers.

Their costumes were faithful copies of a photograph taken early in the '90's of Lady Charlotte and Ambrose. In the photograph she sat upright as a dart in a high-backed chair. He leaned negligently, even a thought rakishly, behind her, against a papier-maché balustrade. A palm in a well-clothed pot on a well-clothed table did its bit to lend an exotic atmosphere to the picture, which had been taken in Bath.

Simon opened the library door and they went in. It was very dark. Not pale and luminous as the fire-light could show it. There was no scent of lilies or cigarettes, expensive or cheap. No hearty voice telling of a good hunt or a good scandal. No laughter. No sound of glasses. The silence was not lazy and rich as any silence here had been for so long. It was of another quality, heavy and chill. It might have come from a place far-off in time. It was so remote. Yet it seemed dangerously near.

Simon put his hand up to the switch near the door and the room was lit.

"It seems so dreadfully real," Sue said, blinking in

the light and talking at once to break the feeling of silence.

"Diana was quite right about the lighting," Simon said. "We had to have it in the old places. I suppose it's a bit bogus but the effect is there."

The effect was indeed there. The library might have been waiting for a dinner-party at any period in its story up to the date of Cynthia's queendom at Garonlea.

Informed by the perfect memory of Diana's perfect hatred, not an ornament, not a sprig of asparagus fern, not a photograph was out of its place. The exact smell, cold, fragrant, a little musty—of chrysanthemums, absence of dogs or scent—that had been the library smell for so long had quietly taken the air again. It stirred in the length and fullness of the red velvet curtains that bellied opulently under the swags and fringes of their canopies. Even the Saxon black boys seemed less exuberant in its breath, more of the page and meek slave about them, less of the curiously pampered favourite. All sofas and chairs had found their own places and wore their clean antimacassars. There was a sort of glum smugness about the portraits. They sank back with a conscious sigh into their proper setting of dark red wall.

Sue sniffed at the air.

"I don't think this would have been quite my favourite period," she said, "what about you?"

Simon took a deeper breath.

"It has its points. Anyhow, it's a good purge for the room now."

"I do think you are brave not to let them drink in here before dinner."

"One couldn't drink in here, not cocktails."

"Perhaps you're right." She giggled at nothing and

shivered, moving closer to the neat coal fire. "Not even a glass of champagne?"

It did not seem easy to talk. It was not altogether the faint feeling of panic before your own party. Each word seemed silly and flat and yet was eagerly listened for as if the least word had importance in a huge dullness. Suddenly Sue felt herself in a panic for something to say to Simon—Simon to whom she said everything as naturally as she breathed or drank water, Simon with whom she examined the details of a pain in her stomach or a spiritual ecstasy. She was apart from him as if a great station full of trains was between them. She longed for Sylvester to come in and pick his way over to them, avoiding tables and sofas. For Diana. For some one to dispel this strangeness. Suddenly and strangely she thought of Cynthia and wished for her most of all.

It was Muriel who came in first. The door had been open. She turned round and shut it gently and came towards them easily, knowing the old tracks between the tables and chairs.

Sue and Simon were a little scared by her look. She wore an expression of extreme disquiet as if she sought for love within herself and only found fear.

"Simon, goodness me," she faltered, "you look so like dear Granny. And the dear old room. It's quite a shock." She looked round it distressfully. "Oh, Sue," she took her in at last with a little squeak of awe, but although the clothes were there she did not convey the same impression as Simon.

"Well, anyhow, I'm in time," she said, as if suddenly it mattered a great deal not to be late. "And how do you like my dress, Simon?" She stepped away from them and turned slowly, meekly, waiting for criticism or condemnation. It was more in the gesture than in the dress that the years of independence in the ever-thrilling flat of her own fell away from her and she was left poor little Muriel in pale turquoise satin, a tiny belt round her tiny waist, a white net guimpe and vest veiling her faint shoulders that sloped into nothing, softening the collar bones from which her neck rose silly as a cygnet's, still. She twirled meekly before Simon, and when she turned to face him again, one could have sworn it was not Simon she expected to see, all powerful on the hearthrug.

"Quite charming," Simon pronounced kindly. "Yes, quite charming. And so lady-like."

Sylvester came in and Sue flew to him. He looked almost normal except for his smoking-cap which he wore with style, and the blue silk, tasseled cord that supported his trousers, and of course, his collar was rather tricky too. He came out of *Trilby*.

"Simon has just told Aunt Muriel that her dress is so ladylike," Sue breathed. "Where have we got to now?"

Sylvester pulled her ear. "It's only a game for one night," he said, "but if you feel hysterical come to me."

"I will. Oh, look at Aunt Violet all in mauve."

"That's Violet for her name. She'll go straight to her photograph, you'll see."

She had swept with dignity and beauty back into a youth that made Sue and Simon the only grotesques. Her hair had gone back into its old crimps. Her figure obeyed its corsets. If the floor had been polished she would have floated across it like a dyed swan. The gentlemen should have held their breaths, emitting, "By Joves!" hands to smooth moustaches. She was no joke. She was gorgeous in mauve. Her eyes took their true iris from it. Sylvester was right. She went straight across to her photograph on the shawled grand piano.

"Gracious, what an old lady it makes me feel," she cried gaily, for she was fresh from her bedroom mirror. "Why, Simon," she crossed over to the fire, "you gave me quite a little start. You might *be* Mother, mightn't he, Muriel? It's so odd in trousers." Her voice was as fresh and flat as usual.

"It's tough on me," Sue whispered, still holding Sylvester's hand, "in all her clothes too. He's stolen my act away."

"Do you mind?"

"Oh, Sylvester, ask me do I mind again. Do you know, I could go wrong on one of those buttoned sofas to-night, just to prove to myself I'm not grand-mamma."

XLII

THE smart chaps came in, a riot as themselves in '04—white pelisses and lace hats and pretty disgusted not to find a drink. Then Enid in Blue and too oppressed by the library to speak at all. She glanced round it, nervously warming her hands at the fire and whispering to Muriel. Then thinking she caught a certain look in Simon's face, suddenly raised her voice to a note of strained uncertainty. It was as if she obeyed a voice saying, "Speak up, my child. We should all be most interested to hear anything you may have to say—Nothing so vulgar as whispering in corners."

An early cricketer came in, Uncle Arthur, very much in period. Jason had forgotten to be anything, but he wore a paper hat to show he meant well. Nancy looked really comically successful in a lady's cycling costume of the wrong date. Cecil had lost every breath of horsiness and developed a tremendously romantic likeness to Enid. She vibrated within an apricot brocade, a veiled, fringed and beaded model that became her beyond any words. Reuben (a Bush Ranger) grew every moment more dangerously enamoured.

"Well, if we're all here," Simon said, "shall we go in to dinner."

The door opened again and Diana came in—Herself by night, she had said. Her costume was warm, modest and yet in effect a sharply discordant note in that restored room, among those newly resurrected busts and naked shoulders and puffed heads of hair, those behinds caged and basketed so formally. Herself as she would never have dared to appear by night in those tortured years of her youth.

She wore a pale-blue flannel dressing-gown, very gored and full to the ground and pieced in the back, corded in blue silk, collared and cuffed in prim white muslin. Underneath it a fine nainsook nightdress, yoke a l'empire, buttoned to its round, close neck-collar, buttoned at the wrists, threaded heavily with blue ribbon. On her bare feet were quilted, heelless slippers of blue satin. Two dark plaits of hair were tied at the end by two blue bows.

She put a silver candlestick down on a table near the door and blew out her candle. The room applauded.

"Diana, you're marvellous."

"You look the cosiest, the sweetest——"

"I'd have chosen you——"

They clamoured round her, laughing, touching, examining as if she was a perfectly-dressed doll. Even forgetting that they wanted drinks.

Enid did not move from the fire. She had started obediently into life together with Muriel at Simon's summons to dinner. Now they stood side by side, different thoughts of the Blue room and the Pink room overcoming them. The chill, the candlelight, the white quilts, the curious, ornamental tatteries they had devised and found decorative breaking back on their minds like waves out of a mist. Enid could see Diana doing her Swedish drill in black silk stockings and knickers, undressing not always as modestly as she might and diving into such a nightdress. Cross, dark, un-communicative, unusually unattractive to gentlemen. That was Diana. Then she had none of the things that counted and now she seemed to have all that mattered.

Muriel whispered inevitably, "What *would* dear Mother have said to her?" Violet calmly aloof, expressed ably and without words that it was perhaps a pity. Simon, on the way in to dinner, paused with icy ceremony while one of the chaps relit Diana's candle. He wanted her to know that her joke dress did not amuse him a lot. They all shouted with laughter, thinking how brilliantly he played up to his clothes.

"Though I was always the one for the stage," Sue said. "The elecution mistress at school thought a lot of me—do you hear me, Sylvester? I remember she nearly cried once when I recited, *Play Up! Play Up! And Play the Game.*"

"Do it now. It really would be riotous in that dress."

"My pretty gown. Look, Sylvester, is this party going to flop badly? Is there only to be one glass of champagne for the ladies? Game *and* a joint. Well, fancy! It's right for the date, I suppose. A white tablecloth looks nice, why don't we always have one?"

Except for a white cloth and an array of small flower vases arranged on a lacey and beribboned table-centre, the dining-room had not been changed. But as in the library, easiness had withdrawn. The party seemed to sit more straightly in their chairs—to converse rather than to talk to each other. If anybody thought of a good crack or a dirty joke it was made furtively and as likely as not suffered a change in the telling towards extreme unfunniness. Under the flowing tablecloth in real 1900 style, Reuben pressed Cecil's foot and sometimes touched her knee. She looked lovely and rather wild with excitement. Arthur felt a curious note of memory sound to him as he looked at her. Clean across all his present occupation with food and wine the sensation of acute unease with which Garonlea had inspired him in youth came fluttering indeterminedly back to consciousness.

Muriel pecked at her food and was quick in ready,

obvious replies again as though she knew some one
listened. Some one waiting for a suitable moment to
say, "Really, my child, you must try to make some
impression. At least answer brightly when he speaks
to you." The delightful stable thought of her own flat
had retreated beyond consciousness. So with Enid, the
little men who ran up your tweeds and all the domestic
implements called gadgets had lost personal importance.
She was a long way previous now to the Enid who had
gossiped happily to Violet over the library fire, warm
in the lily-scented room, pleased with her two attractive, horsey daughters who did not even treat her as a
human being.

Diana, sitting between Sylvester and one of the chaps
in pelisses, was the only person who kept up a real fight
for gaiety. The chap in the pelisse was her child. They
maintained a children's party-joke for about three of
the endless courses. With Simon suddenly attentive
it became in a moment quite pointlessly silly.

Throughout dinner, Simon talked with able dignity
to Violet on his right and to Enid on his left. Each
minute Sue thought he grew farther away from her,
less tolerant of her giggling to Sylvester, more
venomous in his maintenance of polite conversation
with Violet and Enid. And neither was the easiest
person to converse with after a week spent at close
quarters. Simon was good though, he got Violet on to
the McGrath pedigree with such success that by the end
of dinner their blood (on the distaff side) trickled
practically Royal in their veins.

Violet was all right. She was delighted with herself
in mauve. She was undisturbed, calm, unaffected by
memory, not haunted like Enid, who thought she had
forgotten. Or like Muriel who thought she had loved.
Nor was she in arms like Diana who knew how long

and bitterly she had feared and hated all those things which had been brought back to shadow nightmare life at Garonlea to-night.

After dinner when at last the gentlemen joined the ladies, Sylvester said to her uneasily:

"I feel a little as if we had put on such a good puppet show that the Puppets had come to life."

Diana said, "No. Parts of it are too grotesque."

"The pelisses and the cyclist. But other parts of it? He indicated particularly Cecil, the virgin queen of outdoor sport, who sat now swaying at Reuben with tremendous effect. She made a world of separate romance behind her great, soft, feather fan.

"Yes. That's just how Enid used to go on, and then terrible scenes and tears with Mother."

"Poor, oversexed girl. Happily for her she married young?"

"Well—Yes."

Simon came over to them, a cup of coffee in his hand. "I enjoyed dinner," he said, "I think a little restraint must be good for one's digestion. I'm not sure we won't always have a table-cloth now."

"I thought dinner seemed endless," Sue said. She was beginning to feel a little cross and to resent her hideous brown gown. "Why did you want to'have all that food?"

"You'll get used to it, my dear," Simon said. "We're often going to have dinners like that. They soothe me wonderfully. I feel myself after them."

"You don't seem like yourself." She looked at him, picking at the rolled gloves in her hand, raising her striped, uncertain eyes, dropping them, sulky and despairing.

Simon paused as though to consider whether she was worth answering. Then he turned to Sylvester. Diana said, "Come and have a look at the ballroom with

305

me," because she thought Sue might conceivably cry for twopence.

The drawing-room had been stripped and garlanded plentifully with evergreens. Even the window curtains had veils of ivy running up them, producing the maximum of naturalistic with the minimum of decorative effect.

"I think it looks unspeakable," Sue said. "Why did we think it would be amusing to do this? Everywhere I go in the house I feel choked, and I don't know what's happened to Simon. What has happened to him, Diana?"

"I don't exactly know." So hopeless and negative. A lie to this child who had been imprisoned for a night in this parody of another age. And what could one say to her? It was all fantastic. Like shouting in dreams that can't make sound. For the moment as dreadful as that can be.

Diana remembered, Diana knew this sense of being blinded and choked by the sadness of Garonlea, the sadness that was evil, the thing that Cynthia had hunted out and kept at bay, but which they had loosed again, pillared and supported by unhappy memory. Herself, Enid, Muriel, the knowing and remembering past. It was not strange that the old vibrations should stir in the air for them.

But that Cecil should find herself no better equipped for love than Enid, in her youth, that Simon should seem possessed of a spirit that Diana did not name for fear, that darling Sue should be as near to tears as they poor, uncertain girls had ever been, all these things seemed an improper, disproportionate sacrifice and spending of emotion for the cause in hand. They had done too much, gone further than they ought on Cynthia's behalf.

XLIII

AND now the party was on them. It was in being.

"I asked lots of girls," Simon said placidly, "because I wanted the good old wallflower atmosphere. A stiff upper lip in the ladies' cloakroom."

He and Sue, posed as in the photograph that was their original, received their guests in the hall. They made a good group, what with their palm and their balustrade. This unkind remark of Simon's was the first he had made as Simon for a long time. And he would not let Sue leave him, though half an hour of sitting on a hard chair, being Grandmamma's photograph, had got her down and for nearly the first time in her life she badly needed a drink.

"There are far too many. I'll have to make all my chaps dance with them instead of me."

"Well, dear, your partners won't think the less of you for that——" He had gone back to it again. One could not get near him. One gleam of unkind humour and the mask was down—"Mrs. Hughes, I'm so glad you brought *all* your young people, Evelyn, Adela, Dorothy, Barbara, delightful to see you *all*——" On and on it went. Eyes and mind gaped wearily at an endless series of strange dresses and glaringly familiar faces. Plucked eyebrows and varnished nails were not affected by the leaders of society in 1900 but Sue grew grateful to them for their unreality—they were a faint hint that this party could not last forever—that it could sometimes be laughed at and forgotten.

But not yet. Not now, though she had escaped from

307

Simon at last and had her glass of champagne, the party seemed to her hopelessly stagnant. Clogged with failure and unhappiness. Ranged tragically round the rather chilly drawing-room, girls who could not hope to dance, sat with their mothers, or stood about in little groups talking brightly to each other of hunting, that glazed, hurt look about them which is so pitiful to see. Over the scene there was a horrid air of truth. Things had been like this and were again. Mothers looked anxious, watching. Over-polite to one another about daughters who danced or did not dance. The party was no longer a joke. It was real. The dresses had become familiar. Soon they did not even serve as subjects for conversation. The band played waltzes and polkas without any remarkable verve. Simon danced with the ugliest girls, other men danced only with the prettiest or the most amusing. Sue thrust her partners on her friends to the embarrassment of both. Supper seemed endlessly far off. The unwanted girls migrated to the library fire and tried to cheer themselves with weak champagne cup, which was all the drink Sue could procure. She found it a terribly stiff task entertaining them with her stories when they only wanted men. She felt almost wild with despair.

Enid had moments of some enjoyment selecting those old friends whose daughters were not dancing to talk to while Cecil and Nancy twirled continuously round the room.

Simon was in a curious state of satisfaction beyond him to account for. He demanded this unhappiness as a sort of blood offering in his purging of Garonlea. Beyond any idea of Sylvester's he had schemed and planned just such an evening as this, in complete contrast to every party he could remember at Garonlea. It entirely satisfied some instinct against pleasure in his nature. He had never before to-night felt Garonlea to be his own. Now he held a strange power over it, or rather with it. The house itself was his mate and equal in power. Together they avenged the insults of freedom and coarse taking of pleasure that had filled the easy years.

After to-night there would be other parties. Parties for witty talk and restrained pleasures, he and Sue would give them, delighting their chosen friends, themselves cool and happy. But to-night this avenging was required. Even Sue's unhappiness was not enough of a blood-offering for all that he hated in Cynthia and resented in her power at Garonlea.

Diana and Sylvester watched him from a doorway in the garlanded ballroom.

"Sylvester, do you think he's possessed?" Diana said. "I've only known one person like this before. Not minding the unhappiness——" It was her mother, iced above all young turbulence of spirits, calm, unconscious, untouchable. Diana could feel her in the room again, commenting coldly on some miserable young girl who had no success, quite unhurt by the dreadful failure of her rare and awful parties. This was Simon. Simon, to-night recreating the atmosphere among his guests so that the moments, long past, lived again with unspent strength.

"I do think it is rather dangerous," Sylvester said. "You knew more about it than I did when you were so frightened."

"Have you been in the library?"

"I can't bear to see all those girls and know I can only dance with one. And I hate to dance."

"Their soured up, awful silence."

"Better than the gay bursts of girlish chatter."

"Sue didn't get many laughs."

"Is she now? Listen."

"Yes, listen. Do you hear a difference?"

They went back across the hall and stopped inside the library door, holding their breaths in the change, the warm difference fighting with the chill difficult airs, in the room.

Cynthia was standing with the group on the hearth-rug. She looked so of another world and time from them and from the room that Sylvester and Diana hesitated, shocked with surprise in the doorway. She was wearing a black velvet dress of the latest possible mode. It was simple and inevitably clever, flattering her out of two stone of weight and ten years of age. Among all the puffed bosoms and spread hips and frilled shoulders she looked like a very clean, black fish. She looked lovely and clear-lined and active. Beyond any of them she suggested an extremity of luxury and cleanliness. She wore her pearls and diamond bracelets with that sort of bold carelessness that no one could impart to jewels in the days of lockets or in the days of cameos. Her hair was brushed, curling away from her ears. She looked only like herself. Where she was, there was the place to be. There only was strength and laughter and warmth and the reality of present time and the true sense that the past was dead. All these girls who had been cold, stiff and blasted in the hell of Simon's party, were better now—Cynthia with her extraordinary, almost male power of flattering women, had restored in them a sense of their own interest and glamour. It was strange and beautiful, this radiance flowing from Cynthia to the girls and outwards in lessening circles through the terrible room. And it was incomparably stronger than all the chill ghostly currents of the night.

Very soon a servant brought a bottle of wine.

"Bring us another bottle, Thomas," Cynthia said, somehow including him in the lightness and life of her group. "One won't be nearly enough for us. . . . Jean, darling, but you hate champagne. Scotch for Miss Arkwright, Thomas. A double one. Oh, girls, we need a drink up, don't we? You mustn't blame me for this celebration. It's not my idea of fun. I'm all for lots of chaps and sport. Even at my age——"

"She'll steal the whole party," Sylvester whispered to Diana. "You'll see."

"I want her to, Sylvester. Even if it ruins our plans."

"Our plans? Oh, what the Hell? I want her to win it too. Genius putting on that dress——"

"And coming down when it was all touching bottom——"

Sue came flying in in her brown silk.

"Mamma! How marvellous! You are better?"

Cynthia laughed and laughed. "My pet! My poor little McGrath! You do look awful. I hope you won't catch diseases from Granny's old clothes—they never went to the cleaners. Have a nice glass of wine, darling, and take off that monstrous little hat. It gives me back my headache to look at it."

"Oh, Mamma, come and improve the party—you always can." It was odd that Sue who left things half finished, not caring, not even completing her own jokes, should mind so much all this constriction and unhappiness.

"All right, Darling, we'll do our best——"

On the band's platform she looked like a cabaret turn from another life. A preview of Gertrude Lawrence, ageless, enchanting, years before her time. All round the room eyes turned to her. She only saw one person's—Simon's. It was the first time she knew fully the truth of his distrust and hatred. For

311

that was what she saw and she felt towards it exactly as she had felt so long ago towards Lady Charlotte and her bitter powerless hatred. But Simon's was not powerless. Perhaps only for to-night she would be able to defeat it. To-night she felt endlessly strong.

"Listen," she spoke half-apologetically, half alluringly to the waiting listening faces. "The Bar is open—in the schoolroom."

It was nothing and everything. It snatched Simon's party back from reality to masquerade. She was real. She was Cynthia. She knew the horror going on and she would not endure it. She could not suffer its continuing.

XLIV

A BAR—who ever heard of a bar at such a party?
Cynthia was quite right. It was the break up of Simon's
party and the starting point of hers. The schoolroom
empty and pale, nothing there but a lot of bottles
and glasses and the flower piece strong on the wall.
Soon it was stuffed and crowded with people having
a drink, people feeling better already. Girls finding
one another gay, amusing. Not spies and observers of
unsuccess. Cynthia everywhere, with this one, with
that one, giving all that was herself. Taking Simon's
party away from him and from Garonlea and from the
power of the past. Minute by minute changing it
back into to-night. Soon the sedate misery in the
ballroom was broken up. They played musical chairs
and hunt the slipper, and when they were a little
drunk, charades in which one of the mousiest and
dreariest girls was such a success that even Sylvester
was impressed. The party stopped trying to be a ball.
People played Poker and Bridge. If they did want to
dance the band played a little soft music, but most of
the band was playing games soon. Rumour had it
that there were oysters somewhere. And it was true.
All the oysters that you could eat. Really enough
oysters were being opened in the billiard room.
Oysters and champagne and stout. One of the band
turned out to be a truly funny comedian. Encouraged
by Cynthia his cracks grew better and better.

Quite pale with disgust, Violet retired with Muriel
and Simon to the library before the end of that turn.

The library was no longer real, no longer an outpost of dignified restraint. Some one had popped Sue's little hat on one of the black boys. There were forests of empty glasses on all the little tables, plates of oyster shells on the shawled piano. Most curious insult, in the middle of the floor sat a white chamber pot that had figured a little unduly in one of the charades. Violet and Muriel shied violently at the object.

"Well, dear," Violet said smoothly, coming out of her shy on a placid curve, "it's been a wonderful evening, hasn't it, Muriel? Some of the dresses were as pretty as possible. Perhaps now it's time we old people went to bed. What do you say, Muriel? Ah, here's Enid! Are you ready for bed too, Enid?

Simon moved over to the door with them, for all the world as though he would light their candles and watch them up the staircase. There were no candlesticks but there were good-night kisses.

"Good-night, Simon dear."

"Good-night, Simon dear."

"Good-night, Simon dear."

They went upstairs one behind the other, wearing the dresses that belonged to their youth. They had never escaped their youth. They would never all their lives be free of it.

Simon went back to the library. The gentle accompanying blur of the piano came through the door from the drawing-room and the husky half-heard voice of the comedian singing soft Bo-Hoo songs now, cowboy songs, cleanest sentiment, whistling bits of them. There were bursts of applause, wild true enjoyment. It was all an excessive emotional success.

Simon picked up the chamber pot and stood with it held absently in his hand listening to his party shaken into ruins around him. His power was gone. The purging fire was dead. The disease he had thought to burn out raged more strongly for its checking. He felt angry and hurt, but principally very tired in his defeat.

Sue came in and found him standing like that.

"Oh, Simon."

"Darling, I've been beastly to you all night. I do deserve this."

"You haven't, Simon. It was my fault. I couldn't play up."

"Where shall we put this? It's such a nuisance to me."

"Behind the curtain, perhaps."

They put it behind the curtain together.

"And your hat, Sue? She took it off the black boy's turbaned head and put it back on her own.

"The thing is, Simon—Have you had some oysters and Black Velvet yet?"

"No, Sue, I've been too proud. Only that awful cup and a chicken pâté."

"I haven't either. Loyalty to you, I expect. Shall we?"

"Well, we might, I suppose. It will help me to take my defeat like a chap."

They left the squalid library hand in hand.

On the party went and on. No one knew that this was Cynthia's last party at Garonlea, this party that she had snatched so wildly from Simon and from Garonlea, from failure to the highest note of success. Only Cynthia knew and she could not own even to her inmost self all that this told her. To-night her determination to defeat Garonlea again was the only thing. She gave herself to it. For to-night, only for to-night. Never had there been such a spectacular moment as this with the house restored and marshalled against her. Never while she lived had Lady Charlotte's power meant what it did to Cynthia, seeing it in Simon's eyes to-night. She saw defeat. She fought for a fitting exit. A death in music. It would never be Cynthia to creep away from Garonlea in weak surrender. She would go out at her own will and time. Not at her child's wish. Not at the insolent insistence of the house and its ghosts.

So great was her effort against Garonlea that the other part of her defeat slackened in urgency. Reuben and Cecil lost their importance as symbols of a more terrifying defeat. For the greater part of the night she did not see them. It was a dream, a panic, her youth and beauty slipping. She felt ageless and secure. Power could not leave her. All night she felt its flow through her, into her, from her. She could never be defeated.

At last the party ended. Every good-bye was a sort of curtain and Cynthia took them all. The thanks, the praise, the love. All the strange emotions that came out of Simon's party had been changed into these things which must always be hers. Always to the end. Was now the end? She found herself standing alone in the hall. The last good-bye over. The sound of cars fainter down the valley.

Cynthia went out through the open door, saying to the tired servant, "I'll shut it when I come in, Thomas. Good-night. You were all marvellous. You looked after us too well." Out on the dewed heavy grass she looked back at the house; pale, immense, sprawling in the night, its creepers like great deep stains spreading on the walls. She walked across to where Diana had planted one of her groups of lilies near trees. Branches pieced the night sky, caging the scent of lilies, that terrible wild scent at night, and she stood there looking

316

back at the house, holding on to her feeling of triumph, her sense of domination. No, she did not have to hold on. It was flowing out of her, she was bathed in it still. She felt beyond triumphing. She was maintaining a sort of ecstasy of power. She had really won. Now if she chose to give back all to-morrow—to-night, she did it out of her own power.

In another minute she would go back into the house. Find Diana—darling Diana, how dreadful to-night must have been to her—and say, "what would you like most? I know—Rathglass. We'll go back. I know about Simon now. I'm not going to sour him up any more."

For another minute she stood in the lilies' scent. It was like drinking the air to stand there, heavy sharp exciting drug of lilies. Another minute she would wait there, looking at the house, conscious of all the forces that she had overcome.

If she had not waited. Ah, if she had not seen them. They came round the wide flagged turn from the terraces, Reuben and Cecil. They walked slowly, their arms round each other, pausing, whispering, head bent, head raised. It was as if the strain of parting must be beyond them. Outside the light of the doorway they embraced. They parted and again embraced. Cynthia watched a mime of good-nights that must be said. Farewells to love in ardour and despair for even such a short good-bye.

She watched till they had gone, standing trembling and cold now in the lilies' bitter rich breath. She saw them still, Cecil in that long dark overcoat lost against him in the darkness, she knew it was good-night they had said, leaving each other till to-morrow. Cecil was too ignorant, too prudish—— Not that—— Too young—that was it—that was the terror and the

317

truth. He would not sleep with her lightly. She was too young. It was all she had. It was everything.

Back to reality a moment came flying. Not softened by time but with its own twist and edge complete. It came back, the first sight she had of Garonlea, immense, pale, river misted in the depth of its valley ... feeling as though she receded from Desmond. As though impossibly they were parted—their warmth and understanding a cold forgotten breath. Their youth that could never end finished. No more Love. All the meaning of that moment came to her now beyond any meaning it had held then, in its quick passing. He lifted her down from the high dog-cart; decorous, solicitous, tremendously proud. Together terribly emotional. Embraces impossible. Love not spoken then.

And now, all tears shed, Passion unspent, still strong in her. She stood again outside the house, cold in the luxurious animal scent of the lilies and a voice within her was crying and protesting, "Nothing they tell you about Life is true. Nothing. Especially nothing they tell you about old age."

Cold she was now. The night was ending. Mist from the river was taking great shapes like white and silver cows under the dun sky. Cynthia dragged her smart little coat across her breast, and bowed her head and went back across the heavy grass and the wide gravel sweep to the house. She always walked strongly and beautifully. This morning she was like a person walking in a storm or a dream, blown along. She did not remember or trouble to shut the door or put out the light. Through the halls, up the wide stairs, her head still bent, her coat dragged about her for comfort.

Diana was in her room, cosy as though she had

318

just got out of bed in her fancy dress flannel dressing-
gown and the plaits swinging awkward and rather
stuffy. As though she had just got out of bed twenty-
five years ago. She was slipping a hot-water bottle
down between Cynthia's sheets. There was a spirit
lamp burning on a low table near the fire, clear special
smell and blue flame under a bright little pot.
A tray with two glasses and spoons. A new neat tin of
something. How comforting, just for the moment in
the world's whole emptiness. Could she tell Diana?
Could she say to her, "I'm lost." Am I outside life for
ever? No more love for me? Could you say this to
Diana who had lived so vestal a life? Cold caves of
life with no love ever and all that it means in tears and
dreams. This was her only interpretation of Love, this
warmth and care; hot-water bottles, spirit lamps,
hot milk. No more. But far more than that. Thank
God, one need not speak, need never explain oneself,
apologise, admit defeat or demand praise from her.
She was love itself. With her there was ease and peace.
The drama of saying, "We're going back to Rathglass."
slipped from Cynthia almost, not quite, because she had
to say it, looking over her shoulder from the fire.

"Darling, I know you're right. It's not all because
it's so lovely for me," Diana breathed faster. "I can't
believe it's true." She went to the window, pulling
back the curtain, looking out into the early metal
light as if she could see Rathglass through the mist.
As if she could see into the kitchen as it had been, the
warm air wavering with hot sweet smells. In other
rooms the furniture used daily their own again. . . .
Should she leave her favourite flower vases behind at
Garonlea? Certainly not. . . . The thought of purple
flowers and red flowers was like wine in her mouth.
The toil and peace of having your hands in earth you

loved in the place where you lived came back to her, fortifying in her a curious strength for age. No ends of old dreams to startle her into a moment's wild regret. Each present day and hour complete in its own strength.

She saw Cynthia by the fire and knew that somehow, out of this evening, defeat as they had planned had come to her. But she had found and admitted it to herself. No one else knew. It had been as they had planned. But beyond their schemes as she was beyond them. Out of their reckoning. She looked haggard and heavy now, wandering about, the make-up off her face, so that now her skin was clean and old, much older. She had taken off her little coat too and the tight jewelled shoulder-straps of her black dress bit into the solid flesh of her shoulders. She murmured something to herself, putting a Cachet Faivre in a glass of water to melt. Her high-heeled shoes, rather cruel shoes, were off and her black dress seemed yards longer without them. Her figure had lost its balanced lengthy poise. She was taking the earrings out of her small high-set ears and unclasping her pearls and stripping the rings from her faintly swelling fingers. Diana watched her laying earrings and bracelets and pearls and rings in a heap beside Desmond's photograph on her dressing-table. That expressionless picture of a handsome young man in uniform. You could see he had wide-set eyes and a sweet and generous mouth. Otherwise the likeness had no particular character. Cynthia was so accustomed to this picture that she did not see it any more. As they say—"Time is a great Healer."

THE END

320

www.virago.co.uk

To find out more about Molly Keane and
other Virago authors, visit
www.virago.co.uk

Visit the Virago website for:

- News of author events and forthcoming titles
- Features and interviews with authors, including
  Margaret Atwood, Maya Angelou, Sarah Waters,
  Nina Bawden and Gillian Slovo
- Free extracts from a wide range of titles
- Discounts on new publications
- Competitions
- The chance to buy signed copies
- Reading group guides

PLUS
Subscribe to our free monthly newsletter

GOOD BEHAVIOUR

Molly Keane

Introduced by Marian Keyes

'A masterpiece . . . Molly Keane is a mistress of wicked comedy' Malcolm Bradbury, *Vogue*

Behind its rich veneer, the estate of Temple Alice is a crumbling fortress, from which the aristoctratic St Charles family keeps the realities of life at bay. Aroon, the unlovely daughter of the house, silently longs for love and approval, which she certainly doesn't receive from her elegant, icy mother. And though her handsome father is fond of her, his passion is for the thrill of the chase – high-bred ladies and servants are equally fair game. Sinking into a decaying grace, the family's adherence to the unyielding codes of 'good behaviour' is both their salvation and their downfall. For their reserved façades conceal dark secrets and hushed cruelties . . .

'A remarkable novel, beautifully written, brilliant . . . every page a pleasure to read' P. D. James

'Wickedly alive' Victoria Glendinning, *Sunday Times*

'Dark, complex, engaging . . . a wonderful tour de force' Marian Keyes

**You can order other Virago titles through our website: *www.virago.co.uk*
or by using the order form below**

☐ Good Behaviour	Molly Keane	£7.99
☐ Devoted Ladies	Molly Keane	£7.99
☐ Time After Time	Molly Keane	£7.99
☐ Loving and Giving	Molly Keane	£7.99

*The prices shown above are correct at time of going to press. However, the
publishers reserve the right to increase prices on covers from those previously
advertised, without further notice.*

Virago

_____   _____

Please allow for postage and packing: **Free UK delivery.**

Europe: add 25% of retail price; Rest of World: 45% of retail price.

To order any of the above or any other Virago titles, please call our credit
card orderline or fill in this coupon and send/fax it to:

Virago, PO Box 121, Kettering, Northants NN14 4ZQ
Fax: 01832 733076   Tel: 01832 737526
Email: aspenhouse@FSBDial.co.uk

☐ I enclose a UK bank cheque made payable to Virago for £ . . . .
☐ Please charge £ . . . . . . to my Visa/Access/Mastercard/Eurocard

Expiry Date ☐☐☐☐   Switch Issue No. ☐☐

NAME (BLOCK LETTERS please) . . . .

ADDRESS . . . .

. . . .

. . . .

Postcode . . . . Telephone . . . .

Signature . . . .

Please allow 28 days for delivery within the UK. Offer subject to price and availability.

Please do not send any further mailings from companies carefully selected by Virago ☐